Death Goes
to School

Mary Edward

Death Goes to School

By Mary Edward

Published by Author Way Limited through CreateSpace
Copyright 2014 Mary Edward

This book has been brought to you by -

Cover design by Diane Edward

Discover   other   Author   Way   Limited   titles   at   -
http://www.authorway.net
Or to contact the author mailto:infp@authorway.net

ISBN:	1500197033
ISBN-13:	978-1500197032

With thanks to the Anns, for their interest and encouragement.

Chapter 1

'It's the Khan girl – she's missing!' Half a dozen words, each one like a blow to the stomach for Sarah Blane. She sank into her seat by the edge of the dance floor, squeezing her hands together under the table.

Mary Stephens' face was pink. 'Look! There's her father with the Head.' She pointed to a table on the other side of the room.

'Maybe he's invited to the wedding.' Sarah's dance partner, David Smythe, tugged at his black jacket. 'Provided George with his kilt perhaps.''

Sarah shook her head. 'I don't think so.'

The reception for George and Marilyn, fellow teachers in Fruin High, was in the Glen Falloch hotel, on the banks of Loch Lomond.

Sarah had been teaching there for almost year. It was a large 1960s, concrete and glass box on the outskirts of Helensburgh. Seriously different from the venerable sandstone grammar school which she had left behind along with her marriage in the south of England. She edged back her sleeve to glance at her watch. Soon she would slip away over the hill to the peace of her flat. Her new shoes were killing her. Besides Henry, her cat, had been left long enough for one day.

'What's this about Rubina?' Willie Armstrong removed his unlit pipe from his mouth and shook his head.

He was a ponderous man, and Sarah often felt a sneaking sympathy for his pupils. His major fixation, apart from his garden, was the poetry of Philip Larkin. Start him off and a whole lunch hour could slip away to the sound of Willie eulogising the dead poet.

Mary Stephens said. 'Poor man.'

Anwar Khan was leaning over, speaking to the Head, wiping his face on a handkerchief.

David said. 'Not much we can do about it. Let's have another dance.'

When he reached out to Mary, she leapt to her feet, almost overturning her chair.

Sarah and Willie watched the couple whirl off into the middle of the dancers. In a flowery dress which emphasised her broad backside Sarah thought Mary looked a bit like a dancing sofa, and felt guilty. 'It's nice to see Mary enjoying herself, isn't it, Willie?'

William removed his pipe from his mouth. It was empty. It had to be a nostalgic prop for the man, since smoking in public had been banned in Scotland for a while. 'Mm, she doesn't get out much.'

When the music stopped Keith Birkmyre stood and cast around as the dancers straggled back to their places. Finally, spotting Sarah, he waved her over.

As she crossed the floor Sarah reflected that he was probably making do, considering how extensively the Head had ranged around the hall before settling on her. In the months since she joined his staff it seemed that Keith Birkmyre hadn't warmed to her.

He flapped a hand.' Right, eh...Sarah...'

Mr Khan sat at the table, head bent, while Annette Birkmyre looked on. She gave Sarah a half-smile as her husband continued, 'Mr Khan's daughter seems to be missing.'

It was true. Sarah felt dread slide coldly into her gut. The music began again, loud and discordant, and she strained to catch what he was saying.

'...from Miss Aitken's theatre trip, last evening.'

Sarah looked at the father, rigid with fear, and saw her own father, all those years ago...

'Miss Aitken, Judith's, theatre trip?'

The Head brought his hands together with a little clap. 'Yes, Mr Khan tells me that his daughter...' He turned, 'What's her name...?'

'Rubina,' Sarah said.

'Yes, she was allowed to go to Glasgow with Miss Aitken's theatre trip last night on condition that she phoned her father when she got back to town.'

Anwar Khan rose and looked at Sarah. 'Miss Blane, yes, you know, to see the play, you said she should go.'

'Hamlet, for their exams,' Sarah bit her lip. What a bloody stupid thing to say. The girl had not come home, that's all that mattered. Ruth had never come home either 'Did she phone...?'

'Yes, from the bus, you know. With the mobile.' He twisted the handkerchief between his fists. 'She said they were nearly home. But she did not come...'

'Has he...have you contacted the police, Mr Khan?'

He shook his head and Birkmyre answered, 'Mr Khan has not been in touch with the police, yet. But that's where he must go now. Can you perhaps throw any light on where the girl might have gone.'

'No, none at all. What about Miss Aitken, what does she..? Oh, she was flying out of Glasgow first thing this morning.'

'Precisely, and so she allowed the pupils to travel home by themselves.'

'Well, they are senior pupils Dr Birkmyre, most of them seventeen. The mini-bus was a private hire and it was bringing them back to the school gates.'

'But Rubina was not there!' Mr Khan looked as if he

might collapse. The Head gripped his arm and turned to his wife. 'I'm going with him now to the police station, Annette.'

'Mr Khan. Have you spoken to Lynn? Her friend.' Even as she spoke Sarah knew that it was a pointless question, because that's where Rubina's father would have started, trying to bury his worry under irritation at careless kids.

'She has not seen my daughter.' His voice shook, 'No-one has seen...' His last words were lost as Birkmyre ushered him towards the door. Sarah looked after them, the Head's brogues clicking on the polished floor and the swinging kilt exuding efficiency: the father of the missing girl almost running to keep up.

There was a sigh from behind her. 'Thank God we've got boys! I don't think I could cope with adolescent girls. Probably hopped off to spend the weekend with her boyfriend, they're always doing things like that, Keith tells me. Parents having hysterics and the girl turns up on Monday like the cat that got the cream.'

Sarah shook her head.

A huge cheer went up and guests began to rush to the door. Sarah jumped, until she realized that Marilyn and George were on the point of escaping on their honeymoon.

Driving home, Sarah switched on the radio and refused to think about what she knew was waiting for her in the seclusion of her flat. Rubina and Ruth. Ruth and Rubina.

When the door closed behind her Sarah eased her feet out of her shoes, fed Henry, then changed into a dressing-gown and made coffee. The cat joined her, purring and wrapping himself around her legs, as she took the cafetiere and mug to her seat by the bay window. She stroked his sleek black and white coat and was amazed anew at how the little parcel of skin and bone which had been

Henry when she found him shivering on her doorstep had turned into this lovely animal. She'd never had a cat before and she hadn't wanted one even when he'd followed her upstairs and into the flat, but she loved him now. She'd named him after the solicitor who'd handled her divorce. He'd been a whiskery sort of fellow, whom she'd never seen wear anything but a black suit and white shirt. Tucking her feet beneath her, Sarah looked out at her view.

The flat was a two-bedroom attic conversion overlooking the promenade and the Firth of Clyde. When she'd come as a prospective buyer, the outlook had won easily over the several flights of stairs. To Sarah, living high above the roof of the main house, it was as if the view was entirely her own. Now, on a clear October night, the street lamps cast rippling reflections on the water below, and the lights of Greenock on the opposite bank flickered like signals. The faint outlines of the hills beyond the Gareloch were just visible as a more solid darkness against the sky.

Settled in her chair by the window, she unlocked the safe of her memory and let the demons out.

It was a December night when the first threads of the horror that was to be Ruth's disappearance snaked into the lives of the Marchegay family. December 13th 1988. Sarah, ten years old, watching television with her mother when her father left to pick up her sister from the pantomime in Edinburgh.

She had been bathed and in her pyjamas when her father returned, white-faced, with no Ruth. The air had filled with frightening electricity as her parents reassured each other that she would walk in the door any minute. Sarah had sat the bottom of the stairs, eyes fixed on every wavering reflection beyond the glass door, willing it to be Ruth.

Was it like that in the Khan's house last night?

Rubina. Sarah shivered.

7

The police had done what they could, but invariably returned to the fact that Ruth was seventeen, old enough to leave home. Eventually, all the photographs of Ruth had disappeared from the house, while her father had gone back to his work as an insurance salesman, a grey shadow, fading as hope faded, until his first heart attack.

Her mother had given up teaching – there were too many children.

Too many children, even Sarah. As she grew into her teens her powerful resemblance to Ruth didn't help: the combination of very fair hair and dark eyebrows made them stand out in a crowd. Sarah had more or less got through these years by herself, studying and getting to university, while her parents lived in the vacuum that was home after Ruth disappeared. Sometimes she had wished Ruth dead, so that they could have buried her and started over again. Her parents might have been grateful for the daughter they still had.

She took a mouthful of cold coffee, then got up and made herself a gin and tonic. The street below was quiet. When the phone rang, she stared at it as if she'd never seen it before.

'Sarah? Keith Birkmyre here. Sorry to trouble you but I can't seem to contact Moira.'

Moira Campbell, the Deputy Head. 'She's gone down south to another wedding, that's why she wasn't...'

'Damn, of course, I'd forgotten for the moment.' He breathed heavily, 'Well, sorry and all that but I think you should come down here...as her form teacher ...'

'Down where?'

'To the police station! All kinds of family have turned up, all talking at once - the desk sergeant's losing his patience, I'm afraid. So, if you will?'

Her first instinct was to refuse - who did he think he

was? School was out, it was the autumn holiday. Then she remembered her mother's face on the night Ruth had not come home.

She pulled on a pair of denims and a sweater, and ran down to the car. The police station was only a few streets away.

The door opened with a bizarre 'hee-haw' signal. Mr Khan was sitting on a bench with his face in his hands, while two men were arguing with a stout desk sergeant.

Keith Birkmyre looked almost pleased to see her. 'Good, you're here. Speak to these people, will you?'

The sergeant pointed his pen and said, 'Look Miss, could you ask these fellows to speak English?'

The older of the two men said, 'You are a teacher? My brother-in-law says you know about Rubina?'

Mr Khan got to his feet when he saw her. 'Please, Miss Blane, this is my wife's brother, Shahid Ashrif, and my nephew, Hakim. Please, can you help us here - the policeman does not understand...'

Sarah recognised the men: she sometimes shopped in the clothes store run by Mr Khan and his brother-in-law. And Hakim was often to be seen driving around town in his black Range Rover, but she hadn't known he was Mr Ashrif's son. While the father was a quiet-spoken man, tall and slim with fine aquiline features, Hakim was heavy and coarse-skinned, and looked about twenty-three.

The sergeant shook his head. 'Will you explain to them, please, that I'm not in a position to send out men on a hunt for this girl, just because she hasn't come home.' He pointed to a computer. 'It's all in there, and when the day shift come on they'll look into it. And we'll put it on the radio and the night boys can keep a look-out for a girl answering her description.'

Hakim Ashrif pushed past his father. 'Keep a look-

9

out?' He stared at the policeman. 'Is this all my little cousin matters?'

The sergeant pushed his pen behind his ear. 'Listen son, keep calm. We've written it all down - Rubina Khan, 17 years of age...Asian, dressed in...' he shot a look at Sarah... 'Western clothes? Went on a theatre trip to the city - authorised by the school. Phoned her dad here to say she'd be home around 11pm, would walk with her friend - aye, Lynn Cameron, but didn't come home.' Now he looked at Mr Khan. 'This was last night.'

Hakim leaned closer to the sergeant. 'Is this how you do it for anyone who is reported missing?'

The sergeant straightened. 'Yes, sir. That's exactly how we do it. Only sometimes we get to start a bit earlier.'

Sarah said, 'Is there anything I can help with...?'

The sergeant looked weary. 'Only if you can convince these gentlemen that the disappearance of Mr Khan's daughter will be dealt with properly, but that we don't send out posses at one in the morning.' He added quietly, 'Especially when the girl is 17 years of age.'

Hakim shouted, 'What are you saying about my cousin?' and Mr Khan said, 'Oh no sir, my daughter is a good girl.'

Shahid Ashrif put his hand on Anwar's arm. 'Come on, let's go home. There will be no help for us here.'

The sergeant raised his hands and shrugged. 'Make sure they bring us in a photograph of the young lady, will you?'

Sarah looked round. The Head was reading an anti-drugs poster on the wall, his arms folded and his back straight. With his smooth grey hair, chiselled profile and in full highland dress, he looked like a poster himself. She turned back to the sergeant. 'You will keep in touch with Mr Khan, won't you..?'

Outside, the men were getting into a dark-coloured Mercedes. Hakim and his father were speaking in what Sarah took to be Urdu. Mr Khan turned to Sarah. 'Thank you, Miss Blane, it was good of you to come.'

'Mr Khan... if I can be of any help? She hesitated, 'I do know something of what you're going through...'

He tried to smile. 'Yes, thank you...'

'Yes, thanks, Sarah.' The Head was behind her. He shook his head and yawned, covering his mouth with a gloved hand. 'Well, I don't think there's much we can be expected to do anyway. Just a pity that the girl was on a school outing. Doesn't look good. Hope she turns up.' His wife had come to wait for him by the kerb in his SUV.

As she got into her car Sarah saw Hakim Ashrif wave to the Head's car to stop. She hoped he was about to berate her boss for his insouciance in the face of their desperation. Of the family, Hakim seemed most likely to let rip, and it looked that way when Hakim stuck his head inside the window of Keith Birkmyre's car. He appeared to shove the young man away.

Home again, Sarah knew she wouldn't be able to sleep; she made herself another gin and tonic and resumed her seat at the window.

It couldn't have been much after ten when the pupils came home from the city last night. At that time on a Friday the streets of Helensburgh were busy with people celebrating the weekend. This was a town with many of its houses close to the centre - not like those places where all living forms vanished like victims of the Pied Piper when shops and offices closed. Helensburgh - a tidy town new in the 19th century, named for his Lordship Colquhoun's wife - a broad main street, a promenade and the streets laid out in squares for the most part. Commuter distance from Glasgow. Certainly the town was widespread, many of the streets and

11

avenues running uphill, away from the waterfront, but Rubina and Lynn lived very close to the centre. The Khans, in fact, lived in a large flat overlooking the town square, and Lynn Cameron in the next street. So what had happened to Rubina?

Young voices drifted up to her window - quarrelling, she thought. Probably the shirt-sleeved youths she'd seen on the way home from the police station.

Suddenly the desk sergeant's words came back to her. '... said she'd be home around 11pm.' Sarah rummaged in her school briefcase, thrown on a chair for a week's freedom from its contents, until she found the notice which Judith Aitken had passed round the department...

"Theatre....Hamlet....7.30pm - 9.30pm... drop-off at school gates at approx 10.30, possibly earlier."

Sarah needed to see Lynn Cameron. She would go in the morning. It would be Sunday - it was Sunday now - but she had to see her. Lynn had gone on the theatre trip. She would know what time it was when they came back. The two girls walked home together.

Ruth had been with friends that night too - but they'd left her to wait for her dad on the pavement outside the theatre.

*

Sarah woke early, Rubina at the forefront of her mind. She liked most of the pupils in her senior English class, but particularly the bright Asian girl.

She lay for a time wondering if going to see Lynn was such a good idea. It might not be appropriate. But Lynn must be feeling awful. She got out of bed.

Lynn wasn't a popular girl. Plain too. Rubina's exotic beauty didn't help in the comparison, but they seemed to be good friends. Sarah thought it might be because Rubina's background kept her at arm's length of a classroom culture that perhaps Lynn wasn't welcomed into.

The Cameron home had long since left behind all pretensions of 'cottageness'. The house was white, with a red pantiled roof showing a couple of dormer extensions. A driveway of tawny mono-bloc led through a landscaped front garden to a porch and a storm door of the glossiest green, flanked by ornamental trees in fat glazed urns. On one side stood a double garage, its doors a matching green, and the front door was an intricate pattern in leaded glass.

Sarah was surprised by Lynn Cameron's mother. They had never met. Lynn's father had attended Sarah's only meeting this year with the parents of the senior pupils. Had it not been fairly early on a Sunday morning Sarah would have taken the woman who opened the door for a visitor, so unlike Lynn was she. So slim, raven-haired and glamorous was she, in skin-tight white jeans, that Sarah was taken aback.

'Mrs Cameron?'

'Elizabeth Cameron, yes.' Perfect red nails held the door open half-way.

'I'm...my name is Sarah Blane...Lynn's English teacher?' Sarah had never felt her surname to be so apt as under Elizabeth Cameron's scrutiny.

'Well, I wondered if I might see Lynn....you know, about Rubina?'

Could it be boredom which flitted across the woman's make-up?

'I suppose so. You'd better come in.' She opened the door and led Sarah into a broad hallway. 'You know we've had the police here this morning already,' she added, showing Sarah into a room on the left of the front door.

'Oh, of course...'

Elizabeth shrugged. 'Just one of those things. Wait here, I'll give Lynn a shout. Take a seat.'

Sarah looked around; cream leather sofas on either side of a marble fireplace looked so shiny and unused that she feared she might slide off on impact - so instead she sat gingerly on a faux-Regency chair with gilt legs and a pink-striped seat. The room was cold and had the air of a furniture display, the carpet a pale beige which she might have been the first to tread upon, and a huge Chinese rug between the sofas looking equally untouched.

Lynn came into the room; her eyes were red and she was holding a box of tissues to her chest as if they were about to be snatched from her. She was wearing a brushed cotton dressing gown printed all over with teddy bears. When she saw Sarah she began to cry and pull out an untidy string of paper hankies. The opening in the thin cardboard was ragged and the box was almost empty.

Sarah led her to one of the sofas. 'Come on, Lynn, sit down.'

She removed the box from Lynn's grasp and held her hand while the girl wept, pushing up her glasses to wipe her eyes with the ball of tissues. Sarah waited until the sobs became hiccuping breaths.

'Tell me what happened, Lynn.'

The girl shook her head.

Sarah spoke quietly, 'Do you know where Rubina is, Lynn?'

Lynn slid away to the far corner of the sofa, 'No! That's what the policemen kept asking me!' her fist went to her mouth. 'How would I know?'

'Rubina is your best friend.'

Lynn bent her head and began to shred the paper hankies.

'Lynn, she is, isn't she?'

The girl nodded.

'Then surely you want to help - to find her.'

Sarah waited in silence for a moment then got up and stood by the fireplace. 'Well then, why don't you just tell me about yesterday?'

Lynn looked up. 'But you know, Miss Blane. You know that we went to Glasgow to see Hamlet with Miss Aitken.'

'Did you enjoy it? Was it a good production?'

'Oh yes, Miss, it was great.' She smiled, 'The actor playing Hamlet was terrific, Rubina said...' She returned to shredding the tissue.

'Come on, Lynn. You came back together in the mini-bus - you and, how many others?'

'Seven, Miss. We all started walking from the school together, laughing and carrying on. Leslie Watkins, you know, the one we call Grasshopper, was dancing round Rubina, calling her his Ophelia...' Then people started to go off, until there was only Rubina and me - and Leslie. He was going to thumb a lift to the peace-camp.' She sniffed, 'He said the Base Patrol would give him a lift in the jeep they use to round up the sailors.'

Sarah said, 'The what?'

'Oh, the navy police, you know, for the submarine base. Rubina told him he was betraying his peace-loving principles, but she was just teasing him.'

Lynn was brightening, as if she'd forgotten why they were there. Sarah was about to press home the advantage when the door opened. Lynn's mother had her car keys in her hand.

'Popping out Lynn, don't forget to do your washing, it's still lying on floor of the utility room, love. Oh, and see if, Miss...Blane isn't it, would like a drink or a cup of tea or something. Nice to have met you, bye.'

Somehow Sarah didn't think the 'love' was an endearment, and when she turned again to Lynn it was confirmed by her expression.

'My mother the councillor. Always at the beck and call of her constituents, you know, even on Sundays.'

'Oh, I wasn't aware that your mother was a councillor.'

'Don't you read the local paper, Miss, she's never out of it. Do you want tea or coffee?'

'Coffee would be nice.' As Sarah followed Lynn to the kitchen she wondered how to put it - but civic responsibility didn't seem to chime with Elizabeth Cameron's lack of interest in what had become of Rubina...

Lynn seemed to guess 'This isn't her ward Miss Blane, it's further out, includes the base.'

'Yes, the base. So what time was it when you left Leslie?'

Lynn took mugs from the rack. 'I'm not sure. We left him at the corner of John Street, he was going to wait outside the pub.'

'Then?'

Lynn had her back to Sarah, spooning instant coffee into the mugs.

'We split up at the next corner.'

'And went home?'

'Yes.'

Experience had taught Sarah to spot dissimulation a mile off.

'Lynn? Please.' Sarah looked directly at the girl as she accepted the mug of coffee.

Lynn turned away and began to rattle a tin of biscuits. Under the noise, Sarah just made out the words, 'She was meeting someone.'

*

16

'And that's why she told her father she wouldn't be home until 11 o'clock, isn't it? You really must tell the police this, Lynn, you know you must.'

The girl was back in her corner of the sofa, the coffee mugs empty on a glass-topped table. Sarah wondered if they were making rings, then thought, so what?

'But I promised Rubina.' The words were becoming a mantra.

Sarah breathed in, 'Let's begin again. You have given your word and you don't want to break it, and that's fine. But trust carries with it a kind of responsibility too, doesn't it, Lynn?'

'I suppose so.'

'You promised not to tell that Rubina had gone to meet someone instead of going straight home, but surely everything changed when she didn't come back?'

Lynn thought for a moment, then nodded.

Sarah felt truly sorry for the girl: her face was blotchy with weeping, her glasses were smeared and her mousy hair was badly in need of a brush. She could understand too, how important to Lynn Rubina's friendship must be, and how hard she would try to protect it.

Sarah gritted her teeth. 'She might be in danger.'

The girl whispered, 'I know.'

'Then will you tell the police?'

'Can't you do it, Miss?'

'Of course I can, but they'll want to know more than I can tell them. How did Rubina convince her father about the time -11 o'clock?'

'Well...when she phoned from the bus? She said it had broken down.'

'But surely her parents would find out that was a lie?'

Lynn shook her head. 'Not really, no one else from

17

school goes to Rubina's house, just me.'

'And you were colluding.'

For the first time the girl looked more worried than sad. 'Do you think I'll get into trouble?'

Sarah chose her words with care. 'Not because of the time thing, no, that was Rubina's doing. But it is quite different if you know more than you are telling.'

Lynn's eyes widened behind her glasses. 'No, honestly!' She halted a gesture which might have been crossing her heart, but remembered in time that she was seventeen. 'She just said she was going to meet someone.'

'Was it a boyfriend?'

'No, it couldn't have been,' she said, too quickly.

'Why are you so sure?'

Lynn began rubbing at a small coffee stain on her dressing gown. 'Oh well, you know

Miss, how, Rubina being Asian and all that...she isn't allowed...'

'To mix with boys from the school?'

'Yes.'

'Was there anyone special at school that she might have wanted to meet without her parents knowing?'

'No.'

'You're sure, Lynn.'

'Yes, Miss.'

Sarah left with Lynn's promise to phone the police when her mother came home. She didn't feel confident of Elizabeth Cameron's support for Lynn, and her father Commander Cameron, had sailed on exercises from the submarine base at Faslane a week ago.

*

It was still bright when Sarah left the house for the second time. She hoped the weather would hold for the next few days for her visit to Irene in the Lake District. Irene Wilson was her closest friend, and had been her bridesmaid ten years ago when she had married Simon. It was to Irene that Sarah had gone between leaving her marriage and moving back to Scotland. Irene had wanted her to stay, but somehow, the marriage ended, Sarah had been drawn back to the country she'd fled when her mother finally died. No father, no mother, no Ruth.

Still, Irene understood what Simon never did - how Ruth couldn't ever be put away in a drawer marked 'the past', no matter how hard Sarah tried. It had made her husband nervous every time Sarah saw a woman who might have been her sister - sometimes with children - even when they'd moved as far as Southampton. Her parents had given up on Ruth quite soon, and it took Sarah a long, painful time to realise that they had found comfort in their fatalism. Sarah had never given up - Simon called it giving in - to the truth.

Should she go to the police before she left, or should she leave it to Lynn? What if Rubina turned up? Anyway, was it really any of her business?

As it was, on her way to the cattery where Henry would board while she was away, she had to drive past the police station.

This policeman was whistling. He smiled at Sarah. 'Good morning.' A shaft of sunlight filtered in from a high window and created a spotlight for him. 'It's a lovely morning, isn't it?'

Sarah smiled back. 'It's about the girl who's missing, you know...'

'Rubina Khan, yes indeed.' His smile had gone,' Do you know something, Miss..?'

'Blane, Sarah Blane. Not really, but I'm on eof her

teachers at the High, and, well, I've been speaking to her friend this morning.'

'Councillor Cameron's daughter.'

'She told me you had been to see her.'

'That's right, CID went round. Do you have other information?'

Sarah swallowed. 'Yes.'

'Wait there, I'll get DI Hamilton.' He lifted a telephone.

Detective Inspector Steve Hamilton was casually dressed, but in well-creased slacks and a short-sleeved shirt. When he appeared from somewhere in the bowels of the station and beckoned Sarah to follow him it was with none of the bonhomie of the uniformed man on the desk. As she followed him down a corridor Sarah wondered if she had perhaps disturbed him at the Sunday papers. A broadsheet lay on the floor near his desk, and the rich aroma of coffee filled the room from a machine in the corner.

He pointed to a seat, sat down behind his desk and said, 'Sarah Blane, a teacher of the missing girl.' He rubbed his nose with his thumb and forefinger, 'I'm told you were in here last night too, Miss Blane.'

The 'too' wasn't lost on Sarah, and she realised that this man thought she was a busy-body. It was written all over his bored expression and she felt her face grow warm.

'Dr Birkmyre, my head teacher, asked me to come last night. I am Rubina's form teacher, and she is in my senior English class, so he knew that I was involved in the theatre trip.' She added, 'And I know Rubina quite well.'

'I see. But you didn't go on the theatre trip?'

'No, there were only a few pupils from my class interested - Lynn and Rubina and one of the boys - so Miss Aitken took them by herself.'

'But she didn't come back with them?'

'No...o, because she lives in Glasgow, and senior pupils are old enough to come home by themselves.'

He smiled. 'Are they now, Miss Blane?'

Her face was burning.

'Detective Inspector Hamilton, I thought you knew all this?'

'Oh I do, Miss Blane, I do. So that brings us back to the original question. Why are you here?'

Sarah had an overwhelming urge to get up and walk out.

'I've been to see Lynn Cameron this morning and she has given me some information which I understand she withheld from you,' Now I can see why, you smug sod, she thought.

He had thick reddish eyebrows which he raised like a couple of animated toothbrushes. 'Did she indeed?'

'Well, she said, being loyal to Rubina you understand - that she wasn't wholly frank with you about Friday night. Rubina left Lynn to go and meet some other person. Of course, she'll probably phone you very soon with this information, I've persuaded her that she should tell you.'

'Oh, that's very kind of you. And what is Councillor Cameron saying about this?'

'Actually, she wasn't there, so that's why Lynn didn't phone while I was with her. I thought her mother should be supporting her.'

'Mm...then you thought you'd tell us yourself, just to make sure we didn't miss anything, eh, Miss Blane?'

Sarah gripped her handbag strap. She'd been right, it was none of her business. She rose to her feet.

'I'm sorry, DI Hamilton, I shouldn't have come.'

The policeman got up too, and came round his desk. He was about the same height as Sarah and she found herself thinking he was small for a policeman. She hoped he wasn't going to see her out, but as she put her hand on the door, he said.

'By the way, since you're here. What can you tell us about this Khan family?'

'What do you mean?'

'Well, as you said yourself, you know the Khan girl quite well. Did she ever tell you things, confide in you like?' He sat down on the edge of his desk.

'Absolutely not! And if she had, I wouldn't have come here to tell you!'

He was rubbing his nose again, 'Ah, but that's where you'd be wrong Miss; in a criminal investigation there are no secrets.'

'Criminal investigation?' Her heart thumped at the words. 'But, surely, this isn't...I mean, we don't know what has happened to Rubina..?'

'Exactly, Miss Blane.'

Chapter 2

When she returned on Friday, Sarah was pleased to be going to Moira Campbell's for dinner. Carrying a bottle of wine and a bunch of flowers she walked the half mile or so to the Campbell's Victorian villa. The huge garden was, for the most part, Moira's department, and Sarah smiled at the mass of unruly greenery blurring into the dusk of the autumn evening as she walked up the drive.

The weather had been good for her trip to Keswick, fine for some serious walking, but it wasn't enough to block out Rubina Khan's disappearance. Each day she'd scanned the papers and watched the news, mindful of the cliché about the value of no news. On Wednesday she'd phoned Moira Campbell, deputy head of the school, who was back in town.

'The police have searched the school, you know,' Moira said, 'I had to go with them.'

Sarah remembered her parents' shock when the police came to search the house after Ruth disappeared. They tried to understand that it was part of the routine, but it had seemed so callous in the face of their agony.

'Why did you have to go in?' she asked Moira.

'Well, you know what Bobby's like - our dear janitor. Not even the police were gaining access to his dominions without one of us being there. Obviously it should have been the Head, but he's gone off to his cottage up north for the week. He doesn't have a landline there, likes to do a bit of quiet meditating, says he.'

'Don't we all,' Sarah smiled. 'Anyway, searching the

school, all these nooks and crannies - it must have taken ages?'

'It did, all of a morning in fact, and I couldn't imagine her being there, but the police line is that they always search places which are familiar to the missing person - apparently it's the kind of thing people sometimes do.

'I suppose they would go to her home too?'

'I expect they would, Sarah, but I don't know, I haven't actually seen any of the family. I do know they went to see the Watkins boy. Apart from Lynn Cameron, he was the last person to see her.'

'The boy from the peace camp?' Although she had seen it many times, Sarah was still bemused by the rag bag of tents and caravans which made up the peace camp. Multi-coloured graffiti on the caravans, home-made slogans, and ban the bomb symbols mixed with lines of washing and toddlers' prams on what had once been a broad grass verge on the road. There it rambled, in tawdry defiance of one of the most powerful weapons of mass destruction yet conceived by man, opposite the high fences and banks of razor wire designed to repel all comers from the naval base and home of the Trident submarine.

'Yes, I'd like to have been a fly on the wall at that interview. His mother would hardly welcome the police into her little tin home in the west.'

*

When Moira opened the door garlicky smells wafted out to Sarah. Moira looked more like a cook than she did a senior manager in a large secondary school. She had dark, untidy hair which resembled one of the things which grew in her own garden. Moira had befriended Sarah when she came to

Fruin High. She enjoyed dinner-parties there, mostly in the company of other friends, or colleagues of Moira's husband Peter, a solicitor in the town.

'Come into the kitchen, it's warm in there.'

Moira took her coat and Sarah followed her into a large room which had a smooth, oak table set for two. She loved the well-used feeling of this kitchen, with its racks of pots and pans and bunches of garlic and herbs.

'Where's Peter?' Sarah asked.

Moira was stirring something on the Aga. 'He's at a meeting in the city, and having dinner with a client.' She waved behind her, 'If you don't mind, I thought we'd eat in here since it's only the two of us.'

'I like it in here. It's comfortable.'

'Pour us a glass of wine, will you?'

The red wine bubbled cheerfully into the glasses. Sarah proposed a toast, eyebrows raised. 'Here's to the holiday, eh?'

Moira came to the table with two steaming bowls of soup. 'Some holiday!' She shook her head, 'A pupil missing. Since I was in London, you'll know more of the detail than I do.' She held out a basket of warm bread. 'Poor Mr Khan, having to gatecrash the wedding and everything.'

Sarah nodded, 'But aren't there any further developments?'

'Not as far as I know. I have seen Lynn Cameron, but she doesn't seem to know anything either. She's in a bit of a state though, that girl.'

'I know. Did Lynn tell you that Rubina was meeting someone that night? Or, for that matter, did the police?' Sarah wondered if she should be revealing this.

'Lynn didn't, but sharp little DI Hamilton said something about it - wanted the list of boys who had gone on the theatre trip.'

'And they went to see Leslie, the one they call Grasshopper?'

'Leslie Watkins, yes.' Moira pointed with her spoon. 'They wouldn't be welcome, that's for sure. Franny Watkins claims to be a dedicated opponent of the establishment. She came to live at the peace camp about five years ago, when Leslie was just due to start secondary school. I think Leslie's homes until then were a series of protest venues all round the country - you know motorways, tree-houses; places like that, and strange though it may sound, he's actually had some stability at the peace camp.'

'Living in a caravan on the side of a main road?'

Moira was bringing a fragrant stew and dishes of vegetables to the table now. 'As ever, this all looks and smells wonderful, Moira. But there's so much!'

'Well, do help yourself - you can afford to put on a bit of weight, unlike me!' She patted her plump stomach. 'I'm always planning the diet, for tomorrow, next week, you know how it is...'

'Actually, Moira, I've always meant to ask: how come the great and good of this affluent little town tolerate the peace camp? I mean, I admire the commitment of the protestors, but the camp is a bit of an eyesore, isn't it?

'Oh...years ago a leftish council gave the peace camp long periods of planning permission. Even gave them toilets and a telephone line. Imagine? The chagrin of some?'

'It's still the focus for anti-nuclear demonstrations, isn't it?'

'Yes, and Franny Watkins is always in the thick of them. She's been arrested more times than I've had hot dinners.'

'What does Leslie do then?'

'Oh, he's a very resilient boy, he just gets on with his life now that he's a little older, comes to school, works quite hard.'

Sarah said, 'Yes, he does.'

'It wasn't like that when he was younger; Franny had more than one battle with the school over what she called our 'brainwashing' of her son. Since knowledge is power and all that, she wanted him to be literate, but she wanted to censor the knowledge. I remember once there was a terrific battle with Bill MacGregor in History; something about the Industrial Revolution, I think it was.'

'I like Leslie,' Sarah said, her mouth full of creamy pudding, 'I admit his outlandish appearance was a bit of a shock at first glance, but I soon got used to it.'

'I don't know how they can stand these awful dreadlock hairstyles - and washing facilities can't be great in a caravan.'

'He's clean enough, but the layers of clothes are off-putting. The girls like him anyway; he seems to have some kind of charisma.'

Moira didn't answer for moment, but went to the stove to fiddle with a cafetiere. 'Have you, at any time, Sarah, thought Leslie's attraction might be to do with his ability to procure certain illegal substances?'

'Surely not!' Sarah surprised herself by the vehemence of her reply.

'Oh, I don't know,' Moira said, pouring coffee and passing a cup to Sarah. 'Someone in the school is definitely a source, but we can't trace it.'

'Leslie's mother would surely have you for that if you wrongly accused her son. Stereotyping, she'd call it, and she wouldn't be wrong.'

'I know. It's just, Keith has a bee in his bonnet about Leslie's type of boy, so different from his own fine sons, with their private education.'

'Did they go to Millig?'

27

'No, Glasgow. I think it was easier to look other parents in the eye if they didn't see his boys trotting up the hill to the independent school. Hardly a vote of confidence for his own fiefdom! The eldest graduated this summer and he's just left to do a year in America - Harvard or MIT - somewhere august, you can be sure. I don't think Malcolm, that's the other one, has made up his mind yet. He's got another year or two at school. Their mother is a specialist in a Glasgow hospital and Keith says Malcolm is showing an interest in medicine too.

'I met the boys at the school fete; they seemed all right. Gordon, that's the older one, isn't it? He helped to clear up afterwards and he was talking to me about his favourite writers. I found him quite likeable.

'Yes. He was here for most of the vacation. I don't think they'll turn into such stuffed shirts as their father, but you never know.'

They took the tray with the coffee into the sitting room and sank into Moira's squashy, sofa cushions. It was very dark outside now, and rain had begun to lash at the tall windows.

'Oh Lord! Look at that and I walked up!'

'It's all right, I'll get Peter to run you home when he comes in.'

Drowsy with the food and wine, the comfortable sofa was almost enough to lull Sarah into sleep.

On the other sofa Moira lit one of her rare cigarettes. 'We haven't spoken much about Rubina, after all, have we Sarah?'

'No.'

Moira spoke quietly, 'Or Ruth?'

In her new life Sarah had told only Moira about her lost sister, and about the breakdown which had ended her marriage, and put an interval in her teaching career.

Sarah rubbed her forehead. 'I don't think I can bear it, Moira. I know the girl really is nothing to me, but no-one knows what hell it is to lose someone like that...maybe never to find out what has happened to her. I can't stop thinking about her parents. Can you imagine how they feel?'

'Yes, I'm sure I can.' Moira shrugged. 'Being childless doesn't rob one of empathy completely, I suppose.'

'Oh, Moira, I'm sorry, I didn't mean it like that.'

'Don't be daft! I'm not that sensitive now. Anyway, I spend my whole life with youngsters, don't I? I know a lot about them even if they're never going to be my own.'

'What do you think has happened to Rubina?'

'I wish I knew.' Moira shook her head. 'The thing that's worrying me is this drug business. I'd hate to think it was anything to do with that.'

Sarah sat up. 'Surely not!' She repeated the phrase she'd used about Leslie and began to question her own judgement. What, after all, did she know about these kids? Just because she liked them didn't turn them into angels. She felt a sudden jolt. Had Ruth been an angel?

'Anyway, I just can't see it. Rubina is the child of very different parents from Franny Watkins!'

Moira smiled, 'Stereotyping, Sarah?'

*

Next day Sarah was restless. Painfully conscious of her freedom slipping away - it was the weekend again, school on Monday - she couldn't settle to her normal Saturday routine - cleaning the flat and shopping. She drifted around with a duster in her hand most of the morning, wondering if she should give David Smythe a call, maybe meet him for lunch. Still, she knew it would simply end up in more discussion about Rubina. Anyway, he'd hardly be back from his exotic holiday. He'd told Sarah where it was, but events had put it out of her mind. Sarah had never met a teacher as well-heeled as David. His was the only Aston Martin DB7 in the staff car park, for example. Sarah didn't know much about cars but she heard the boys often enough. They never remarked on her modest Fiesta except to tell her when the tyres were needing air.

She knew that David lived in his own flat, attached to his parents' house; that must help. His father was the eponymous owner of Colin Smythe Cars - a huge national concern. She had often wondered how David came to be a teacher, for that matter; more lucrative pickings would surely have been waiting for him in his father's business. And she'd gathered from remarks made here and there that his father wasn't exactly thrilled by his son's chosen profession. Anyway, David liked it well enough. Besides, the good-looking young man seemed to be a magnet to the teenage girls.

She threw down the cloth and made herself think about going to see the Khans. She felt so sorry for them. Then she picked up the duster again and began to scrub at the bookshelves. It wasn't her role. When the bell rang she thought for a moment she'd summoned David - but it was Lynn Cameron's voice she heard on the intercom. Sarah pressed the button.

While she waited for Lynn to climb the stairs, Sarah put the kettle on and fetched the instant coffee out of the cupboard.

The girl looked better than she had on Sunday. She smiled at Sarah when she opened the door. Her hair was clean and her jeans and sweater were fresh-looking, as if she'd taken some trouble with her appearance.

'Come on in, Lynn, I'm just making some coffee.'

Lynn Cameron was the first pupil ever to have entered the flat and Sarah wondered if the girl would be self-conscious, but she seemed to be calm. In normal circumstances Sarah would have thought twice about letting a pupil enter her home - it was seldom a good idea when a teacher lived alone - but for the moment at least, this was a different time.

Lynn walked to the window and looked out. 'What a brilliant view!'

'Yes, isn't it? Sit down Lynn, and tell me why you've come.'

The girl nodded and sat down on the window seat with her back to the light. Henry investigated her shoes then, deciding to approve, sat up beside Lynn.

'I hope it's all right to be here, Miss Blane, but I needed to tell someone!'

Sarah said. 'Yes, I think so. Depending, of course, on what it is.'

'Oh, it's nothing bad!' A seagull on the windowsill screeched. Lynn jumped and Sarah thought that she was probably nervous after all.

'Okay, tell me.' Sarah sat on the chair in the bay window, close enough to Lynn to watch her as she spoke.

'I've been thinking and thinking all week, about Rubina, you know?'

Sarah nodded.

'My mother even got mad at me for moping around so much. She keeps saying that Rubina's just gone off for reasons of her own, and if she didn't choose to tell me what they were, it was up to her.' Lynn smiled. 'She said all girls weren't as lucky as I am, with such a good home.' She hesitated, 'And that Rubina maybe wanted to get away from some trouble in the house.'

Sarah was still.

'Anyway, it made me think, and I began to remember something Rubina had told me. She was pretty angry about it.'

'Did she tell you in confidence, Lynn?'

The girl bit her lip. 'I suppose she did, but I mean now...it's such a simple explanation...'

'You're right. Of course...' Sarah put her cup down. She wasn't sure that she wanted to hear this confidence.

'You know how Rubina is Asian, Miss? She was born here but her family came from Pakistan years ago.'

'Ye-es.'

'Well, apparently there's some cousin in Pakistan and they want her to marry him!'

'What?'

'Oh, it's to do with this guy being able to come and live here if he marries her, or something. Rubina said her mother wasn't very happy about it, but her dad was determined she would meet him when he comes to Scotland.'

'I see.'

'Rubina wants to go to university, she's really clever, but her father doesn't seem to agree. You know, women's place in the home and all that - just like her mother. Rubina told me he even hates it because she won't dress as a Muslim woman should. You know, with the trousers and scarves and things.'

'So what are you saying, Lynn? That Rubina defies her father?'

Lynn jumped off the window seat. 'Yes! She's run off, hasn't she? She's gone to stay with some auntie in Glasgow or something to avoid this cousin from Pakistan. If they can't find her they can't make her marry him, can they?'

'But surely someone would know where she was?'

'Well that's it! Maybe her mother does and she's not telling!'

Sarah studied the dregs in her coffee cup. Still

absorbed in the conversation with Moira, she'd braced herself to hear something about Rubina and drugs. But this? This put an entirely different slant on the girl's disappearance. If Lynn was right.

'Why didn't you say any of this on Sunday? Heavens, it's more than a week since Rubina disappeared!'

Lynn began feeling in her pocket for a hankie and Sarah regretted her tone.

'Honestly Miss Blane, I just didn't think about it then. It seemed so...' she waved the tissue, 'ridiculous! I actually thought Rubina was making it up at the time, but don't you see, this could be the perfect answer!'

Sarah stood up and moved to the window. Below, people were walking dogs on the esplanade, couples strolled arm in arm or pushed babies in prams. One father was steering his toddler's cycle, laughing and holding on to the saddle as the ambitious child pedalled furiously.

'Why are you telling this to me, Lynn?'

'Well, because you came to see me...and you seemed so...concerned about Rubina.'

'And what do you want me to do?' She turned. 'Your instincts may have been right, Lynn; Rubina could have been teasing you.'

Lynn had begun to shred the handkerchief; little flakes of tissue were falling on Sarah's as yet unvacuumed carpet. The girl was starting to look tearful.

'It's just that...well...if it's true, it means that Rubina could be safe - she could be all right, couldn't she?'

'Sit down again, we'll have to think about this. I'll make some more coffee.' She switched the kettle on again.

'So, what could we do, Lynn? We can't just knock on the Khan's front door and ask them if Rubina was being lined up for an arranged marriage, can we?'

Lynn shook her head as she took the cup from Sarah.

'I know.' She sighed as she sat down on the sofa. 'But I just feel there must be something!'

Sarah joined her 'And, if you're right - it wouldn't be any of our business.'

Lynn sat up straight, 'No, but I know someone who would make it his business!'

'Who?'

'Hakim, of course! You know, her cousin. He really fancies Rubina, but she can't stand him. He'd have, like, a fit if he knew there was someone from Pakistan on the go.'

Lynn got up and placed her cup on the kitchen counter, then walked back to the window.

'Lynn, calm down! We can't just go asking Hakim then, can we?'

The girl smiled, 'Ah, but we can ask Mohammed.'

Sarah said again, 'Who?'

*

Lynn explained as she and Sarah walked from the front to the main shopping street,

'Mohammed is not bit like Hakim. Even although he's his brother. Rubina likes Mohammed a lot - in fact, he's her best friend,' she glanced sideways at Sarah, 'apart from me, that is.'

Sarah recalled the young man she had seen in the store on several occasions. 'Is he a pupil at Fruin High then?'

'No, he left last year. He's going to college but at the moment he works in the shop. It gives him something to do, because he never goes out anywhere, he's very quiet.'

'So what makes you think he'll talk to us?' Sarah skirted a pram.

'I think he'll be just as worried as we are. And if the cousin from Pakistan story is true, he'll know about it.' She stopped, her eyes wide. 'He might even know where she is!'

'But Hakim wouldn't?'

They turned the last corner and ran across the road on the green signal.

'Well, Rubina wouldn't have told him, that's a certainty. Maybe Mr Khan did, but Rubina said she wasn't to speak about it outside the house.'

They had arrived in front of the plate glass windows of the store. It was an establishment of some class, and the window displays were of a range of well-known labels.

'Except to Mohammed?'

'She didn't count Mohammed.' Lynn moved to the edge of the entrance and peered into the store. 'I can't see him just now.'

Sarah said, 'Look, you can't see properly that way. Why don't I go in and look around, and if I see him I'll come out and tell you?'

'Okay.'

Inside, Sarah approached a rack of winter coats and began to pull the hangers along one at a time. As the uncle, Shahid Ashrif, was about to come forward, Sarah mouthed, 'Just browsing,' and he smiled and retreated to the counter. She didn't think he would remember her from the police station. Anyway, she did shop there sometimes. Behind, in a little office, she could see Mohammed reading a newspaper, so, with a final rattle of the hangers and a shrug she left the store.

She edged Lynn away from the window. 'He's there. What are you going to do now?'

Lynn wriggled a bright green mobile phone from the pocket of her jeans; and they stood aside until Mohammed answered.

'Quick, he's going to meet us in the park!'

Sarah was a little out of breath by the time they reached the meeting point, a long disused bandstand in the centre of the town park. The weather was growing colder as the end of October approached, and she shivered in her light jacket. Beginning to feel a bit silly about this assignation, she wished she had waited in the flat for news.

She was just about to suggest this to Lynn when Mohammed appeared round the bandstand. He walked with a slight limp. Sarah thought he looked as confused as she felt.

'Hi, this is Miss Blane,' Lynn said. 'Rubina's English teacher.'

Mohammed's frown deepened. 'Yes?'

'Listen Mohammed, she's just as worried about Rubina as the rest of us, and I thought you might be able to help us.'

Sarah tried to smile at the boy. 'Yes...if you know anything...'

He looked at her directly. 'But why should I tell you...'

Forgetting how cold the stone was going to be, Sarah sat down on the edge of the bandstand. She nodded. 'You're right of course, it's none of my business.'

Lynn's voice rose, 'No, it is...we're all worried sick. Mohammed! If Rubina was running away from something...'she hesitated, 'like this cousin from Pakistan or what...she'd have told you, I know she would.'

Mohammed put his hands into the pockets of his black anorak and looked away towards the park gate. It was getting colder and the park was deserted. He spoke with his back to them,

'She did tell me. But she wasn't going to run away from it. She just said she would refuse to meet him when he came.'

'But wouldn't her father be very angry if she did that?' Sarah said.

The thin black shoulders moved in a shrug. 'Yes.'

Sarah began to feel the need to tread gently.' What about your brother, Hakim, did she tell him about this?'

Mohammed smiled. His teeth were very white. 'No, he would go ballistic!'

Lynn moved forward. 'So you don't know where she is then, do you?'

He had begun to shake his head when Sarah added, 'Or who she was meeting that night?'

The boy stopped. 'Meeting someone? But...'

Lynn said, 'Yeah, you might as well know. She left me to meet someone. No one knows who...'

'Does Uncle Anwar know this?'

'I think the police will have told him now, 'Sarah said.

'But Uncle Anwar...he hasn't mentioned...look, I've got to go now.'

Suddenly he vanished into the shadows.

Sarah was surprised. 'So, what do we do now?' She got up, and with Lynn started walking towards the park gate.

Lynn was despondent. 'I was sure Mohammed would know something.'

'Actually Lynn, I think he does.'

At home the heating had come on and the flat was warm. Sarah was turning on the lamps when she remembered that she hadn't eaten since breakfast, apart from a couple of biscuits with Lynn. The fridge held only a couple of eggs and a yoghurt or two, probably out of date. Besides she had no milk or bread. She had intended shopping in the afternoon and she had forgotten all about it. Moreover, Henry was moping around looking distinctly hungry. With a sigh, she picked up her jacket again.

She headed into Dumbarton for the late opening supermarket. It was still bright and noisy, and she wondered what all these other people had been doing all day. Not the same as she had, she was quite sure of that. The warm cheerfulness of the store was foreign to the dark places of Sarah's mind, and she pushed her trolley hurriedly up and down the aisles, conscious that the contents were piling up haphazardly. Well, at least she wouldn't starve.

At the check-out her heart caught at the sight of a young Asian woman a few places in front of her. It wasn't Rubina; this girl was older and was wearing the shalwar kameese; the tunic and trousers worn mainly by women of Pakistani origin. She had a scarf held lightly on her dark hair. The sight stirred something in Sarah's memory.

It was an article from a Sunday supplement about arranged marriages in the Asian community. Sometimes Sarah took articles into class for discussion and stimulus to writing but she remembered that this one hadn't seemed like such a good idea with Rubina there. It could have been tough on the girl to take on the argument on her own. Sarah had pushed the article back into her file. How long ago...two months?

Back in the flat, she contained her impatience until she had cooked herself a pasta dish, then she sat down at the table to eat with the article in front of her.

The material was a series of case histories; personal testimonies ranging from those who favoured the idea of marriages arranged by their families on all sorts of grounds, to those who spoke, not of mutually agreed arrangements, but of the horror of marriages forced on unwilling and powerless girls. The article spoke of refuges which had been set up to help those Asian women who needed to escape from abusive partners, and there was also reference to 'safe houses'. The piece also referred to 'bounty hunters'; men who were paid high sums to find and return the reluctant bride or fiancee. Even in Britain, the strangely named 'honour killings'were known to take place on occasion, when 'a woman deemed to have blackened the family name is murdered by her own or her husband's family.'

Sarah shuddered, and put the paper aside.

*

Before classes started on Monday morning she climbed the stairs to Moira's office with the article in a brown envelope. The last thing she wanted was for rumours about Rubina's disappearance to be given lurid and probably mistaken credibility by what she had been reading. All the same, she thought that Moira should see it. Her room was empty and Sarah stuck a yellow sticker on the envelope with the words, *'Read this when you have a moment',* and left it on her cluttered desk.

In the corridor she met Moira leaving the Head's room. The deputy head looked grim and Sarah held her breath, dreading news of Rubina.

'Oh, Sarah, I'm just going to call a whole school meeting.' She jerked her head at his door. 'Orders of the boss.'

Sarah clenched her fists in her jacket pockets. 'Is it Rubina?'

'Rubina?' Moira looked distracted. 'No...worse than...I mean...' She ran a hand through her hair. 'What am I saying? No, we've just had word that a fourth year girl is critically ill in hospital. Elaine Godfrey?'

Sarah shook her head, she didn't know the pupil.

Moira leaned one shoulder against the wall. 'Ecstasy. She was at a youth club disco on Saturday night and she took an Ecstasy tablet. A youth club! Would you believe it? She's...I can hardly bear to say it...her life is in danger. The police are on their way to talk to the school and Keith wants

39

all the pupils to be there.' She shoved herself off the wall. 'And all the staff.' Her last words were almost drowned out by the bell and Sarah hurried to her classroom.

It was a subdued group of pupils who filed into the room and sat at their desks - quite different from the usual noisy gathering after a holiday. Sarah wondered what she should say - about Rubina? About this other girl, Elaine?

With her head down she called their names from the register: Lynn Cameron's response was muffled. Sarah looked up. The girl sat in her usual place, biting at her knuckles. Beside her was Rubina's empty seat.

A young pupil knocked at the door and gave Sarah the note about the whole school meeting in the assembly hall.

After the interruption the class waited in silence, until she was finished.

Then Leslie Watkins raised his hand. 'Miss Blane, can we ask you something?'

She nodded.

'Do you know what's happened to Rubina, Miss?'

Sarah took a deep breath, 'No, I'm sorry, Leslie. I don't know any more than anyone else, I'm afraid.'

'Lynn says you are trying to help.'

Some of the other pupils were nodding. Sarah glanced at Lynn, who was staring at her with a pleading expression.

'I would if I could,' She tried to smile, 'but the police are the best people to find Rubina, don't you think?'

Leslie Watkins barked. 'Ha! The police!'

Sarah had just raised her eyebrows, daring him to go no further, when the bell rang for the end of registration. As the class began to move she waved the note. 'Meeting in the hall, 5C.'

The shuffling, talking and coughing amongst the

pupils in the assembly hall ceased abruptly when the Head, followed by DI Steve Hamilton, walked on to the stage. Sarah thought Keith Birkmyre looked at his most imposing beside the smaller figure of the detective. He introduced the policeman then, after a tension-building pause, broke the news about Elaine Godfrey.

Hysterical sobbing began amongst the girls in her year group, and Hamilton's face made it clear that he wasn't best pleased to have his authority usurped by a teacher, however senior. Holding up both hands for silence he began to speak in a way which suggested that this custodian of the populace knew damn all about kids.

'Now boys and girls, we adults know what it is like to be young.' Leslie Watkins snorted. 'We all remember how easy it is to be tempted to do the wrong thing at times.' His teeth showed in a smile. 'But a little bit of mischief can have some very dangerous consequences, and you all know what I am talking about, don't you?' He pointed. 'This morning one of your friends is lying in hospital very seriously ill because she was tempted to do a bad thing. So,' the finger swept around the hall like a gun, 'who is going to tell me where little Elaine got her ecstasy tablets, eh?'

Pupils and teachers gasped, and Keith Birkmyre intervened.

'What the Detective Inspector means, I'm afraid, is that there is some evidence that ... illicit substances...drugs...are being sold in the town, maybe even,' his voice dropped, 'the school. We are very sorry, but what has happened to Elaine is a warning for all of us, and if anyone...I repeat, anyone, knows anything at all about this, you must come and tell me...or Mrs Campbell. Any information you may have will be treated in the strictest confidence.'

The Head and the inspector then took it in turns to

hammer home the penalties for experimenting with ecstasy. The burning skin, the foaming at the mouth...the possibility of death. Nothing was too graphic. Pupils became restless, and teachers muttered warnings along the rows. At last the Head gave permission for a return to classes. Suddenly, over the sound of talking and scraping chairs, there was a shout. 'What are you doing about Rubina Khan then?'

Sarah stopped, as did others, and the platform party turned back and began to scrutinise the hall for the speaker. Leslie Watkins had become fascinated by the exit sign above their nearest door. Sarah looked at him. As they left the hall Keith Birkmyre and the inspector were still scanning the room.

The next couple of lessons passed without much work from her over-excited pupils and Sarah was glad when the interval came and she could escape to the English department staff-room.

It was another surprise to discover that David Smythe had failed to show up for school. In the time that Sarah had been there David had never been absent; he remained the picture of health when all around were felled by the various bacteria which ran wild in schools every winter.

'We have heard from him.' said Willie Armstrong. 'He seems to have picked up some kind of bug in Sri Lanka and he's not at all well.'

'Sri Lanka, of course, I knew it was somewhere hot.' Sarah nodded. 'But poor David, he must be miserable.'

Judith Aitken spoke from behind her newspaper. 'On the contrary, quite happy, I'd say, to be missing this vale of tears today.'

Mary Stephens turned from the kettle. 'I think that's a bit unkind Judith, David would never miss school deliberately.'

Judith lowered her paper and stared at Mary, who flushed.

'I never said he'd done it deliberately, did I?'

'No but...I thought you were implying...' Mary was obviously regretting her little burst of nerve.

'Yes, you thought I was implying something about the Khan girl, didn't you!' Judith threw her newspaper on the floor and left the room, slamming the door.

There was a silence, eventually broken by Sarah. 'Well, well, what was that all about?' She looked from one to another of her colleagues.

Mary Stephens clattered the lid on the kettle. 'Since I appear to have started it Sarah, I should give you an explanation, I suppose.'

The principal teacher put down the essay he had been reading. 'It's all right, Mary, I'll tell her.' Roger Bullough shook his head like a man who couldn't believe that yet another problem had reared its ugly head and it was only Monday morning.

'No, look, I'm sorry I asked, it's none of my business.' Sarah said quickly.

'Well, sometimes the truth is simplest, and best.' Roger continued, 'And it's as well that you know, under the circumstances.' He paused to blow his nose on a greyish handkerchief and Sarah was reminded of the invalid wife who had kept him from attending the wedding. 'As you must be aware, David is...very attractive to some of the younger girls, and for a time, Rubina Khan was no exception. She would be about fifteen then. The difficulty arose because David seemed to be, I suppose - flattered - by Rubina's attentions. 'She is...' he stopped and rubbed his hand over his mouth, '...a very lovely girl. Anyway David was seen several times chatting to her outside school.'

Sarah opened her mouth, and Roger raised his hand.

'Oh, I know what you are going to say. Where's the harm in that? But her cousin Hakim didn't see it that way. He reported it to Rubina's father and a complaint was made to the school. The upshot was that Rubina was removed from David's English class.'

Mary Stephens was red in the face. 'And Judith Aitken has been trying to make something of it ever since. She simply hates David!'

'Now Mary, that's not helping the situation.' Willie pulled himself out of his chair and patted Mary's shoulder. 'Sit yourself down. I'll make the tea.'

Chapter 3

On Tuesday morning the school got the news that everyone had been dreading. Elaine Godfrey had died from massive hemorrhaging caused by the ecstasy tablet she had taken to celebrate her fifteenth birthday.

In the days which followed it seemed the entire school had gone into mourning, an atmosphere deepened by the presence of the drug squad in a large stationery cupboard become interview room, while they questioned every pupil from third year and above. Sarah's own senior pupils, however, were able to tell her that the police were drawing a blank every time. Elaine, it appeared, had been in possession of one Ecstasy tablet, which she'd shown to friends in school before the disco, but no-one knew, or was prepared to say, how she had acquired it.

Sarah felt sorry for Moira, who was to be glimpsed rushing here and there all over the building. Keith Birkmyre too, must have been deeply affected by the tragedy which had befallen his school, but if so he was better at hiding it than his deputy. Moira was pale with exhaustion as she tried to cope with the stream of worried or angry parents who crowded into the school every day. Some were there to be with their under-age children during the police questioning: others were just there.

It was not surprising that these terrible events overshadowed the disappearance of Rubina Khan, who could after all, still turn up at any moment. Sarah reflected that perhaps she had become too influenced by her own experience. Ruth's disappearance and Rubina's were not identical happenings.

At the end of the week she decided to go and visit David Smythe, who had still not returned to school, although William reported him to be much better. After lunch on Saturday she set out to drive to David's place: she had never been to the house, but she'd often passed the end of the long driveway.

It was bright and fairly sunny for the last day in October, and Sarah watched the street, busy with shoppers, while she waited at the traffic lights. And when her eye was caught by what looked like a banner in the side street, she was reminded that it was Hallowe'en. She had time only to register that the banner was being carried by a youth with long dreadlocks when the lights changed and she had to drive on, passing a police car turning into the street.

Squeezing into a minute parking space she got of the car and started to run back - feeling sick at what she thought she'd glimpsed in blood-red lettering on the white cloth.

When she reached the corner her fears were confirmed. There was more than one banner, more than one protestor, and, until the arrival of the police, they had been parading outside Khan and Ashrif's clothing store. Leslie's banner proclaimed, 'DOWN WITH FORCED MARRIAGE', while Lynn's carried a question - 'WHERE IS RUBINA?'

A small crowd had gathered; at the heart of it a distressed-looking Mr Khan, the policeman and Leslie and Lynn. As the officer spoke Lynn's banner drooped further and further towards the ground, but Leslie's remained upright.

Sarah stood, uncertain what to do. For a second she thought of slipping away pretending she hadn't seen anything, then she found herself walking towards the scene.

She was relieved to see that the policeman was the friendly one who'd been in the station on that Sunday morning.

Lynn gave a cry when she spotted Sarah and dropped the banner completely. Her eyes were wide. 'Miss Blane, he's going to arrest us!'

The policeman turned. 'Oh, hello there.' He gestured towards the two young people. 'Do you know anything about this?'

Sarah shook her head, and turned to Leslie. 'I suppose this was your idea?'

'So?' His ropes of hair swung as he looked away.

'So? What on earth are you doing? And getting Lynn involved!'

The policeman said, 'I've just informed them that this is breach of the peace.'

Leslie turned back. 'No it isn't - it's not a police state yet. We have the democratic right to peaceful protest!'

The policeman groaned, 'Oh, give it a rest, son. We all know where you're coming from. Listen Miss, why don't you tell them to apologise to Mr Khan here, and we'll say no more about it.'

'But...'

'Leslie, just do as he says.' Sarah pulled at the banner. 'I'm so sorry about this, Mr Khan.'

The man looked from one to the other of the young people and shook his head. 'I do not understand...' He walked back into the store.

'Right then, off with you before I change my mind. And get that rubbish in the bin!' The policeman got back into his car and the small crowd of onlookers drifted away.

Sarah held out a hand and waited while the two ripped the makeshift banners from their sticks. She folded them up into small squares, then she used them to point at

Leslie and Lynn.

'I've got to be somewhere in the next five minutes, so I can't do anything about this just now. But I'll see both of you in my classroom on Monday morning. All right?'

Leslie, scraping the point of his stick on the pavement, nodded without looking at her, while Lynn sniffed and began to search the pockets of her anorak.

Sarah wasn't sure how she felt as she walked back to her car. Angry yes, because such a stupid stunt wasn't going to help find Rubina, but at the same time struck by their determination. At least they were doing what they thought was right.

She threw the cloth parcels into the back of her car and switched on the ignition. The radio came on. Manoeuvring out of the tight space she didn't give it her full attention; until the voice said; 'News just in...', and the word 'body' leapt out of the speakers.

'The body of a young woman, believed to be of Asian origin, has been recovered from Loch Lomond, close to the village of Luss. The woman was found by a man walking his dog on the shore. At this stage police are not revealing how she died, but say only that the death is being regarded as suspicious. Police frogmen have been called to the scene ...'

Sarah switched off the radio and made a u-turn, oblivious to the blasting horn of another driver. Leaving the car on the double yellow lines outside her house she ran upstairs. Her whole body shook as she tried to get the key into the lock. Once in, she made straight for the bathroom. Kneeling by the toilet bowl, she vomited.

*

The phone was ringing. Wiping her mouth, she got to her feet and went to answer. It was David.

'Sarah? What happened, I was expecting you almost an hour ago?'

'I'm...I'm sorry David. It's ...I was on my way...but I couldn't...You haven't heard?'

'Heard what? What is it?'

'They've found a...a body...in the loch...it was on the radio.' She could smell sick on the hand holding the phone. 'I...I think it's Rubina.'

There was silence at the other end of the line.

'David?' Another wave of nausea swept over her. 'I've got to go...'

'No, Sarah, wait....talk to me.'

'I'm sorry...'

She hung up the phone, slumped on the sofa, and stared into the blackness of her cold fireplace for a long time.

When the phone rang again, she knew that it was David, and she let it ring.

What could she do? There was nothing for her to do. 'Police have found a body...' Those were the words the Marchegays had lived in terror of hearing for so long after Ruth disappeared: lived in helpless terror, for there was nothing to be done then either - but wait.

Now that awful message was being given to another family

.Maybe she should speak to Moira. Maybe Moira already knew. Then there was Lynn Cameron. Oh God, Lynn! What would this do to the girl?

Sarah rose and paced her small sitting-room. She had no role in this. No role. Because she'd lost her own sister didn't make it her tragedy. But, somehow, she felt as if it was. Rubina's smiling face - then Ruth's dimly remembered features - swam into her mind, and she wept for both of them. Sarah was crying so hard that when the phone rang again she didn't get to it in time. She called back. Lynn was incoherent. Sarah's throat hurt when she spoke. 'Oh Lynn, Lynn - try to calm down.'

The girl's hysterical sobs continued until a sharp voice in the background could be heard and the phone clicked into place. What now? She couldn't bear to sit in the flat, but she didn't want to see David. She would go to Lynn. Instinct told her that any kind of emotional crisis would not be well received in that immaculate place, and she felt desperately sorry for the girl. So, welcome or not, she would go.

The Cameron house was close enough to walk. It had started to rain heavily, and by the time she arrived her jacket was wet through and rainwater was running from her hair.

Elizabeth Cameron opened the door and peered out at Sarah on the dark path as if she were some bedraggled stray. 'Yes? Oh, it's you. What do you want?'

'Sorry, I was wondering …about Lynn?'

'Oh…Lynn? You were wondering about my daughter?' The woman's tone was hostile.

'I just…' It had been a mistake to come. She was turning away when Lynn rushed past her mother and threw herself into Sarah's arms.

Elizabeth Cameron walked back into the house, leaving Sarah clutching Lynn in a wet embrace. 'There, there Lynn…try to hold on.'

Lynn dragged Sarah into the house. 'Come to my room.'

Her mother nowhere to be seen, Sarah followed reluctantly. Lynn's bedroom had the same designer perfection of the rest of the house; now it looked entirely wrong for the shuddering mess that was the teenage girl. Sarah sat down beside Lynn on her frilled duvet cover, put her arm around her.

Lynn raised her swollen face. 'My mother doesn't like scenes.'

Sarah said, 'Yes.'

'But I loved Rubina, Miss.' Tears overwhelmed her. 'Now somebody has killed her! How could anybody...'

As the girl's voice rose, Sarah said. 'Shh...we don't know that yet.'

Suddenly Lynn pulled away. 'We don't know...? She stared. 'Then how did she die?

'I mean...we don't...' the words stuck in her throat. 'Might she have taken her own...'

Lynn jumped off the bed, shouting. 'What are you saying? What are you saying?' Rubina would never have done that...'

Sarah waited until the sobs died away. 'I'm sorry, Lynn.'

The girl went to her dressing table. 'I didn't lie to you Miss, when I said that Rubina never went out with any of the boys from school. But she did have a boyfriend.'

She turned back with a photograph in her hand and Sarah's heart thudded.

'Look.'

It was a fuzzy snap of a smiling Rubina - the background somewhere on the shores around Helensburgh: Greenock could be seen in the distance - and across her shoulder was what looked like a male arm. A blue sleeve could be seen, and a watch. That was all, because the photograph had been neatly cut to show only Rubina.

'Who is this, Lynn?'

'I don't know.'

Sarah said, slowly, 'Rubina was your best friend - and she never told you?'

Lynn wiped her eyes with her knuckles. 'No, it's the truth, honestly. I was the only person who knew she had a boyfriend, but she wouldn't even tell me who he was.'

'How do you know it wasn't one of the boys from school, then?'

The girl almost laughed. 'Because we talk about them all the time. Plenty of people in school fancy Rubina, but she says...said... they were all just little boys.'

'Even Leslie Watkins?'

'No, Grasshopper's all right. He's just our friend.' Lynn began to chew her thumbnail, and her next words were almost inaudible. 'But it wasn't only the boys in school who liked Rubina?'

The room was cold, and Sarah shivered in her damp jacket. 'How did you come by this photograph, Lynn.'

'Rubina asked me to keep it safe for her. She didn't have any other photographs of herself...her dad didn't approve of photos or something...and she didn't want anybody to find it.'

'You'll have to show this to somebody.'

'Somebody?'

'The police.'

'No! No! I couldn't do that!' Lynn broke down in another torrent of weeping,

Sarah stayed silent.

'Miss? You know what? I'd like to go and see Rubina's mum and dad.'

'I...I think that would be kind.' Sarah said carefully. 'With your mother.'

Lynn stopped crying. 'My mother?' She wiped her eyes with the bottom of her sweatshirt. She appeared to have run out of paper hankies. 'My mum...didn't really approve of Rubina.'

'What?'

The girl checked the closed door and lowered her voice. 'Oh, you would never guess, from what she says in the council - about welcoming asylum seekers and all that. But I hear her talking to Wilson Toner.'

'Wilson Toner?'

'Yeah, the newspaper guy.'

Sarah didn't read Toner's paper, but he was well known for the extremist views he expressed in The Clarion, a daily tabloid published in Glasgow.

'Is he a friend?' Sarah whispered.

Lynn came closer. 'Only of my mother, when my dad's not here?'

Sarah got up. 'I see. Listen, I think I should go now.'

'No, wait Miss, please.' She touched Sarah's sleeve. 'Would you go with me to see Rubina's parents?'

Sarah felt ill. 'Oh, Lynn, I don't know...it's not my place...'

'Please.'

'We'll see. Phone me tomorrow.'

Once outside, Sarah regretted the half-promise, and knew that she had taken the easy way out of that sanitized environment. She was exhausted now, but she walked quickly, longing for the comfort of her own home. On the way a pirate and a couple of witches loomed up out of the darkness; kids in fancy-dress, and she was reminded again that it was Hallowe'en. She wondered if they still called them guisers, as they had when she'd been a child in Edinburgh. The children laughed and shouted as they went on their way.

Legs aching, Sarah trudged up the three flights of stairs to the flat, to find David Smythe sitting on the top step, outside her front door.

David got up and put his hands on Sarah's arms. 'I saw your car downstairs, so I knew you hadn't gone far.'

She moved back a little. 'Why have you come?'

'I wanted to see you.' He was brushing the rain from

53

the shoulders of her jacket. 'And I thought you...needed someone. You sounded dreadful on the phone.'

Wearily, Sarah unlocked the door. 'You'd better come in.'

Inside, David shook his head when she offered him coffee. 'And you look as though you could do with something stronger.'

Sarah took glasses and a bottle of whisky from the cupboard, and handed them to him. He poured a large measure of whisky into each glass.

'Take that wet jacket off and come and sit down.'

The first mouthful of whisky made her cough. 'I've been to see Lynn Cameron,' she said.

David ran a hand through his hair. 'God, of course. That poor kid.'

They drank without speaking for several moments, then Sarah said, 'You haven't said anything about Rubina yet, David.'

He looked over his glass at her. 'I can't find the words.'

She felt an edge of panic. 'Words? A teenage girl, who was your pupil - more than your pupil if gossip is to be believed - has just been pulled out of Loch Lomond, and you can't find any words!'

His hand jerked, and some whisky spilled down the front of his shirt. 'More than...more than my pupil? You can't think...' He shook his head as if to empty it of Sarah's accusation. 'You couldn't think something like that. The girl used to be my pupil, yes, but she was always hanging around my car when I parked in town. All she wanted to do was talk. I kept trying to tell her that it wasn't a good idea, but well, you know the rest.'

'Now she's dead, David.'

He covered his face with his hands. 'What sick

bastard could do something like that.'

'Like what? What do you know?'

He removed his hands. 'She's been murdered. My father - he's pretty well in with some senior guys in the police.'

Sarah poured more whisky. 'What do you mean?'

'Well, when the news came in...about Rubina...he phoned someone, don't ask me who. It seems she was strangled, but they won't know any more until the post-mortem's been done.'

'But why does your father want to know?' Sarah looked closely into David Smythe's face. He didn't look well. His holiday tan had a patchy, yellowish appearance. She remembered that he had been ill.

He shrugged. 'My father is a very big noise in this town. Worked himself up from dodgy second-hand car salesman to millionaire? Nothing happens in this place that he isn't going to know about.'

Sarah was beginning to feel light-headed. 'And it's got nothing to do with you...and Rubina?'

He leaned forward, till his knees were almost touching her. 'No, Sarah, I swear. It's got nothing to do with me.'

'What about the police?'

'What about them?'

'Father or no father, they'll hear about your connection to Rubina. They'll probably want to interview you.'

The implications for the school struck her. Elaine Godfrey, now Rubina. How could a school in small town cope with so much in such a short space of time? There must be very few precedents. A pupil? An Asian girl - strangled and dumped in Loch Lomond? Sarah felt very, very tired.

55

Chapter 4

She awoke in the morning with a thumping headache and a dry mouth. It was Sunday, she didn't need to get up early. Then all the events of the day before rushed back, and with a sick feeling she knew that she was probably going to see the Khan family with Lynn Cameron. But she had no personal locus in this, and if she was representing the school it would have to be authorised.

When Lynn phoned, Sarah explained the difficulty and persuaded the girl to wait. Then she phoned Moira, but Peter told her she was at the school with the Head and the police. 'I think they are trying to work out a strategy for the coming week.'

Well, phoning was out of the question, she might interrupt a meeting. She would go to school and wait for an opportunity to speak with Moira.

As she drove into the car park a television van was already there, and a cameraman was filming some bunches of flowers which been had tied to the school railings. This affair would not be the kind which merits a small paragraph in a newspaper. This was the second death in just over a week. This was news.

The first person she met in the corridor leading to the Head's room was Judith Aitken, dressed more casually than Sarah had ever seen her, in jeans and a baggy jumper. 'Judith? Is everyone here?'

'No - just me. The police wanted to ask me again about the night the kids went to Hamlet. They were going to send someone to interview me at home, but I thought I might as well come down before all hell breaks loose.'

Sarah said, 'It's going to be unbearable, isn't it?'

Judith shrugged. 'Can't do anything about that. We'll just have to try to keep going.' Moira appeared and Judith left. Moira was deathly pale, and she had huge dark rings under her eyes.

'I need to talk to you, Moira.'

'Come into my office.'

Sarah unearthed a kettle in Moira's untidy office and filled it from the washbasin.

While she waited for it to boil she found the teabags and some sugar.

Moira said, ' I can't believe this is happening.'

Sarah brought her tea. There wasn't a clear space, so she laid it on a pile of folders on Moira's desk.

The depute head had the glazed look of someone who has just witnessed a terrible accident. 'What on earth can we do?'

Sarah took the chair in front of the desk. 'The awful thing is – nothing.'

Moira looked at her. 'But - we have the welfare of over a thousand pupils to think of! Think of tomorrow - think of the panic! One pupil dead of drugs and another murdered on the way home from a school trip! It's beyond ...anything...'

A nerve in Sarah's knee made it jump. 'How do they know already that Rubina...was mu...died on that first night? She was missing for two weeks. She could have been anywhere.'

'No. They could tell how long her body had been in the water.' She shuffled papers around on her desk. 'Apparently, they...bodies...take about two weeks to come to the surface. Oh, there's that file, I thought I'd lost it.' She put on her glasses, opened a folder and stared at the pages inside.

Sarah was reminded of the envelope that she had left on Moira's desk. 'Oh, those articles!' She looked at the cluttered desk. 'It might be a good idea to put them away somewhere, Moira, in the light of...'

'What articles?'

Sarah said, 'The ones about marriage in the Asian community...remember? I left them...with a yellow sticker.'

Moira patted the papers on her desk aimlessly. 'I never got them.'

The two women looked at each other. Into Sarah's mind flashed the blood red letters of Leslie Watkins banner about forced marriage. That would have to wait.

'What about Rubina's family? Has the Head, or have you, been to see them yet?'

The depute shook her head. It was obvious that the enormity of what had happened to the school had, temporarily at least, dulled her awareness of what had befallen one family. She let her glasses fall around her neck on their chain. 'Oh Sarah...no...we've been so caught up...with the police and people from head office and everything.' She pushed back her chair . 'I must talk to the boss...'

'Wait. Lynn Cameron has asked me to visit the Khans with her and I don't want to go without, you know, some authority.'

'Come with me. We'll see what the Head says.'

The room was full of people Sarah didn't recognise, apart from DI Hamilton. The Head was wearing a diamond-patterned golf sweater which made him look out of place amongst the filing cabinets and bookcases in his office. He agreed readily that Sarah should make an initial visit to Rubina's family. 'But do impress upon them, that I will be there in person soon, to discuss...arrangements.'

The detective said, 'You will pass on anything you think may be important, now, won't you, Miss Blane?'

She closed the door behind her.

*

Sarah's stomach was churning as, with Lynn, she made her way to the Khan house. She had taken the precaution of phoning rather than turning up unannounced. Shahid Ashrif had gently given her the message that the family would welcome her condolences. She bought some flowers from a garage forecourt and hoped that she was not making any blunders.

The Khan flat was large and well-furnished, with a mixture of very modern furniture and many rich artefacts from the sub-continent. A pleasant odour of unfamiliar spices greeted them as they passed soundlessly on thick Indian carpets from the hall into the large sitting room. The room was almost silent, although a number of people were present, sitting on the sofas and chairs. Sarah recognised Mohammed as first he, then Hakim rose at Mr Khan's unspoken signal. Hakim left the room and Mohammed went to stand at the window, gazing down into the quiet Sunday square. Mr Khan led Sarah to where a slim woman sat in the corner, seeing nothing, twisting the end of a white shawl which covered her head, round and round between her fingers.

'Please, this is my wife.' To the woman he said, 'Jaswinder, it is Miss Blane, Rubina's teacher.'

She did not respond. 'Jaswinder...'

'I am sorry, but my wife is...'

'I understand.' she handed him the flowers and he bowed his head, then he led her to a chair next to Lynn and

59

they joined the silent group. Sarah realized that several women near-by were quietly weeping, their fine scarves covering their faces. Lynn too had begun to cry.

Moments passed then Sarah was aware that Mr Khan was in the hallway, conducting a whispered conversation with Hakim. Why became apparent when the younger man burst into the room and confronted Sarah.

'What have you come here for?' His angry voice shattered the silence.

Sarah put her hand on Lynn's. 'We have come to offer...our sympathy. Rubina's friend here...and the school....'

'The school! The school let my cousin be taken away to be...'

Shahid Ashrif touched his son's shoulder. 'Hakim, please. This will not help,' He forced him away from Sarah. 'We must wait for the police...'

Hakim's face twisted in a sneer. 'The police? They will do nothing for us.'

Rubina's father said. 'Allah, praise be his name, will help us. This terrible deed will not go unpunished. And the police will do their duty.'

Sarah stood up. 'I think we should go, Mr Khan ...' She moved to where Mrs Khan still sat, staring at the silk she twisted and untwisted in her hands as if it were a task requiring all her concentration.

'Mrs Khan,' she bent over the woman. 'please, I am so sorry. And...if I can do anything to help...'

As she turned towards the door, Rubina's mother rose, and grasping Sarah by the arm, began to speak very quickly in Urdu. She didn't need to understand the words to know that the woman was entreating her in some way. Sarah tried to murmur her understanding.

MrKhan moved to his wife's side. 'Shh...Shh...Miss

Blane...my wife is asking for your help. Please...' his voice broke... 'if you know...help us to find whoever has done this terrible thing to our daughter...'

Sarah left the flat with Lynn behind her, the sounds of the woman's agony seared into her consciousness.

*

By the following Friday afternoon when Sarah left school the playground and the car park were, at last, almost deserted. The reporters and the TV cameras appeared to have found other sensations to follow. For a moment she stood, blankly trying to recall if she'd brought her car to school that morning.

It had been almost two weeks of sheer hell, and now, like everyone else on the staff, she was exhausted. DI Hamilton had brought in reinforcements and the questioning had been relentless, day in, day out, in an attempt to find out, not how Rubina Khan had died, but how Elaine Godfrey had obtained drugs in Fruin High. Sarah had wanted to scream with frustration until he'd told her an hour ago that he would appreciate it if she would be at home later since they wanted to talk to her about the Asian girl.

She hated the thought of her sanctuary invaded, but rather her territory than his.

At last she spotted her car behind the Head's big SUV. Fishing for her keys in her handbag she lost her grip on her briefcase and it fell, scattering papers on the ground. She sighed and bent to pick them up. They were mostly pupil exercises but done so badly in the light of events that she wouldn't have the heart to mark them down.

As she scooped the papers up a hand appeared and presented her with a couple of sheets which had drifted out of her sight. She straightened and looked at the man - a stranger - but vaguely familiar.

'Thanks.'

He smiled, 'No problem. I wanted to speak to you anyway.'

Sarah's heart sank. 'Another reporter?'

He raised his eyebrows. 'Another? You suppose we hunt in packs?'

Sarah nodded. 'Don't you?'

'Well, even pack animals have varied markings. Or don't you agree?' He stuck out the hand again. 'I'm Mark McKenzie - journalist, Sunday Standard,'

She shook it. 'And I'm Sarah Blane.'

She turned to go to her car and he walked beside her.

'Oh, I know who you are, Sarah Blane.'

She stopped as the doors unlocked with a click. 'You do?'

'Yes, DI Hamilton pointed you out to me this morning.'

Sarah stared at the man. 'DI Hamilton did what...you mean...have you been skulking around the school all day?'

He backed away from her anger. 'No, no...well, in truth, yes. I want to know about the girl...'

'Elaine Godfrey!' Sarah snapped.

'No, actually. I wanted to ask you about Rubina Khan. DI Hamilton sort of suggested...that you were pretty close to the girl.'

'Well DI Hamilton is wrong. She was my pupil no more, no less.'

Sarah wrenched open the car door and got in but before she could close it Mark McKenzie leaned in, 'Look, I'm sorry. I know this is a terrible time for all of you, but I'm really interested in what has happened to this girl. She's not the first, you know.'

'Not the first what?'

'Asian girl to meet a violent end.'

The words cut into Sarah like a knife. She turned on the ignition. Had Ruth met a 'violent end'?

The journalist stood up, out of her line of vision. 'Sorry, I'm intruding; I'll let you go now.'

Surprise stopped Sarah - a journalist who apologised? Was this man unique? She switched off the engine and stepped out of the car.

'No, I'm sorry. I was rude. I wasn't actually close to Rubina, as DI Hamilton likes to put it, but I did think highly of her.'

McKenzie nodded. 'Maybe you'd let me buy you a coffee or something and we could talk about her? My interest is completely genuine. I mean, I'm not a reporter on a daily tabloid. I've been looking into this kind of situation with Asian girls for quite some time.'

'Honour killings, you mean?'

'That, and other things.'

Sarah's jaw began to ache. 'Look, I've got DI Hamilton coming to talk to me tonight. I think that will be enough, don't you?'

He held up his hands. 'Fine. Tomorrow then? I don't want to put pressure on you.'

Sarah almost laughed.

He went on. 'What about lunch in the Glen Falloch? Get away from the town.'

The memory of Mr Khan's distress on the night of the wedding came back to her, making it impossible to believe in anything suspicious in that quarter. Perhaps she should meet Mark McKenzie and save him from a false trail. Besides, he appeared to be sincere - a far cry from the tacky sensation-mongers. And he might even be helpful. Taking a deep breath and hoping she was right, she said, 'All right.

One o'clock in the Glen Falloch.'

But before that she had the company of DI Hamilton to look forward to.

He came accompanied by a WPC. She was an attractive girl, far too young-looking in her neat uniform to be a real policewoman. Sarah wondered what the protocol was. Should she offer them coffee? All she could remember from her family's dealings was that the police hastened to the kitchen to make tea for her grief-stricken parents.

In the end they refused her offer and the DI settled himself on the couch while the WPC sat in the window seat with her notebook. It gave Sarah a strange sensation to be the subject of a police interview. In spite of herself, or perhaps because of the intensity of Hamilton's gaze from under the bushy eyebrows, she felt distinctly uncomfortable, as if she had something to hide. Henry, apparently, felt the same, since he had disappeared into another room as soon as the police arrived. She smiled at the disloyalty.

'Why don't you take a seat, Miss Blane,' he said, pointing at the only other chair in the room - a leather-covered rocker designed for relaxation. Sarah sat and the chair swung backwards. The policeman smirked, and she knew he had the advantage.

He sat forward on the couch and clasped his hands between his knees. 'Right, what do you have to tell us? '

'What...? I told you all I know...when I came to the station that time.'

He ran his thumb and forefinger, up and down the length of his nose, and she realised it was something he'd done before. It was obviously a habit, or perhaps a tactic, intended to distract an interviewee.

'Now, now, this won't do. What about that little disturbance in the street a week or so ago?'

'Disturbance? I don't know what you...oh, you

mean, the business of the ...' She stopped, reluctant to name Leslie and Lynn. She raised a hand. 'Oh that? It was nothing. I'm sure your constable would tell you that.'

'Nothing? And yet there you were. Ready to intervene as soon as the law showed up, eh?'

Sarah gritted her teeth.

'I was not 'ready to intervene' as you put it. I simply happened to be passing.'

Hamilton leaned back and folded his arms. 'Coincidence figures a lot in your connections with this case, does it not?' The eyebrows were becoming active.

Sarah didn't reply.

He went on. 'A girl is reported missing - an Asian girl - and within the week a teacher and two of her pupils, friends of the girl, are involved in a demonstration, outside the business premises of the girl's father.'

'Her friends were worried about her.'

'And so were you, Miss Blane, as I recall.'

The leather squeaked as Sarah forced herself upright on the chair. 'Just what are you suggesting, DI Hamilton? I'm finding it difficult to follow the direction of your inquiry.'

'All right. I'll make it easy for you. We have reason to believe that you are interested in the subject of forced marriage in the Asian community. And considering that you were so fond of the girl Khan, we have to wonder how much, call it encouragement, she and her fellow pupils were given in this matter - by yourself.'

Sarah recalled the disappearance of the articles she had left in Moira's office. Obviously Leslie Watkins had not been involved in their loss, since Hamilton knew about them. A chill touched her when she knew that someone else had taken them and passed the information to the police. She didn't have time to wonder why. 'Inspector, what has all this to do with Rubina's death?'

'Well, that's what we were hoping you could help us with.'

The chair squeaked louder as Sarah got to her feet. Her legs were shaking.

'But none of this makes any sense!'

Out of the corner of her eye Sarah saw the WPC's pen jump at the force of her words.

Hamilton was shaking his head again. 'On the contrary, it makes a great deal of sense. Look at it from our point of view. A girl goes missing on a school trip - you come to us suggesting that she may have been abducted - remember, it was you who told us she was meeting someone that night? You are in possession of paperwork concerning forced marriage in the girl's community, and then you join in a demonstration against the girl's family on the very day that she is taken from the loch, murdered by person or persons unknown.'

Sarah felt queasy.

'So,' Hamilton moved forward, his expression grim. 'What exactly do you know?'

It was no use. It was apparent that no matter what she said Hamilton was not inclined to believe her. Sarah sank into the chair again.

'Rubina's family is devastated. You must know that. I mean, what you're implying...it's unthinkable.'

'I asked you what you know.'

'I told you what I know.' Unbidden, the crumpled picture of a blue sleeve came into her mind. Had Lynn told them about that? Was she herself withholding information if she didn't tell? 'The Head asked me to meet with Rubina's family the night she went missing - Lynn Cameron later told me that Rubina was meeting someone - then ...then Rubina was found...' Weariness swept over her like a veil. 'That, literally, is all I know.'

'You knew about the cousin from Pakistan that Rubina was promised to, didn't you?'

'No, I didn't know as such, I simply heard from Lynn that Rubina had spoken to her about it. That doesn't make it true.' So, Lynn had passed that on to the police. 'Besides, surely Rubina's family is best to tell you about that?'

The eyebrows went in to overdrive.

'Let us be the judge of that, Miss Blane.'

*

Sarah awoke with her teeth clenched. Another Saturday, another problem. Why had she agreed to meet that journalist; what was his name? She searched her bag for the card he had given her. Mark McKenzie. And his mobile phone number was there. As she showered and made breakfast she told herself that she would phone and call off the lunch. The last few weeks had been so draining that she longed just to do something aimless, like drive to Glasgow and potter around the stores, anonymous and impervious for once.

But as she lifted the phone, card in hand, it rang. It was David Smythe. His voice shook.

'Sarah?'

'David?'

'I need to see you. I've had that policeman round here this morning.'

Sarah looked at the clock. 'Hamilton? This early?'

'Yes, he got me out of bed. I think he was trying to catch me unawares or something...'

She hesitated. 'Ye-es...so?'

His voice rose; 'So? So? He thinks I killed Rubina!'

'Oh, David, that can't be true!'

'It is. He went on and on - not actually accusing me

67

but question after question until I didn't know what I was saying…'

Sarah thought she was beginning to understand Hamilton's tactics - shake every tree hard enough and something was bound to fall out. Last night she was sure that he had Rubina's people in his sights, and yet this morning he appeared to be challenging David Smythe? Which suggested that he didn't think for a second that Sarah had any involvement in Rubina's disappearance, just that she might reveal anything she knew, however incidental.

David added, quietly. 'He knows about what happened, with me and Rubina…'

'But you told me it was harmless, didn't you, David?'

For moment there was silence at the other end.

'I thought you, of all people, believed me, Sarah.' His voice was cold.

'Why 'of all people'? No-one in school thinks otherwise.'

'Really? Why don't you ask Judith Aitken? She'll give you a different slant on the whole thing.'

'Look David, I don't have time to deal with this right now. I've got to go out - I've got a …a lunch date. Why don't I phone you this evening?'

*

On the bleak November day Loch Lomond's scenic beauty was hard to discern. Dark, funereal clouds hung around the mountains and the water looked black and menacing. Sarah shivered as she parked the Fiesta at the hotel.

In the restaurant a log fire warmed the air, and the atmosphere. A waiter led her to Mark McKenzie's table, and as he stood to greet her Sarah chose a seat with her back to the panorama of the loch.

'I thought perhaps you weren't going to come?' he said.

'I almost didn't.'

He nodded. 'It's understandable.'

Sarah had time to study the man as he called the waiter and ordered their food.

There was a wedding ring on his left hand. Then she noted how unusually symmetrical his features were. Even his short dark hair was smooth and immaculate. So much perfection in the face of a man could be disconcerting. He wore the newspaperman's garb of sweater and open-necked shirt, chinos and battered suede shoes. She reckoned he was in his late thirties.

When he turned back to her and smiled she felt a little pang of embarrassment at the closeness of her scrutiny. 'What is it…you want from me?'

He laughed, and raised his eyebrows. 'Nothing, until we've eaten, if that's all right. I don't know about you but I'm very hungry.'

She felt herself relax. Maybe it would be fine. Maybe it would just be a pleasant meal with a man she hardly knew, tension-free. She thought of how fraught all her current relationships were - with her colleagues, even with her pupils. The horror of the past weeks hung over all of them, with its potential for tainting every association. Quite suddenly it came to her that she had stopped trusting David Smythe.

While they ate they avoided the subject uppermost in both of their minds. Instead, Mark McKenzie told her about himself - born in Gourock - Glasgow University - worked on various newspapers until he became social affairs editor for the Sunday Standard. Father retired GP, mother retired teacher, brother a surgeon in California. Sarah listened, waiting for the object of the wedding ring to enter the conversation. She didn't, until Sarah told him that she was divorced, then, concentrating on crumbling a bread roll, he told her that his wife Sally had died of breast cancer three years before. They had no children. In the small pool of silence that followed Sarah thought to tell him about Ruth - but how could twenty-three years of absence equate to the raw grief of a young wife lost to such a disease?

He looked up again and smiled. 'Coffee?'

When the plates were cleared away, he said. 'How did it go with Steve Hamilton?'

Sarah clattered her cup on the saucer, 'Oh. That man irritates me beyond belief! I hope he's not a friend of yours.'

'No, a professional acquaintance at most. When I was a crime reporter in Glasgow our paths crossed frequently. Then he was promoted to this area. He's a bit of a terrier, isn't he?'

'He confuses me. Last night he more or less suggested that I had encouraged Rubina to defy her family - and her culture for that matter - to the point where she …disappeared. Then this morning I had a colleague on the phone, bruised and battered by the inspector's insinuations about his relationship with Rubina.'

'Did this colleague have a relationship with the girl?'

'Well…it seemed like a storm in a teacup at the time. He's a very attractive young man, all the teenage girls fancy him, as far as I can see. He's single and rich - drives an Aston Martin, would you believe? It appears to be an irresistible combination. However, Rubina's family asked to have her removed from his classes.'

'What about the cousin from Pakistan; do you think there is any mileage in following that line of inquiry?'

'Even there - I don't know if it's true. Lynn Cameron, Rubina's friend, got very excited about that before

Rubina was found, thought the perfect answer to her disappearance was that she had run away from a forced marriage.' Sarah shook her head. 'Who knows what, if anything, Rubina was running from.'

'How many people knew where Rubina was likely to be on that Friday evening?'

'Well, let's see. Her immediate family of course. I don't know about the cousin Hakim - he's a pretty fiery type - and of course everyone in the department at school. It may be that people from other departments knew about the theatre trip, but it was organised by our principal teacher, Roger Bullough. And it was only for senior pupils, it wasn't a big group.'

'Did he accompany them to Glasgow?'

'No, that was Judith Aitken. Roger's wife is an invalid - multiple sclerosis. Roger isn't really able to take much part in school life outside the normal timetable, other than occasional duties at in-service or parents' nights, for example. Dorothy, his wife, is paralysed. He doesn't talk about it much but I think his life is very difficult.' Sarah frowned. 'Anyway, I cannot imagine for a moment that anyone in the department, or the school for that matter, could have anything to do with…with…'

'But someone killed her, Sarah.'

'Oh, God, I can't bear to think of it!'

'Apparently she set off to meet someone, didn't she?'

Sarah was beginning to feel uncomfortable with McKenzie's questions. 'I thought you wanted to talk to me about forced marriage in the Asian community?'

He leaned back in his chair and opened his hands. 'Sorry. You're right. Old habits die hard. Hamilton suggested that you were also interested in the subject?'

Sarah leaned back in her chair and copied his

actions. 'Well, he's wrong. I don't have a smidgeon of interest - or knowledge - about such things. I just happened to come across an article about it after Rubina went missing and I took it in to Moira Campbell - our deputy head.'

'Ah, I see. So, you don't wish to discuss it further?'

She felt boorish. 'Oh, I don't mind discussing it, I just don't see how I can help you.'

'Did this article refer to honour killings?'

She nodded. 'A strange concept. But surely it must be rare in this country?'

McKenzie leaned forward again. 'Not so rare as you might think. I can't get hold of any official figures - the government is unusually reticent about the subject - but it happens more often than the man in the street might imagine. Of course, sometimes it can be covered up - especially when the women concerned are recent immigrants or whatever - and sometimes the deaths are suicide, like when a girl can't escape from an abusive marriage. In fact, not so long ago an Asian woman in England was given a life sentence for strangling her daughter. She believed the girl had brought shame on the family by getting pregnant outside her arranged marriage.'

Her own parents' love for their lost daughter echoed in Sarah's mind. Surely that kind of love is always unconditional?

It had to be the blazing log fire, but Sarah had begun to perspire. 'Murdered? By her own mother? It defies belief.' She passed her hand across her forehead.

'I wish it did.' Suddenly he was signalling for the bill. 'I must apologise, Sarah - it's okay if I call you that? I can see that I'm upsetting you. Let's get out of here. Maybe some fresh air is what we need.'

Outside the weather had not improved and when Mark McKenzie suggested a walk on the shore Sarah's instinct was to refuse. She didn't know exactly where Rubina's body had been taken from the loch and she hoped that he didn't either. But for once she was reluctant to go back to just the company of Henry, and her heart sank when she remembered the promise she had made to David Smythe to phone him in the evening.

It was becoming so dark in any case that the walk would, by necessity, be very short.

As they picked their way along the shoreline, avoiding flotsam and unexpected hummocks in the pebbly sand, Sarah burned with a question which had been troubling her since Rubina died. With his contacts Mark McKenzie probably knew the answer.

'Maybe…this isn't a fair question, but would you know if Rubina was - assaulted in any way?'

The journalist stood in front of her. 'There was no evidence of sexual assault - but I can see why you'd want to know. If it turned out that Rubina was a victim of her own community it would be a great comfort to the school, wouldn't it? Since they were in *loco parentis* when she went missing.'

'Rubina was almost seventeen. The police certainly didn't see her as a minor when she disappeared!'

Sarah's step quickened as they turned to walk back to the cars. 'They don't search too seriously for girls of that age, you know.'

She could barely make out his features in the gathering gloom.

Chapter 5

On Monday morning there was further bad news - another pupil had fallen victim to drugs. This girl was still alive, at least, but she wasn't telling the police or her parents where the stuff had come from.

Last period before lunch was the English departmental meeting, and as they settled around the table in the workroom Roger Bullough said. 'Two things: Moira and the head will be joining us shortly, and, as you will know by now, David is still absent. I'll talk to him some time today.'

Sarah said, 'I spoke to him at the weekend. He's not... coping too well.'

'With what?' Judith Aitken's voice was sharp.

'Oh, but he's sick, we all know that.' Mary Stephens' pale skin flushed. 'I called up to see him when I was walking the dog yesterday and he's far from well. That virus from his holidays has laid him low. It was like when Mother and I came back from that cruise to...'

Judith said, flatly. 'Yeah, we remember that...'

Roger said, 'Anyway, we must get on.'

Departmental business was almost concluded when Keith Birkmyre and Moira Campbell joined the meeting. Moira sat beside Sarah and the Head placed himself at the vacant end of the table.

'I have decided to attend each departmental meeting in the week ahead. The problems facing the school are such that we will all have to pull together. We must be vigilant about any signs of substance abuse: so you must pass any information to me.'

'How is Sharon?'

Moira answered. 'Still in hospital, but it looks as if she'll pull through.'

'But saying nothing!' The Head went on, 'However, perhaps we'll get to the bottom of it soon. That... boy...what's his name, Moira, who has been arrested for questioning...?'

'Leslie Watkins.'

Sarah gasped. 'Leslie - arrested? For what?'

'If you'd waited...'

The head frowned and it was as if his brow moved independently of his hair. She wondered, ludicrously, if he wore a hairpiece.

'He has been picked up as part of an inquiry into drug use at the camp. Not surprising really, if that were the source - all these hippie types.'

Willie Armstrong mumbled. 'Give a dog a bad name.'

Birkmyre ignored Willie. He leaned back in his chair and folded his arms. 'In fact, I'm almost coming round to the view that the inquiry may throw up more than drug use...'

He looked around the table. Roger Bullough, on Sarah's other side, was doodling on his pad - a series of intricate little whorls and diamond shapes.

'What do you mean?' Roger looked up.

The head cast his eyes over each person, then dropped his voice. 'Between ourselves, I wouldn't be surprised if our Mr Watkins had something to do with the Khan girl. After all, he was the last person to see her alive.'

'Apart from the killer, of course,' Willie said quietly.

Sarah swallowed: 'And how would Leslie Watkins get Rubina to the loch at the dead of night? A distance of what...eight or nine miles...without a vehicle?' She was trying hard to keep the scorn out of her tone. 'Anyway, what possible motive could one seventeen year old have for murdering another? And a classmate at that?'

'I think we have plenty of evidence from the United States that disturbed teenagers are perfectly capable of killing their classmates.'

Beside her Moira sighed.

'As for motive, she may well have found out about the drugs, and, who's to say that the boy's supplier doesn't have a vehicle?'

The bell rang and the relief in the room was palpable. Birkmyre looked at his watch and hurried out, to yet another meeting with the police.

Lynn Cameron was waiting outside Sarah's classroom. 'Miss Blane, have you heard about Leslie?'

'Yes, Lynn, I'm afraid I have.'

'Some of the others have asked me to come and speak to you. To see if you can help.'

'I don't...' Sarah was jostled by a horde of pupils rushing to their lunch.

'Help in what way?'

'Tell someone that Leslie has nothing to do with drugs. He hates them, in fact.'

'I don't honestly think, Lynn, that I have any place in this. Surely his mother..?'

'That's just it! His mother's been arrested too! She went mad when the police began to search her caravan and hit one of them!'

'How do you know this?'

Lynn put out a hand, palm upwards, 'My mother? The peace camp's in her ward. Besides, Wilson Toner would tell her.' She made her eyes wide. 'He just happened to be passing when the police were raiding the camp?'

Sarah hid a smile. 'I'm really sorry, Lynn. I can't

76

interfere in this.'

'But, we thought…' She put her hand into her pocket and pulled out an assortment of coins and notes. 'We thought you could maybe bail him out. We've collected all this money.'

'I see.'

'You don't think Leslie has been selling drugs, Miss, do you?'

Sarah hesitated, wondering how to respond. Honesty was best, she decided.

'I simply can't say.'

'But we thought you were different.' Tears, never very far away, began to well up in Lynn's eyes. 'You helped when Rubina went missing…and…we don't know who else would be on Leslie's side…'

Sarah took a deep breath, 'All right. Wait for me when school closes and we'll go to the police station and see if Leslie needs anything.' And pray that DI Hamilton is miles away. 'But I'll have to check it with Mrs Campbell.'

Moira signalled Sarah to push the door until it clicked shut when she entered the office. There was a cup of coffee and the remains of a sandwich on her messy desk. She rose.

'Coffee?' She waved at a chair in front of her desk. 'Have a seat.'

The aroma from the coffee machine was good. 'Mm, yes thanks…'

Moira brought the coffee to Sarah and sat down again. 'So, what do you think of this morning's little ordeal by theory, eh?' She cocked her head to indicate the head's office on the other side of the wall.

Sarah said. 'Frankly, I'm amazed at his lack of discretion. I can't imagine every single person on the staff can be trusted not to let his words go any further.'

77

'Ah, but, do you think everyone will hear it? Or just the English department?'

'What do you mean?'

'Look at it this way. As he sees it the English department was responsible for the girl and - remember we're talking about Keith here - let him down.' She shrugged. 'I think he just wants to make the department feel uncomfortable.'

'Hardly appropriate behaviour for a head teacher, though, is it?'

'Oh, I agree. I don't think for a minute he believes that Leslie had anything to do with Rubina's death, but he does have him in the frame for the drugs, I know that.'

Moira took an unenthusiastic bite from her sandwich.

'Anyway, that's what I've come to see you about. Lynn Cameron has been appointed by her classmates to ask me to go to the police station and see if Leslie needs anything.'

'What?' Moira choked on the bread and began to cough.

Sarah held up her hands. 'I know…I know. She even came with a pocketful of money to bail him out!'

Moira said, her eyes watering, 'I think she's been watching too much television. If it wasn't so awful it would be funny. But seriously - the school can't be seen to intervene in a police matter.'

'His mother has been arrested too, so he's on his own.'

Moira swung on her chair. The room was quiet, except for the muffled sounds of pupils from the playground. The chair-spring bounced as she sat up.

'All right, Sarah. If you give me your word that you are going to help Leslie as a private individual, ok? Not as his teacher. If there's any trouble from that quarter Keith will go mad.'

'Ok.' Sarah got up to leave. 'I'd better have something to eat before my third year come next period. They require all the strength I can muster. Then after school - as a private individual, of course - I'll give you a ring and tell you how it went with Leslie.' Her hand on the door she turned. 'By the way, did you ever find those magazine articles?'

Moira shook her head, slowly. 'No. It was strange. Mind you, the door's unlocked all day every day - so anyone could have taken them, I suppose.'

At the end of the school day, Sarah and Lynn made their way to the car park to find Mark McKenzie leaning against Sarah's car.

'What, no social affairs to edit these days?'

He smiled. 'Lots, but I wanted to speak to you. I know I can't phone you in the middle of classes so there's nothing else for it but to waylay you, and here I am.'

Sarah said. 'This is Lynn Cameron.'

McKenzie raised his hand. 'Hi, Lynn.'

'Lynn and I are just off to the police station to see if Leslie...'

'He's not here, he's in Dumbarton. At Divisional HQ.'

'Oh.' Sarah and Lynn looked at each other.

'Here, why don't you let me drive you there - since, with respect - I'll certainly get further past the desk than would a teacher and a friend.'

His car was a dusty BMW which had seen better days. On the way to Dumbarton, Sarah mulled over something which had been troubling her since the Head's remarks in the morning. Much as she hated the idea, she had to know. Horses were grazing in the fields they were passing, and Mark was commenting about them over his

79

shoulder to Lynn in the back, when Sarah twisted around in her seat and blurted it out.

'Lynn, is there any chance that Rubina told Leslie she was meeting someone that night, you know, when you came back from Glasgow?'

For a moment Lynn stared at her as if she hadn't understood the question. 'Oh no, Miss, she only told me.'

'Can you be sure about that?'

Lynn nodded furiously. 'Definitely! She was far too worried that anyone else would find out.'

'Where did you part?'

'Like I said before. We left Rubina at Colquhoun Street and Leslie and I walked along to John Street. Leslie thought Rubina was going home.'

When Lynn began to sniff Sarah changed tack. 'And no-one else on the bus knew where she was going?'

'No. Everyone says the police have been to their houses to ask them that already. Nobody knew, honestly!'

'Of course.' Sarah smiled to reassure Lynn, and turned back as they drove into the car park at the police station.

Leslie was making his way down the steps.

'The infamous Leslie Watkins, I presume,' Mark said dryly as he pulled up. Convinced by Lynn's presence that his troubles were no worse, Leslie was persuaded to get into McKenzie's car.

Sarah whispered to Mark, 'As you can guess, journalists don't rate much higher than police in Leslie's estimation.'

Mark snorted, quietly. 'That doesn't surprise me,'

He headed back to Helensburgh.

Sarah turned. 'Right Leslie, tell us. Why have they let you go?'

He shook his head and shrugged. 'Seems they just

wanted to talk to me. No charge. Anyway, they can't do anything else, there isn't any evidence.'

'So how did they explain it?'

Leslie laughed, 'Oh, you know, the usual, reason to believe, da, da, da... and all that crap - oh, sorry, Miss.'

'What about your mother?'

'She'll be all right. She's been arrested loads of times. She's cool with it. They'll let her out and she'll appear in court and get a fine, more than likely. That's what always happens'

Mark said, 'And if we take you home...will you be all right?'

'Yeah, thanks.'

For most of the short journey the two young people talked quietly in the back of the car, while Mark drove and Sarah sat next to him in near silence. As they entered the town Sarah said, 'I should thank you too. It was kind of you to come with us to Dumbarton.'

'Not at all. As I said, I wanted to speak to you anyway.'

Sarah looked at his smooth profile. 'Yes...you said?'

They dropped Lynn at her luxurious home and then carried on to Faslane and Leslie's scruffy home in the peace camp.

As Leslie jumped out of the car Sarah said, 'They didn't mess up the caravan, did they? The police, you know, when they were searching?'

Leslie grinned, 'Not so you'd notice. Thanks again for coming for me, Miss - and Mr McKenzie.'

Mark leaned over Sarah, 'Before you go, Leslie. Did the police ask you anything about your friend, Rubina?'

The smile left the boy's face and he nodded. 'They did ask me a few questions but I don't think they were very serious about it. Where I was concerned, I mean. They asked more about Rubina's family and that - what did I know about her cousin Hakim? Stuff like that.'

'Thanks, Leslie.'

As they drove back along the seafront Mark said, 'Look Sarah, why don't we stop off somewhere for a drink, or a meal perhaps?'

She grimaced. 'In these school-saturated clothes? I don't think so.'

'You could always go home and change.' He smiled at her. 'I don't mind waiting?'

Mark McKenzie wandered around Sarah's living room, drink in hand. When she re-appeared, in black trousers and a cream silk shirt, he was holding one of several photographs from the shelves of the bookcase.

'Is this you?'

'No, it's...my sister.'

It was a picture of Ruth, aged ten, posing awkwardly for the camera wearing shorts and a tee-shirt, in the garden of their home in Edinburgh.

'And this one?'

Ruth again, in her first long dress, for the school Christmas dance, a week before she disappeared.

Sarah took the photograph from his hand and put it back. 'That's my sister too.'

'You're very alike. You know, the hair, the eyebrows? ' He touched above his own eyes with a forefinger. 'Is she a teacher too?'

Sarah picked up her bag. 'I know. No, she's not. Are we going then?'

Mark McKenzie looked closely at her then lifted his jacket from the sofa. 'Right.'

He had suggested Italian, in the city, and as he drove the silence between them was deeper than before. Sarah wondered what she was doing there, sitting next to this person - on a date of sorts for the second time. They drove across the river on Erskine Bridge, and while she observed the myriad lights shimmering away towards the city and reflecting in the water below, she felt a small stirring of pleasure in the company of a man, which she had not experienced since her marriage ended. For the moment at least she would stop questioning his motives and just look forward to dinner.

It was a small *trattoria* in the Merchant City, that atmospheric gesture to Glasgow's rich commercial past, as Mark described it. Sarah inhaled the garlicky odours of Italian cuisine, and felt hungry.

The waiter poured Sarah a large glass of red wine, and Mark a mineral water.

He held up his glass in a toast, 'To an enjoyable evening, Miss Blane.'

Sarah replied, 'And an abstemious one for you, I note, Mr McKenzie.'

He laughed, 'The curse of the responsible driver. I've got to get you back to Helensburgh, after all, without attracting the attention of the police!'

She shuddered. 'Not more attention, please! Seriously though, what do you make of the questions they asked Leslie about the Khans? Or, perhaps more to the point, what do your sources tell you?'

'That's one of the things I wanted to discuss with you. How well do you know the Khans?'

Winding spaghetti on to her fork Sarah took a minute to answer.

'In truth, not well at all. I know that Mr Khan is ...was pretty strict with Rubina. Apparently he didn't approve of her choice of clothes or the way she wanted to spend time. I do know that he didn't want her to continue her education, as Rubina had hoped, because he told me that when he came to the parents' meeting. He made it clear that her future was to be a life of domesticity.'

She took a mouthful of wine. 'Then there was that business with David Smythe.'

'Yes, tell me more about that.'

'We spoke about it last time, Mark.'

'I know, I just want to be clear about it.'

'Well, you have to remember it was just before I came to the school, but Rubina's father had her removed from David's English class because he thought they were being too friendly.'

'And were they?'

Sarah shrugged, 'David says not, as he tells it she took to hanging around his car when he parked in town, just to speak to him. The cousin, Hakim, saw this a couple of times and well - you know the rest.'

'Are you sure he's telling the truth?'

Sarah laughed, 'I'm not sure of anything any more! This morning the boss was casting suspicion on poor Leslie Watkins - David appears to be suffering some kind of nervous collapse - and your major interest is in ferreting out a possible honour killing?' The wine was loosening her tongue. 'It's all so...so bloody incredible!'

'Somebody killed her, Sarah.' Mark spoke quietly.

She was reminded of Willie Armstrong's words at the departmental meeting.

'And,' he went on, 'if that girl lost her life because of her culture, I want to find out. It's as simple as that. Because it's something which needs to be exposed.'

His words sobered her.

'Do the police have much evidence?'

'Some, but not a great deal. She was strangled with her own scarf. They are testing the scarf for DNA of course, and if they find any which didn't belong to Rubina then they'll probably start taking samples from people she knew.'

'Men?'

Mark scratched his chin, 'Well, that's just it. Since there was no sexual assault, it doesn't rule out women, does it?'

'But surely…would a woman be strong enough to…kill like that?'

'Depends on the woman, doesn't it?'

Unbidden, a picture of Judith Aitken's short, compact body leapt into Sarah's mind. Judith was gay. She didn't hide the fact, neither did she advertise it. She had a steely personality. Sarah wondered what caused so much friction between her and David Smythe. Could it be…competition?

She shook the thought out of her head.

'But then, it could be any number of people.'

It was Mark's turn to shake his head.

'No, only those who knew where Rubina would be on that Friday night, and, more to the point, only those without an alibi.'

Every member of the English Department knew where Rubina would be that night. Every member of Rubina's family knew where she would be that night.

Sarah said, 'Mohammed.'

'Mohammed?'

'He's Rubina's pleasant cousin. Hakim's brother but not at all similar. He was

Rubina's special friend too. He must be devastated by her death. He was certainly worried enough about her when we spoke to him, during the time she was missing. And he seemed to know more than he was telling.'

Mark pointed his coffee spoon at her. 'Aha! So you have been interested in this since the beginning. Steve wasn't that far wrong, was he?'

Sarah held up her hands, 'Guilty as charged. Actually it was Lynn Cameron who involved me - no, on second thoughts it was Keith Birkmyre, ordering me to the police station that first night to deal with Rubina's family. Then, afterwards, when I began to think there was something iffy about the timings for the Friday night, I went to see Lynn.   Since then she's recruited me as a sort of ...spokesperson...as you saw today.' She looked into the cup as she stirred her coffee. 'Don't ask me why...'

Mark tapped the back of her hand with a finger. 'Because you seem to have understanding and compassion, that's why, Miss Blane.'

Sarah felt heat rise and covered her face with her hands. Understanding? Compassion? Try anguish...for another lost teenager.

'Would you care to talk about it?' He said, gently.

Sarah removed her hands and looked into the face of the man who had lost his wife.

'Perhaps.' she said, 'But not tonight.'

He nodded. 'Well - what about this Mohammed? Would he talk to us again, do you think?'

When they left the restaurant it was raining; a fine, misty drizzle. As they passed George Square the first Christmas decorations were appearing, the rain creating ghostly haloes around the lights. Sarah's heart sank: another Christmas approaching, without Ruth.

In the morning Sarah asked Lynn to stay after class for a moment, to find out if she had Mohammed's mobile phone number. Lynn's eyes were full of questions. Sarah said, 'I'll tell you later. If there's anything to tell.'

When she called, Mohammed agreed to come to Sarah's flat in the evening to meet with her and Mark McKenzie. She told him plainly who Mark was, and so she was impressed when the boy, albeit reluctantly, said he would be there.

To her relief, Mohammed arrived before Mark. Sarah was prepared to employ some of her usual methods with young people in order to engage him, but found it wasn't necessary. Mohammed had an agenda of his own. Once settled on the window seat with a soft drink, and after the usual comments about the wonderful view, the boy said,

'Miss Blane. Please tell me about David Smythe.'

Sarah knew the shock must have shown on her face. 'What on earth do you want me to tell you?'

'About this teacher, and my cousin.'

'Honestly, Mohammed, there's nothing to tell... as far as I know.' She suddenly remembered the cut photograph and the blue sleeve, and heard the conviction leak out of her words.

'My Uncle Anwar was very angry with Rubina at that time...'

Sarah nodded.

'...and so was my brother, Hakim.'

She didn't think it wise to ask what business it was of Hakim's.

'Really?' she asked.

Mohammed smiled. 'He thought she would bring dishonour to the family.'

It was an opportune moment for Mark to arrive. He shook the cold from his shoulders as he entered the room, and held out his hand to Mohammed, who had risen to his feet.

'Yes, it's a very cold night.' Mohammed said. His tone was reasonably friendly and Sarah relaxed. She poured coffee for Mark and he sat on the sofa and removed his jacket.

'Mohammed was just telling me about his brother, you know, Hakim...'

'Do you know my brother, Mr McKenzie?' Mohammed looked surprised.

'Not really, but I have heard him mentioned. He is known to have, how shall I say...strong views about your culture.'

It was Sarah's turn to be surprised. Hitherto it had been her impression that Hakim was simply a young man with a short fuse.

'I know that he frequents a *bhangra* club in the city.' Mark continued. 'But I've never seen you there, Mohammed.'

The boy shook his head. 'Hakim and I are different. When he was a baby he was sent to Pakistan, and my grandmother brought him up. My mother sewed, at home, helping my father to get the business started. He is nine years older than me. I was born in Scotland.' He shrugged. 'It changes things.'

Sarah said, 'Mohammed tells me that Hakim was very upset by ...Rubina's behaviour...with David.'

Mark nodded. 'About bringing dishonour to the family? Yes?'

Mohammed's eyes opened wide. 'How do you know this?'

Mark laid his cup on the table before he answered. It was apparent that he was choosing his words with care.

'It's like this, Mohammed. As you know, I'm a journalist. And for quite some time now I have been looking into certain aspects of marriage in the Asian community.'

Mohammed laughed. 'Everyone wants to know about arranged marriage.'

'That may be so, but it is my view that a marriage arranged between two people who give their consent is probably as good as any. It's the other kind I'm concerned with.'

Mohammed's head went up. 'You're not a social worker or something, are you?'

Mark gave a laugh. 'Point taken. No, but part of my work as a journalist is to bring injustices of one sort or another into the open.' He paused, but the boy didn't speak.

'And that, for many people, includes forced marriage - or abduction - or, at worst, extreme forms of punishment which are, in fact, against the law.'

Mohammed cast his eyes down. Sarah thought it was perhaps time to ease the pressure.

'How is Rubina's mother now?'

He looked up again, relieved.

'Not good. The police visit the house nearly every day to ask her questions. Uncle Anwar has to interpret for her. My father says it's making her ill.' He turned to the window when there was a noise in the street. 'They want to take Rubina to Pakistan for burial, but the police say not yet. Not until they know ...who...'

'Do you have any idea who might have killed her, Mohammed?' Mark asked quietly.

Still looking out of the window, Mohammed whispered. 'I'm scared that it might have been...my brother.'

Sarah's voice was high. 'Because of David Smythe?'

The boy moved his shoulders. 'Or because of the cousin from Pakistan. Who knows?'

Mark said, 'Why the cousin from Pakistan?'

Mohammed turned back, his dark eyes focussing first on Mark, then Sarah. 'Can I trust you not to tell the police?'

Mark nodded. 'We could only go to the police with evidence. Do you have evidence?'

Mohammed shook his head. 'But I do know that Hakim wanted Rubina for himself. He nearly went mad

when Rubina got into trouble over the teacher. He said he
was going to keep his eye on her until Uncle Anwar agreed
they should be married. He wasn't happy about her going to
Glasgow that night because he knew there would be boys on
the bus. He had a big argument with Rubina and told her he
didn't want her to go.'

Sarah raised her eyebrows. 'How did Rubina take
that?'

'She told him where to get off. She said if he didn't
leave her in peace she would maybe even consider the
cousin from Pakistan.' Mohammed smiled. 'She didn't mean
it.'

'How did Hakim react to that idea?' Mark asked.

The boy began to observe his fingers tapping on the
glass Sarah had given him. 'He said he'd kill her first.'

Sarah caught her breath, and Mark McKenzie ran his
hand through his hair.

'No, Mohammed. We couldn't go to the police with
this.'

'But, thinking like this,' Sarah said, 'it puzzles me
why are you are still so interested in David Smythe?'

Mohammed carefully laid the glass on the coffee
table, then stood up.

'Because, if the teacher was to …to blame…it
wouldn't be Hakim.'

When the boy had gone Sarah and Mark looked at
each other across the room.

Sarah said, 'I can't believe I just heard all that.'

Mark stretched his arms along the back of the sofa. 'I
know. Unfortunately, I don't think we can do anything about
it.'

'But if it's true…'

'What seems to be true is that Hakim threatened
Rubina, yes, but it may have ended there. On the other hand,

if Hakim carried out his threat, then the police will find the evidence they need, I'm sure. We wouldn't want to create another victim if we're wrong, would we?'

Sarah rocked on the leather chair. 'No...o.'

Mark looked at his watch, and removed Henry from where he was sound asleep on his lap. He brushed a few white hairs from his trouser legs.

Sarah said, 'Sorry about that, but Henry doesn't sit with just anyone.'

He smiled. 'I'm pleased about that - and neither do I as a matter of fact. Anyway, I must go. It's getting late.' As he shrugged himself into his jacket he said, 'What's the chance of Hakim giving us an interview, do you think?'

'Not high, I'd say.' Sarah walked him to the door of the flat, 'But I suppose we could try.'

As Mark started to go downstairs she called after him. 'By the way, what's *bhangra?*'

He raised a hand. 'I'll tell you tomorrow.'

Once in bed Sarah was unable to sleep, her thoughts filled with the events of the evening. What were the classic ingredients for any crime? Motive, means and opportunity? If Mohammed was right Hakim certainly had motive, regardless of how obscene. He also had the means - his flash car. Opportunity? Sarah sat up. It couldn't be Hakim! Rubina would never have agreed to meet him in secret by any stretch of the imagination. She threw the duvet back and found the piece of paper with Mohammed's mobile number. Afterwards she would phone Mark; there would be no point in trying to have a meeting with Hakim.

She started to dial Mohammed's number with the good news, then stopped as yet another thought struck her. What had Mohammed said of his brother? That he was going to keep an eye on Rubina? Who was to say he hadn't been spying on her when she came back from Glasgow that night? Had seen her with whoever she was meeting, in fact, fuelling his anger to the point of no return. Not good news at all.

Slowly, Sarah went back to bed.

Chapter 6

Another uneasy week passed, until, on her way to school one morning, Sarah stopped off at the newsagent. She handed over the money for her usual morning newspaper, then stared in disbelief at the bold headlines which screamed from the next shelf - on the front page of the Clarion.

"WHO KILLED RUBINA ?

Police in Dumbarton yesterday refused to confirm allegations that the death of Asian teenager Rubina Khan has been linked to the deadly practice of 'honour killing' in some sections of this community, when the life of a young woman is forfeited when she is found to be in breach of the rules laid down for relationships between the sexes thus being seen to bring dishonour on the family. On October 30th Rubina's body was taken from Loch Lomond. She had been brutally murdered. To date, no-one has been arrested for her death.

And so, we pose the question. Who killed Rubina Khan?"

As she left the shop the newsagent called that she had forgotten her change. She stood on the pavement, coins in hand, apologising automatically when another customer bumped her from behind. The coincidence of the headline, reflecting what had been going round in her head all night, was staggering.

In fact, it was too much of a coincidence. Someone must be talking to the press. Mark McKenzie came to mind, but she couldn't see how it would be in his interests to offer ideas to a competitor. Unless he had some kind of subtle strategy that he wasn't prepared to share with her. And Mohammed would have to hate his brother passionately to give stuff like this to a tabloid.

She got into her car and drove to school, all the personnel connected to this drama parading across the stage of her thoughts. Hakim - Mohammed - Lynn - Leslie - David Smythe. David Smythe? Such headlines would certainly take the heat off him. And his father had no end of influential contacts. She wondered if he would be back to school today.

As soon as she set foot in the building, however, all of it was driven from her mind. Moira, looking as if she hadn't been to bed for a week, was waiting in the English base to tell them that Roger Bullough had been taken to hospital with a heart attack.

'We'll have to get some supply in, but meantime, Judith, as assistant principal, will be in charge of the department.'

Judith said, 'Is Mr David Smythe likely to show up any day soon?

'No. There's been a sick note - he's suffering from stress.'

Judith's hard laugh bounced out into the corridor. 'I wonder why?' she said, as she slammed out of the room.

Moira sighed. 'I'll let you know when the supply teacher comes. I know it isn't easy to cover for two absent members of staff , but we've already farmed out as many of David's classes as we can.'

'How long will Roger be off?' Mary Stephens asked.

'Who can say?' Moira shrugged.

'What about Dorothy? How on earth will she manage?'

'Well, in the meantime, her sister from Paisley is looking after her. But that's only temporary; she has a family. And if Roger can't cope she may have to be put into somewhere residential...Oh, let's hope it doesn't come to that.'

The bell rang and Moira stopped at the door. 'I'll go to the hospital and find out what I can about Roger to-night.'

'What about Dorothy?' Mary Stephens said, 'I'd go, but there's the dog, and mother...'

'Would you like me to visit Dorothy, Moira?' Sarah asked, 'You know, after school.'

'Oh, would you? That would be a great help, Sarah. Give her our best and tell her I'll be there to see her as soon as I can.'

The others hurried to their classrooms. Time and teaching wait for no man, Sarah thought, as she squeezed through groups of pupils trying to enter their classrooms.

The busy day which followed pushed even the morning's headlines to the back of Sarah's mind, until her senior class came last period and settled to a writing task. In the quiet room her gaze rested on Leslie Watkins, then Lynn Cameron. What if Mohammed had expressed his fears about Hakim to Lynn? And what if Lynn had then spoken to her mother, and her mother had passed on the suspicions to Wilson Toner?

Sarah knew that she would have to speak to Lynn again. It was altogether too simple to suppose that Rubina had not confided in her best friend about the owner of the blue sleeve. Sarah knew there had been someone, she'd seen the photograph. If Lynn knew who that someone was, it was time to tell.

Otherwise, every member Rubina's immediate family, were in danger of being tried and sentenced by a tabloid newspaper. As the class streamed out of the room at the end of the day, Sarah quietly asked Lynn to stay behind.

Sarah perched on the edge of her desk and invited

Lynn to move into a front seat.

The girl was eager to comply, obviously wanting to find out what had happened with Mohammed.

'Have you seen today's Clarion, Miss?' Lynn's eyes behind her glasses were huge. 'Do you think it's true?'

'Yes, to the first part, and no to the second, because there is nothing in the report which can be said to be true at this stage.' Sarah folded her arms. 'But what I'd like to know, Lynn, is what made the Clarion splash unfounded suspicions all over its front page like that?'

Lynn, said, her brow furrowed. 'I wouldn't know.'

'Have you seen Mohammed recently?'

Lynn scraped at a mark on the desk . 'Yeah, I met him in the library one day.'

'And did you talk?'

The girl looked up, her glasses were beginning to mist over. 'Yes, we talked on the way home. Mohammed is really, really sad about what happened to Rubina - and he knows I'm ...was...her best friend.'

'Did he talk about anyone else?'

'Anyone else? No...I don't think...oh, wait, he did. He asked me what I thought about Mr Smythe.'

'What did you tell him?'

Lynn removed her glasses and started to polish them on a tissue. Without them, her face looked blank. 'I told him we liked him. He's a good teacher. I think he was asking because of that stuff with Rubina, you know? Yonks ago. I said it was really silly, we all fancied Mr Smythe - it wasn't just Rubina.'

'And was that all?'

'Yes. Miss? Did you...talk to Mohammed?'

'We did. Mr McKenzie wanted to ask him a few things about Rubina,,.that was all.'

Lynn looked at her suspiciously. 'Oh?'

Sarah felt guilty but if Lynn didn't know of the talk about Hakim then it was better left like that.

'Ok, Lynn, thanks.'

As the girl reached the doorway Sarah said, 'Oh, by the way, Lynn, you never did tell me who was in that photograph with Rubina. You know, the one that was cut?'

Lynn turned back. 'Honestly, Miss Blane, she never told me.'

'And you didn't guess?'

She shook her head. 'I just know it wasn't a boy from school.'

'How can you be so sure?'

'I was teasing her one day, going over all the senior boys, trying to get her to tell me. She just said, 'No way - I wouldn't risk my father's wrath for any of these kids! I remember, because I thought it was such a ...a fancy word to use - wrath. Like, sort of, Shakespeare?'

When Lynn left, Sarah gathered up her papers into her briefcase while she thought about what the girl had said. If she was right then all the boys in the school could be eliminated. So who on earth could it be? With her restricted home life - no clubs or discos for Rubina - it hardly seemed likely that she would meet many others of her own age.

She was still thinking about it as she made her way along the corridor and turning a corner, bumped into Keith Birkmyre. 'Oh, sorry!'

He was smiling broadly. 'No, pardon me, Sarah!' He spoke more cheerfully than he had for weeks. 'Rotten news about Roger, isn't it?'

Sarah stared for a second. Roger's illness was no reason to be jumping for joy. 'Yes, it's very worrying. I'm on my way to see Dorothy now, deputising for Moira.'

'Dorothy? Oh, Roger's wife, of course. If there's anything we can do for ...er...Dorothy, you'll let me know, won't you?'

Sarah nodded.

The head started to move off, then turned. 'Rubina Khan was your pupil, was she not?'

Keith Birkmyre started to nod too, so Sarah stopped.

'Interesting stuff in the paper this morning. Did you see it?'

'I did. Very unpleasant insinuations, weren't they?'

'Well, you know the old saying ...no smoke without fire...' and he was off, striding down the corridor in his usual brisk manner, booming at a lurking boy near one of the exits.

Sarah went out to the car park. His final words had revealed the source of the head's cheerfulness. If the paper was on the right track the school was in the clear. Both pupil and teacher-wise, if he'd had any suspicions of David Smythe.

*

Roger and Dorothy Bullough lived in a modest bungalow in Rhu, a village a couple of miles out of Helensburgh. While the house had no stairs to make life more difficult for Dorothy, Sarah wondered at the hilly terrain which had to be negotiated before reaching the front door. Even the garden was laid out in terracing.

She'd been to the house before. Not long after her arrival at the school Roger had invited her to dinner. At that time Dorothy had been able to move about quite smoothly in her wheelchair, and had, in fact, cooked dinner with a little help from Roger.

Now, it was the garden which first struck Sarah. Even allowing for the time of year and the sad appearance of most gardens during the winter, the Bulloughs' was much neglected. She had to wade through the piles of soggy leaves from the chestnut tree on the pavement, which had found their way almost to the front door, while bare, grubby windows suggested that Christmas was very far away from this house. All around, the dark afternoon was brightened by winking Christmas trees or garlands of lights on many of the houses.

Dorothy's sister Ann let her in. She resembled her, a round-faced smiling woman, who looked capable of handling any crisis, as Dorothy once had been. She had taught art in a Glasgow secondary school until multiple sclerosis had ended her career.

'She's in the bedroom.' Ann said, leading the way to the back of the house.

Sarah was shocked by the change in Dorothy. She was propped up on pillows, looking towards the darkened window, her eyes dull. Her hands resting on the duvet were white, the fingers curling inwards.

'Sarah.' She smiled. 'It's good of you to come.' Her voice was weak, but clear.

She gestured towards the chair beside the bed and Sarah sat down. Ann switched on a bedside lamp and left the room. 'I'll make us some tea.'

Sarah stroked the hand closest to her. 'I'm so sorry about Roger. None of us had any idea that his heart...'

Dorothy said, 'Neither did he. He hasn't been feeling too well for some time - but...we put it down to stress.' She gestured again. 'It's... I'm not easy for him.'

'School's not easy, Dorothy.'

'I know. And he's been so upset about that girl, the one who died.'

'Yes, Keith has been going mad trying to find out where the drugs are coming from.'

'No - the other girl - the one who was found in the loch.'

'Rubina?'

The woman nodded, and closed her eyes.

'Oh, Dorothy, I'm tiring you.'

She opened her eyes again. 'No...no...you're not. It's good to have the company. It's a long day when Roger's at school.'

'Can you...still manage the wheelchair?'

'Yes, if Roger comes home at lunchtime. The nurse comes in the morning, then Roger gives me lunch and helps me into the chair. I can usually sit up until dinner, then he puts me to bed.' She smiled. 'Not today, though.'

'Moira is going to see Roger in hospital this evening to see if there's anything she can do.'

'Moira is kind. What about Keith? Will he go?'

'I really couldn't say. He asked me to pass on his concerns to you when I told him I was coming.'

Dorothy didn't answer for a moment, and Ann came in with a tray. Gently, she placed a mug in Dorothy's bent hands. It had a closed lid and a spout, like a baby's cup.

Unable to speak, Sarah busied herself with stirring her tea.

Dorothy's throat moved painfully as she sipped at the cup and after a moment she handed it to Sarah.   'I've had enough.' then she added, 'So Keith is concerned?'

'He says so.'

The other woman grimaced as she changed her position in the bed.

'Don't believe him.'

'What?' Sarah thought she had misheard.

'We used to work in the same school, you know.'

'No, I didn't know. In Glasgow?'

Dorothy rolled her head on the pillow. 'In Aberdeen.

It was before I met Roger. Keith was Assistant Head then.'

'Didn't you get on?'

'It wasn't so much that. He just wasn't popular with any of the staff. We all thought teaching seemed to be beneath Doctor Birkmyre, if you know what I mean.' She took several laboured breaths. 'Assistant Head in a comprehensive school was way below his expectations, and it showed.'

'Well, I can't say I have a lot of time for him, but he's reasonably efficient. And he seems to be a good enough father, I haven't heard anything to the contrary.'

'What are the boys doing now?'

'Oh, Gordon, the elder son went off to America a couple of months ago for his gap year, and as far as I know the younger one is still at school in Glasgow.'

'Maybe he's a better father than teacher then, eh?'

'Well, Moira is undoubtedly the human face of the senior management team.'

'Yes, Roger has a high opinion of Moira. She's been so understanding about...you know, having me to look after and running his department.'

'He's a very committed principal teacher.'

'Oh, I know. Why, he even worried so much about his pupils coming back on their own that night he went into town to meet the bus.'

A small bomb went off in Sarah's chest. 'What night was that?'

'You know, when they went to Glasgow to see some play or other...and Judith didn't come back with them. Roger felt he should be there but,' she lifted a pale hand '...he's got me.'

Sarah drove back to Helensburgh: things which were confusing before had just become chaotic. One thing stood out. While all the rest of it; Hakim, the Clarion's innuendo

101

about Rubina's family, or David Smythe for that matter, was no more than speculation, it was a fact that Roger had gone to meet the bus on that Friday night. Or as close to a fact, since it came from his wife.

This was something she couldn't discuss with Moira. It would have to be Mark McKenzie.

Mark was in his office when she phoned him from the flat, at around 6pm, and they agreed that she would drive to the city and meet him in Rico's, the restaurant they'd eaten in before.

He was there when she arrived. He got out of his chair and helped her off with her jacket, smiling so widely that she thought he must be pleased to see her. She realised that she was happy to see him, and found herself hoping he was not the source of the stuff in the Clarion.

'I'm walking tonight.' Mark raised his glass of wine. 'So I can give you a toast. To my favourite teacher.'

'I may not be so popular with you when you hear what I have to say,' Sarah retorted.

The smile left his face. 'Go on.'

'I expect you've seen the Clarion blast? 'Who killed Rubina?''

'Of course I've seen it. Didn't like it much…'

Sarah crossed her fingers under the table. 'So you didn't aid and abet it?'

Mark laid his glass down very deliberately. 'How can you say such a thing?'

'Well, let's face it - it's quite a coincidence when Mohammed sits in my flat more or less accusing his brother - and there's headlines in the paper the very next day.'

He twirled his wine glass by the stem. 'Unless Mohammed confided in someone else?'

Sarah sighed. 'I've thought of that. The only person I could ask was Lynn - because of her connection to both

Mohammed and to Wilson Toner - by way of her mother, but she was totally bewildered by my questions.'

She sat back while the waiter served her with a fragrant risotto, and nodded for black pepper from a mill so huge that could it have done service as a cannon.

'So, Miss Blane, have you come all the way to Glasgow just to ask me if I share information with my colleagues on the more salacious organs of the press?'

'Mark, I'm sorry. I had to ask.'

'Listen Sarah, if and when I next write about such matters in the Asian community, it will be properly researched and honestly written, with my by-line. I don't hide behind innuendo, ever.'

Chastened, Sarah concentrated on the food in front of her. They ate in silence for a while then she laid down her fork.

'I …need your advice…about one or two other things.'

Mark held her eyes as he signalled for coffee. 'I'm intrigued.'

She told him about the photograph and the fragment of blue sleeve. 'I promised Lynn faithfully that I would never tell, but I think the time has come to try to find out who he is.'

'Is Lynn likely to give up the photograph?'

'Possibly, if I can convince her that it would help find Rubina's killer. Of course, it might be totally innocent - but at least it's somewhere to start. After all, the police don't seem to be making much headway, unless you know different?'

He shook his head. 'Why didn't you tell DI Hamilton about this?'

'For exactly the reasons I'm giving now. A promise to Lynn, and for fear of implicating some perfectly innocent young man.'

'Ok. If you can persuade Lynn to part with the photograph, I'll see what can be done with it here. There's some fairly sophisticated technical equipment around these days, and we might be able to extract a bit more information than is evident just by looking at it.' He leaned over the table towards her. 'You said one or two things?'

'I don't really know where to start with this one.' She took a deep breath. 'Our principal teacher, Roger Bullough?' Mark nodded. 'He had a major heart attack last night. His wife, Dorothy, has multiple sclerosis and I volunteered to visit her, to see if we could offer any help.'

She took a gulp of almost cold coffee. 'Ugh!'

Mark laughed. 'I'll get some more.'

Sarah waited until the fresh coffee had been served. She focused her gaze on a mural depicting Venice, then she poured cream carefully and stirred her coffee as if something important depended on it.

'Sarah?' Mark said. His tone told her that she been found out.

'Roger Bullough went to meet the mini-bus on the Friday night that Rubina disappeared.'

'What?' Mark sat back, his eyebrows raised. 'And?'

'And nothing. What could I say to Dorothy? But this throws a whole new complication into the works, doesn't it? It's the first thing Lynn or Leslie would have mentioned when Rubina disappeared.'

'Yeah...and if no-one saw him it can only mean that he didn't actually meet the bus.'

'So where was he? Dorothy said he wanted to see them safely back because he felt responsible. She also said that he's been very upset about Rubina's death.'

'He certainly didn't tell the police about it, because teacher or not, Steve would have had him in for questioning.'

Sarah touched his hand. 'You won't tell them just yet, will you? Roger might not even survive the heart attack.'

Mark patted her hand where it lay on top of his. 'Not yet. There may be a simple explanation. But you will have to tell them sooner or later, if no-one else is caught for Rubina's murder. Because - don't shake your head like that, Sarah - it makes Roger Bullough a suspect, in no uncertain terms.'

Sarah opened her mouth to speak but Mark cut in: 'I know what you're going to say, you can't believe it. But let me remind you again - somebody killed that girl.'

'Well, at least I've found out from Lynn that it was none of the boys in the school. Rubina herself scoffed at the idea that she would risk her father's anger for any of them. In fact, she called them kids, which suggests that the person she was seeing was significantly older.'

'But not Roger Bullough, you think?'

'Oh no - Roger must be almost forty. I expect we're looking at someone in his twenties.'

'David Smythe then?'

Sarah started to say no to that idea as well, then stopped herself. As Mark said, it had to be someone.

'I don't know. I mean, if the Clarion is right in its hints about 'honour killing' it could be a complete stranger who is responsible, couldn't it? Someone...hired...to do the job.'

'A bounty hunter, you mean.'

'Something like that. It could mean the killer might never be found.'

'Mohammed wasn't thinking along those lines.' Mark said.

'No. But if Hakim did kill her, I think we're looking

at a crime of passion rather than a murder coldly done for cultural reasons.'

'On that subject, I have got one piece of information. Forensics found only Rubina's DNA on the scarf.' Mark held up his hands. 'The killer must have been wearing gloves.'

'But surely that suggests premeditation!' Sarah burst out, and people at the next table glanced over.

Mark shrugged. 'Or a cold night.'

'Not that cold!' She said, crisply. 'I was in Edinburgh at the opera; the ticket had cost the earth, another reason I wasn't at Hamlet, and when I came out of the theatre I thought how chilly it always seems to be in Edinburgh. I was late getting back to Helensburgh and noticed that it was a lot milder.' She smiled. 'And that mattered, because I was wearing rather a light suit to the wedding next day.' Her voice dropped, 'It was at the wedding we discovered that Rubina was missing, when her father came to ask if we'd seen her. You know, when I think back to that night, before it all got totally out of proportion, the idea of bounty hunters or whatever becomes a complete nonsense! Mr Khan was distraught, just like any other father of a teenage girl.'

Mark caught both of her hands. 'You're determined to see the best in everyone, aren't you?'

Sarah didn't answer for a moment.

'Well, maybe it looks that way, but it's just that I can imagine how awful it is for these parents. Their only daughter.' She thought of Ruth. 'At least my parents…' She looked at her watch. 'I'd better go. It's getting late.'

'I'll walk you to your car.'

They strolled towards the car-park. It was cold, but dry and Sarah pulled the collar of her jacket up around her neck. There were more Christmas lights since last time; the city was preparing for the usual burst of Christmas revelry. It was one of the things which hadn't helped her marriage: Sarah's lack of enthusiasm for wild, festive celebrations didn't go down well with Simon.

Mark's foot caught a discarded beer can and sent it into the gutter. It made a rolling clatter in the quiet street.

He said, 'Would Roger Bullough have a motive?'

The picture of Dorothy in the bed, scarcely able to move now, flashed into Sarah's mind. She said, slowly: 'Who can know what fantasies fill people's dreams.'

'You think he may have had a thing for Rubina?'

'It's happened before. A forty-year old teacher in my last school got a teenage pupil pregnant! And Rubina was a very lovely girl.'

'Sarah, we've got to get that photograph!'

They walked up the ramp into the car park. Sarah said, smiling, 'I can manage on my own, you know.'

Mark took her by the elbow. 'Well, you don't have to when I'm here. These car-parks can be dangerous places at night.'

At the car, he seemed reluctant to let her go. 'Of course, we may be on the wrong track. The person in the photograph and the person who killed Rubina may be two different people.'

The locks clicked open. 'I've thought of that too,' Sarah said. 'But we have to start somewhere.'

On the drive home Sarah reflected on the fact that she and Mark McKenzie had now eaten together three times in less than a week. She was amazed at how familiar and, she had to admit, essential, to her he had become in that short time. Of course, these times were far from normal. Next, her thoughts turned to strategies to get hold of Lynn without raising any comment in school. She'd been seen with Lynn so often recently that she didn't want it to become a problem. Teachers and pupils didn't normally spend that much time together, and the fact that she was a female wasn't going to cut much ice these days. At the finish she decided to phone Lynn and invite her to the flat on Saturday morning for coffee. She'd been there before, after all. Saturday would be soon enough; the picture wasn't going anywhere, she hoped. Besides, Sarah felt that her work was falling behind - however unavoidable, there had been too many distractions in the past weeks.

At home, there were several messages on her answering machine. The first, from Moira, said that Roger was out of intensive care. He would recover, but it would probably be after a lengthy absence. The second was David. He made no mention of Rubina, just asked her to call him when she had time. And the last was Detective Inspector Hamilton. He too, would like her to call him at her earliest convenience. They would have to wait: she wasn't about to make phone calls at this time of night, nor would she before school in the morning.

Chapter 7

Last period before lunch on Thursdays Sarah was free. She remained in her classroom, and had settled at her desk to get on with some marking when the door opened and DI Hamilton entered the room.

'You didn't return my call, Miss Blane.'

Sarah raised her head. 'I was too late in getting home last night, and,' she waved her pen at him, 'you can see I'm busy now.'

'Murder investigations can't wait.' He came forward and rested one buttock on the edge of a table in the front row.

'You've interviewed me already, DI Hamilton.'

'Oh, this is not an official interview.' He spread his arms wide as if to demonstrate that he wasn't hiding a PC inside his jacket. 'This is just a chat.'

'About what?'

'Well, you know,' he rubbed his nose. 'I find it hard, very hard indeed, to believe that every one of these youngsters who went on the theatre trip knew nothing about Rubina's...assignation. You remember, you told us about that?'

Sarah stood up. Sitting put her at a disadvantage.

'Well, if they do, why would they tell me?'

'Ah, now, that's the point. You spend a lot of time with one or two of these young people, in and out of the classroom from what I hear.'

109

Sarah sighed and shrugged her shoulders.

The inspector smiled and the eyebrows jiggled. 'Do you want to know what I think?'

Sarah leaned against the wall behind her desk and didn't reply.

He got up suddenly and began to pace the classroom 'I smell a little conspiracy here, Miss. Not one of these kids will tell us anything, and we find that hard to understand. Girls especially, are very wont to confide in their pals, are they not?'

'Conspiracy?'

'Yes, a conspiracy of silence.'

Sarah pushed herself off the wall. 'Why on earth would they do that?'

The inspector stopped. 'Protecting someone? Someone they like?'

'I can't see them liking anyone enough to hide evidence of a murder, for Heaven's sake! They liked Rubina too, you know.'

'Maybe they did.' He cocked one eyebrow in her direction. 'But you have to admit, she was every different from them, wasn't she?'

Sarah looked at the floor. For the first time she noticed how small his feet were. 'Rubina was a perfectly normal teenager, from what I could see, Inspector.'

He returned to sit on the table, and rubbed his nose with his thumb and forefinger. She wondered again if it was deliberate, to give himself the look of a deep thinker.

'But that's it, isn't it? She wasn't allowed to be a 'perfectly normal teenager', was she?'

She thought for a moment. 'I think that's a subject for Rubina's family, rather than a teacher. I can only tell you what I observed.'

DI Hamilton got up. 'Rubina's family...yes now.

Thank you, Miss Blane.'

When he left the room Sarah threw her pen down. The man had an unerring power to wrong-foot her. He'd made it sound as if Rubina's family had never entered his mind until she mentioned them.

Anyway, she reflected, as she made her way for lunch, the police obviously have nothing to go on, or smarmy little DI Hamilton wouldn't be snooping around her so much. He hadn't even implied anything about David Smythe. David Smythe! She'd completely forgotten about his phone call.

Sarah walked home from school. It was, for once, a mellow day, more autumnal than wintry. The firth was its usual rolling grey, but a low sun glinted on the waves, tipping them with gold.

When Sarah called David from the flat he sounded better than last time: more in control. She apologised for taking so long to get back to him. 'Anyway, why did you call? Was it something important?'

David said, 'Well, actually I wanted to know about Roger, how he is. Mary Stephens phoned me about his heart attack, but it had just happened.'

'You didn't phone school?'

'What? And get that bitch, Judith? She'll be in her element now, running things.'

Sarah switched on the kettle, nursing the phone under her chin. 'You know, David, she might be running things for a while. Roger's out of intensive care - apparently it was a reasonably mild heart attack - but we don't know how long he'll be off. After all, you know as well as I do that school's no place for a man with a dodgy heart.'

She heard his sharp intake of breath. 'Well, in that case I won't be back at Fruin High! Hell will freeze over before I'll work for that woman!'

'Come on, it's not that bad.'

A faint note of hysteria was creeping back into his tone. 'It is that bad! It was her fault that Rubina was taken out of my class!'

Sarah was silent.

'Sarah? Are you there?'

'Yes, David,' she spoke slowly, 'What exactly do you mean? How was Judith involved? I thought it was Hakim who...'

'Yes it was! Hakim Ashrif actually challenged me in the street one day. He wouldn't listen to reason, said he was going to have me dismissed and a whole load of rubbish like that! I brought it up at the departmental meeting to prepare Roger, just in case, you know? Then Judith Aitken made a big scene of it and insisted that the boss should know. He phoned Rubina's father, to keep the school right, he said, and well,' he said truculently, 'you know the rest.'

'But what will you do if you don't come back?'

'Oh, I daresay I could find a job abroad, teaching English, in Japan or somewhere...'

Suspicion crept into Sarah's mind. He'd been thinking of this before now, she could swear. It was far too pat.

'Well, that's up to you, David. But you know it won't look good.'

There was a crash, and for a moment she thought he'd slammed down the phone. Then he spoke again. 'I don't care how it looks, Sarah. If I want to leave this nasty wee town I will, and no-one can stop me!'

Except Detective Inspector Hamilton, if he gets wind of your impending departure, Sarah thought. Or perhaps even Hakim Ashrif?

She sank into the sofa with her coffee, but soon found her eyes closing in the quiet room. She put the cup on the table and lay back, giving in to the need for some rest, and was deeply asleep when the intercom buzzed and startled her. She stared around stupidly. As she rose and stumbled towards the handset it gave another insistent ring. 'Hello? Who is it?'

In her fuzzy state she had difficulty in making out the name, and she asked again.

'Who?'

'Hakim Ashrif.'

For a moment Sarah thought she was still asleep, until he said, 'Please, Miss Blane. My uncle has asked me to speak with you.'

She pressed the button. 'Come up.'

While he made the climb Sarah went to the bathroom and splashed water on her face. She needed to be alert for this interview, though she couldn't think what he wanted from her. Or what his uncle wanted, if Hakim was telling the truth.

To her surprise the young man seemed embarrassed once she had shown him into the living-room. He stood in the middle of the floor, dressed entirely in black, his bulk almost filling the cam-ceilinged space. His obvious discomfort took the edge off his menacing appearance, and Sarah waved at the sofa.

He ignored her and took the window-seat. She almost smiled at the observation that the seat with its back to the window seemed to offer some protection, or, perhaps the possibility of escape, to uncomfortable visitors. It was Mohammed's choice, and Lynn's too when she had come first time.

'Can I offer you something? Coffee? A soft drink?'

Hakim shook his head.

Sarah shrugged, and sat on the leather chair. 'Then how can I help you?'

He lowered his brows and stared at the floor as he spoke. 'It is not my wish to be here, but my uncle has asked me to come.'

Sarah nodded. 'Mr Khan?'

'Yes, Mr Khan, my mother's brother.' The young man clasped his hands in front of him and Sarah saw his knuckles whiten. 'The family wants to take Rubina to Pakistan for burial.'

'But, what...I mean...how...?'

Hakim Ashrif looked up. 'The police will not allow it.'

'Oh, but...' Sarah searched for a suitable response and failed. 'Why?'

His eyes were black pools of anger. 'The police say that Rubina's body cannot be released until the investigation is over.'

'But what can I do?'

He unclasped his hands. 'My uncle thinks you might have some influence. To be honest, I don't share his view.' He looked directly at Sarah, 'If you couldn't even get her safely home from Glasgow...'

Sarah's insides lurched, 'Oh, no...you can't say that! What happened had nothing to do with the school!'

His head went up, 'How can you say that? What do you know?'

'Nothing, nothing!'

Her forehead grew damp as she felt an overwhelming urge to tell him everything - about Rubina's mysterious appointment that night - about the photograph of the blue sleeve. She took a deep breath. 'Look, Hakim. I know how awful this is for your family.'

He snorted.

'And if I could, I would do anything to help. But please tell your uncle that I have no influence with the police. Really, I wish I had.'

'It's as I told him. But he's clutching at anything. So I agreed to ask you.'

She nodded. 'I'm sorry.'

He stood to leave, filling the room. 'But I have a question of my own.'

'Yes?'

'Why is David Smythe not at work?'

'Oh...I ...he's not well.'

'What's wrong with him?'

'I don't know. I think it's a virus or something, from his holiday.' She was floundering. 'Remember he went - oh, you wouldn't know that - but he was abroad during the October week holiday, and he seems to have brought something back.'

'He was abroad?'

'Yes, he'd arranged to go away as soon as the school stopped - on the Friday evening I think - or he'd have gone to the theatre, you know...with...'

Hakim Ashrif was shaking his head. 'He didn't leave on the Friday. I saw him that night, in Glasgow.'

'Are you sure?'

'I'm sure. I was worried about Rubina, and the boys, you know, and when I saw Smythe in town I knew at least that he wasn't one of them.'

'Where did you see him?'

'In Sauchiehall Street. About eight-thirty. I was parking my car and I saw him going into... a club.'

'And you're sure it was him?'

He smiled. 'Quite sure, Miss Blane.'

When he left Sarah struggled to remember the various conversations which had taken place all these weeks ago, when the theatre trip was being planned. Judith Aitken had agreed to accompany the senior pupils because Roger couldn't leave Dorothy - or so he said - Mary Stephens never left her mother in the evenings - none of Willie Armstrong's pupils wanted to go - she herself had the opera booked and, she was sure of it - David had said he was leaving straight after school. Why? Was it because he had a secret meeting lined up for later in the evening? In fact now it seemed that half the English department could have been skulking around in Helensburgh that night.

Her thoughts turned to William Armstrong. Where was he on the night in question? She would have to find out.

A moment later she laughed at herself. Never in a million years could the lugubrious pipe-sucking Willie be any young girl's idea of a secret lover. Nor would Roger Bullough, in Sarah's eyes, but at least he had more going for him than William.

On Friday morning it was winter without any apology, and Sarah hurried into the car for the short journey to work. Needles of freezing rain hit her then struck the windscreen with force as she started to drive. In the poor visibility it took her some time to realise why she was stuck at the traffic lights on West Clyde Street, until she saw a low-loader manoeuvring with difficulty out of Sinclair Street. Her first concern was that it might keep her late for school, until she saw what was being carried on the long vehicle. A gleaming black Range Rover. She noted it with passing interest, then the big truck swung round and she saw the personalised number-plate. HAK 08. She reflected with a little bit of envious amusement that even up-market cars broke down from time to time, until she saw the police vehicles which were escorting the transporter.

DI Hamilton had moved on to a new angle. Or the police had uncovered some fresh evidence, possibly at the crime scene? Mark would know perhaps, but she didn't have time now to get in touch with him.

But at the end of the day, he was waiting for her in the lane outside the flat, sitting in his car avoiding the worst of the weather. Sarah squeezed past, making for her garage at the back of the house, cursing mildly, until she saw that it was Mark.

Together, they ran upstairs, shaking off rain, until they got inside to the warmth. Sarah left Mark putting on the kettle while she went into the bedroom to change out of her school clothes. When she came back he was searching in one cupboard after another for the coffee, Henry prowling the worktop for attention. Sarah pushed past him and found the cafetiere, then she fished the milk out of the fridge.

'It's ok, just go and sit down and I'll make the coffee.'

He stood at the window looking out at the dark scene. The lights of Greenock were almost obscured by sheets of rain and the hillside silhouettes had completely vanished. 'What a day!' He turned, and smiled. 'But it's cosy in here.'

Sarah laughed. 'For cosy, read pokey!'

'No, I like it here. It is comfortable.'

'At least I never have to draw the curtains, so I have all the space outside, except for days like this when there's nothing to see!'

Mark sat on the sofa and stretched out his legs. He did look more comfortable than any of her recent visitors. Especially Hakim.

'I had Hakim Ashrif here last night.'

The smile left his face. 'Wasn't that a bit risky?'

Sarah came from behind the counter with the coffee pot.

'Well, since I saw his car being taken off by the police this morning, maybe it was.'

'Yes, about that…but first, what did he want?'

She shrugged, 'Ostensibly to ask on his uncle's behalf if I had any clout with the police in that matter of releasing Rubina's body for burial in Pakistan.'

His eyebrows rose. 'He didn't seriously think that you could influence that?'

'Not for a minute. But who knows, Mr Khan may think differently. After all I was at the police when Rubina disappeared. No, I think he used it as an excuse to ask about David Smythe. Wanted to know why he isn't back at work.'

'If he's fishing for information about David Smythe it makes him look innocent himself, doesn't it?'

'I suppose it could be a distraction. Anyway, what about his car? You obviously know something about that.'

Mark helped himself to a biscuit. 'I don't know much, but the word on the grapevine is that they are going to take it apart for evidence. Apparently someone has come forward to report seeing a similar car parked in a lay-by on the loch shore that night.'

'But that means the police must suspect Hakim!'

'Yes, they've picked him up too.' He crunched the biscuit for a moment then he said, 'All along I think Steve Hamilton's been looking to find an honour killing. It simplifies things for the police if it is. I mean, in Manchester the other day two guys went to prison for burning out the home of a girl they didn't approve of. The girl died, and nine other people in the house nearly lost their lives too. Unlikely as it seems in a place like Helensburgh, it does happen.'

Sarah held out the biscuit plate again. 'All the more reason we should get hold of that photograph. If we knew who it was it would tell us so much. We can be sure it's not Hakim, but we can't be sure it's not someone that Hakim found out about? He seems to have kept a pretty close eye on Rubina.'

Mark leaned forward. 'So close it's incredible that

someone else could have found an opportunity to murder her.'

'I know. I hate to put pressure on her but I'll have to use all my powers of persuasion on Lynn, when she comes for coffee tomorrow morning.'

'On the subject of coffee, Sarah, the pot's empty. What are you planning for dinner? No school tomorrow, you can indulge yourself.'

Sarah went to the window and looked out at the dark, unwelcoming evening.

'How does take-away Chinese and a bottle of wine sound?'

Mark laughed. 'You took the words out of my mouth.'

She fetched the menu from a drawer in the kitchen and they amused themselves for the next half-hour choosing food then changing their minds, until eventually Mark made the phone call.

While they waited Sarah set the small table in the corner, then lit candles around the room. Mark opened a bottle of wine.

Dinner over, the dishes washed and put away, Mark lay back on the sofa and Sarah rocked gently on the chair, as Mozart's flute concerto played quietly in the background. They had already discovered a mutual love of several composers, but especially Mozart. She continued to be amazed at how well they fitted each other's company in such a short time.

After a spell of quiet listening, Mark said. 'Tell me about your sister.'

So she did. She told him everything, including the fact that it had damaged her marriage beyond repair.

When the story was finished it was late, and she asked Mark if he wanted to stay. Without involvement, but simply because it would be hellish to drive back to Glasgow on such a night. And there was a second bedroom.

He nodded, 'I understand. Thanks.'

Mark was still there when Lynn arrived in the morning. She was wearing a huge, parka-like jacket which made her look as if she was just about to enter a spacecraft. As she waited to take the jacket from her Sarah ignored her knowing look, instead nodding at a thick envelope in Lynn's gloved hand as the girl began to remove her arms from the sleeves.

'Oh, yikes!' She laid the envelope on the sofa while she completed the removal of the bulky garment, and Sarah took it out to the hall to hang it up.

She shook her head when Mark offered her coffee, but agreed to some hot chocolate. 'That would be fabulous, Mr McKenzie.'

Sarah said, 'Sit anywhere,' and wasn't surprised when the girl chose the window-seat.

The weather was worse than ever, the scene beyond the window a whirl of grey sleet. They spoke about it while Mark completed making the hot drink for Lynn, then, mug clutched in both hands, she said. 'I'm glad you invited me, Miss Blane, because there's something I want to ask you about...' she added, 'after you, of course...you wanted to speak to me?'

`Sarah glanced at Mark, who gave her an encouraging nod. 'Yes, Lynn. I don't want to do this...but I think you're going to have to give up that picture of Rubina...you know...with the other person...'

Braced for the usual negative reaction, she was astonished when the girl smiled widely. 'No problem.' She lifted the bag at her feet and produced the photograph. 'Here it is.'

Bemused, Sarah took the picture and passed it to

Mark. 'But, Lynn, what's changed? You were so adamant that...'

There was a spark of excitement in the girl's eyes. 'I know, but that's not necessary now!'

She jumped to her feet and retrieved the package from the sofa. 'Look at these!'

In her haste she opened the envelope at the wrong end, and out poured sheet after sheet of A4 paper; coloured images of Rubina cascading on to the sofa cushions.

Sarah picked one up - two dark-eyed Rubinas smiled at her from each page - and two blue sleeves - tumbling over and over as some of the sheets slipped from the leather sofa on to the floor. She held it out to Mark, who looked as stunned as she was.

'What on earth...?'

The girl smiled. 'Great, aren't they? Leslie and I got them done. We used a copier in the supermarket in Dumbarton because we didn't want to be seen doing it until we were ready.'

'Ready to do what?'

'That's what I wanted to ask you. We could only afford to pay for fifty copies - that's a hundred when we cut them - and we're going to hand them out in school next week - but do you think we should just give them out to the seniors?'

Sarah said, 'You are what?' She looked at the swirling sleet outside the window and felt dizzy. 'What are you thinking of, Lynn? You can't just...' She waved the sheet in her hand.

Mark picked up another copy of the two identical pictures. 'Why don't you explain, Lynn.'

She set her lips in a line and looked from Mark to Sarah.

'It's like this. Leslie and I are really sick that

121

nobody's been caught for Rubina yet. In the end I told Leslie about the photo, you said Miss, remember? And he had the idea that if we got copies and showed them around in school somebody might just recognise this other person.'

Sarah clutched at the only straw she could think of, 'But, haven't the police already arrested someone?'

Lynn knelt on the floor to slide the photocopies back into the envelope. She looked up, 'Yes, Hakim, but they've let him out again. Obviously they don't have the right evidence, because Leslie says they can only keep somebody for six hours if they're not charged'

Mark said, 'Leslie is a very resourceful young man, isn't he?'

'Defin-ately. He wanted to speak to Miss Blane too, but he thought it would be rude to come when he wasn't invited.'

'Lynn,' Sarah spoke as gently as she could, 'What if Rubina's parents, or someone close to her... saw these? Think how awful that would be.'

'We thought of that, Miss. We showed them to Mohammed. He's all for us doing this because he wants to know what happened to Rubina too, and he said nothing can make them feel any worse than they do now...'

Lynn jumped to her feet. 'We've just got to do something! We've got to!' Nobody is doing anything!' Her voice rose and she felt in the pocket of her jeans for a tissue. 'And we can't stand it any more. So don't tell us not to!'

Mark said, 'Lynn, sit down, please.'

She went back to window, her expression mutinous.

'Has you mother seen these? Sarah asked.

Lynn looked out of the window as she spoke, 'No, but it won't bother her.'

'I wouldn't be so sure.' Sarah told Mark. 'Lynn's mother is a councillor.'

'Anyway,' Lynn said, 'I'll tell her that Leslie had them done and I was just helping to give them out.'

Mark got up and leaned against the kitchen counter. 'Has it occurred to you, or Leslie, that this might be a dangerous game you're getting into?'

Lynn's head turned sharply. 'Dangerous?'

Sarah nodded. 'Yes, Lynn, dangerous. What if the person in the photograph is the same one who killed Rubina?'

The girl's eyes widened behind her specs. 'We're only going to show it round the school.' She shook her head vigorously. 'And we know it's not any of the boys there. It's just that some of them might know who...whose arm this is?' She looked at the blue sleeve as if seeing it for the first time.

Sarah sighed. 'Well, Lynn, if you take my advice, you'll tell Leslie that giving out this photograph is not a good idea.'

She didn't say much as Sarah fetched her jacket. At the door she said, 'I'll speak to Leslie.'

When Sarah returned to the living-room she spread her hands out. 'What next?'

Mark said, 'Do you think they'll take heed?'

'I think Lynn might, but I'm not so sure of Leslie. He's a very determined lad.'

She was thoughtful as she rinsed out the cafetiere and spooned fresh coffee into it. Mark was quiet too and when she turned she saw that he was studying the picture of Ruth.

'Do you think we should go and speak to Leslie then?' Sarah raised a cup in Mark's direction and he nodded. 'What, more coffee or go to see Leslie?'

He didn't answer until she had placed the coffee in front of him on the table.

'Thanks. Why don't you sit down Sarah, so that we can speak about one or two things.'

Sarah did as he asked. 'What things?'

'Right. First, if you think it will help, we can pop along and see how persuasive we can be with the young rebel.'

Sarah looked at him over the rim of her cup, 'And second.'

She watched as Mark appeared to take deep breath.

'Ruth.'

The rocking chair swung as Sarah bolted upright, and Mark held up his hands. 'I know... I know, Sarah, how difficult this is - but...have you ever attempted to find out what happened to her?'

She laid her cup on the coffee table and covered her face with her hands. 'No.'

'Why not?' Mark's tone was gentle.

She took her hands away and shook her head. 'To begin with, I was very young when it happened, and then...later...well, my parents were so distressed...it would have been cruel. And then they died and, I suppose I thought then the door had closed on it all.' She shrugged. 'I tried to get on with my own life.'

'But the door hadn't closed, had it?' Mark leaned forward. 'Think about it Sarah, almost every step in life you have taken since then has been coloured by your sister's disappearance all those years ago. You've never been able to put it behind you, have you?'

Sarah got up and returned to the window - a watery sun was struggling to replace the sleet and the sky was faintly blue in places.

'It looks as if it might clear up.' She spoke without turning.

'Sarah. You're doing it again. Come on, sit down

and let's talk about it.'

She felt a rush of fury - how dare he! This stranger! She turned back to the room, angry words at the ready, but they faded away when we she saw Mark's expression. There was a brief glint from his wedding ring as he passed his hand over his eyes.

'Let's go and see Leslie,' she said.

Mark smiled and shook his head. 'Ok, you win, for the moment.'

Mark's car slithered to a stop on the verge outside the peace camp. In such weather conditions the camp-site appeared deserted, apart from a straggle of smoke from a battered van at one end, and they struggled over the slippery rough ground on the way to the caravan they had seen Leslie approach.

'I hope this is the right one,' Sarah whispered as they came round to the door side of a medium-sized caravan. But when Mark pointed to the Che Guevara poster in a window she smiled and nodded.

Franny Watkins opened the door. Her red hair was tied up in a messy bun and her face was pink. She was wearing jeans and a dark sweatshirt with what looked like a streak of egg down the front and she was holding a wooden spoon. A blast of gassy heat came out of the caravan. She took in Sarah's leather coat and Mark's Barbour jacket.

'Yeah?'

Sarah realised that Franny didn't recognise her. Leslie's mother hadn't appeared at any parents' meeting since she had been teaching at Fruin High.

'It's eh...is Leslie at home?'

Franny's eyes narrowed. 'Who wants him?'

Feeling distinctly foolish as they stood at the foot of the caravan steps in the slush Sarah said, 'I'm Sarah Blane and this is Mark McKenzie. I'm Leslie's teacher...'

125

In a slightly less suspicious tone Franny said, 'Right, got you.' She almost smiled, 'Fetched my boy from the cop shop the other day, didn't you. He told me. Ta for that.' Suddenly, in the tone of a hostess, she said. 'Oh, please, come in.' She stood back and waved the spoon in welcome.

Sarah was surprised at how tidy the cramped space was, apart from a long shelf above one side of the curving bench which ran around the end of the living space. It was crammed with books and papers, and she reflected on the skill required to live like this and keep any sense of order.

As Franny turned the gas off under a pot Sarah said, 'Oh sorry, are we disturbing your lunch?'

Franny shook her head, then sat down at the other side of the table. 'What's Les been up to then?'

'Oh nothing Mrs…Watkins'

The boy's mother laughed, 'Franny will do.'

'No, it's…you know about Rubina Khan?'

Franny's eyes narrowed again. 'Leslie had nothing to do with that.'

Mark said, 'We know, that's why we're here. Leslie is trying to help, but we're worried that might put himself in danger.'

'What do you mean?'

Sarah was sweating under her thick coat. 'Leslie and Lynn Cameron have a photograph they want to…'

The door opened and Leslie came in carrying a loaf of bread. He turned back to knock the slush off his trainers, then he registered that they had visitors.

'What…?'

Franny stood up. ' Come on, son. Get the shoes off. What's this I'm hearing about a photograph? By the way, does anyone want a cup of tea? It's herbal. Cranberry and thyme?'

'No, but thanks.' Mark and Sarah spoke together.

In his stocking-feet Leslie came and sat at the spot his mother had vacated. 'What are you saying about the photo?'

Sarah smiled. 'Hi, Leslie. It's just,' she pointed to herself and Mark. 'We don't think it's a very good idea to ...well...give it too much publicity.'

Franny was back, carrying a striped ceramic teapot. 'What is this?'

Leslie said, 'We're just trying to find out who killed Rubina?'

'Just!' Franny's hair shook. 'Are you mad?'

Leslie folded his arms. 'Rubina gave this torn photo to Lynn to keep for her. We got copies done - it's got a bit of some guy in it... and we're ...' He hesitated.

'You're what?'

With a defiant look at Sarah, he went on. 'We're going to give it out in school.'

Franny put the teapot back on the draining board and held out her hand. 'Let's see it.'

Leslie shrugged. 'Lynn's got them.'

Mark took from his pocket one of the copies he'd rescued from the sofa. He smoothed it out on the table.

Franny studied the double image of Rubina for some time, then she sighed. 'What a waste. Does anyone know where this was taken?'

'Somewhere around Helensburgh, isn't it? Sarah said.

Franny took a spectacle case from a shelf and put on a pair of narrow metal framed glasses. 'You know, yeah, I'm sure...I think this has been taken somewhere around the Rhu Marina.'

She turned the picture so that Mark and Sarah could see, 'Look, there, I'm sure that's a bit of a boat, and the other side from there...I pass it often on the bus and I could

127

swear that's where it is.'

Now that she had been alerted, Sarah thought she could see a fraction of what looked like a mast behind the shoulders of Rubina and her unknown companion. And, a greater expanse of water. 'We've got to give this to the police.'

As soon as the words were out of her mouth Sarah regretted them, when she was met by the outraged gasps of Leslie and his mother.

'Anyway, Leslie, they'll soon get it if you pass it out willy-nilly in Fruin High.'

'Yeah, they'll be on to it like a shot. And we don't know - maybe this poor guy in the photo has nothing to do with any of it. Let the pigs get hold of it and the poor sod won't have a chance.'

Mark coughed. 'That's true, but we're also concerned about Leslie and Lynn. If they make this picture public they could be putting themselves at risk, if he's not an innocent party.' He nodded at the photograph.

Franny went on, 'The other question is, who took it? That's the person who will definitely know! Showing it around will alert him, or her, won't it?' She leaned back against the sink. 'No Les, old son. I think the teachers are right for once. This is not a good idea.'

Sarah saw Leslie tense and knew that if he had the space he would be slamming out of the room. He stood up and faced his mother, 'Oh, this is great, isn't it? You're the one that's always on about acting because you think something's right and not being put off by,' he waved around the caravan, 'the conventions.'

Franny touched him on the arm and spoke quietly, 'I know, son, every time. But this is different. This is murder.'

It was as if all the air left the boy and he slumped back on to his seat.

Sarah said, 'Leslie, I admire your conviction, and Lynn's, but I agree with your mother. Murder is in a class of its own, isn't it?'

In Rhu, as they drove past the marina, Sarah gazed at the forest of masts visible from the road.

Mark said. 'We can go in if you want?'

She shook her head. 'I don't think I'm prepared for that.'

Mark took his eyes from the road. 'Ruth?'

Chapter 8

'They'll have moved or be dead by now, I'm sure. ' Sarah said, as they drove up St John's Road in the leafy suburb of Clermiston, in Edinburgh. She gnawed at the finger of her leather glove. 'If I could even have phoned.'

'Well, since you couldn't find their number there was nothing else for it, was there? We have to start somewhere, Sarah, and if there's a chance that the Buchanans are still at that address it could be a major step forward.'

'Only if they know anything.'

'Oh, I'm sure they will. You said they were close - good friends.'

Nerves were making Sarah feel slightly nauseous as they returned to the streets of her childhood, which, surprisingly, were much as she remembered them. A new building society on one corner and a hairdresser on the other, but otherwise, there wasn't a lot of difference. When it became apparent that Ruth was never coming home they'd moved away from Edinburgh to the relative peace of North Berwick on the south coast of the Firth of Forth. Sarah had hoped, with her parents, that the clear, cold air of the little resort would blow away at least some of their grief.

Now, apart from a modern house or two squeezed into the gardens of big villas, the district was relatively unchanged.

She caught her breath as, at her direction, Mark turned into the quiet Sunday street of semi-detached villas and drove until they were outside what used to be her home. It had been stone-cleaned, the front doors painted a glossy blue. The glass door behind which 12 year-old Sarah had waited on that terrible night had been replaced by a smart double-glazed door with fancy panelling. Two cars were parked on the widened driveway. Next door, on the other hand, had retained the familiar, slightly scruffy gravelled driveway, and the original glass door. Its frontage appeared dull next to the pale sandstone of the other house.

They sat in the car, Sarah making no attempt to move, until Mark touched her on the shoulder. 'Go on, Sarah.'

She turned to Mark. 'Will you come in with me?'

'Don't you think this is something you'd best do alone?'

Sarah looked from Mark to the curtained windows. 'No.'

The woman that opened the door was instantly recognisable to Sarah. Nancy Buchanan hadn't changed that much in twenty-three years, but she looked doubtfully at Sarah and Mark . 'Can I help you?'

'Mrs Buchanan? It's me - Sarah? Sarah - Marchegay?'

'Oh, Sarah!' Nancy Buchanan took Sarah's hands and drew her into the house. 'I thought it was you but I just wasn't sure. You look so like...' She hugged Sarah. 'And this is?' She turned to Mark.

'This is Mark McKenzie, a...my friend.'

The woman smiled, 'Come in, come in - Oh, I'm so pleased to see you, it's been so long.'

She led them into the warm sitting room, and made them sit near the fire. For a moment Sarah thought it was real until she recognised the flicker of a living flame gas fire. Sunday newspapers were scattered on the floor, and there were the remains of a sandwich on a table beside an easy chair. Again Sarah found herself apologising for disturbing someone's lunch.

'Not at all,' Nancy Buchanan was still on her feet.' What about yourselves - are you needing some lunch.'

Mark said. 'No, thanks all the same, Mrs Buchanan. Sarah and I ate on the way here.'

'You'll have a sherry then, yes?' She was a small, quick woman, her slim figure unchanged from Sarah's memory of her, dressed in neat grey trousers and a lilac cashmere sweater. Her hair was well-cut, and had the rich golden shade that Sarah associated with regular visits to a good hairdresser.

She handed them crystal glasses of pale, dry sherry. 'And no more of the Mrs Buchanan, it's Nancy, please.' She nodded towards next door. 'Heavens, even the kids call me Nancy, not like you and...Ruth...The adults were always Mr or Mrs in those days. Anyway,' she settled herself back in her chair, smiling. 'tell me, what brings you back, Sarah?'

Sarah looked around her. 'Bill?'

The smile left Nancy's face. 'Bill died four years ago. Heart attack. He was only fifty-nine.'

'I'm sorry.'

'Och, I know. But you've just got to get on with life, haven't you.' She put a hand to her face, 'I suppose you know that better than anybody, Sarah.'

'That's what we're here about, Nancy. You know how Mum and Dad were after...we could never talk about what happened.'

The woman nodded.

'I don't know if there is any point to this....but Mark here has persuaded me that...that maybe I should try to find out something more about...'

'Your sister?'

'Yes. I was much younger, so young in fact that I just had to accept...I remember that there was a police inquiry but not much more. All I ever knew was that dad had gone into town to fetch Ruth from the pantomime and she didn't turn up.'

Nancy Buchanan laid down her glass and clasped her hands in front of her. She said quietly, 'Ruth wasn't at the pantomime that night.'

Sherry splashed on to Sarah's hand. 'What?'

'They didn't want you to know, Sarah'

'Know ...?'

'What they found out afterwards. Oh, Ruth left to go to the pantomime all right - only she had no intention of going. She got a couple of her friends to cover for her while she...she went off to meet this lad she'd been seeing.'

'Lad? What lad?'

Nancy sighed. 'Well that's it, they never found out.'

'But surely the school noticed she was missing, they must have - it was their job!'

The woman shook her head. 'The girls told the teachers that Ruth was sick, so they weren't looking for her.'

'They damned well should have been!'

Mark said, gently. 'Easy Sarah - she was seventeen?'

'Then how did they find out she'd been seeing someone?'

'The other girls told the police. They had to, they knew it would come out. They thought he was a student at the university or something. She told them she'd met him in the library when she was, och, I don't know, looking up something for school.'

Mark said, 'And he didn't come forward when she disappeared?'

She shook her head. 'Never.'

Sarah said, 'But the girls - her friends - they must

have known something about him, his name, where he came from, what he was doing at uni...he can't simply have vanished!'

'No Sarah, I'm afraid she kept him a secret from everybody. That night, she said she'd be at the meeting-place in time for your dad, but, well, you know what happened...'

'Didn't the police make inquiries at the university?'

Nancy smiled. 'I'm sure they did, love, but,' she opened her hands '...thousands of students?'

'Thousands of...Ruth and a student? I can't even begin to think what this means...'

She stared at Mark and he leaned over and took her hand. 'It's all right Sarah, it's all right.'

Nancy Buchanan jumped up. 'I'm putting on the kettle. Tea's what you need when you've had a shock - tea with plenty of sugar.'

Sarah sipped at the tea, trying not to gag on the syrupy liquid. Nancy must have emptied the sugar bowl into the cup.

She waited, speaking to Mark about the weather in the west, until she saw that Sarah had calmed down.

'Why didn't they tell me?'

Nancy bit her lip. 'Because the thought that she'd run away of her own accord nearly killed them. Nothing would convince them that they hadn't totally failed as parents.'

'They almost did with me.'

'I know. Your mother would talk to me about it - she and your dad - they just couldn't communicate after it happened. And your mum kept saying that they must have interfered too much in Ruth's life, put too much pressure on her, with her school work, and her music. Driven her away.'

Sarah laughed; it was a hard sound. 'So that's why

they let me give up the piano!'

Nancy nodded. 'Ruth was such a clever girl. They had great hopes...'

'But not for me.'

'Oh no, Sarah, you mustn't think like that. They adored you...but after what had happened with Ruth, they became...I suppose scared is the word...to put any pressure on you. Thought it best to let you develop more naturally.'

'And here was I thinking they just didn't care.'

Mark stroked her hand. 'That wouldn't be possible, Sarah.'

He turned to the other woman. 'Those girls, the ones who covered up for Ruth, do you remember who they were?'

Nancy Buchanan grasped her chin with one hand while she thought about the question. 'No...no...I can't say that I...unless, wait. Yes, there was one girl - d'you not remember Sarah, a quiet wee thing with dark hair. Used to come home with Ruth sometimes? What was her name...Gillian? Jill? Something like that.'

Sarah shut her eyes, 'Jill...Jill....no, Julie, that's what it was. Julie Robertson!'

Mark said, 'Is it likely she's still around?'

Nancy sniffed. 'No, I remember these people now. Moved to England when the father got some fabulous job offer. In fact, it's coming back to me. Bill used to play the odd round of golf with a chap called Robertson, the girl's dad.'

'But you didn't keep in touch afterwards?'

'I'm sorry...no...I wish I could tell you more, but that's it. I'm afraid I can't even remember where they went, if I ever knew.'

Back in Glasgow, as Sarah was unlocking her car, which she'd parked outside Mark's flat in the west end, her mobile phone rang. Mark had been inviting her into the flat for supper, but she'd shaken her head. She had work to do for school on Monday, and she was exhausted by the events of the day.

When the phone rang Mark was holding Sarah's car door open for her.

'It's Nancy Buchanan,' she mouthed. She listened for a minute then said, 'Oh really, that's great, Nancy - hang on while I get a pen.'

She gestured to Mark, who wrote down the phone number as Sarah repeated it.

'I can't thank you enough, Nancy, that was very good of you...yes, of course I will. Bye.'

Mark held his notebook so that Sarah could see the number. 'What, another feat of memory from Nancy?'

'Better still. After we left she kept thinking about it, until it occurred to her to check Bill's old address book. It was in a suitcase full of stuff she'd put in the attic after he died.'

'And?'

'And, there it was, a phone number for Alex Robertson, Julie's dad. The English one, no less. The Edinburgh number scored out and this one written in its place.'

'Do you want to come in and phone now?' Mark dangled his keys, but Sarah slumped against the car.

'Mark, I'd love to, but I'm shattered. I think I've had enough for one day.'

He turned her by the shoulders into the car, then kissed her quickly on the cheek. 'Ok, off you go. Drive carefully; in fact give me a call when you get home then I'll know you're safe. We'll do it tomorrow.'

On the drive home, Sarah could still feel the place on her cheek where Mark had kissed her, and his careful touch on her shoulders. She hoped it wasn't just weariness, but she felt ...cosseted was probably putting it too strongly, but her sense of security when Mark was around was growing all the time, and she was getting to like it. But it wasn't until she reached the outskirts of Helensburgh that she admitted to herself that, whatever she was involved in now, she wouldn't have the strength to do it without him.

Once in bed, Sarah allowed herself to dwell upon the coincidences thrown up by the disappearance of the two girls. Ruth and Rubina, both seventeen, both on school trips, supposedly, and both vanishing. Rubina's disappearance, however, soon solved by the discovery of her body. But Ruth ? Her heart began to beat faster. Was she alive somewhere? Could she have a sister living a normal life somewhere - a woman more than forty? But, on the very edge of sleep, as Sarah's thoughts became chaotic, she was jerked sharply awake again by a voice in her head. As clear as a bell, it said. 'Ruth is dead too.'

*

It was a full week later before Sarah got the chance to do anything about Julie Robertson. Sharon, the second ecstasy victim, had come back to school, little the worse for her escapade, almost basking in her new notoriety, but still saying nothing about where she had obtained the drug. After holding her breath for a few days Sarah had relaxed when no pictures of Rubina appeared, and had begun to believe that Lynn and Leslie had taken the advice given to them. In any case, things were building up for Christmas, and more or less every evening had been spent in school, preparing for the Christmas concert which the Head had decreed must go ahead as planned.

Roger Bullough was still in hospital and not

expected to return to teaching even in the new year, and David Smythe had submitted a doctor's certificate keeping him on the sick list until at least the new term.

The murder of Rubina Khan had even slipped from the pages of the newspapers, replaced by the tally of accidental deaths from a train derailment near Glasgow and a couple of festive house-fires. In Helensburgh itself, the killing of a young man by stabbing after a drunken party appeared to be exercising DI Hamilton, since he hadn't been seen around the school all week.

And while they'd spoken on the phone, pressure of work had kept Mark too out of Sarah's life for a few days. In spite of everything she welcomed the breathing space; the intensity of the last weeks was hard to live with. And while she knew that it was all far from over, she welcomed the distractions offered by routine. Perhaps Keith Birkmyre was right, and things had to proceed as normally as possible. Even Moira's air of desperation, Sarah noticed, had been replaced by that of the usual panic surrounding school events.

By Saturday, Sarah acknowledged that she must even do some Christmas shopping in town, and she agreed to go to Mark's home for dinner afterwards. She trawled the shops, not for long since she was in danger of being squashed by the crowds, and at one point considered a rather elegant fountain pen for Mark. It was only for a moment, however; they weren't that stage yet, if they ever would be.

The flat was enormous, but beautifully warm, even allowing for the high ceilings. Sarah was impressed by light wooden floors and Swedish-style furniture that had never seen an IKEA catalogue. The cool uncluttered surroundings were oddly suited to the century-old property, as were several unusual pictures and pieces of sculpture.

They were to eat in the large kitchen, and Mark

settled Sarah at the table with a glass of wine while he put the finishing touches to the meal he was preparing.

'This is a lovely flat.' Sarah said. 'And the art work...'

He smiled over his shoulder. 'Sally's. She was a lecturer in fine art...'

'Oh, I'm sorry.'

Mark turned from the stove; he was shaking his head. 'Sarah, I haven't changed a thing since Sally died. Not because I've been in denial, but because ...I suppose...I've just wanted to keep something of her...her spirit around me, if that makes sense.'

Sarah nodded, 'It does. I've kept some of Ruth's music. I couldn't understand it when my parents just packed up all her things and...God knows where they went. I just came home from school one day and her room was empty - it was awful, as if she'd never existed. Anyway, I had this piece of music that she'd been working on - oh something way beyond me, and I've kept it ever since. It sort of, goes everywhere with me.'

He placed a dish in front of Sarah and sat down opposite her. 'I hope you like smoked salmon...maybe I should have asked you?'

'I love it. And avocado.' Sarah took a piece of very thin brown bread.

'So, have you brought the Robertson's phone number with you?'

Sarah looked up, buttery knife poised, 'Yes, it's in my bag, but, I thought...'

Mark grinned, 'You thought you were getting off the hook, is that it?' He tilted his head. 'Look Sarah. I know that if we don't pursue this thing you'll lose your nerve. We've started now, so let's keep going, eh?'

Sarah shrugged. 'I suppose we should.'

'Oh, and by the way, I've got some news on the photo. I gave it to one of the boys on the paper.'

'And?'

'After dinner.'

Later, in the warm living-room, Sarah relaxed. She longed to kick off her shoes and relieve feet weary from the day's shopping, but resisted. On the coffee table in front of her she had a very small cognac, since she intended to drive back to Helensburgh.

Mark came into the room with a laptop computer and laid it on the coffee table. 'This is what Ross came up with.' He sat down beside Sarah and brought up on the screen a blown-up version of the torn photo. 'He thinks it is definitely Rhu Marina, see, the skyline on the other side of the Clyde is quite good now...and he's even managed to identify the watch, by some piece of technical wizardry. Digital enhancement, actually. You can't tell just from the enlargement but he says it is a Dreyfuss...a pretty expensive watch for a kid.'

'A Dreyfuss? I've never heard of that.'

'Nor had I, but I did a little research this afternoon. It's a Swiss watch of course, but hand-made. They come in a range of prices, all high. And Ross thinks the sweater is probably a quality garment too.'

Sarah leaned forward to get a closer view of the picture. 'Who on earth would Rubina know that wore such things?' She pointed at the screen. 'Unless...what about Hakim? He has expensive tastes.'

Mark pursed his lips. 'Sarah, it's not Hakim. In the first place we know that she wouldn't have posed with his arm round her, and in the second - look at the skin.'

She felt her face grow warm. 'Oh, of course, how stupid of me...' On the bright screen it was quite possible to see the pale, freckled wrist of the watch-wearer.

'Anyway,' Mark closed the file and shut down the computer. 'There's nothing much to be done with this tonight, so let's get phoning.'

He got up from the sofa and came back holding out a cordless phone.

She ran her hand over the smooth plastic. 'Isn't it a bit late?'

'Oh? I don't think...' he glanced at the clock. It was quarter to eleven. 'Well, maybe you're right.' He took the phone back. 'So, we'll do it in the morning.'

Sarah raised her eyebrows. 'Are you planning to be in Helensburgh in the morning then?'

Mark reached over and ran his palm gently down the side of her face. 'Unless I can persuade you to be here?' He looked directly into her eyes, his meaning unmistakable.

She didn't answer, as her thoughts raced each other around. It would be so easy...this man was so easy to be with. She placed a hand on his chest. 'No, Mark. Not yet, I think. There's too much...'

He caught her hand. 'I know.' Then he kissed her on the lips, very lightly, and rose to fetch her coat.

Driving home, Sarah found herself trying to picture the wrists of her male colleagues. The watch would definitely be within David Smythe's budget, but did he have such fair skin? She thought back to the night of the wedding, and tried to visualise David's wrists against the black jacket of his Highland dress as she danced with him. Or Roger? No, that was ridiculous. Even if Roger Bullough had a fancy for Rubina there was no way he'd be embracing her in a public place like Rhu Marina. And that was another thing. What was the connection with the marina? Her heart thudded. David Smythe kept a boat there! He'd offered to take Sarah sailing more than once, but she'd declined; she wasn't happy with small boats and big expanses of water.

There was nothing else for it. She would have to visit him.

On Sunday morning she phoned David Smythe early. He sounded pleased with the prospect of a visit from her. As she reached his driveway she recalled her last, aborted attempt to see David, on the day that Rubina's body had been found. It all seemed very long ago.

When he opened the door to her she was shocked to see how ill he looked. His usual tan, natural or otherwise, had faded to a sickly yellow, and his body seemed lost within a dark blue jogging suit. He led her into his sitting room and stood in front of her as she sat down. He pointed at himself. 'You're surprised, Sarah, aren't you?'

She shook her head as if to deny it, while out of her mouth came, 'Yes...I'm...you don't look well, David.' She noticed that, although the room was suffocatingly warm, his long sleeves almost covered his hands. He sat in an armchair opposite Sarah.

'Have they...do you know what it is?'

He slumped back in the chair. 'Tests. They're doing tests. They think maybe it's something I picked up in Sri Lanka.'

'Well...I suppose...'

'Anyway, do you believe me, now that you have the evidence of your own eyes?'

'David...I ...'

'Oh,' He struggled out of the chair. 'You must have coffee. I won't be a minute.'

Left in the room Sarah examined David's bookcases, unsurprisingly similar to her own with the exception of a shelf of books about sailing, then she studied the pictures on the walls. Mostly photographs, they showed David and other young men in sports gear of one kind or another, and several of the pictures were of a sailing dinghy, with or without David on board. She was gazing at one of these, obviously

142

taken at Rhu Marina, when he came back carrying a tray with two mugs and a plate of biscuits.

'Admiring the Lynx, are you, Miss Blane?'

Sarah turned. 'It must take a lot of your time, looking after a boat, I expect.'

'Not so much, it's just a dinghy really. Some of the members have much fancier craft than my wee boat. Come and have your coffee.'

There was a moment or two of silence while she lifted the mug and put it to her lips. David offered the biscuit plate and she shook her head, then he said.

'So tell me, what brings you here, now?'

'I...I just wanted to see how you are...'

He lay back in the chair again and clasped his hands in front of him. 'So that you can convince my esteemed colleagues that I really am sick.'

'No, not for that reason...'

He leaned forward again. 'And, that I'm not just hiding myself away because I'm guilt-ridden about Rubina Khan?'

Sarah put her mug on the tray and it rattled. She opened her handbag and found a handkerchief before she answered.

'Well?' He stared at her. His eyes had a yellowish tinge.

'I've never thought that, David, you...you must believe me.' She hoped that she was convincing.

'Anyway, what's being said now, down yonder?' He gestured with his head towards the lower part of the town, and the school.

'Well, nothing really. We've got a couple of supply teachers in for you, and Roger, but we'll soon be finishing the term, then we'll see.'

David got up and walked to the window. 'Don't tell

143

me the murder of a pupil isn't still the biggest talking point, eh?'

'Well, the police aren't around so much now, and the press...and with Christmas...'

'Christmas, for God's sake!' He whipped round. 'Tell me the concert isn't going ahead!'

Sarah got up. 'David, you know what the Head's like. Everything has to be as normal as possible.'

He laughed; it was a hard sound. 'Good old Keith. Nothing's ever to be allowed to stand in the way of his big ego-trips, eh? Not even the death of a pupil.' He pulled at the sleeves of his sweater as if he was suddenly too hot, and she saw the edge of his watch.

Sarah pushed her own sleeve. 'Damn, I've left my watch. I'll have to go in a minute. David, I've got someone coming. What time is that now?'

He pushed the cuff back far enough to see the face of the watch. It was a chunky stainless steel affair, and there were no freckles on his wrist.

As she made her way to the door the question she longed to ask was about the night of the play, and David Smythe's presence in Glasgow when he was supposed to be away, but how to raise the subject? And she was out of the flat, about to descend the stairs, when he suddenly made it possible.

'I heard the police arrested Hakim Ashrif, is that right?' he said.

Sarah stopped, her hand on the railings of the staircase, 'Well, I don't know if arrest is the right word. They certainly had him in for questioning, but they let him go.'

'Well, at least they haven't dragged me in yet, I suppose that's something to be grateful for.' His features were sharp in the cold daylight.

'Anyway, apparently he was in Glasgow most of that night; he seemed to have proof of that.' She gripped the icy railing until her hand stung. 'Oh yes, and actually, he said he'd seen you there.'

*

'I thought he was going to faint, Mark. He leaned against the side of the door and closed his eyes, and he swayed. I got such a fright!'

'And he didn't answer?'

'No, he just sort of, slid back into the house and closed the door.' Sarah rubbed her forehead. 'It gave me the most horrible feeling. I've always liked David, so much. But he was like a stranger!'

Mark came and put his arm around her shoulder. 'Maybe that was the only thing he could do, in the circumstances.'

'But it makes him look so...suspicious.'

'I know, but if he is hiding something the police will surely find out.'

'Should we tell them?'

Mark leaned against the kitchen counter and scratched his nose. 'What would we say? That he was in Glasgow when he was supposed to be winging his way to...where was it?'

'Sri Lanka.'

'And then will you tell them that Roger Bullough was skulking around Helensburgh that night too, instead of being at home with his sick wife?'

'Yes, well...'

'Listen, Sarah. Not one of these things is evidence as such. Even if David's watch was exactly the same as the one in the photograph, it wouldn't constitute evidence. Nor would the fact that he has boat at Rhu.' He shook his head. 'Not evidence, just grounds for suspicion. Hamilton wouldn't thank you for that, would he?' He pushed himself up. 'Besides, we still don't know if the damned photograph has anything at all to do with Rubina's death, do we?'

Sarah stood holding her jacket, ready to hang it up in the hall. 'You're right. I think I keep forgetting that. We've got so tied up with the mystery of the photo that the whole culture thing is slipping away.'

'It certainly isn't slipping away from the police, I can guarantee that.' He took the coat from her hands and spoke as he moved out to the hallway. 'I hear their investigations have moved down south.'

'Down south?' Sarah echoed.

Mark came back into the room. 'I don't know if they have a central data base or whatever, but I know there is considerable liaison with forces in the south who have this to deal with more often than we do. They have contacts in the various Asian communities - women's groups, refuges - things of that sort. People who would know if Rubina's secret relationship, if that's what she had, would be enough to...' He let the words hang in the air. 'Anyway, we've got work to do. To the phone, Miss Blane.'

Sarah glanced at the clock. She could hardly claim eleven-thirty on a Sunday morning to be an inconvenient time. She fished the paper from her bag and dialled the number which Nancy Buchanan had given her. The number rang out for several minutes and Sarah was about to hang up when a woman answered. Her 'hello' was almost whispered.

Sarah found herself lowering her own voice. 'Is that Mrs Robertson?'

'Yes, please, what is it?'

Sarah raised her shoulders at Mark. 'It's about Julie, Mrs Robertson.'

'Oh no, what's happened?' There was an edge of hysteria in the woman's voice.

'No, nothing - it's just that I used to...' There was a faint scuffle at the other end then Mrs Robertson's voice was replaced by that of a man. He didn't whisper.

'Hello! Hello! Who is this?'

'Mr Robertson?'

'Yes, this is Alex Robertson. And you are?'

Sarah took a deep breath.

'My name is Sarah...Marchegay, Mr Robertson. I believe you used to live in Edinburgh, is that right? And that Julie Robertson is your daughter?'

There was a silence.

'What do you want?'

'Oh, I don't want...I tried to tell your wife. I'd just like to get in touch with Julie, if it's at all possible.'

'Where did you get this number?'

'Nancy Buchanan? She said you were friendly with her husband, Bill. The Buchanans were our neighbours when we lived there. You may remember...Ruth Marchegay, my sister, who ...disappeared in 1988? Julie was her friend.'

'And what's that got to do with anything now?'

Sarah took an even deeper breath.

'Well it's...actually, Mr Robertson. I was very young at that time and my parents are both dead now. And I ...I feel that I should like to know more about what happened.'

There was an angry snort on the line. 'What do you hope to gain from troubling my daughter with this now?'

'Oh, I don't want to trouble her - no - she's the only friend of Ruth's that I can remember, and I just thought...' she stopped, the will to pursue this uncomfortable conversation dribbling away.

Mark was watching her with a puzzled frown. Sarah

looked over at him and jumped when the next sound over the line was a harsh laugh.

'Right, Miss, whoever you are. You want Julie? I'll give you Julie. My daughter was last heard of living in some dump or other. This was the last phone number we had, but God knows where she is now.' He read out the number and Sarah scribbled it down. 'We don't communicate very much - so the best of luck!' The phone was hung up noisily.

Sarah said, 'Whew! They don't communicate, he says - and I'm not surprised.'

Mark sat next to her and looked at the phone number. 'I could hear him from over there. It didn't seem very positive.'

'It wasn't. The woman sounded absolutely terrified of what I was going to tell her.' Sarah fell back in the chair. 'And guess what? I forgot to ask if her name is still Robertson!'

'Anyway, one good thing Sarah, this is an Edinburgh number. She's not far away, if she's still there.'

'She could be anywhere, if her father is anything to go by. Something strange seems to have happened to Julie. And she was such a quiet wee thing.'

Mark took the phone. 'Will I do it this time?'

'Oh please, do. That was no fun.'

But when Mark dialled the number, which also rang out for some time, it seemed that he was speaking to someone in a shop. 'It's what? Freddie's Fish and Fries? Is that what you said?'

Sarah's eyebrows shot up and she went to the kitchen for a glass of water. An air of the bizarre was floating around in the room.

Mark said, 'I'm looking for Julie Robertson.'

She could still make out a faint gabble.

'Yes, that's right. Julie Robertson. Does she work

there?' He listened. 'No, nothing like that. Just an old school friend trying to get in touch.'

For the next few moments Mark listened intently, then he said, 'Thanks, mate. Ok. We'll try. Yes, soon.'

It was Sarah's turn to lean on the counter, arms folded. 'We'll try what? The fish?'

Mark's face bore the expression of one who knows he isn't about to give good news. 'Julie did work there for a while. That's when her parents got the number.'

'Where is she now?'

'Well, he says she's still around, told me the address, but his advice is that if we want to catch her we'll have to be quick.'

'Why, where's she going?'

Mark shrugged. 'Wherever she can get her next fix, as he tells it.'

'Oh no!' Sarah folded herself on to the sofa. 'That's awful. I mean, she's not a kid.'

*

The address was in a part of Leith which so far had escaped the rampant modernisation and upmarket developments of the harbour area. The tenement was still dark and grey, its disreputable air redolent of the area in seedier times. There were paper nameplates stuck here and there on the battered door, but none for Robertson. It didn't seem like a good idea to enter and knock doors randomly in this building. Mark and Sarah looked at each other.

'Maybe we should try Freddie's first?'

Sarah nodded.

The fish and chip shop was a couple of streets away. It was still closed, but they were spotted through the glass by the person inside who came and opened up for them. It was bright and spotlessly clean as was its proprietor - a ruddy, fair-skinned man in his fifties wearing an overall so white it was almost blinding. Fat bubbled in the fryers as they passed to the back of the shop, its smell not unpleasant. Freddie waved them to a couple of stools set in the space left by cartons of pickles, sauce bottles and salt containers.

'The name's not Freddie, you know.' He laughed. 'It's actually John - John Phillips. Freddie was the former owner and it was just too good to waste.'

He looked from Mark to Sarah, and back, as if taking a measure of some sort. 'So, you're looking for Julie. You don't look like social workers, or cops, so what's the score?'

Mark turned to Sarah - it was her story.

'She was a friend of my sister, when they were at school, and I need to see her.'

John Phillips drew his brows down. 'A school friend? Julie's forty if she's a day.'

Sarah nodded. 'I know. My sister was the same age.'

'Was?'

She sighed. 'All right, Mr Phillips, I'll tell you. My sister disappeared in 1988. Recently we discovered that she might not be...dead...as I've thought, and since Julie was around when it happened we just want to know if she remembers anything which might help us.'

'Who was your sister?'

'She was called Ruth Marchegay.'

She was surprised when he said. 'Yeah, December 1988. I was made up to sergeant that month and I remember that case. The unusual name.' He produced another stool from somewhere amongst the boxes and sat down.

Mark pointed to the shop. 'The fryers?'

'No problem - thermostat. Aye, I was in the police then. Lothian and Borders.' He nodded around the room. 'Bought this place when I retired after thirty years. I remember when that lass went missing. I felt really sorry for your folks when we stopped looking because of her age, you know? Your dad haunted that station for months, asking us what we were doing to find her.'

'I never knew that,' Sarah said.

`Oh, she went into the files all right, but wasn't there a guy involved or something? I think the official line was that she was more a runaway than a missing person.'

Sarah said, 'I've just found out about the...guy. That's why I want to speak to Julie. She might have known something about him.'

John Phillips smiled. 'You'll be lucky. I doubt if Julie's got a working brain cell left. She can hardly remember who she is herself most of the time.'

'I can't imagine her like that. What happened to her?'

'It's hard to say. She would never tell very much. I gave her a job when I opened at first. I knew she had a problem like, but she was fighting it, trying to get back on her feet. Didn't last long. I got the impression that there had been a few men in her life. Kids too, but I think they were taken off her. Anyway, she's up in that flat now and she's just going from bad to worse. Next thing she's going to be evicted, because there's no way she's paying rent. No,' he heaved himself to his feet. 'I don't think you'll get much change out of Julie.'

Back at the tenement they climbed to the top floor and the flat. There was a smell of decay and old, old food clinging to the scarred walls and the worn steps.

They stood outside a door which looked as if it had had a rough life. At one point some optimist had started to slap on a greenish paint and had given up half way down. It was as if the door had suffered an outbreak of mould.

Mark smiled at Sarah as he knocked.

She said, 'I'm not looking forward to this.'

151

The woman who opened the door was wearing a fairly clean shirt and black leggings, and apart from the lines and the grey puffiness of her face looked better than Sarah had expected.

'Julie?'

The woman screwed up her eyes against the smoke of a cigarette which hung from the nicotine stained fingers of her right hand. 'What?'

'Julie, I'm Sarah Marchegay. Do you remember me?'

'What?'

Mark said. 'Julie, we've just come from John - you know John Phillips? He told us where to find you. We really need your help. Do you think we could come in?'

She stepped back automatically and they followed her into the living room. There was a worn sofa which might once have been blue check and a couple of dining chairs. A sticky looking TV in the corner was on, the picture shimmering with poor reception.

Sarah attempted to smile at the woman. 'I knew you when you were a teenager.'

'Marchegay? Is that what you said?'

'Yes. Do you remember Ruth, my sister?'

Julie Robertson didn't answer, but gazed into the distance as if she was watching some other picture of her own. Then she smiled.

'She was a nice girl.'

They waited.

'Ran away, didn't she?'

Carefully, Sarah said, 'Can you remember who she ran away with, Julie?'

The bloodshot eyes turned on Sarah. 'You weren't there.'

'I was, Julie, but I was only ten. I didn't know as

much about my sister as her friends did. Like you.'

Julie sat down suddenly on the sofa and Sarah sat beside her, while Mark took one of the chairs.

'Mm...yes...her friend.'

Sarah touched her on the arm.

'I was going to be a doctor you know,' the woman burst out. 'Ruth was going to play in an orchestra.' A light came on in her eyes. 'Yeah, I remember that.'

'That's right. Ruth was musical. Was her...her boyfriend - was he musical too.'

Julie puffed hard on the cigarette while she struggled with her memory. 'No...no...he was like me...a doctor?'

Mark said, 'A medical doctor?'

She looked at him as if seeing him for the first time. 'What? How the hell should I know. I failed my highers...got pregnant, didn't I? My dad was raging...' She smiled. 'I think I ran away as well.'

Sarah said, 'Can you remember anything else about this...doctor...of Ruth's. No...oh wait...I saw him once.' She hugged herself as if she had a secret, then rolled her eyes.

'What was he like, Julie?'

'Very handsome,' she said, in a parody of a polite Edinburgh accent. 'She never knew, nobody was supposed to know. Then she disappeared.'

She focused on Sarah. 'Why did she disappear?'

Sarah shook her head.

'Ask Sheila.'

Sarah looked at Mark.

'Sheila who, Julie?'

She waved the cigarette. 'Sheila something - how should I know. She was her best pal.'

As they got up to leave Mark took a card from his wallet. 'Listen Julie, my number's on there. Give me a call if you need anything, OK?' He placed the card and some folded banknotes on the arm of the sofa.

On the street Sarah breathed in the cold air. 'I think we might have got ourselves a new friend there, Mark.'

He shrugged. 'I know. But if I hadn't done it you would, wouldn't you?'

She smiled. 'Yes, I reckon.'

Chapter 9

'So, the next step is to find this Sheila, ' Mark turned towards Sarah as he drove.

She punched him lightly on the arm. 'You don't give up easily, do you?'

He laughed. 'Really? So who went off to visit to David Smythe this morning then, eh?'

'Ok. Point taken.'

It had started to rain. She listened to the rhythmic sweep of the wipers for a moment, then she said. 'Anyway, Sheila Whoever must be a non-starter.'

'Why do you say that?'

'Well, we can't go back to Nancy Buchanan, she won't know - and I certainly don't remember any Sheila amongst Ruth's school-friends.'

'Ah, but what about that? School. They'd all be in the same year those girls, wouldn't they? Don't they keep records or something?'

'Yes, school logs. But Julie Robertson might not be that reliable, under the circumstances.'

'Did you go to the same school as Ruth?'

She nodded. 'For a time. Until we moved to North Berwick.'

'There you are then. A phone call to the school, that's all it would take.' He stopped at a traffic light. 'I'd be happy to do it but I think it might come better from a former pupil.' He pulled away again as the lights changed. 'And if it's a dead end, then we're no worse off, are we?'

155

Sarah sat quietly on the journey to the motorway between Edinburgh and

Glasgow. Mark's use of 'we' gave her a little spurt of warmth every time he said it. Bit by bit, the dark hollow inside had begun to recede since Mark entered her life. She hoped she wasn't fooling herself. Mark had a painful past to get over too, and maybe finding the truth of her story was helping him come to terms with his own. Anyway, she'd take the comfort while it was there.

'You're off in a dream,' Mark said. 'Want to share it?'

'I was just thinking what a difference it makes to have you doing this with me.'

He took one hand off the wheel and twirled a strand of her hair. 'And for as long as you want. That's the deal, Sarah. As soon as you feel I'm poking my nose too far in, just cut it off.'

Sarah laughed. 'No no, that's far too regal a nose to be tampered with.'

At lunchtime on Monday Sarah took her phone out to the car to make the call to the Edinburgh school. She wanted no interruptions, and since the car park was on the other side of the building from the playground it was relatively quiet. Besides, it wouldn't be the easiest of calls to make. The school personnel would have changed completely in twenty-three years, and a query with only a first name might seem ridiculous. She shivered while she got the number from directory inquiries. It was colder than ever outside and she turned on the car heater.

The school secretary answered the phone, and to Sarah's astonishment, revealed that she been working there for no less than twenty-six years. And she remembered very well the girl called Ruth Marchegay. 'It was such a sad story. I often wonder what happened to her. Every time a youngster goes missing it comes back to me.'

'And a Sheila something or other, who was one of Ruth's friends?' Sarah held her breath.

'Sheila...Sheila...' She seemed to be tapping the phone as she thought. 'No... but I'll tell you what. I bet Miss Ferguson would! She's retired now but she seems to remember all her former pupils. What if I speak to her this afternoon? I can either ring you back this evening or I can get Wendy, Miss Ferguson, to do it? That's a Sheila something who was in Ruth's class, or at least her year? Would that be a help?'

Wendy Ferguson. Sarah actually remembered her, and how incongruous the rather girlish name had sounded when someone told her it was that of the starchy English teacher. Sarah had thought her old then, what age must she be now? She smiled at the thought. As her own experience had shown, teachers always seem old to children - Miss Ferguson probably had been little more than thirty then.

At afternoon interval Moira dashed into the staff-room and asked if anyone had been to see Roger since he came home from hospital. The Christmas rush was keeping everyone busy and no-one had yet been to the house.

'I know it's only been a few days since he got out, but I haven't had a minute and I hoped one of you might..?'

Sarah said, 'I'll go after school, Moira.'

Moira's thanks vanished out of the door with her as she hurried away.

Mary Stephens showed her gratitude by jumping up and offering to wash Sarah's coffee cup and William too said a gruff thanks. He was a reticent man and Sarah suspected that although he worked well with his colleagues, a private visit to one of their homes would be an ordeal too far for him.

Judith, needless to say, hardly raised her head from

the Guardian crossword. At the first opportunity Sarah intended telling Moira of her visit to David Smythe, but thought better of mentioning it in the staff-room in view of the minor explosion last time.

It was with a heavy heart that Sarah approached the Bullough's house. Afternoons were so dark at this time of year that the neglected garden was almost invisible from the door-step. As she waited for someone to answer she reflected on how many doors she had knocked in the last forty-eight hours - David Smythe's, Julie Robertson's - not to mention the diversion to Freddie's Fish and Fries - now Roger Bullough's.

He was slow in answering and when Roger let her in at last Sarah was struck by the stale odour in the house, which brought to mind the fetid air of Julie Robertson's flat. He was obviously in no fit state to be doing housework. He didn't look so much sick as battered. There were heavy dark circles under his eyes, and his usual sallow skin looked grey in the dim light of the sitting-room.

He gestured vaguely, 'A couple of the bulbs need replacing.'

'Roger, you know you only have to give me a ring if you need anything - shopping or whatever.'

'It's all right Sarah, thanks anyway. I think the Council is arranging for some help.'

'What about Dorothy?'

'She's fine, come and see.'

Dorothy did look cared-for, the nursing help was coming in twice a day now. She said it with a bright smile, but Sarah knew that it meant her condition was worsening.

'Anyway, sit down and chat, Sarah. Roger will bring us a cup of tea, won't you love?'

He nodded and left the room. 'How is Roger, Dorothy?'

The smile left her face. 'I'm not happy about him. Oh, the hospital have discharged him with some drugs and advice, but it's as if he's had more than a heart attack.' She stopped for breath and Sarah waited.

'He just doesn't seem like the same person, Sarah.'

'Oh, but surely, a heart attack - it must be a life-changing experience - don't you think?'

Dorothy rolled her head on the pillow. 'It's as if there's something...' She stopped as Roger came into the room. 'Do you need sugar, Sarah?'

'No, oh please Roger, don't bother. Come and talk to us.'

He raised a hand and disappeared again, to come back moments later carrying a tray with two cups and Dorothy's drinking mug.

Conversation was difficult. Dorothy struggled with talking because of her illness and while never loquacious, Roger in school was friendly towards everyone, even Judith. Now he seemed to Sarah withdrawn and sad. He asked about events at school but he didn't show much interest in the answers.

Finally it was Dorothy who brought up the subject of Rubina by asking about the investigation into her death.

Out of the corner of her eye, Sarah could see Roger's grip tighten on the handle of his cup, while she related what had, or had not, taken place in recent weeks. 'If the police are getting anywhere it's not obvious to any of us, because they've stopped asking questions in school.'

Roger said, 'They spoke to me on one occasion, but after that...of course...I became ill.'

As Dorothy started to speak he laid down his cup, staring intently at the tray as if placing the cup required all his concentration.

'Roger was so upset, weren't you, that the girl hadn't

got home safely that night.' She took a breath. 'He felt responsible.'

Sarah also concentrated on putting her cup on the tray.

Roger said, 'I...I seemed to be just too late...?'

Sarah turned to him. 'Yes, Dorothy said something about you going to meet the bus?'

He nodded, looking down as he spoke, 'I did. But I must have missed it because there was no-one around when I got there.'

'He told the police that, didn't you, Roger?' His wife said.

He was silent for a moment then he raised his eyes to Sarah and nodded again.

Soon afterwards Sarah got up to leave and as they stood at the front door Roger started to speak. 'About that night, Sarah, I need to tell you...'

Just then the door bell rang and the nurses came in to attend to Dorothy. Sarah raised her eyebrows at Roger before stepping out but the moment had obviously passed. Whatever he was going to tell her would have to wait.

It was Wendy Ferguson who phoned Sarah in the evening. She started by saying that she remembered Sarah too, even although she had not been long in her class. And of course, like the secretary, that Ruth's disappearance had impacted greatly on the school then and for some time afterwards, so that it was not difficult to recall.

Sarah said, 'I can understand that.'

The teacher said, 'And you were asking about Sheila Simpson?'

'Simpson, is that her name? It's just that recently I've discovered that Ruth was involved with some young man at that time and I'm trying to find out if any of her girlfriends knew anything. I've already tracked down Julie

Robertson, and she mentioned Sheila.'

'Oh, and how is Julie?'

'In a very bad way, Miss Ferguson. She's addicted to drugs.'

'Oh dear, I didn't know that. She was a quiet little thing too. And please, call me Wendy.'

Sarah was glad that Wendy couldn't see her smile.

'Actually, I don't remember Ruth being friendly with a Sheila Simpson.'

'Ah', the teacher's tone was brisk. 'that's because she wasn't. Sheila was, how shall I put it, a very knowing girl, and although they were in the same class Ruth didn't have much to do with her.' She stopped for a moment. 'Unless, wait a minute...it might have been through the music. I've just remembered that Ruth was musical too. Sheila plays the violin.'

The use of the present tense alerted Sarah. 'Plays? Now?'

'Oh yes, Sheila Simpson, or Macdonald now, is a music lecturer in Dundee University. Still sends me a Christmas card every year.'

Mark phoned shortly afterwards and Sarah filled him in on her visit to Roger Bullough. When she told him about the interrupted conversation Mark gave a little whistle. 'Do you think he was about to reveal something meaningful?'

'That's just it - it's so frustrating. What's more, when Dorothy said he'd told the police about that night I had the distinct feeling that it wasn't true. Oh, Dorothy thought it was, of course, but I'm not so sure.'

'What will you do, will you go back again?'

'Well, I don't know. Roger's certainly hiding something.'

'You know it might not be a good idea to provoke him.'

'But it would be fine, Roger's not...' She stopped. 'Oh...I see what you mean. Anyway, I've found Sheila Simpson.'

'Have you? Well done! Where?'

'Would you believe Dundee University? Apparently she lectures in music. Ruth went for extra piano lessons after school in those days and that's possibly the connection with Sheila - Doctor Macdonald as she is now.'

'Great. I'll find out where she lives and we can go and see her.'

Sarah laughed, 'Just like that?'

'I'm not an investigative journalist for nothing, you know.'

'But why can't we just phone?'

'You know why, Sarah. There is no comparison between a disembodied voice on the phone, and meeting a person - body language, facial expressions, all of that. I mean, look at how Roger Bullough almost revealed something to you. Besides it's much harder to fool two people, if that's what someone is trying to do.'

However Dr Sheila Macdonald, née Simpson, wasn't as easy to find as Nancy Buchanan or Julie Robertson. It appeared that Sheila was out of the country at a conference and wouldn't return until the third week in December. It was frustrating, but there was little they could do. Still, Mark had her address.

Meanwhile, he insisted, they should do a recce at Rhu Marina.

'What do you expect to find there?' Sarah asked. 'Besides, we can't just wander around with no good reason, can we?'

'Ah, but what about the chandlery - there's bound to be one. I've always fancied one of these jaunty caps the sailors wear.'

Sarah laughed. 'Done. I'll buy you one for Christmas.'

The marina shop was an Aladdin's cave of all things nautical. Sarah breathed in the combined odours of ropes, paint, boating gear of all sorts, mostly unrecognisable to her uninformed gaze, and clothes for every kind of weather. There was even a gift section, and she made an effort to keep her face straight as Mark tried on caps ranging from the useful and weatherproof to the apparently frivolous. As Mark pondered over his choice various members of the sailing community came and went, and while they attracted a few sceptical glances, no-one challenged them.

Afterwards, cap in a bag, they set off to wander around. It was cold, but bright and sunny, so that an interested stroll looking at the various craft didn't appear entirely inappropriate and in fact one or two people working around the boatyard greeted them in a not unfriendly way.

'If anyone asks, I'm thinking of buying a sailing dinghy.' Mark said, pausing beside a canvas-covered boat.

'In December?'

'Well, so that I'm prepared for spring and the start of the season.'

'Ok. Look, there's a 'used craft', section. That should be right up your...oh my, look who's here.'

Mark looked, 'Who?'

'Of course, you've never met him. It's Keith Birkmyre, the Head. Maybe he won't notice...'

'Uh, uh - too late.'

Keith Birkmyre came striding towards them. He was in working garb of jeans, a dark green oiled jersey and heavy boots. Sarah hid a smile when she recognised a much battered version of Mark's new hat on the boss.

'Well hello there. This is a busy place, but I didn't expect to see you here.' He spoke to Sarah but looked at

Mark.

She nodded. 'Hi. This is Mark McKenzie. Mark, Keith Birkmyre, my Head Teacher.'

The two men shook hands.

'Right,' Keith Birkmyre rubbed his palms together, 'Cold, isn't it? Anyway, what brings you here, Mr McKenzie? A sailor are you?'

Sarah waited, a spectator, while Mark went into his pitch about hoping to take up the sport, but of course...not knowing much about what to buy.

'Ah, well.' The other man folded his arms. 'If I were you, new to the game, it might be a good idea to consider a power boat - you know, as opposed to sailing? Yamaha, for example, do some that are ideal for the novice. I believe there's a new one, now, what's it called...yes, the Terhi, a nippy little number.'

Mark said, 'Of course, I've been doing some research, books, the net, as you will, but I just wanted to get the feel of the real thing here.' He put his arm across Sarah's shoulder, 'And Sarah here agreed to give me her company.'

The Head glanced her way. 'Yes, good. Well, I suppose you're doing the right thing. I'm not so keen on the motorised craft myself.' He laughed. 'No, no, too much of a 'yotty', too fond of the canvas, but my son Gordon likes them a lot. He doesn't know it yet but we're going to buy him one when he finishes his year in the States.'

'Oh, right. I'm sure he'll be pleased.'

'Well I think he'll have an even bigger taste for such things after his year at MIT...the Massachusetts Institute of technology, you know?'

Mark raised his eyebrows. 'Really? MIT?'

Keith Birkmyre nodded. 'Yes, he's a bit of a boffin in the making. We're very proud of him. Anyway, must get on,' he nodded towards the chandlery, 'maintenance, you know…' He turned back. 'And if you need any further help, Sarah knows where to find me, all right?'

When his back was turned Mark sketched a quick salute.

Sarah said, 'So now you've met the boss. Enlightening, what?'

'And to think I thought editors were bad? Did you know he kept a boat here?'

She laughed. 'No, but even if I had, I can't honestly see him cuddling Rubina in full view of all his 'yotty' friends, can you?'

He smiled. 'Not really.'

Later, as they threaded their way back through the yard to where they'd parked the car, Sarah gripped Mark's sleeve. 'I don't believe it. Look!'

Lynn Cameron and Leslie Watkins were sneaking out from between two of the larger boats. Lynn clapped a hand to her mouth when she saw Mark and Sarah.

Leslie grinned. 'Hi, four minds with a single thought, Miss, eh?'

Sarah and Mark looked at each other.

'Is that so?' Sarah pointed to the bag Mark was carrying. 'As it happens, we're here on a legitimate errand. What's your excuse, as if I didn't know.'

Lynn gave a despondent shrug. 'We've been here before. We're just trying to do something, anything…'

'Did Dr Birkmyre see you?'

Leslie bristled. 'Yeah, so what, we've as much right to be here as he has.'

'I don't know about that.' Mark said. 'Did he speak to you?'

Lynn sniffed. 'He wasn't very nice. He said it could be dangerous for unsupervised youngsters to be fiddling about in a place like this.'

'Youngsters!' Leslie scrubbed the toe of his trainer on the ground.

'Anyway, have you found out anything from your mooching around?' Sarah walked towards the car. 'Do you want a lift?'

'Into town would be great, Miss.'

They were in the car before Leslie answered. 'We just hoped to bump into someone wearing a blue pullover, but no chance.'

'But I'm sure that picture was taken in the summer, Leslie, or at latest, autumn. The blue sweater doesn't look very thick, and it appeared to be a nice day.'

'It would look like a nice day today, Miss,' He pulled a copy of the photograph out of his pocket. 'but you're right, the sweater looks quite thin.'

Lynn produced her copy of the photo. 'Fine wool. Maybe even cashmere. That's what my mother would say.'

'She hasn't seen the picture, has she, Lynn?' Sarah turned in the passenger seat.

'No way, Miss. She'd blab to that Austin Toner and next thing, he'd like, have it all over his newspaper.'

Mark coughed. 'Eh, you never thought of that when you were going to pass it round the school, did you?'

Sarah caught the look which passed between the two young people.

'You haven't, have you?'

Lynn said, 'What, Miss?'

'You know, shown it around.'

Leslie folded the picture. 'We might as well tell.'

They were driving along the front, and Mark drew the car to a halt outside Sarah's building.

Mark and Sarah turned round to face Leslie and Lynn.

At last Lynn spoke, almost in a whisper. 'We showed it to the Head.'

'Why?'

Leslie stuffed the photo in his pocket. 'He kept asking us why we were in the boatyard and we couldn't come up with a cool answer so...'

'I showed him the photo.' Lynn said.

'What did he say?'

'Well he was a bit surprised I think, when he saw that it was Rubina. He just said he couldn't imagine what we hoped to find out from a bit of sleeve. Anyway, he said, they could just have been passing and stopped there for the picture.' Lynn went on, 'That could be true, couldn't it?'

Sarah smiled. 'Yes, that could be true. Oh well, I don't suppose any harm's been done.'

Mark nodded. 'But you might have run into someone other than the Head. So, just be careful, won't you?'

They left Lynn and Leslie heading for the town centre.

Back in the flat Mark picked up the daily paper while Sarah went into the kitchen. He leafed through the pages for a bit, then he said, 'By the way, Sarah, what about this son of Birkmyre's?'

'Gordon?' she leaned on the counter and shook her head. 'I doubt if he would even know Rubina. Anyway, he went off to America several weeks before Rubina was killed.'

'To MIT?'

She smiled. 'Yes. To be a boffin.'

*

167

It was on the day of the staff Christmas dinner that the Clarion ran lurid headlines about the death of another Asian girl. Once more a body had washed up on the shores of Loch Lomond, but on the east side this time, near Balmaha.

Sarah's stomach churned as she read the report, which detailed how two teenagers working with a rowing skiff had come across the girl tangled up in the undergrowth bordering the shore. As yet there was no name, and no cause of death. In spite of that, Wilson

Toner had been unable to resist hinting at serial killing in the Asian community.

When she had a free period Sarah phoned Mark, who said he would get back to her when he found out more. It couldn't be that evening, she said, because she was committed to the Christmas outing.

The dinner was held the week before end of term in the biggest hotel in town. For reasons of their own not everyone on the staff took part in these functions and this year the party seemed less festive than usual. Not that Keith Birkmyre didn't do his best to raise the collective morale, with a speech about new beginnings: a new term, a new year, a time to put the past behind, particularly since the drugs issue appeared to have gone away for the time being. He cemented it with a toast to his industrious and committed staff, a surprise to many, judging by the bemused expressions Sarah noted around her.

After dinner, Sarah joined Moira and Mary Stephens in the lounge for coffee. A few noisier parties began at other tables with some of the younger staff, and Sarah was saddened to feel herself past all that. She knew it wasn't her age - but rather her circumstances, which had brought her to a serious view of life long before it should have been necessary. She thought of Mark then, and the sense of lightness which he seemed to bring and hoped, when and if they solved the riddle of Ruth, that there might be a less complicated future ahead for both of them.

As if she'd read her thoughts Moira said, 'And what about your journalist friend? Are you still seeing him?'

Sarah felt her face warm. 'Yes, as a matter of fact I am.'

Mary Stephens patted Sarah's knee. 'Isn't that nice. So, what's everyone doing for Christmas,' she continued in a bright tone, which belied the fact that she would be spending it, as she did every year, with her ailing mother.

Moira said, 'Oh, as usual I have the hordes at Christmas.'

'Peter's family?'

'Och, I don't really mind, it's lovely to have the house full at Christmas but it's usually the middle of January before I get things back to normal. And I'm still finding needles from the tree in July!'

'Still,' Sarah said, 'It's always more like Christmas to have a real tree - that lovely resinous smell...'

'And are you spending Christmas with your nice journalist?' Mary Stephens said with a tilt of her head and a coy smile.

'No, no...I'm going to my friend in the Lake District.'

In fact Mark had invited her to join him at his parents' house for Christmas, but apart from her commitment to Irene, Sarah knew she wasn't ready for that yet. It would be enough to come back and spend time with him after the festivities but before the new year. As yet they hadn't managed the visit to Dundee and Sheila Macdonald, so that was planned for a few days after Christmas.

Suddenly over Sarah's shoulder came the Head's voice. 'Well, Sarah, did your friend buy a boat?' He pulled out the chair next to her and sat down.

Moira gave her a puzzled look.

'Oh, eh, not yet. He's still sort of, at the research stage.'

'It's a great sport you know. If not for the faint-hearted.' He smiled. 'Anyway, what is Mr McKenzie's line of business?'

'He's a journalist.'

The Head nodded. 'Right, I see. A bit of a landlubber then, eh?'

Sarah braced herself for the next cliché, but his attention turned to his Deputy Head.

'Seen the Clarion today, Moira?'

She nodded.

'Dreadful. Terrible for the communities involved. Where will it end, one has to ask?'

Mary Stephens leapt in. 'Well at least this girl has no connection with Fruin High. That's a blessing in itself.'

The boss got up and leaned on the back of the chair. 'It certainly is.'

When he moved away Moira nodded to Sarah. 'How about a nightcap at my place? And you too Mary, if you like.'

But Mary Stephens had to hurry home to her mother.

Ensconced in Moira's comfortable sofa Sarah kicked off her shoes and folded her legs under her. The big Christmas tree winked in the corner, the lights reflecting in the glass of pictures and mirrors. Sarah gazed at it, mesmerised by the glittering display until Moira appeared with two gins and tonic. She lit a cigarette. 'Now, come on, give. What was all that nonsense with Keith about boats?'

So Sarah told her everything, Moira listening intently until hot ash fell on her hand, making her jump.

'Lynn and Leslie? - this photograph? - David here when he should have been out of the country? Roger

170

apparently sneaking around town on the night Rubina disappeared? I can't take it in. And those boys, Mohammed and his cousin...all coming to you. Why didn't you tell me, Sarah. I'd have tried to help.'

'Moira, I know that. But you've had plenty to deal with - pupils and drugs?' She felt herself blushing again. 'Mark's been - is - a tower of strength.' She unfolded her legs. 'Besides, I'm not finished.'

Moira's astonishment grew as Sarah outlined the steps they'd taken so far to trace Ruth. She got out of her chair and came to sit beside Sarah, covering her hands with her own. 'Sarah, I'm really pleased about this, and I agree with Mark. You need to do this and you won't have any peace until you've...it's...reached some conclusion.' She smiled. 'So, tell me about this tower of strength. Is he very good-looking?'

When she got home there was a message on the phone from Mark. It was about the Asian girl. Her name was Jaswinder Saeed, but she preferred to be called Janice. She was nineteen. Jaswinder had been born in Glasgow, had two older brothers, and she had worked in an office in town. She wasn't married but the wedding was planned to take place very soon when the groom arrived from Pakistan. He didn't know when the post-mortem results would be available but he'd get them as soon as possible. He finished with, 'Accident, suicide or honour killing? We'll have to wait and see. And for any connection to Rubina? That too.'

As she had on the night Rubina disappeared Sarah curled up on the window-seat in her flat and watched the lights flickering on the surface of the river. Another death in Loch Lomond, another watery grave for a life hardly begun. She hoped that her sister had been spared such an end.

*

The only definitive news from the death of the second Asian girl was that she had been alive when she had been put into the loch. Bruises on her face and body were consistent with a struggle - 'In other words,' Mark said, 'Jaswinder appears to have been held under water until she drowned.' The results of other tests would take longer, but the post-mortem had also shown that she was pregnant.

'Poor girl,' Sarah shivered at the implications, 'So no husband from Pakistan then - for her or Rubina.'

'Well, in this case it does look as if there is a connection - but what is it?'

'Rubina wasn't pregnant.'

'No. But she didn't have to be, if you know what I mean.'

Sarah nodded.

They were en route to visit Sheila Macdonald. Her home was in Broughty Ferry, and as they drove into the town the Tay estuary opened out before them like a dark grey plate; the castle glowering on the headland. And while they weren't invited, they were expected. Mark had seen to that, overcoming Dr Macdonald's reluctance by stressing how much they needed her help.

'Although I wonder how helpful she will be, in fact,' he said now, as they drew up in front of a large detached house which looked as if it had been built in the 1930's. Nets hung close on the bow windows on either side of the door, giving the front of the house a blank, opaque look. The car doors closing were like small claps of thunder on the quiet street, and a ginger cat shot across their path. The air had a cold, salty odour, the sky streaked with yellowish cloud.

It was a man who opened the door. He was extremely tall, with a helmet of metallic-looking grey hair. He gestured to them to enter, then, opening a door on his right, he said, 'It's your visitors, Sheila,' and disappeared.

The room was elegant, if dark. A baby grand piano filled one corner and there was a lot of mahogany and ornate lamps. There were no Christmas decorations on show, but candles burned in several places, casting shadows around the room.

Sheila Macdonald got up from a dark green sofa with roped corners and waved to them to sit on the chairs opposite. She too, was very tall, and she too was elegant, but far from dull-looking. She had thick black hair and a deep tan, which she hadn't obtained in the Scottish winter, and Sarah reckoned that her conference had taken place somewhere tropical. She was wearing a dark red knitted suit and large, presumably ruby, earrings swung as she sat back down on the sofa. She didn't smile.

Sarah found her chair very deep and had to move forward to keep her feet on the floor. 'I must thank you for seeing us...eh, Dr Macdonald.'

'Sheila will do. Yes, well, Mr McKenzie here,' she waved long painted fingernails in Mark's direction, 'was very persuasive, but I doubt very much if I can help.'

'You did know Ruth at school though, didn't you?'

'Of course. We were in the same year.'

Mark said, 'As a matter of interest, were you on the pantomime trip that evening?'

She looked at him and frowned. 'What pantomime?'

'The night Ruth disappeared. Some of her friends covered up the fact that she hadn't been with them, although her parents thought that's where she was.'

Sheila Macdonald shrugged. 'Oh, that? No, I wasn't there.'

Sarah said, 'Did you know she was seeing someone?'

The woman's eyes dropped. 'I...heard that.'

Mark sat back in his chair, as if he was settling in.

173

'Tell us about your music lessons then. We know that you and Ruth went together for extra lessons.'

Sarah, surprised by the certainty in Mark's words, said nothing, but Sheila Macdonald nodded. 'We did. We went to the university '

'And sometimes you would go for coffee, or a coke or something, afterwards.'

It wasn't a question. Then he added. 'You had a boyfriend too, Sheila, didn't you?'

Her mouth almost, but not quite, dropped open. 'Wha...who told you this?'

Mark moved to the edge of his seat. 'Well, let's not bother about that right now. Let's concentrate on the boyfriends, yours and Ruth's.'

Sheila Macdonald cast around the room, as if she'd find answers in the shady corners.

Mark said. 'Sheila?'

The woman still didn't answer, and Sarah found herself holding her breath. She looked at Mark and opened her mouth. He gave a slight shake of his head.

Suddenly the other woman got up from the sofa and went to the fireplace, where she took a cigarette from an onyx box and lit it from the candle on the mantelpiece. She blew out a stream of smoke. 'Yes, I had a boyfriend, then.'

'And Ruth?'

She sighed. 'Yes.'

'And they knew each other.'

She looked at Mark with a puzzled expression. 'How do you know all this?'

He laughed. 'Just accept that we do. And tell us what we want to know.'

'But what is it you want to know?'

Sarah could wait no longer. 'Who he was, and did Ruth run off with him?'

174

Sheila Macdonald narrowed her eyes, as if in thought. 'Ah. Sorry, I don't remember his name.'

'But you knew him!' Sarah could hardly stay in her seat.

Mark got up then and went to stand beside Sheila Macdonald at the fireplace.

He pointed to her cigarette and she opened the box and offered it. Mark took the cigarette and as she had done, lit it at the candle. Then he smiled at her.

'Do you remember the name of your own boyfriend?

She shrugged and laughed. 'Just about. I think it was Michael something. It wasn't serious you know, just a bit of flirting really.' She turned away to knock the ash from her cigarette. 'We never went to their flat or anything. We just met them in the library, and sometimes we'd go for coffee or whatever. They were a good bit older than us, of course - PhD students.'

Mark said, 'What was his subject - Ruth's boyfriend?'

'Oh, heavens, I wouldn't know. It wasn't the main topic of conversation, as you can imagine.' She furrowed her brow. 'Chemistry? Physics? - something like that.'

'Was it just a casual thing with Ruth then?'

'I thought so at first, but it seemed to get a bit more serious.'

Sarah spoke through clenched teeth. 'His name?'

She shook her head. 'No. It's gone.'

Then she added, so quickly that Sarah's heart thumped. 'But I know she didn't run off with him!'

Sarah jumped to her feet. 'How do you know that?'

Mark put his hand on her arm, and Sheila Macdonald sat down again on her sofa. When she answered her voice was so low they could hardly hear. 'I saw him afterwards.'

Sarah also had to sit down again. The blood pounded

in her ears and she felt faint. Mark held her shoulder, and said, quietly. 'Where did you see him, Sheila?'

'Oh, Dundee I think. I never saw him, or Michael after...you know, what happened. ' She straightened her shoulders. 'Michael had left Edinburgh a couple of months earlier anyway, some trouble at home. But I know Ruth went on seeing...' She screwed up her face, 'seeing...no, sorry...I just can't remember.'

She drew heavily on the cigarette. 'No, it was years later. At some award ceremony or other. My husband,' she gestured out of the room, 'is in pharmaceuticals , and it was something to do with that. It was a corporate thing. We met in the queue for the buffet lunch. I wasn't sure if it was him - Ruth's boyfriend - but when he spoke I recognised his voice. He didn't seem to recognise me.'

'How do you know Ruth wasn't around?'

'Because he was wearing a wedding ring, and I saw him with a woman. They were speaking to other people and it was obvious from his manner that she was his wife.'

'Why didn't you tell him who you were?' Mark sat down again and stubbed out the cigarette, while Sheila Macdonald rose and took another. When she had it lit she turned round and spoke directly to Sarah.

'Because I didn't want to talk about what had happened with Ruth. I hadn't said anything about him at the time, to the police, you know, and I felt, least said...'

Sarah felt tears come to her eyes. 'My parents thought she was with him. Why didn't you tell anyone the truth?'

'I'm sorry...I...my father was very strict. Everything was about my music, and boyfriends just weren't allowed. If I had told about Ruth and...me, then, you see, they'd have found out...'

Sarah said, 'Have you any idea where this man is

now?' Her voice was husky.

The ruby earrings shimmered in the light from the candles as Sheila Macdonald shook her head.

'None at all.'

She continued to shake her head as Mark asked, 'And you're sure you can't remember his name?'

Chapter 10

Sarah was silent as they drove away from Broughty Ferry. She felt as if there was a lump of lead in her stomach.

Mark glanced sideways at her. 'Well that wasn't so bad, was it?'

'It wasn't so good either. We learned nothing.'

'No, no, Sarah, I don't agree.' He stopped talking to negotiate a narrow space between oncoming cars. 'We know now that Ruth had a boyfriend, it's not supposition any more.'

'And if Sheila Macdonald remembers his name we might get a little further.'

'Actually, Sarah, I think she does know his name. Oh, she's not telling - in fact she told us more than she was planning to as it was...'

'Yes, by the way, what was all that about us knowing this and that?'

Mark smiled. 'It works every time. If someone thinks you already know things they sort of fill in the rest for you.'

'A technique of investigative journalism, I take it. And the smoking?'

He patted her hand. 'Whatever it takes. Anyway, we now know that the boyfriend was indeed a student at Edinburgh University and that Ruth almost certainly didn't run off with him.'

'Surely she could have, for a time. Then, maybe, changed her mind?'

He drove in silence for a moment.

'If it had ended, Sarah, don't you think she would have come home?'

The lead rose into her throat at the import of his words, and she thought she might choke.

Mark looked at her again, 'Let's stop for a coffee.'

He drew off the road into a service area. As if blindfolded Sarah followed him into the café and sat where he placed her. She stared at the surface of the red formica table. There was a watery ring on it, and she moved it with her finger into an oblong.

Mark returned with two beakers of steaming coffee. 'I think you need something stronger, but this'll have to do for the moment.'

The café was fairly quiet. There were a couple of families going or returning from holiday trips and several couples. Most of them had plates in front of them, and Sarah suddenly realised that they'd eaten nothing since breakfast.

'Oh, Mark. You must be starving.'

He smiled. 'Only if you are too.'

'I'm not hungry.' There was waft of fried bacon as a waitress passed carrying dishes. 'Please, have something, Mark.'

He nodded. 'All right. Then we'll talk.'

He came back from the counter with several bacon rolls. Sarah made the effort to nibble at one of them, then put it back.

'I wish we'd never started this.'

Mark swallowed, then he wiped his mouth with a napkin.

'I'm sorry.'

'She's dead, isn't she?' Sarah raised her eyes and looked into his.

He reached across the table and grasped her hands. 'I think she must be.'

Sarah said, nodding, 'Because she wouldn't have been able to survive on her own - she had no money, nothing. She was too young - and she had no reason to run away - except this boy.' She pulled away from Mark and wiped her eyes.

'He must have killed her,' she said, her voice high.

The people nearest glanced their way.

'Sarah,' Mark spoke quietly, 'we can't say that.'

'But what other explanation is there?'

He rubbed his face. 'There could be any number of explanations.'

'Well then,' Sarah almost spat the words, 'why don't you tell me what they are? After all, it's your ...your crusade, isn't it? Help poor Sarah to solve a mystery! It might occupy you sufficiently to displace your own...' She stopped as Mark rose from the table.

'If you are finished your coffee, let's go. It's getting dark.'

The sky had blackened while they were in the café and a biting east wind cut through to Sarah's bones. She huddled in her seat in the car and Mark pushed the heater switch to full. The fan was noisy and they didn't speak. The silence lengthened with the journey as the new reality hammered into Sarah's consciousness. Ruth was dead, murdered by this unknown young man. She had been dead for twenty-three years.

She could see no point in trying to share how she was feeling with the person sitting next to her, or for that matter, with anyone, so far removed from normal human experience this thing had to be. Mark's expression was difficult to read in the darkened car, but she was aware of a new distance between them, and that she was its cause, but she could do nothing about it.

For the next few days Sarah avoided Mark. She

switched off her phones and she cancelled his text messages. Once, the intercom buzzed and she thought it might be him, but she didn't answer. Nor did she leave the flat.

Instead, she let herself drown in wave after wave of pain, washing over her in a vicious tide. Who, after all, could begin to share this; all the love that had gone to waste, and all the hope stripped away, layer by layer, like skin - down to the raw acceptance that more than twenty years of her life had been hostage to the belief that her sister might be alive? She found herself envying the Khans the quick release that Rubina's body had brought - then she found herself ashamed of such thoughts. Their pain was no less for knowing that their daughter was lying in a mortuary somewhere. What was more, they may never know who had taken her life. And nor might she.

On Hogmanay, that most festive of Scottish occasions, she had settled herself on the sofa with Henry, a bottle of gin and the television, when Peter Campbell arrived with strict instructions from Moira to join them and some friends to bring in the New Year. Reluctantly, she changed her clothes and tried to enjoy herself when she got there.

*

It was with some relief that Sarah went back to school in January. Mark had stopped trying to contact her. She had begun to miss him and had lifted the phone more than once, but each time the memory of her outburst in the café came back to her. She couldn't blame him if he'd given up on her; what she'd said had been unforgivable.

But four days into the new term Mark phoned her during the lunch break. Sarah answered cautiously but there was no note of reserve in his voice, and when she began to apologise he cut her off.

'Don't worry, we'll deal with all that another time. No, I'm phoning because I've had a call from John Phillips'

Sarah said, 'John Phillips?'

'Yeah, remember, Freddie's Fish and Fries?'

'Oh, that John Phillips?'

'It's about Julie Robertson. Apparently she's pretty ill in hospital and the social services people are trying to trace some family or whatever. John knew that you had a connection with her from before, and I'd left him my card, so he called me. Did you keep the phone number?'

'Of her parents? Yes, I'm sure I've still got it somewhere. Do you want to pass it on to John Phillips?'

There was a silence then Mark said quietly, 'Wouldn't it be better if you phoned them?'

Sarah recalled the unpleasant nature of her last call to Julie's parents. She didn't answer, but gazed at the picture of Ruth on her bookcase.

'Sarah? Are you there?'

'What's wrong with Julie?'

'I'm not sure, but it's pretty serious according to John. He said something about an overdose. They don't think she's going to make it.'

'I couldn't tell her parents that.'

'No, but whatever you say, wouldn't it be better coming from you than from a total stranger?'

Sarah's eyes remained fixed on the picture of Ruth, then she said. 'I want to see her.'

Surprise filled Mark's tone. 'Who? Julie?'

'Yes. I will phone her parents but I'll do it after I've seen her. I'll drive through after school. Where is she?'

Mark told her, then added, 'Can I...I mean...would you...will I come with you?'

The bell rang for the end of lunchtime. 'I've got to go, eh, feel free, to come I mean.'

'Right, I'll meet you at school.'

Sorry as she was to hear of Julie Robertson, Sarah found her mood lift as the afternoon progressed. She knew she would be glad to see Mark McKenzie again.

When she got into his car he smiled at her. 'Do you want to get out of the 'school-saturated' clothes before we head off?'

When she hesitated he said, 'I'll wait in the car.'

She nodded. 'Okay, five minutes.'

As they set off on the journey to Edinburgh and the Western General hospital, Sarah said, 'I must owe you a fortune in petrol.'

Mark glanced at her, 'You don't owe me anything, Sarah,' and she knew by his tone that he wasn't referring to petrol.

Sarah looked out at the passing fields as they drove out of town. She spoke quietly. 'I do, Mark. I owe you a great deal.'

He touched her hand briefly, then he started to speak of the investigation into the death of Jaswinder Saeed. 'It's not looking good for her brothers.'

'What do you mean?'

'My sources tell me that there's lots of DNA evidence of their involvement with Jaswinder. But of course, they lived in the same house, so it's hardly surprising. Their story is that the person who made her pregnant must be the guilty party.'

'And is that not likely?'

Mark shook his head, 'Not very. The young man in question is absolutely distraught at her death. The police have had him in for questioning more than once, but they are pretty well convinced it wasn't him. As he tells it they wanted to get married but Jaswinder was absolutely terrified at the thought of her brothers' reaction.'

Sarah thought of Hakim Ashrif.

'In fact, he told the police that they'd planned to run off together the very weekend that Jaswinder was killed.'

'And maybe the brothers found out? Anyway, at least it looks a bit more straightforward than Rubina's death. The man in that scenario remains a mystery. Unless you've heard anything to the contrary.'

'No. I spoke to Steve Hamilton yesterday, as a matter of fact; they're no further forward.' He braked to avoid a suicidal pedestrian. 'And they're no further forward with the drugs either. They know there are plenty of hard drugs swilling around in the district, but not ecstasy; the tablet of choice for reckless teenagers.'

'Moira tells me that there haven't been any more incidents in the school. It would be good if that source has dried up.'

'Sources for drugs never dry up - they might fade away for a while but someone else always takes up the supply.'

'The Head has organised a big meeting in the school - police, staff, parents - and other interested parties - all working together, that sort of thing.'

'About drugs?'

'Certainly not about Rubina. I suspect that Keith feels that Jaswinder Saeed's death lets the school off the hook where that's concerned.'

Mark shook his head. 'I don't think there's any connection there at all.'

'Not even if it turns out to be an honour killing?'

He shrugged. 'Even then.'

Julie Robertson was in a small side room of the hospital. She was unconscious, and that she was close to death was obvious even to Sarah's untrained eye. The nurse who had shown them to her bedside asked about their relationship to Julie. Sarah told her she was willing to phone the Robertsons, but asked for some more information. The nurse led them to a small office and told them to wait until she fetched the doctor.

The doctor was a pale young man with a very tired expression. He declared himself pleased to see someone there on Julie's behalf. She had been in the hospital for ten days and they had despaired of getting any contact with family members.

Sarah said, 'Would an...overdose...usually make a person ill for so long?'

'Well, not always. But paracetamol - that's different...'

'Paracetamol? Not...heroin...or...'

Mark said, 'That's slow to act, isn't it?'

As the doctor nodded Sarah said, 'So, couldn't she be saved?'

The doctor shook his head. 'No, I'm sorry. We didn't get to her quickly enough. And in fact, even when we do, paracetamol does its work gradually, destroying the liver mainly, until it becomes fatal.'

'But she was a drug addict.'

'That didn't help. She was already in a weakened state when she took the overdose.'

'Could it have been an accident?'

The doctor rolled a pen on the desk in front of him. 'Maybe.'

'May I tell her parents that?'

He shrugged. 'If you think it might be a comfort.'

Mark said, 'How long has she got?'

The doctor looked at Sarah. 'I should contact her parents right away, if I were you.'

Once outside, Sarah said to Mark, 'I think I should speak to John Phillips, before I phone. He knows Julie better than we do.'

'Okay, let's do that.'

The shop was doing a brisk trade at this point in the evening - but when John saw Sarah and Mark enter he left the other two staff to continue and nodded towards the back. 'How is she?'

Sarah said, 'We've been to the hospital. She's hasn't got long.'

John Phillips drew his hand across his eyes. 'It's a bloody shame. Have you let her folks know yet?'

'No, I wanted to speak to you first.'

'Right. Look, sit down.' He pulled out the stools. 'Would you like something to eat?'

All of a sudden Sarah became conscious of the appetising smells from the shop, telling her that she was hungry. She looked at Mark, who grinned and gestured that the decision was hers.

'Maybe after we talk?'

'Right, whenever you're ready, just say the word.' He pulled out another stool. 'Anyway, it's great of you to come. Thanks. I hated it that the poor lass had nobody.'

Sarah said, 'She didn't have nobody, John - she had you, by all accounts.'

'Aye, well.'

'What happened? They said it was paracetamol. How did that come about?'

'Well, after that time when you came to see her, I think she got the notion that she might pull out of the drugs, get clean you know. She had some money, and this time she didny run to her supplier, she tried to make contact with the drugs workers, like? She bought some decent food and she was all set for going on the methadone if they would let her - even spoke about getting her kids back, God help her...'

'So what happened?'

He spread his hands, 'What happens to them all? The supplier came knocking and down she went. She hated herself for it, and I think that's when she went out and bought the paracetamol.'

'You mean, it was deliberate?'

'What else?'

Sarah turned to Mark, 'What do I tell the Robertsons?'

Mark said, 'Nobody really knows if it was deliberate, do they?'

John said hurriedly, 'No, no…we don't.'

Sarah got up and went outside to the street. She waited until some raucous shouting passed into the distance then she dialled the number. She was grateful when Julie's mother answered the phone. She remembered Sarah's earlier call. When Sarah gave her the news she gasped, began to weep, then repeated, with what Sarah recognised as a note of hope in her voice, 'And they think it might have been an accident?'

Sarah went back into the warm, vinegary fug of the chip shop. 'They are coming to Edinburgh. They are leaving tonight. I hope they get here in time.'

Mark clasped her by the shoulder. 'Well done.'

On the way back to Helensburgh Sarah and Mark spoke easily about Julie Robertson. Obvious to them both was the fact of yet another wasted life.

'At least the Robertsons might get the chance to say goodbye to their daughter - unlike the Khans, or for that matter, Jaswinder's family.'

Mark nodded, and Sarah knew he had picked up on the unspoken reference to Ruth.

*

A buzz of conversation filled the school hall as people waited for the meeting to start. As Sarah chose a seat she noted the good turnout, and she was studying the platform party when Annette Birkmyre slipped in beside her.'

Sarah smiled, 'I'm surprised to see you here.'

'Oh, wifely support and all that, you know. 'Besides,' she jerked her thumb and Sarah saw her son Malcolm next to her, 'it won't do this one any harm to get the message too.'

The content of the meeting was entirely predictable - input from the Head, DI Steve Hamilton and a drugs worker, whose message was aimed at telling parents how to spot suspicious behaviours and demeanours on the part of their teenage children: a film on how to recognise certain harmful substances, and at question-time a few attacks on the authorities by the more belligerent parents.

Afterwards there was tea and biscuits in the cafeteria. Sarah was about to make her excuses and leave without the tea when Malcolm Birkmyre began to talk to her about his choice of book for an essay he had to write for English. They were still speaking as they reached the cafeteria.

'Anyway, check with your English teacher at school before you start, Malcolm, and see if she approves.'

'She won't. I can't stand her,' the boy said. A few biscuit crumbs dropped on his school sweatshirt, and one landed on the raised golden threads of the Latin motto.

'Tsk, tsk, that won't do. We English teachers have to stick together, you know.' Sarah said, keeping her voice light. 'I'm sure she's perfectly nice.' She looked around, but his mother was engaged in conversation with the drugs worker.

The boy gave her a sheepish look. 'Actually, I think the problem is that she doesn't like me.'

Sarah frowned. 'What makes you say that?'

'She had a fight with Dad about something or other when Gordon was in her class, and since then I don't think she likes any of us.'

'I'm sorry to hear that, Malcolm. Anyway,' Sarah looked for an escape route, 'how is Gordon getting on in America? Was he home for Christmas?'

'No. He was going to come, but Dad fixed him up with some friends of his in New York or somewhere for Christmas. Lucky pig.'

'I take he enjoyed it then.'

'Yeah, he said it was cool - he went to loads of parties and he said the girls were well...' he blushed, and Sarah laughed.

'Never mind, your turn will come soon enough.'

She left shortly afterwards, and made her way to her car in the darkened playground. She was ahead of the crowd and when she stopped to find her keys she was grabbed from behind. She twisted around, taking a panicky breath to scream for help when she recognised her would-be assailant.

'David! What the hell!'

'Shh... Sarah, I just want to speak to you.'

She was still breathing heavily as figures began to appear from the lighted doorway of the school. David Smythe turned away from them.

'Look, I don't want to be seen. Can we get into the car, please, Sarah?'

Once inside the car, she said, 'You gave me the fright of my life there. What's with all the cloak and dagger stuff?'

'I'm sorry about that. I've phoned the flat a couple of times but you don't seem to be taking calls.'

A faint yellowish beam from the security lights caught his face, making it all angles and shadows, and Sarah thought how little he resembled the handsome young man who had whirled around the floor at the wedding just a few months before.

'Oh. That's a long story. Anyway, what do you want to speak to me about?'

He looked nervously out of the window. 'Would you mind driving away from here?'

As Sarah started the car her first idea was to take him home with her, then she thought better of it. He wasn't the same David Smythe any more. Instead she drove to the large car park on Helensburgh pier. Granted it was dark there too and almost deserted, but at least it was an open space. She could hardly believe that she was thinking in a way that was so alien to all her natural instincts but, she reminded herself, there was still a murderer around.

'So, let's talk.'

The dim interior of the car didn't disguise David's smile, nor the slight nod he made towards the choice of parking place. Sarah decided to ignore it.

'Actually, I want you to tell me what you know about the other murder.'

'What other murder?'

'Come on, Sarah, you know. The other Asian girl.'

'Why on earth would I know anything about it? Besides, what about your father and his important sources? He knew everything about Rubina in no time at all, it seemed to me.'

He turned away from her and mumbled something, and Sarah said, 'What did you say?'

'I said, I can't ask him,' in a louder voice.

'Why not?'

He turned back to face her. 'You know why not.'

Sarah lifted both hands off the wheel. 'For heaven's sake, David, you're not making any sense. You'll have to spell it out for me.'

'It's about Rubina, isn't it?'

'Rubina?'

'Yes, he's been funny with me ever since it happened. And, you know, he doesn't like it that I'm not very well, keeps on about more tests.'

'Have you had any test results?'

He looked away again and nodded. Sarah didn't pursue it.

'So, what does your father think about Rubina?'

David punched his knee with a clenched fist. 'That's just it - he never comes out and says anything definite - he just has a kind of ....attitude about it that makes me uncomfortable.'

'And why should that be?'

He shook his head then slumped in his seat. In the poor light Sarah was sure she could see tears glistening on his eyelashes. They didn't speak for a moment then he said,

'So, you see, that's why I want to know about that other Asian girl.'

Sarah said, 'Yes, I do see. Well, all I can tell you is that no-one has yet been arrested for her death, but there are quite definite suspects, if that helps.'

He gave a harsh laugh. 'And I'm not one of them!'

'Oh David! Come on, I'll drive you home. I take it you didn't bring your car?'

'It's locked in the garage until I'm well enough to go back to work, says my father.'

'And when is that likely to be?' She glanced at sideways at him.

'Never.'

At the flat there was a message on the phone from Julie Robertson's father. Julie had died, and there was to be an inquest, then they were taking her south for burial, so there would be no funeral in Scotland. His last words were a gruff thank you to Sarah for giving them the chance to be there - and hoping that she would soon make contact with her sister.

Sarah made herself a gin and tonic and sat on her window seat. As she sipped the drink she reflected on the complex organism which families sometimes were - David Smythe and his father, who showed his worry over his son by bullying him, and Julie Robertson, whose parents disowned her when she was alive and yet were anxious to claim her when she was dead. At the end of the day it seemed the bond was unbreakable.

As January wore on Sarah relaxed as much as she could into the routines of her school life. At times it even felt as if all the activity of the previous months was fading into the background, almost as if it had never been. She had a couple of meals with Mark McKenzie, but he made no further mention of the quest to find Ruth. Sarah was conscious that the issue hung between them, but they made an effort to steer their conversations away from that area. Instead, they concentrated on getting to know each other better, something which was much easier without the slightly frenetic edge which had been there in all their previous meetings.

Even Lynn and Leslie appeared to have settled down to some acceptance of Rubina's death. They had important exams coming up which would affect their chances of getting into university, and they had begun to give serious attention to their work.

Sarah herself, however painfully, was coming to the conclusion that she was never going to find out what had happened to Ruth, although she still wished fervently for Rubina's killer to be caught. In a way which she couldn't fully explain to herself, it would be some kind of retribution.

And she was almost disappointed when the news came that Jaswinder Saeed's brothers had confessed to her killing, seeming to remove any possibility of that link with Rubina's murder.

When she discussed this with Mark he said, 'Unless they were in the business of killing to order - and there's not a scrap of evidence to connect them with her. Of course the police went down that road, but they concluded that Jaswinder's death was entirely personal, and apparently, aided and abetted by her their mother because the girl had brought dishonour on the family.'

And Sarah thought, so much for family bonding.

They were relaxing in Sarah's flat after a takeaway meal, and she got up to put the plates in the kitchen.

'But the whole thing could throw suspicion back on Rubina's family, if they found out she too was seeing someone? Don't you think so?'

Mark stretched his arms along the back of the sofa.

'No, I don't actually.'

Sarah came back and perched on the edge of the leather chair. 'What makes you so certain?'

He shook his head. 'I'm not certain at all. I suppose it's just a feeling I have. There are too many people in this town with dodgy alibis for it to be that simple. Besides, family killings don't usually take that long to solve. Things leak out, because there's always more than one person in the know.

But a few days later it seemed that a breakthrough in the Rubina Khan case might be coming closer, when a gent's leather glove turned up on the shores of Loch Lomond, not far from the point where her body had been found. Lynn Cameron broke the news to Sarah, when she stuck her head into the classroom between lessons.

'But how do you know about this?' Sarah's voice got

lost in the clatter of thirty first year pupils entering the room.

Lynn managed to say, 'I'll come back at the interval, Miss,' before disappearing along the corridor. Sarah's heart sank at the thought of the glint she may have seen in the girl's eyes. However, the next two periods spent engendering some creativity in the souls of a bunch of ten-year olds drove it out of her mind until the bell rang for the morning interval.

When Lynn returned Sarah saw that she had not been wrong, and she could detect suppressed excitement in the girl.

'It's a breakthrough, Miss.'

Sarah resolved to do without her coffee and told Lynn to take a seat.

'One glove? A breakthrough? How's that?'

'Well, actually someone came to my mum with it. I could hardly believe it! This guy was fiddling about with a metal detector or something on the shores and he found it...'

'But why did he take it to your mother?'

Lynn shrugged. 'He's pretty scruffy - I don't think he'd go to the police - I don't know,' she smiled. 'maybe he just fancies my mum. And everybody knows her. Anyway, he came to our door with it. Said he 'minded about the dead lassie.' She gave a fair imitation of a coarse voice.

'I'm sure your mother was delighted.'

Lynn laughed aloud. 'No way! She was for chucking the glove in the bin when Austin Toner phoned and he went ballistic! He said it could be important evidence and he'd come down and take it to the police himself.'

Sarah said, 'Ha, that way he could get it into the paper before anyone else. If it really is evidence, that is. When will they know?'

'Ah, but that's it, Miss - the glove was found last week and he phoned my mum early this morning.' Her eyes behind her glasses were huge. 'Rubina's DNA is on it,' She lowered her voice, 'and someone else's.'

Sarah felt a jolt. This was a breakthrough.

'Who knows about this, Lynn?'

'I don't know, Miss. I told Leslie, and my mum and Wilson Toner know - he's got this 'friend' in the police - she made commas with her fingers - who gives him information, but I don't know about anybody else.'

At lunchtime Sarah left the school and walked to the nearest newsagent's to buy a Clarion, but someone's advice, or orders - had so far kept the news out of the paper.

She phoned Mark when she got home.

'Yes, I've heard. I wasn't actually going to tell you.'

Sarah bristled. 'Why not?'

'Because someone might make themselves unavailable if this knowledge becomes too public? Besides, the DNA is quite badly degraded because the glove has been in the water for so long, and the police have got to eliminate all the people who handled the damned thing , quite apart from its original owner.'

Sarah though how pleased Lynn Cameron's mother would be about that.

'They've also got to start a search for the other glove, and they don't want hordes of tourists helping them on the bonny banks...'

'Of course, that makes sense. Oh well, I just hope Lynn Cameron will be more discreet than she usually is, and Leslie.'

'Would you have another word with them, Sarah? In a worst case scenario it could be a bit dangerous? The killer is likely to become edgy if he thinks these kids can get inside knowledge from the police?' He added, quietly, 'Which is why I wasn't going to tell you.'

Sarah felt her face warm. 'Should I perhaps say

something to Moira Campbell, the deputy?'

'She will be careful?'

'Undoubtedly.'

Sarah phoned Moira. She was at home, and expressed herself delighted by the prospect of a chat.

She was locking her car in the driveway when Moira opened the door. 'Oh, you've driven up? And here I was just opening the wine?' She made a disappointed face and Sarah laughed,

'Oh well, if you insist, I'll just walk back home.' But as she said the words the thought came to her that she wouldn't feel safe walking home late at night; not now. It would be a taxi if need be.

'So, I thought it might be best if you speak to Lynn and Leslie about the seriousness of this?'

Moira laid down her glass and ran her fingers through her already messy hair. 'I don't know, Sarah. That would make it formal, if you know what I mean, and I'd have to tell Keith. We couldn't risk Franny Watkins storming the gates because we were trying to influence her son in a criminal matter.'

Sarah said, 'Right enough, I hadn't thought of it like that. It's just that I'm worried about these youngsters knowing things which, quite honestly, they shouldn't.'

'What about Councillor Cameron? Perhaps you could have a word with her.'

Sarah raised her eyebrows. 'You think so? Besides, it's her doing that the kids are involved in the first place.'

Moira laughed, 'Point taken. Anyway, once the police start testing all Rubina's contacts it's bound to come out...but I know, up until then...'

They drank quietly for a moment or two then Sarah raised the subject which had been niggling at her since she heard about the glove. 'I'm worried about Roger.'

Moira nodded. 'I've thought about him too.'

'If he did tell the police that he was roaming about that night they'll probably want to test him, but if he didn't tell...?' Sarah ran her finger round the top of her glass.

They were sitting one on each side of the big kitchen table. Moira got up and switched on the kettle. 'Let's have some coffee, it'll help with the thought processes.'

Sarah said, 'What will we do if the police don't know about Roger?'

Moira rattled the coffee tin. 'Lord, Sarah, I just don't know. I mean, he said he'd told the police, after all, and we can't be sure that he didn't.'

Sarah shook her head, 'Moira, I'm just as sure that he didn't tell them. You should have been there. He was so shifty when Dorothy mentioned it that I just knew he was lying.'

Moira sighed. 'Roger's not the kind to do anything like that.'

'Like what? Lie to the police, have a relationship with a young pupil or take to murder?'

'Sarah!'

'I know, Moira, it's a shocking idea isn't it? But maybe it's time to start thinking the unthinkable. If I was sure that Roger didn't tell the police about that night I'd tell them myself.'

Moira sat down on her seat with a thump, banging down the cafetiere. 'Sarah, what's happened to you? It's not like you to be so...so ruthless.'

Sarah laid her hands flat on the surface of the table. 'I know, I know. But all these years ago, if people had been more honest about what was going on, my sister might still be alive.'

Moira poured coffee into mugs with great care, then lit a cigarette. She blew out the smoke. 'You don't know that she isn't.'

'Moira, I do. She's dead, and that's all there is to it.'

'And you think by telling the police about Roger that you'll be doing a service for Rubina, is that it?'

Sarah took a mouthful of coffee before she answered. 'If need be, yes.'

'Even if in doing so you damage the reputation of a good man?'

'Oh, for heaven's sake, Moira, if he's such a good man then he's got nothing to fear, has he?'

In the end Sarah did walk home, anger fuelling her steps to the extent that she feared nothing, and distress that she had upset Moira.

When she reached the flat she phoned. 'Moira, I'm sorry to have been so difficult. But I can't let this rest.'

'I understand. It's just that I've known Roger for such a long time...'

'Listen, I'll go and see him again. I'll find an excuse. And I'll give him the chance to explain himself, if he can.'

'You won't say anything to him about the glove, will you?'

'No...no, that wouldn't be wise.'

Next day Sarah planned to visit Roger and Dorothy after school. To give her visit some validity she asked Judith and William if there was anything they wanted her to pass on. Willie said just his good wishes and Judith said, if she didn't find time to phone him maybe Sarah could ask him where he'd hidden the assessment sheets for the SQA - she'd searched everywhere and hadn't been able to find them.

'And tell him I'd visit myself if I wasn't so snowed under with staff shortages.' She went off to chivvy Keith into phoning the education department about a replacement for one of the supply teachers who, it appeared, hadn't found the strength to return to Fruin High after the Christmas holidays. As yet another teacher hadn't been found, and Willie expressed some genuine sympathy for Judith, and the workload which Roger and David's absences placed on her. The mention of David made Sarah think of what was in store for Rubina's male contacts.

The thought was in her mind when Mary Stephens arrived in the department, still in her coat, and it occurred to Sarah that she'd never known Mary to be late for school. Mary's usually pale complexion had a waxen sheen.

Sarah got up and helped Mary off with her coat. 'Sit down, for goodness sake. You look about to faint - what's happened, is it your mother?'

She shook her head, and struggled to get a breath. 'No, it's David. Dear David.'

He eyes filled with tears. 'He's disappeared, and no-one knows where he's gone. His mother just rang me, she's in a terrible state!'

A chill settled in Sarah's stomach as she recalled Mark's words about who might make themselves unavailable. And she thought how Austin Toner wasn't the only one who had a 'friend' in the police.

Chapter 11

'So, what do you make of it?'

Mark had turned up at the flat after a call from Sarah with the news about David.

'Well, it's interesting - but he's a grown man, he can go where he likes.' Mark said.

'Without telling anyone?'

'Ok, begin at the beginning again. Your call was pretty rushed.'

'I know, I had hordes of pupils around at the time. Mary Stephens came in late to school this morning in a state of collapse. She'd just had a call from David's mother, wondering if she had any idea where he could be?'

'Why Mary Stephens?'

'Oh, I suppose because she dotes on David, like a fond auntie, and always shows a great interest in all his doings. She's been very worried about him for months now. She tries not to show it in school - Judith Aitken isn't her best friend, nor David's - and she thinks it's a load of spinsterish frustration which is wrong with Mary.'

'That doesn't explain why his mother would contact her.'

'Apparently she knows his mother quite well. They were at school together and they go a whist club or something. Anyway she'd tried everyone else, Mary was the very last resort.' Sarah looked at clock. 'Listen, I'm going to see Roger Bullough. Why don't you help yourself to coffee or whatever and we can continue this conversation when I get back.'

Mark said, 'Perhaps I should go with you and wait in the car?'

Sarah smiled at his expression. 'I think I'll be quite safe. Dorothy is bedridden and Roger is her main carer. Nothing dangerous will happen in that house.'

Mark raised one eyebrow and as he helped her into her jacket, gave her shoulders a quick squeeze.

'I'll be waiting.'

Roger Bullough wasn't at home. A neighbour sitting with Dorothy said he'd gone out just after the nurses had left for the evening. Dorothy, neat and tidy in a fresh nightdress, her hair brushed smooth, lay propped up in bed. Sarah thought she looked like a waxwork.

She smiled. 'Oh Sarah. How nice…but Roger's gone out.

'That's all right. I just have a couple of questions from Judith, and they're not that urgent. Anyway, I wanted to see how you were.'

'I'm fine.'

'So I see.'

Dorothy forced out the words. 'He'll be sorry…to…miss you.'

Sarah sat by the bed. 'Oh, it doesn't matter. I should have rung anyway. I just expected him to be here, don't ask me why.'

The neighbour hovered behind Sarah, holding some knitting. 'It's his constitutional.'

Sarah swung round. 'Constitutional?'

Dorothy gave a little gasping laugh. 'His evening walk. He needs…a break…you know. Mrs Black…is kind…'

Mrs Black said, 'I come in a few evenings in the week to give Roger a break. I can knit just as easily here as there,' she nodded next door, 'and it gives Dorothy some company. He's never out for long.'

Sarah said, 'It's not very nice tonight to be out walking, it was trying to snow when I came in.'

Mrs Black laughed. 'Oh, Roger doesn't mind that, does he, Dorothy? Out in all weathers. Parks the car at Kidston and walks along the seafront. I often say to my Jack that it would fit him better to be doing something like that than mouldering away in front of the TV.' She scratched her grey hair with a knitting needle. 'But does he listen?'

'Is this part of Roger's recovery programme? I know they usually recommend a certain amount of exercise after a heart attack. My father had heart problems...'

'Oh no, he's always done it, hasn't he, Dorothy?'

Dorothy nodded her head against the pillow. 'Since...I got ill...'

Mrs Black threw the knitting on the bed. 'Here, I'm forgetting my manners. Would you like a cup of tea... eh?'

'Sarah - Sarah Blane. I work in Roger's department at the school. No, I won't have tea, thanks all the same. I've got to go in a minute.' She turned back to Dorothy. 'We miss Roger in the department. He makes all the paper-shuffling look easy. Judith's finding it quite a job.'

Dorothy smiled. 'I know. He...he wants to be back...next term.'

'Oh, that'll be good.' Sarah rose. 'I'll get off now. Maybe you could ask Roger to give Judith a ring, there's something or other that she can't seem to find.'

As Sarah drove back to Helensburgh, slowly, to allow for the slushy road surface, she passed Roger. She wouldn't have noticed him but for the fact that the conditions seemed to have emptied the road. He was coming out of a house at the west end of town. He turned to close the gate and as he moved under the streetlight a nimbus of dancing snowflakes waltzed around his head. He raised a gloved hand to someone at the front door. Sarah could see light in the porch but the house was set too far back to pick anyone out.

'And there's absolutely no reason why Roger shouldn't visit someone in town - apart from the fact that they think he's out walking.' Sarah spoke from the hall, where she was hanging up her jacket.

Mark got up and switched off the television. 'Maybe he was walking too.'

Sarah came into the room. 'Yes, I'm sure there's a perfectly innocent explanation. But he was pretty far from Kidston, if he was walking on such a night. Anyway, I think I'm becoming paranoid, seeing suspicious acts in every corner.'

'It happens. Here, come and have a drink. You look frozen.'

'It's getting pretty foul out there. I think you'll have to stay, Mark.'

'Fine. Now you can give me the continuing story of David Smythe.'

'Yes. I can understand why they're all so worried. He's gone without his car, which, as you recall, is locked in the garage, and he didn't tell anyone he was going anywhere.'

'Did he take luggage?'

'That's it. His mother doesn't know whether he did or not, he's got so much of everything.'

'He's got a boat, hasn't he?'

'Surely it would be madness to go out in this weather?'

'You didn't think he was very rational when you saw him last.'

'That's true.'

'Anyway, I'll see what I can find out tomorrow. I take it the police have been notified?'

'Well that's it. My first thought was that his father is well informed about recent developments, and that David's vanishing act is no accident. But obviously, if that's the case, his mother doesn't know about it.'

'You said his father seemed to be suspicious about him and Rubina, didn't you?'

'All the more reason to get him out of the way before the police come calling again?'

'Would he go that far?'

Sarah went the window to check the weather. 'It's getting worse.' She turned back. 'The words blood and water come to mind.'

In the morning conditions were worse than ever. Several inches of snow had fallen overnight and the situation in the school was verging on chaotic. The school buses from the country couldn't get in, nor could some of the staff who lived in rural locations. Even the trains from the city were disrupted. Sarah was amazed, as ever, at how little snow it took to paralyse this country. Britain must be a standing joke with these European neighbours who coped perfectly well with excessive amounts of snow on a yearly basis.

Mary Stephens was in school and she reported that there was still no word from David. Grown man or not, his mother had contacted the police.

Mark had managed to get back to Glasgow at least, and he phoned Sarah at lunchtime.

'Steve Hamilton is very suspicious about David Smythe's disappearance at this point, as you can imagine. They have started the DNA testing - family first, then moving on to other contacts, and he would definitely be included in that. And Leslie Watkins.'

'Gosh, Franny will go mad. What about other

teachers? She didn't just do English.'

'Well, they're not in a hurry to extend it, until they've exhausted all the obvious contacts.'

'I wouldn't put Leslie in that category.'

'He was the last person to see her alive, don't forget.'

'Ye-es, except the killer. Oh, by the way, what about David's boat? I know it's a stupid question, but I have to ask.'

'No, it's there, safely tucked up for the winter in Rhu Marina. More than we can say for its owner, in this inclement weather.'

'David's a guy with lots of friends He'll be staying with one of them, I'm quite sure.' She hesitated. 'Mark, would you...is it possible that you could find out about Roger, you know - the night she went missing? Did he tell the police he went to meet the bus?'

She heard him take a deep breath. 'That could be difficult. It would mean getting access to the initial interview transcripts. And my sources would want to know why.'

'I see what you mean. Oh well, I suppose we'll have to pass on that for the moment.'

A week passed and there was no word of David Smythe. The snow gradually disappeared and school got back to normal. Mary Stephens grew paler, if that were possible, and became very quiet. It baffled Sarah that she was sufficiently in control to do her job.

For Sarah herself, waiting for something to happen was frustrating. The urgency which had gripped the investigation for a brief time seemed to be draining away and the February mid-term break, a long weekend, was coming up.

Sarah looked forward to spending it with Mark. They were going to a country-house hotel in Perthshire, and tentatively, he had asked about booking a double room. Sarah had agonised for several days then lost her nerve. That step in the relationship was still on hold. She knew her affection for Mark was deepening all the time, and she found him attractive enough, but somehow there were still too many unresolved issues surrounding them. Besides, what if it went wrong? Wasn't the relationship still rather fragile? Still, she was growing very used to having Mark close by, so maybe soon...

Besides, the whole gradual thing was so different from what she'd had with Simon. She'd met him at the wedding of a colleague in her first school. Tall, blond, blue-eyed and charming, he'd laughed Sarah all the way to the altar in a very short time. Afterwards the bitter truth of the aphorism, 'marry in haste and repent at leisure' came to haunt her. Simon, who worked in the butterfly world of advertising, was wonderful when the going was good. And by the time he found out about the lost sister the shine was already coming off the marriage. Mark was shaping up to be a very different kind of man, but she wasn't quite ready to take the risk, especially when they had been drawn together in such unfortunate circumstances.

There had been no arrest. Mark could tell her that the police had tested all of Rubina's male relatives for DNA, but no-one was telling him if they'd got any positive findings. While his sources were good, on this occasion they weren't that good, and Sarah wondered if it would be a step too far to inquire into Lynn Cameron's channel of information. She couldn't stand Wilson Toner's newspaper and its lowest common denominator approach, but she wanted to know.

Then something did happen. She had arranged to meet Mark in their usual Italian restaurant in Glasgow on Saturday evening, and the moment she saw him she knew that he had news. He got up and kissed her on the cheek.

'Sit down, Sarah. You'd better order first, then I'll tell you the latest.'

Sarah frowned at him but did as he suggested. Then she said, 'Now.'

'They've traced David Smythe.'

'Where? How?'

'This golden boy with too many possessions? His mother didn't notice that he'd taken his passport with him, but the team which searched his flat weren't long in spotting its absence. They've traced him to Sri Lanka - apparently a favourite destination?'

Sarah said, 'Oh! I wonder if Mary knows that he's safe?'

Mark smiled and shook his head. 'Tell me, were you the kind of child who brought home stray kittens and rescued injured birds?'

Sarah looked blank, then she laughed. 'Yes, guilty as charged.' She pointed to Mark. 'But look who's talking.'

He pursed his lips. 'Mmm...hard to tell who's rescuing who here.'

She smiled briefly as the waiter laid a dish in front of her. 'But it's very serious, isn't it? David running away like this. Will they be able to make him come back?'

'Not for a while, I shouldn't think. You haven't heard the worst yet. David Smythe is in hospital in Colombo.'

'What?'

'He...attempted to commit suicide. Cut his wrists. The maid found him in his room when she went to clean, or he might not be alive.'

Sarah put down her knife and fork, and covered her mouth with her hand. She felt sick. 'Oh, God. This is terrible. His mother, Mary - they'll be devastated!'

'His mother flew out to be with him this morning. I

don't suppose that's something Mary will be able to do?'

'No...she's got her own mother...and school, of course...I can't imagine...' She looked at her watch, 'I'll have to go and see her.'

'Not tonight, tomorrow surely. This is exactly why I didn't phone to tell you, I knew you'd go rushing off. You've got to relax some of the time, Sarah.' He caught her wrist and spoke gently, 'In truth, none of this is your problem, now, is it?'

She didn't answer right away - but dug with her free hand in her bag for a handkerchief, 'How many times did you take me to Edinburgh?'

He smiled and released her wrist. 'I knew you'd say that.'

Sarah shuddered, 'So, is that it? David Smythe killed Rubina.'

Mark called for the bill. 'Let's go Sarah, we can talk more at my place.'

'But my car...it's parked...'

'We'll come back for it tomorrow. Anyway, you've had too much of a shock to be driving.'

Sarah shed a few tears as Mark drove them back to his flat in the west end. The implications of this news were enormous, and saddening. Once there, he steered her to the sofa and made her sit down while he poured drinks. Hers was a brandy.

She wiped her eyes. 'God. David. It doesn't make sense. Anyway, the police won't be able to get DNA from him in Sri Lanka. Or will they?'

'Actually they don't need to do that. Initially they can get it from any of his personal possessions, combs, toothbrushes and so on.'

'Of course, I hadn't thought of that.' She sighed. 'David Smythe a murderer? I can't come to terms with that.'

208

'He has been behaving very oddly since it happened though, hasn't he?'

*

Mary Stephens lived with her mother on the ground floor of a grey sandstone tenement in one of the back streets of Helensburgh. It was a spacious flat, but Sarah found herself struggling past all kinds of odd furniture to get to the living room. It was equally crowded, and the whole place had the musty odour of old things. Sarah could see that many of the pieces were antiques, but the overall effect was that of a junk shop. So surprised was she by Mary's home that she almost forgot why she'd come.

Mary ushered Sarah into an ancient armchair. Its springs poked into her. Then she looked at Mary and had another surprise. The woman stood before her, asking her if she'd prefer tea or coffee, as if this was a Sunday morning social routine. Gone was the pale, drawn face. Instead Mary's eyes gleamed and her cheeks were pink.

Sarah said, 'Eh, coffee would be…but Mary, that's not why I've come.'

Mary smiled, 'I know why you've come Sarah. Now, coffee…' She bustled out, her broad hips brushing furniture, leaving Sarah to gaze around at the hundreds of objects which filled the room, and, assume from a muffled barking that the dog was shut in another room.

There was an upright piano, its top festooned with dusty ornaments, a venerable organ, and something which looked like a double bass in one corner: it was difficult to tell, since it was half-hidden under a variety of coloured shawls. She'd never heard Mary say she was musical. There were books everywhere, on the high wooden mantelpiece, alongside curios of obviously exotic origin, and piled on every other surface. Of Mary's mother there was no sign, unless she was lost amongst the furniture.

Sarah had begun to feel a touch of hysteria by the time Mary came back carrying a tray with coffee pot, two fine china cups, a small milk jug and sugar bowl and a plate of digestive biscuits. She swiped a pile of books off a small table with her elbow and laid down the tray.

'Sorry about the plain fare, Sarah, chocolate gives Mother headaches.'

Sarah took the cup and nodded. 'Your mother?'

'She's at church. One of the neighbours takes her in his car.' She smiled brightly, 'I'm not a fan of organised religion myself.'

'Oh…really…I wasn't aware…'

Sarah shook her head as the biscuit plate was held in front of her.

'Oh well, never mind.' Mary said, and took one herself. 'You've come about David, haven't you?' She said, and a few digestive crumbs flew in Sarah's direction.

'Well yes, I'm so sorry about…what's happened…and I wondered if you were all right. You've been so worried.'

Mary brushed biscuit traces from her hands. 'As you can see, Sarah, I'm fine.'

'But…'

Mary interrupted, 'Yes, I know what you're going to say, but it's all nonsense, isn't it?'

'But he's…the hospital?'

'Yes, that's not so good. I often wish David wouldn't holiday in places like that - they're full of dangerous people. Obviously he's been attacked for his money or whatever.'

'Who told you, Mary, about David being hurt, I mean?'

'Celia, that's his mother. She phoned before she left.

She was quite cross with him, you know, going off like that and not telling her. But I understand, I told her, it's the stress he's been under recently. You see, Sarah, David's not like the rest of us, he's very sensitive. All these terrible things which have been happening in the school, it's been so much worse for him.'

Sarah said slowly. 'Mary...you know there's suspicion now about David and... Rubina Khan's death.'

Mary's eyes opened wide. 'But it's ridiculous to even to hint at such a thing! Of course all these wee girls go after David because he's so handsome, but he would never have taken up with any of them - especially Rubina.'

'Why especially?' Sarah held her breath.

'Well, let's face it, she was a pretty child, it's true - but that's just what she was - a child. David is a sophisticated young man after all; he doesn't seek his pleasures in little old Helensburgh.' She laughed and waved her hand in front of her face as if to waft away such a foolish idea. 'I mean he would be kind to her, David would never hurt anyone's feelings, but that's all. Why, you remember he even came to George and Marilyn's wedding that time, even although he was going off on holiday early the next morning. That's the sort of person he is.'

As Sarah left she banged her knee on an unidentifiable piece of furniture. The pain saw her through her stunned goodbyes to Mary.

It was half past ten, and when she stepped into the street she was pleased to see a watery sun struggling through the clouds. In her bemused state she didn't fancy a long day in the flat contemplating Mary Stephens' eccentricity. 'That's the sort of person he is', indeed. She obviously didn't know that he was still in Glasgow when Mary thought he was winging his way across the world. The woman was in complete denial about David Smythe's behaviour: granted

211

he had not yet been charged with killing Rubina, but that he had attempted to kill himself was without doubt. Sarah was yet to hear of an attacker who slit his victim's wrists. She took a deep breath to rid herself of the musty smell in her nose, and thought uncomfortably that Mary's certainty bordered on madness. It was just one more example of the fact that working next to someone didn't mean you knew them.

She began to walk towards the esplanade. She would collect her car from outside the house and go for a drive. She would have loved to share these latest events with Moira, but she was worried that the discussion might take a wrong turn, as it had last time. Moira would find out about David through official channels soon enough. And Moira was probably well aware of Mary Stephens' peculiarities; she'd known her for much longer than Sarah had.

She decided to treat herself to lunch in Arrochar, a village a few miles further up on the shores of Gareloch. There was a quaint little restaurant there that she was fond of, which, now she came to think of it, could have been furnished out of the excess in Mary Stephens' house.

As she crossed Colquhoun Square she thought she recognised the slightly limping figure of Mohammed Ashrif coming towards her, and her heart sank. In a thick black anorak with the hood up the figure looked sinister, and she wondered if she might be wrong. However, when they came within speaking distance, she saw that it was Mohammed. Sarah said, 'Not a bad morning. Out walking?'

He smiled. 'No, not a walk, Miss Blane. I've been visiting my Uncle Anwar.' He bent his head, 'And my aunt.'

'Oh…yes…how are they?'

He shrugged. 'They are not good.'

'Well, perhaps it will not be so long now…until…well, they may be able to…'

212

She was floundering.

He looked up at her, his black eyes sharp. 'Not long? What do you know?'

She began to sweat under her warm coat. 'Oh, nothing...nothing...'

Suddenly he said, 'You know we have all been tested for our DNA? Even my Uncle Anwar!' He spat on the ground.

'I'm sorry, Mohammed. I wasn't aware of that.'

'But you are aware that David Smythe has run away?'

'Well...'

'Mr Birkmyre came to tell my aunt and uncle.'

'What? The Head?'

'Yes. It was kind of him. He said that he was sorry, but they have been very patient, and he thought it would help them to know.'

'To know? Did he...Mr Birkmyre...did he tell them where David Smythe is?'

'Yes. So how will they test his DNA? Hakim goes to the police every day to ask when he will be brought back.'

'And, the tests they have done so far?'

'No result yet. I must go.'

She blinked as he walked away, moving too fast for the question which had sprung to her lips, did no results mean negative findings or did it mean they were not yet available. But he had turned the corner and was gone. And what was Keith Birkmyre playing at? Rubina had been dead for months and, as far as Sarah could tell, it was the first time he had made any approach to her parents.

When she turned on to West Clyde Street a gust of icy wind whacked her in the face and stung her eyes. To give the Head some credit, of course, it was probably thoughtful to prepare the Khans for the awful revelations about David.

She longed to discuss all this with Moira. But she couldn't. She would wait until evening and phone Mark. He was working today, but he would phone later. Besides, this wasn't the stuff of a quick mobile phone message. Leaving Helensburgh on her way to Arrochar, Sarah found her way blocked at Faslane Naval Base by a large and vocal demonstration against Trident. While the peace camp was an ongoing reproach to the Ministry of Defence, these frequent demonstrations drew much bigger crowds of activists. Sarah joined a line of cars easing their way through with the assistance of dozens of uniformed police, some of whom had the task of lifting prostrate protestors off the middle of the road. Driving at a snail's pace she got a good look at some of them. She wasn't surprised to see Franny Watkins, red hair flying, carried by the shoulders and feet by two policemen. Her banner was trailing on the ground, and Sarah could see where Leslie had got his protesting techniques. She also recognised a well-known socialist politician, frequently on the news - and even a couple of clergymen - then she spotted someone else that she knew. Incredibly, it appeared to be William Armstrong.

For a moment her view was blocked by a large policeman, then she saw him again. It was Willie. Sarah was astonished. This was turning into a day of surprises. Willie had never mentioned his anti-nuclear principles in the staff-room. Another enigma in the department. She simply hoped that he wouldn't be arrested, staff shortages were bad enough in the English department. Then she felt uncharitable. It was to be admired that someone like Willie was prepared to stand up for his beliefs in public.

Over her ploughman's lunch, Sarah wondered what other eccentricities her colleagues might harbour. Willie, an unlikely rebel; Roger, with his ambiguous behaviour; Mary Stephens with her strange house and her obsession with

David Smythe - and what about him? - the weirdest of all.

She wondered idly what revelations might emerge from Judith Aitken's private life. She could be mud-wrestling champion of the West of Scotland for all the department knew. But then, none of them knew anything about Sarah herself, other than Moira.

'So, you could have knocked me down with the proverbial feather,' she told Mark on the phone, 'seeing Willie Armstrong shoving a large copper. All in all, it has been a pretty eventful day.' Sarah hitched her legs over the arm of the chair and made herself comfortable.

'Mmm, it's interesting about Willie Armstrong. I don't know the man, but from what you've said he seems a stolid kind of bloke?'

'Well, that's what I've thought for more than a year.'

'This puts him in quite a different light, though, wouldn't you say?'

Sarah chewed her lip. 'We-ell, I suppose so.' She had a mental picture of Willie in the staff room, his bulky figure bent over his marking, his bald head catching the beam from the strip-light above. His ponderous discourses on Philip Larkin and his equally heavy contributions about his carrots and leeks at the appropriate time of year.

'No, the more I think of him. No.'

'You'd have said that about David Smythe a few months ago, wouldn't you?'

She sighed and swung her legs round again. 'That's true. But listen Mark, something's bothering me. We're always told that murder is about motive, means and opportunity, right? That was crystal clear in the case of Jaswinder Singh, but if David is our ...guilty party, what's his motive?'

Mark made a tooth-sucking noise over the line. 'I see what you mean.'

'As far as I can tell, the worst that would have befallen him for having a relationship with a pupil would be losing his job. He doesn't need the money so I doubt if that threat would carry much weight with him.'

'Perhaps he's a truly dedicated teacher.'

'If that's the case, his job seems to be the least of his worries now. He hasn't been in school since the October holiday.'

There was a silence. Sarah could hear some Mozart faintly in the background.

'On the other hand, Sarah, he certainly looks like a man who's done something terrible. It takes a lot for someone to cut their own wrists.'

Sarah slumped in her chair. 'I suppose you're right.'

Chapter 12

On Monday morning Sarah wasn't surprised to see DI Steve Hamilton making his way to the Head's office as she walked along the corridor. He had just vanished inside when Moira's door opened.

'Hi Sarah, good weekend?'

Sarah stopped. Moira's wide smile looked pasted on. Sarah said, absent-mindedly, 'Yes, fine. Moira...you don't...are you all right?'

Her expression changed 'Are you free this period?'

Sarah nodded.

'Then come in.'

Moira's office looked in its usual state of urgent activity - papers and folders everywhere. She sat behind her desk and waved Sarah into the chair on the other side.

Sarah said, 'Moira, I'm so sorry about the other ni...'

Moira waved it away. 'Oh, that's water under the bridge now.' She flipped the edge of a folder with her thumb. The paper made a slippery noise. 'What about David?'

Sarah shook her head. 'I know.'

'It seems now he may also be the source of the drugs.'

Sarah's eyebrows went up. 'Also? You mean, as well as...Rubina?'

Moira closed her eyes and gave a faint nod.

'But that's ridiculous!' Sarah laughed. 'That's the

217

last thing he would do. He's loaded.'

'I know, but Keith says that's what Detective Inspector Hamilton thinks. I told the boss what I thought of that theory but he seems prepared to go along with it. As he sees it, the drugs stopped coming into school at the same time as David. Simple, isn't it?'

'And astonishingly tidy.' Sarah got up and went to the window. The playground was empty apart from a few empty crisp bags blowing around in a little circle.

'You know that the Head went to see the Khans the other day?'

She heard a sharp intake of breath from behind. 'Now? Whatever for?'

Sarah turned. 'To give them assurances about Rubina's murderer?'

Moira went back to flipping the edge of the folder. She didn't answer for a time.

Then she said, quietly, 'You know, Sarah, sometime I wonder if I'm going mad.'

Sarah was inclined to similar thoughts when the natty figure of the policeman entered her classroom just before lunch-time. As he squeezed past the departing pupils she observed that some of the fourth-year boys were already taller than he was.

He smiled tolerantly as he was bumped slightly against the door, but the set of the bushy eyebrows told a different story. She noticed, not for the first time, that he favoured the kind of light tan shoes which were almost yellow. She'd never liked the sort of man who wore shoes like that.

'What can I do for you, Inspector?' Sarah continued to sort a pile of essays.

He folded his arms and leaned his rear on a desk. 'It's about your colleague, David Smythe, Miss Blane.'

She looked up. 'Pardon?'

He gave a little knowing smile. 'Now, now, don't look so surprised. We know it's common knowledge about Mr Smythe's hasty departure, and his ...adventure, shall we say?'

She looked back to the essays. 'Is it really?'

Suddenly he stood up, unfolding his arms. 'Has David Smythe attempted to get in touch with you?'

'No.'

'Are you sure?'

Sarah threw down the paper she had in her hand, 'I think I might have noticed.'

'It's a serious offence to withhold information, you know.'

'How can I withhold information when I don't have any?'

'Ah, but I don't think that's true, Miss Blane. You were seen with Mr Smythe very shortly before he... absconded.'

Sarah laughed. 'I hardly think that 'abscond' is the right word.'

'Well, you can decide on the appropriate language for someone who defects from their place of work and their home at a time of...shall we call it...inconvenience?' His light tone altered, 'We want to know who told him about the new evidence?'

'The glove?'

'Yes, exactly. The glove. Maybe you would tell me how you found out about that. It's evidence which hasn't yet been made public.'

Sarah could have bitten her tongue off. She wasn't about to give Lynn away to this unappealing little man, detective or no detective. She said, 'Well, what about Mr Birkmyre? He has visited the Khan family. What was he telling?'

He gave a smug smile. 'Mr Birkmyre does not know about the glove, Miss Blane.'

Sarah raked the content of her conversation with Moira a few hours before. Had she mentioned the glove?

The eyebrows were jigging about. 'Who told you, is what I want to know?' He emphasised the 'you', leaving Sarah in no doubt that he wasn't referring to a general leaking of information.

She didn't answer.

Hamilton began to walk towards the door. 'Let me repeat. Withholding information is a serious offence in a criminal matter, Miss Blane.'

As she opened her mouth, the door swung closed.

In the staff-room Sarah nibbled a sandwich which tasted like mud. She had been drawn into this whole business to an astonishing degree. Had the glove been found before or after her car park meeting with David? She thought for a moment. It was definitely afterwards. She had met David after the school meeting, and before the news broke about the glove. She laid the plate on the work top and reached for her phone. The sooner she told DI Hamilton this the better. Then her fingers slackened on the keys. Phone. He would simply point out that she didn't need to see David to tell him about the glove.

She sighed and dropped her phone back into her bag. It made a solid clunk on the floor and she wondered if she'd broken it.

'Problems, Sarah?' Willie Armstrong raised his eyes from the book resting on the mound of his stomach.

They were the only two in the room this lunch hour. Judith had gone out, the supply teachers had gone to the cafeteria and Mary Stephens had gone home for lunch.

Sarah smiled. 'Not more than usual.'

He puffed out his cheeks. 'What a terrible business.'

'Willie? Do you…I mean…can you see David even being capable of doing something…so awful?'

He closed the book, then got up and switched on the kettle. There was already a half-full cup of tea on the arm of his chair. He tapped the spine of the book on his hand, and it made a doughy sound against his palm. 'How do we know what anyone is capable of?'

Sarah felt a chill at his words, then she had a vision of him struggling with the policeman. 'I saw you at Faslane on Sunday, by the way.' She spoke to his back as he waited for the kettle to boil. 'I didn't know you were into all that, Willie.'

He turned. The light was catching his glasses and she couldn't make out his eyes.

'I'll say it again. We can never tell what another person might do, Sarah.'

Sarah went home after school and indulged in a frenzy of cleaning. She had reached the stage where nothing and nobody seemed to make sense. Her brain felt as if it was being pushed through a sieve, bit by bit. Making order in her own house she could control.

She started by hauling down all the coats and jackets from the hall pegs. Two of them went into a bag for the charity shop and two went into the wardrobe. Opening the wardrobe triggered another bout of throwing out and the black bin bags filled rapidly. From there she went into the bathroom and disposed of every half-used shampoo, shower gel, and some elderly cosmetics. Then she scrubbed every fitting with so much cleaner that it made her eyes stream. With the bathroom assuredly antiseptic, it was the turn of the kitchen - out of date packets and tins joined the rest of the detritus, plus a few jars of jams and other condiments. Henry took refuge in the spare bedroom, obviously fearing to be next into the bin-bag. Finally she emptied the fruit bowl in amongst the rubbish. As she scoured the coffee pot to within an inch of its life the phone rang. So engrossed was she that she almost didn't hear it - and when she did, she looked at the clock. It was quarter past ten. She dried her shrivelled hands and picked up the phone. It was Mark.

'How was school?'

'School - was - hellish.'

'Oh, I'm sorry about that. Is the stuff about David all round?'

'Well, I'm sure it is, though none of the pupils said anything to me. But apart from Willie Armstrong suddenly coming over all philosophical, I had another visit to my classroom from your friend, DI Hamilton.' The name was squeezed through her clenched teeth.

'Steve Hamilton? He's not exactly my friend, but anyway, what did he want?'

'Only to accuse me of withholding important information about the chief suspect in this case. Not to mention passing him classified information about evidence.'

'Listen, Sarah. I can't think what it is about you, he acts as if you were some kind of accessory or something. But Steve Hamilton knows perfectly well that you don't have any real information or he'd be interviewing you in the station, not dropping into your room for a chat.'

'So why does he do it then?'

There was a silence. 'You know, a thought has just struck me. Is it possible that anyone has a grudge against you, maybe slipping ideas, however false or exaggerated, to our policeman friend?'

Sarah almost shouted; 'A grudge? God, of course not!'

'Not even a disaffected parent? Someone you've had a run-in with?'

She took a deep breath. 'No, Mark. I cannot imagine a single person in this town who would have any reason to make trouble for me.' She though fleetingly of Hakim Ashrif, but his family had enough problems of their own. While he would be desperate to see David Smythe behind bars for the murder of his cousin, she couldn't believe that he'd felt that degree of enmity towards her. Still, how could she tell? Maybe he thought that she could have saved Rubina?

She didn't sleep well that night in her pristine flat. It wasn't so much the smell of disinfectants and cleaners which kept her awake, but the unpleasant notion that someone might have her worst interests in mind. As she tried to drift into sleep she paraded the cast of her Helensburgh life through her mind. When she thought about them all, the school staff, pupils, neighbours - and those acquaintances she had made since she came to live there, she couldn't see any one of them in such a role. In fact, she jerked awake at the thought - the one person who really seemed to have disliked her from day one was the policeman - the same DI Hamilton. Maybe she just didn't show him enough respect, or something. She smiled into the darkness at that, and fell asleep.

But she woke in the morning with the name Keith Birkmyre on her lips. He didn't seem to be particularly fond of her either. She didn't know why. Her work was competent and she was never the subject of parental complaints, like some of her colleagues, so what was it? However, once in the shower she dismissed the idea, the Head didn't manifest much warmth and affection for any of his staff. In fact it was a blessing that he left her alone to get on with her job.

*

The following Sunday saw Mark and Sarah on the way to have lunch with Mark's parents. Whatever was going on in the hunt for Rubina's killer, nothing was being made public. DNA test results must have been available, but if the police had found anything damning in the Khan family no-one yet seemed to be 'helping the police with their inquiries.' The Clarion was making much of the fact that David Smythe was still in hospital in Sri Lanka, but was treading carefully as far as accusations went.

Initially reluctant, Sarah had been persuaded by Mark that the trip to Skelmorlie would do her good: give her a break from the intense atmosphere of Helensburgh, school and town. Apart from his prominent identity as a local teacher, Colin Smythe's son was big news.

'It's nice,' Mark said. 'It's the seaside.'

Sarah laughed, 'It's just the other side of the estuary from Helensburgh!'

'Ah, but it's closer to the sea.'

In the end she had given in, and although slightly apprehensive now that it was close, she was looking forward with interest to meeting Mark's parents.

They lived in a blindingly white bungalow on the seafront, with open views of the Firth of Clyde. Skelmorlie was fresh and clean-looking, and almost entirely residential.

Mark's mother led Sarah to the sun-porch at the front of the house. 'At least it's bright today, but in the summer it's just bliss to sit here and watch the sailing - and sometimes the most wonderful sunsets. It's our retiral home, of course, after too long in the hurly burly of the city. 'What about you? Do you enjoy living in Helensburgh?'

Sarah smiled. Mrs McKenzie was making it easy. She was a fine-looking woman with the same, almost perfect symmetry in her features as Mark, and with a cap of silver hair which had once been as dark as her son's, she guessed.

'It's all right. I love my flat, and the school is - well the school is just like any other big secondary these days, but I enjoy my subject.'

'And how did you and Mark meet?'

Sarah's heart jumped. She was on the point of mentioning Rubina's death, but thought better of it. It would strike a very discordant note in this scenario.

She was about to devise an answer when Mark came in, followed by his father with glasses of sherry on a tray. Sarah was surprised at how father and son differed: Mark's father was a big, shaggy man with tufts of grey hair making a tonsure for his otherwise bald head. He had a ruddy complexion which would have suggested a love of sailing which he had not passed on to his son, had Mark not told her that now he spent all his days in the garden. On the Clyde coast that too could produce a weathered complexion.

'Prying already, Mother,' Mark said, smiling. 'If you must know, I met Sarah months ago through some work I was doing in her part of the world, ok?' He bent to kiss his mother on the cheek.

His mother patted Mark's arm. 'Forgive me, Sarah, nosey old mum that I am.' She got out of her wicker chair. 'Now you just sit there and enjoy your sherry while I put the finishing touches to lunch.'

It was a traditional Sunday lunch of roast beef and all that went with it. Sarah enjoyed the food and found the conversation with all three McKenzies interesting and enjoyable, to the extent that she was relaxed and slightly sleepy when it was time for coffee. Mark served Sarah and his mother in the sun-porch, then, with his father he went off to clear the table in the dining room and stack the dishwasher.

Anne McKenzie looked out at the water, 'You know,

Sarah, I haven't seen Mark look this …good…for a long time.'

Her words awoke Sarah. 'We're …really just friends you know.'

His mother turned, eyebrows slightly raised, and gave Sarah a calculating look. 'That's fine. Whatever, it's a friendship which seems to be making him happy.'

'We...ell.'

'You know about Sally, of course?'

Sarah nodded. 'Yes, Mark told me.'

Anne McKenzie shook her head. 'It was so cruel. Did he tell you that she refused treatment, because she was pregnant and she didn't want to harm the baby?'

Sarah felt a lump in her throat. 'No, not that.'

'The baby didn't survive.' Her voice took on the cadence of things told many times. 'They'd been together from school. Then they married, and after a few years Sally became pregnant.' She paused. 'It was all so perfect...then she got the cancer.' She went back to looking out of the window. 'We thought Mark would never get over it.'

Sarah said, 'Mrs McKenzie...Anne...I'm so sorry. It must have been unbearably difficult for you too...'

Anne McKenzie blinked a couple of times, then turned back with a smile. 'So, Sarah, you will appreciate how pleased we are to see him with someone like you...and beginning to look happy again.'

Sarah nodded. 'Yes.'

'Anyway,' his mother jumped to her feet. 'I must show you some pictures of my American grandchildren...they live in California...'

In the car, on the way back to Helensburgh, Sarah said, 'I like your parents.'

Mark smiled, and reached for her hand. 'And they like you.'

'Mark? There's something I need to say…'

He glanced at her. 'That sounds ominous.'

'It's not, but I want to say it.' Sarah took a deep breath, 'If…this…friendship or whatever…is to …flourish, I need to apologise for the dreadful things I said the day we went to see Sheila Macdonald'

'It didn't matter.' he said, quietly.

'It did matter. It mattered enormously. I was so caught up in my own…pain I suppose… that I had to lash out. I think, as I saw it, you were making me confront…my loss.'

A sudden squall of rain hit the windscreen as they crossed Erskine Bridge.

Sarah went on, 'I just want you to know how very sorry I am about that day. It was unforgivable.'

Mark didn't answer as he drove on to the A82. Then he said 'You know, I've thought about it since.

'Perhaps you weren't entirely wrong. Acting with you, let's face it, on something which was so important to you, gave me a focus - you had scars too, I suppose. Maybe it was a bit of a crusade for me…' he reached for her hand again. 'But not now. Now I just want to be with you, Sarah Blane.'

In the darkened car Sarah felt her body glow, and she was sure that if he looked Mark would be able to see it - like a halo round the moon. It made her feel safe. So what if someone was planting odd ideas in the head of Steve Hamilton, Sarah knew that she had Mark , and Mark was security. In fact, she admitted to herself now, she hadn't quite told his mother the truth. It seemed her relationship with Mark was rapidly heading past the friendship stage, and it felt right.

*

Sarah was in her room reading the poetry of Robert Burns with a third year class.

'So, what do you think he meant when he said the mouse was 'blest' because 'the present only toucheth thee'?'

A hand shot up. It was, as ever, Jason Smith - a thin, intense youngster, who took his education very seriously, if his constant enthusiasm were genuine. In spite of herself Sarah sometimes wished, just once, that he wasn't so quick off the mark with an answer. 'All right, please tell us, Jason' she said, a little wearily.

'Miss, Robert Burns meant that the mouse, because it was just an animal, couldn't think about the past or the future the way he could, and that made it lucky, because sometimes it's better not to know what's going to happen next.'

Sarah smiled. 'That's about it, Jason.' She scanned the faces before her. Last period in an over-heated classroom and her charges were looking distinctly droopy. 'Come on, someone else, is it ever better not to know what's going to happen next?'

The door opened, and some pupils giggled. Pleased to see they did not lack a sense of irony at least, she turned to see Moira beckoning. Her face was chalk white. 'Come and see me after the bell,' she mouthed at Sarah, then withdrew.

Sarah felt guilty: the rest of the lesson was carried out with less than her complete attention. Something serious must have happened, to have Moira looking like that.

The Head came striding towards her as she approached Moira's room, and she had a fleeting memory of her strange thoughts about him; almost confirmed when he seemed about to pass without acknowledging her, but at the last minute he nodded. 'Miss Blane.' He too, looked rather green about the gills, and Sarah hoped that they hadn't lost another pupil to drugs.

Moira was staring out of the window of her office when Sarah entered. When she turned, her usual air of urgency was gone. She nibbled at a thumbnail.

'What's happened, Moira?'

The deputy wandered over and sat behind her desk. 'David Smythe is home.' She said it mechanically, as if she couldn't quite believe what she was saying.

Sarah's breath caught in her throat. 'Oh, God. Has he been arrested yet?'

Moira shook her head. Her dark curls swirled around her face. 'He didn't do it.'

'What?' Overwhelming relief swept over Sarah. 'That's wonderful. How do they know?'

'Something about DNA - no match or whatever.' Moira sunk her head between her hands.

'But…Moira…this is great news, is it not?'

The other woman removed her hands from her face. 'Not when the police are about to start testing all kinds of people here.'

Sarah sat down with a thump on the office chair.

'Here? You mean in the school?'

Moira nodded, 'Every boy over sixteen, and every man who ever came into contact with Rubina. Even Bobby.'

'The janitor!' A trickle of sweat ran down between Sarah's breasts. 'Does this mean that the Khan family have been exonerated?'

'They must have been. DI Hamilton came in to break the news. He didn't seem very pleased about any of it.'

'No, he thought he had his culprit, didn't he?' The pieces were taking time to fall into place. 'And is David…do you know how he is?'

Moira shook her head. 'We haven't got that far yet. Anyway, Mary Stephens will be over the moon, as they say.

Her golden boy is innocent.'

Sarah managed to smile. 'She's never been anything else since he was found. He's been innocent all the way for Mary.'

Moira's lips curved. 'Bully for Mary.'

'So, when will they start? With the testing?'

Moira shrugged. 'They have to wait until all the parents have been informed. But they're talking about doing the testing here, in the medical room, rather than going round the homes. Can you imagine it? The place will be drowning in angry parents.'

'And angry teachers.'

Her thoughts went once again to Roger Bullough, and she wondered if the testing would be sufficiently thorough to net all the males connected to the school, or if she would have to carry out her threat to bring it to police attention. It was something she had more or less dismissed, since David seemed so squarely in the frame for Rubina's murder. But now all bets were off. She felt slightly sick. However, if the police did have to be informed of Roger Bullough's antics, she had no intention of being the messenger. She would almost prefer it that Roger would escape the testing than give DI Hamilton the pleasure of humiliating her again.

Mary Stephens was alone in the staff-room when Sarah went to collect her coat and her briefcase. Her head was bent over a pile of exercise books and she didn't look up when Sarah went in.

'Oh, Mary, I didn't expect you still to be here. I thought you'd be off celebrating the good news about David.'

When the other woman raised her head Sarah was shocked to see that her face was pale as it had ever been, her eyes were red and her nose looked raw.

Mary drew a handkerchief out of her cardigan pocket and rubbed it over her face.

'What's wrong?' Sarah sat down next to her. 'I thought you'd be thrilled about David.'

A new flood of tears erupted, sliding to and fro on her face as Mary shook her head violently. 'I am...thrilled. That he's home. But,' the tears flew like spray at the speed of her shaking head. 'he's seriously ill.'

'Oh.' In the euphoria produced in Sarah by David's innocence, she had forgotten how sickly he was before he ran off.

She racked her brains for something that would temper Mary's agony. 'Would it help if I took you to see him?' She knew from staff-room conversations that Mary had a car, bought for the purpose of taking her mother on outings. But she never brought it to school. Sarah suspected that she was actually a reluctant driver.

The other woman continued to shake her head, as if now she'd started, she couldn't stop. 'He's not at home.'

'Then where...?'

'His father arranged for him to be taken straight to a private nursing home. Celia says ...it's all been too much for him, the police and everything.' The crying turned to sobs. Sarah sat there rubbing Mary's back. She couldn't recall a time when she felt more useless.

'Well, at least, Mary, let me take you home.'

*

But when time passed with no sign of the DNA testing starting in the school and no indication that parents were being notified, Moira admitted that she was baffled. However, since Keith Birkmyre was liaising with the police and had not chosen to confide in his deputy, Moira was making a point of simply getting on with her job.

'I'll find out soon enough, when we get to the nasty bits.'

David Smythe was still in his mysterious private clinic, and Mary Stephens had gone very quiet again.

On the Thursday evening after their trip Sarah was expecting Mark for dinner. The weekend had been a success. They had treated it as an opportunity just to spend time together, walking, sight-seeing, enjoying evenings in front of a log fire while they ate and drank and talked about everything that defined them as people. They had barely touched on the troubling state of affairs in Helensburgh. Neither, by an unspoken understanding, had they mentioned Ruth. By the end of the weekend Sarah had come to the happy conclusion that they had much more in common than their personal tragedies.

She had prepared the steaks, and was chopping mushrooms and onions when the buzzer sounded. Wiping her hands on a tea-towel, she went out to the hall, thinking as she did so that perhaps it was time to let Mark have a key. But when she pressed the button to release the door it wasn't his voice she heard. She listened, but, so garbled were the speaker's words that it was some time before she realised that it was Mohammed Ashrif. She opened the door.

When he came into the flat he was breathing heavily. His skin was damp and his hair was sticking up as if he'd been dragging his fingers through it.

'Mohammed, what is it? Come on. Sit down.' She guided him to the sofa and he collapsed into it, covering his face with his hands.

She stood, non-plussed for an instant, then she went into the kitchen and poured a glass of water.

'Here,' She held out the water. 'Try to calm down.

What is it? Mohammed?'

The boy removed his hands. He looked up at her as if he had difficulty focussing, and when he spoke, his voice was thick and she knew he'd been crying.

'My brother has been arrested.'

'Hakim? What for?' Sarah sat down on the leather chair, level with Mohammed. 'For...murdering ...Rubina!' The words exploded out of him as if they were poison, and his mouth twisted. 'My father has been there all day and they won't tell him anything!'

'What?...but...no, that can't be right, Mohammed, the police they've ... the tests...were...' Her words dribbled away as she thought how no-one seemed to know what was happening in this investigation. After all, there had been no further mention of DNA testing in Fruin High.

Sarah noticed that she was still holding the glass of water. 'Take this, then tell me what has happened.' She shook her head, 'I just can't believe what I'm hearing. Why on earth have they arrested Hakim?'

Mohammed took a few sips of water, then gulped for breath.

'Take your time.'

The boy fumbled in the pocket of anorak then, producing an inhaler, sucked at it a couple of times. He held it up to Sarah, 'Asthma.'

She said, 'I know. Quite a few pupils have them.' She waited while his breath settled.

'They ...the police, say they have ...new evidence...'

'Now? What new evidence? I mean...there wasn't...your family, seemed to ...'

She realised she was babbling. 'Anyway, they had him in before, and let him go didn't they?'

Mohammed nodded.

Unsure of police procedure Sarah was reluctant to ask if Hakim had actually been charged with the murder of his cousin, or if this was a repeat of the previous arrest. She was trying to frame the question when it occurred to her to wonder why Mohammed had come to her.

'And...how can I help, Mohammed?'

He laid the water glass on the coffee table. 'We, my uncle...and...we wondered if you would be able to tell us more about this...'

Sarah spread her hands. 'Me? I mean, how would I know any more than ...your family?'

'We thought that, Mark McKenzie... your friend, he can find out things. Lynn told me that he does investigations into...stuff?'

Sarah smiled. 'He's a journalist, Mohammed, he's not a policeman.' She spoke gently, conscious of the boy's febrile state. 'Sometimes he does find things out, it's true but,' she shook her head, 'I don't think he could help with this.'

Mohammed's shoulders bowed, as if in defeat, then he nodded, and got up from the sofa. 'I understand. I'm sorry for troubling you.'

Just as Sarah became conscious that an inordinate amount of smoke was coming from the grill, the door buzzer sounded. She waved at Mohammed to press the button while she turned off the gas, and the smoke alarm went off with a frenzied screech. The cat shot out of the room.

When Mark came into the flat Sarah and the boy were flapping tea-towels at the alarm. He stood there for a few moments, bemused, until the wailing stopped.

Waving trails of smoke away, Sarah opened the living-room window. Cold air and traffic noises entered the room, and she pulled it down again, leaving a couple of inches open to the night.

Mark said, 'That was quite a welcome! Mohammed, isn't it?' He nodded at the boy's anorak. 'Are you coming or going?'

Sarah spoke from the kitchen, 'He was just about to go, but I think he should stay and speak to you.' She pointed with a kitchen knife. 'Sit down, Mohammed and tell Mark what you've just told me.'

'Actually,' Mark said, 'I think I know already. It's about Hakim's arrest, isn't it?'

The boy's eyebrows shot up. 'See, I told you, he knows things.' He sat down again on the sofa, next to Mark.

Sarah came to sit on the leather rocker, supper preparations abandoned. 'What have you heard, Mark? Why Hakim?'

'What have the police told your family, Mohammed?'

The boy shook his head. 'Just that there is new evidence.'

Mark chewed a little at his bottom lip. 'That's true, I'm afraid.'

Sarah said, 'But what new evidence?'

Mark looked from one to the other, then he said, 'The police found the other glove. On the loch shore.'

'What?' Sarah rocked on her chair. 'It certainly took them long enough!'

Mark smiled. 'Loch Lomond is twenty-eight miles long, Sarah - that's a lot of shore.'

'But what's this glove got to do with my brother?'

'I know. It sounds really strange. But,' he leaned towards Mohammed, 'it seems that there are traces of Hakim's DNA on this glove, and Rubina's, of course.'

'But that's impossible!' The boy got up and paced to the window, as if he needed some of the cold air which was filtering through the gap. 'Hakim never wears gloves -

never! And he would not hurt Rubina, he would never hurt Rubina!'

He came back and collapsed on to the sofa, covering his face with his hands. Mark looked at Sarah as same thought crossed both their minds - hadn't Mohammed suspected that his brother might have done that very thing a few short months before?

'Rubina's DNA was also found in Hakim's car that time, when they examined it.'

Mohammed slowly removed his hands from his face. He nodded. 'Hakim told me, but it was okay. Rubina had gone with him and my Uncle Anwar in the car just a few days before...before. They had gone to Glasgow to buy some supplies for my aunt - it is difficult to get the right ingredients in Helensburgh for proper Asian cooking. Rubina was often in Hakim's car, we all are. My uncle told the police this, and they believed... But this glove?'

When the boy left, Sarah half-heartedly returned to her wilting vegetables, while Mark poured two glasses of red wine.

'You know, of course, that I'd just told Mohammed that you couldn't possibly have any information about Hakim, then in you come and it turns out you know everything! How do you do it, Mr Holmes?'

'Elementary, my dear Sarah.' He clinked his glass against hers. 'Actually, I ran into our mutual friend, Wilson Toner,'

Sarah snorted.

'And he wanted to crow. Apparently they found this out few days ago, and were sitting on it until they were sure. Hakim's arrest will be in the Clarion tomorrow.' He shrugged. 'I hate to disappoint you, but it's not down to my sleuthing, after all.'

'Now we know why the testing didn't happen in the

school.' The steaks spat a little as she turned them under the grill. 'Keith and Moira are going to be very relieved.' She passed a bowl of salad to Mark and pointed to the table. 'But still, I feel terrible for the Khans. Rubina's own cousin?'

As they ate they tried to talk of other things but in spite of it, kept coming back to the implications of Hakim's arrest.

'You know, if he never normally wore gloves, according to Mohammed, he must have bought some. That looks like premeditation. So, honour killing after all, you think, Mark?'

He laid down his fork. 'It's beginning to look that way, isn't it? We know that it isn't Hakim in that photograph, but maybe he found out who it was.'

'Yes, maybe he did.' Sarah got up to fetch the cheese and the coffee pot. 'But, wait, didn't he have an alibi for the night Rubina disappeared? It was Hakim who told us that David Smythe was in Glasgow that night, because he was there too.'

'But he could still have made it back to Helensburgh in time to meet Rubina when she came home from the theatre.'

Sarah poured the coffee. 'Ye-es, but didn't we also agree that she wouldn't have a secret meeting with Hakim lined up?'

'Mmm…' Mark broke a piece of biscuit. 'Highly unlikely, but not impossible. In fact, it's possible that he followed her when she went to her secret meeting.'

'But,' Sarah paused, a morsel of cheese on the edge of her knife. 'wasn't Hakim the one beating a path to the police station every day to find out when David Smythe was going to be charged?'

'Camouflage perhaps?'

'I don't know, Mark, I just don't feel very good

about this. Has Hakim actually been charged yet?'

'That, Wilson Toner couldn't tell me. But if he's still in custody he must be charged by now. They can only hold someone for six hours, after all.'

'Mohammed said they'd picked him up at eight o'clock this morning.'

Chapter 13

The news that Hakim Ashrif had been charged with the murder of his cousin, Rubina Khan, dawned on Helensburgh like a new day. An honour killing, while sensational in itself, was nevertheless a very particular kind of crime. While some might have felt guilty about it, the relief in the town was palpable. Hakim was in prison in Glasgow awaiting trial, and his father's business closed its doors. Whether they would ever open again was a matter of speculation around town, but there were plenty of shops in Glasgow.

The parents of teenage girls breathed a little more freely. And for the moment at least, drugs, while still a live issue in the town, had ceased to be a problem in Fruin High.

In the school itself the atmosphere began to lighten considerably. Moira looked less and less like the ghost of Christmas past and Keith Birkmyre was almost cheerful. Snowdrops were pushing through the earth in the flower-beds which edged the school playground, and the days were slowly but surely lengthening. In spite of themselves, the young people in the school were forgetting about Rubina. Lynn and Leslie's crusade to find the stranger in the photograph had perforce been abandoned, and they were preparing for the exams which would start in a matter of weeks.

Even in the English department there were signs of recovery: Roger Bullough had come back to work part-time, and while it didn't relieve Judith Aitken of all administrative tasks, his return to work appeared to improve her demeanour. And as a bonus, she was to be free of David Smythe for good, when the word came that he had resigned from his post in the school. He was home, according to Mary, and she was a little happier now that he was within visiting distance.

It was lunch-time when Roger broke the news to Sarah, while everyone was in the staff-room.

'He's resigned! But that's a shame.' Sarah said. 'Should I go and see him, do you think, Mary?'

Willie Armstrong put down his newspaper and removed the cold pipe from his mouth, waiting it seemed, for a reaction. Judith simply shook her head gently at Sarah as if to wonder why anyone would want to do such a thing, while Roger studied the inside of his teacup.

Mary's eyes skittered from one to the other of her colleagues. 'Oh...eh...I really couldn't say. He's still not at all well.'

Sarah became aware that the temperature in the room was dropping by the second. 'Oh, I see ...well...maybe I'll think about it.'

When the bell rang for the afternoon session she went back to her classroom, wondering if there was something about David Smythe that everyone knew except her. She was an outsider after all, last into the department, knowing only what she had been told about past events. The tension puzzled her, all the same, especially since Rubina Khan's murderer was safely behind bars, thereby removing all taint of suspicion from Fruin High.

After school, when Sarah called in to the pet shop in Helensburgh to buy Henry's preferred cat food, she was surprised to find herself standing next to Judith at the counter.

'Oh, hello - Judith, I've never seen you in here before, Have you acquired a pet?'

The shop was small and as Sarah stepped back to let another customer squeeze between them, she bumped into a box and almost lost her balance. There was a loud nerve-wracking squeak, and she was scared to look down at whatever squashy thing was suffering, until Judith bent and retrieved it from under Sarah's foot.

She held up an orange plastic hamburger. 'No animals were harmed in the making of this purchase.'

She was laughing, and Sarah laughed too.

Judith went on, 'No, I haven't suddenly acquired a pet. It's my next door neighbour. She's got flu' and I said I'd pick up some shopping for her on my way home.' She held up a packet. 'This is for her budgie.'

They left the shop together and walked to the car park. But as Sarah reached her car Judith put a hand on her arm. 'Listen, Sarah, could I have a word?'

A chill wind whistled through the tunnels created by the lines of parked cars, and Sarah shivered. 'Yes, of course.'

'Look.' Judith waved her purchase, 'Why don't we put this stuff in the car and go for a coffee. I'd really like to speak to you.'

Surprise as much as anything led Sarah to nod. 'Right, I'll be with you in a minute.' As she put the bag of cat food in the boot of her car she wondered what Judith wanted to say. It was a complete departure for her taciturn colleague to suggest a cosy chat over a cup of coffee. She shrugged as she banged down the boot lid. It couldn't hurt to get to know Judith better, if that's what she had in mind.

They walked to a bar and restaurant a couple of blocks away. Coffee shops in the town tended to close early, but coffee was served all day in the bar. As they walked Sarah reflected that much further and she would be almost home. Still, it was worth it to have a decent talk with Judith.

She'd been civil enough since Sarah came to the school, but she'd never been all that friendly.

Settled on comfortable sofas in the lounge, which had few customers at this point in late afternoon, Judith chatted to Sarah about school matters while they waited for the coffee.

'By the way, how do you get on with Keith Birkmyre?'

Sarah said. 'Well, we haven't crossed swords, but I never feel that comfortable with him. He's...stand-offish, I suppose you'd say.'

Judith nodded. 'I know. He doesn't do well with women actually, haven't you noticed?'

'Noticed? No, I was more inclined to think it was personal.'

'Take it from me, it's not. Our Keith is a bit of a misogynist, I'm afraid.'

Sarah laughed. 'Well, now you come to mention it...'

Judith smiled. 'You might think it's because I live with my girlfriend, Rosalie - you knew that, didn't you - but it's not that. None of the female teachers seems to find favour with the Head.'

'As long as it doesn't stretch to actual discrimination, I don't suppose there's much to be done.' She nodded. 'And yes, I knew about Rosalie.'

It wasn't until the waiter had brought their drinks, and asked if there was anything else, that Judith got to the point. She scooped chocolate off the top of her cappuccino, licked the spoon, and said.

'I'll be honest, Sarah, I wouldn't be doing this if David Smythe hadn't resigned.'

Sarah looked up from adding milk to her black coffee, 'Really?'

242

'Oh, I don't mean that I wouldn't have a coffee with you - sorry - no, I wouldn't be having this conversation if I thought he was coming back to the department.'

Sarah waited, cup half-way to her mouth, her eyebrows raised.

Judith continued to play with the coffee, swirling the foam around with her spoon. Her dark fringe of hair fell over her eyes and she pushed it back with her other hand.

'It's not easy to say this, but you must be aware that David was the darling of the department?'

'Well, for Mary, certainly.'

Judith sighed. 'Mary, yes. But the others, Willie and Roger, even Moira at times, wouldn't hear a word against him.'

Sarah laid her cup in the saucer. 'But, I don't understand. Why should there be anything against him? He seemed to me to pull his weight in the department before...all this.'

Judith's spoon clattered on to the table. 'Oh, he pulled more than his weight! He pulled every senior girl in the school! It wasn't just Rubina Khan, you know.'

Sarah felt a jolt of surprise at Judith's anger. The fleeting thought returned that perhaps she was jealous of David's success with girls? She hesitated, unsure of her response. Had Judith suggested this meeting just to let off steam?

'Well, at least we won't have any more of that, now David has resigned.'

Judith leaned back on the sofa. 'You must think I'm a real bitch.'

'Why would I think that?'

The other woman sat forward again. 'Okay, I'll tell you. After David Smythe found out that I was gay he was very cool towards me, almost hostile, in fact. It didn't

243

matter,' she smiled. 'the golden boy held no temptation for me, but it could be difficult to work with him at times. I tried to ignore it, until I found out something which really brought matters to a head.'

Sarah leaned back on her sofa while she listened.

'One night, more than a year ago, before you came, Rosalie and I were in a nightclub in Glasgow. And we saw David Smythe.' She swept her fringe aside and looked intently at Sarah. 'A club, all right?'

Sarah nodded. 'A club, yes.'

Judith placed her elbows on the low table in front of her. 'Do I have to spell it out for you?'

Sarah sat up. 'What are you saying?'

'I'm saying it's a club for gays and lesbians.'

'But David, he's not...'

Judith sat back. 'Aha! That's what everyone thinks. And that's why I get so damned angry.'

Sarah said, 'But, Judith, if what you say is true, why would he need to hide it? I mean, all that...it's out in the open these days, surely?'

Judith laughed. 'Not if you are the heir to the Colin Smythe fortune - and Daddy hates all deviants. You name it - he hates it - and he makes no secret of the fact.'

Sarah was astonished. 'Does...anyone else know?'

She shook her head. 'No. He made me promise I wouldn't say anything about him being there, in case it got back to his father. He'd said he'd never been in the club before, but the guy he was with had insisted. It was his birthday, or some damned thing. And it was just David's bad luck that I happened to be there that night.'

Sarah thought of Mary Stephens' boast that David was too sophisticated to find his amusements in Helensburgh.

'But what about all those girls?

'Camouflage.'

It was the word Mark had used about Hakim.

'Why are you telling me all this, Judith?'

She opened her hands. 'Just to be fair. I know I've been pretty grouchy in the department since you came, but it's not easy knowing this, and listening to all the drivel about wonderful David. You can't tell me that Willie and Roger don't suspect anything? Not that poor sap Mary, she just adores him, but men can always tell, I'm sure. And they're so bloody hypocritical about it, playing along with the mockery of removing that girl from his class and all that. Absolute hypocrisy!' She shook her head. 'Rubina Khan was never in any danger from David Smythe.'

'But wait a minute, Judith. David was in a terrible state about Rubina. He was sure he'd be blamed.'

Judith went on shaking her head. 'Sarah. You're such an innocent. More likely he was terrified that when the police started looking into his lifestyle…'

Sarah remembered her visit that Sunday morning, and David's sailing pictures. There was not one girl in any of them.

'But, the suicide attempt? And why did he run away?'

Judith was gathering up her handbag. 'I suppose you'll have to ask him that.'

Sarah fed the cat so absently that she put the food and the water in the wrong bowls - much to Henry's disgust, which he made plain by sticking his tail in the air and marching off.

'Okay…okay…I'll change them back.'

Henry sat on the arm of the sofa and watched over the counter as Sarah changed the bowls around, washing the food out of the wrong bowl before filling it again with fresh water. Only when all was as it should be did the cat deign to jump down and begin to eat.

Sarah's mind was on David. The further away from Judith's assertions she got the harder it was to believe them. She just couldn't see David as gay. And, for all Judith's suggestions, she couldn't go asking Roger or Willie what they thought; that was out of the question. Mark might have been able to tell her but he had never met David. Anyway, she asked herself, what business was it of hers? Besides, he wasn't under suspicion for Rubina any more, possibly never had been by anyone except herself and Keith Birkmyre. He had seemed eager enough to accept David's guilt, especially when it looked like solving the drugs problem.

And now she thought of it, Steve Hamilton had obviously known perfectly well when he was putting pressure on her that David Smythe had nothing to do with Rubina's death. Almost the first thing the police had done when he disappeared was to go through his flat with a fine tooth comb. If they hadn't found any evidence there what did the DI hope to gain by badgering her?

By the time she'd finished her evening meal Sarah had resolved to go and see David. She'd been his friend before all this started, and she was his friend still. She reckoned he must be feeling pretty awful now, sick, out of a job and deserted by his colleagues, except Mary. Sarah smiled to imagine Mary's reaction to Judith's suspicions about David if they were ever to come out.

If Sarah had been shocked before by David Smythe's appearance prior to his disappearing act, she was horrified now. Mary Stephens' darling had become a sad specimen. It was little wonder she had been so distraught that day.

He led her into his sitting room, then stood in front of her while she sat down. 'Don't even try to hide it, Sarah, I know how I look.'

The place was stifling; Sarah loosened the collar of

her coat, then said the first thing that came into her mind. 'I'm sorry about your resignation, David.'

He threw himself into another chair, an exotically patterned throw sliding almost to the floor. 'Oh that? It seemed like the best thing.' He placed both hands on his chest. 'I could hardly turn up in school looking like this, could I?'

Sarah sat on the edge of her seat. 'But surely you will get better, David?'

He smiled, but she could see no humour in it. 'Who knows?' He got out of the chair, catching the silky cloth with his foot and kicking it aside. 'Drink?'

She nodded, and didn't speak while he went to the side table and the bottles. 'G&T as I seem to remember.'

She nodded again.

As he handed her the glass Sarah's eyes were drawn to the long sleeves of his sweater, but there was no sign of damage to the wrist that she could see.

'Anyway, where were we?' he said. 'Yes, when I get better. Well, when I do, I'll be out of here for good.' He jerked his head in the direction of the main house. 'Father and I have never hit it off too well, but my latest…escapade as he likes to call it, has been the last straw.'

Sarah took a deep breath. 'Why…?'

'Did I run away?' He took a long mouthful of alcohol, then looked her straight in the eye. 'Panic.'

'Panic?'

He shrugged. 'I thought I was being set up…you know…for Rubina Khan.'

'But why would anyone do that? Anyway, surely running away made it worse?'

David laughed. 'Well, at the time it did. But I wasn't thinking straight. You know what had happened with Rubina in the past? Then I knew I'd been seen in Glasgow that

Friday night when I'd said I was off on holiday.'

Sarah laid down her glass. 'How do you know you were seen? Did you meet someone from the school?'

He shook his head. 'Worse than that. It was Hakim Ashrif. He came to see me when I came back from holiday and told me Rubina was missing.' He rubbed a hand across his mouth. 'It was terrible. I tried to tell him I'd been away, then he dropped his bombshell. He'd seen me going into...a club in Glasgow.'

Sarah knew that much at least was true. Hakim had told her the same story.

'Then, when she turned up...Oh God, I didn't know what to do...you know that, Sarah. That policeman...what's his name...'

'Steve Hamilton'

'Yes, him - he came round hinting at all kinds of things....and then my father...'

The sweat was standing out on his forehead.

'Surely your father couldn't believe you had anything to do with it?'

He smiled again, sadly this time. 'You'd think so, wouldn't you?' He heaved a sigh. 'I'm afraid I've been a disappointment to him. Not interested in cars, not interested in wheeling and dealing, or rubbing shoulders with all the celebrity golfers, footballers, wags...you name it.' He gazed across the room. 'I'm sure you know the scenario...no son of his...'

Sarah didn't wait for him to end the sentence. 'You know that it's Hakim who has been arrested for Rubina's murder.'

This time the smile was genuine. 'Couldn't happen to a nicer chap!'

'So, you think he did it?'

He stopped with his glass half-way to his mouth.

'And you don't?'

Sarah pulled her collar away from her neck. 'I'm just not sure.'

She jumped back when David Smythe sat bolt upright in the chair. 'You're ..not sure...what the hell does that mean?' He waved his hand at her. 'It was an honour killing - plain and simple. Rubina wanted to be like other girls, free to make her own choices - have male friends like any other teenage girl, and they wouldn't let her. So,' he snapped his fingers. 'her dear cousin gets rid of her, saves embarrassment all round.'

He stared at her, hollow-eyed, his pallor disappearing as his face flushed.

For a long moment Sarah stared back, made wordless by his outburst. 'What...David...what do you know about Rubina's ...male friends?'

The flush faded and he got up to refill the glasses. Sarah shook her head.

'David?'

He shrugged, his back to her as he poured gin into his glass. 'Lynn...Lynn spoke to me.'

'When?'

He turned, and the flush returned to his skin. 'For God's sake, Sarah, what is this? An interrogation? You're as bad as that policeman. I don't know - before I went off...'

He returned to his chair. 'I don't know when it was...before I ...left. I met her in the street, and she said something about Rubina having a friend...'

Sarah got up, fastening her coat. 'I've got to go. But maybe you would tell me one thing, David.'

He smiled up at her.

'Why would Lynn tell you that Rubina had a 'friend' as you put it? She had given Rubina her word and it took a lot of persuasion to get her to open up about it.'

He didn't answer but got up out of the chair and escorted Sarah to the door. When he opened it cold air blasted in from the outside landing. The contrast to the heat of the flat was so great Sarah shivered.

'For example, did she show you the photograph?'

'What photograph?'

'I'm really puzzled, David. Why, exactly, did she choose to tell you about Rubina's friend?'

'You'd best ask Lynn that, hadn't you?' he said, as he closed the door.

As she made her way home Sarah reflected that twice in one day she had been told the same thing, ask the person concerned. She'd tried to do that with David Smythe, but she hadn't got very far. His demeanour was so changed from the David she thought she knew that it had been like talking to a stranger. She'd intended to get him to open up about his sexuality, and show some understanding, and she was sure he was about to when he spoke of his father, but her ill-timed remarks about Hakim had obviously put a stop to that.

By the time she was climbing the stairs to the flat she'd made up her mind, she would ask Lynn.

But all thoughts of speaking to Lynn were driven out when the phone call came.

It was Mark. 'Sarah...I've had a call from John Phillips' For a second the name didn't mean anything as her mind lingered on David Smythe.

'John Phillips?....oh yes...the chip shop...what...?'

'Actually he wanted your phone number, but I needed to speak to you first.' The cat had come to sit by her and she ran her hand over the smooth fur of his back. 'Well...?'

She heard Mark sigh, 'It might be nothing, but he thought you should know...'

Unease crept into her. 'Know what, Mark?'

Her own breath sounded loud in the mouthpiece as she waited for his reply.

'It's...you remember we saw some demolition work going on when we were in Leith that time? The old tenements?'

'Uh-huh...'

'John thought you should know...they found... something...Oh shit! I can't do this, I'm coming down.'

She looked at the clock. 'Mark, it's after ten!'

'I don't care - I'll be there in half an hour.'

'But what is it...what...?'

He'd hung up.

Only when Henry complained and jumped off the sofa did Sarah realise that she had been gripping his fur to the point of hurting him. She patted his head in apology and fetched the gin from the cupboard and a couple of cans of tonic from the fridge. The dull ache in her stomach told her Mark wasn't going to be the bearer of good news. She clinked ice into the glass, poured herself a large measure and waited, frozen in place, until she heard Mark's voice on the intercom.

One look at his face as he came into the flat confirmed bad news to come. Before he spoke he folded her into his arms and hugged her tightly. The zip of his jacket scraped her face as she pulled away.

'What is it?'

He sat down and she handed him a drink. 'There's no easy way to tell you this. The demolition squad found a body in one of the houses.'

She refilled her glass without looking at him. 'So?'

'Sarah, come and sit down, please.'

She sat opposite him on the leather rocker. 'But...what's it to do with me?'

He smiled and reached for her hand. His voice was soft. 'It's... a female.'

'And..?'

'It seems she's been there for more than twenty years.'

'And he...the man...' his name had left her. 'thinks it might be...'

Mark nodded, 'Ruth. Yes.'

She set the chair to rocking and the leather squeaked in tandem with her movements.

'But he said it might be nothing.'

'I know. He really just wanted to warn you - it will be on the news tomorrow - in the papers, you know how it is. They won't be able to identify her right away, but they'll be checking the missing person files, and her name will come up...' His words died away as he got up from the sofa and removed the glass that was drooping from Sarah's hand. 'I think you need tea more than gin.'

'What should I do, Mark?'

She stayed in the chair while he busied himself in the kitchen. She knew her legs wouldn't support her if she tried to get up. The news that she'd dreaded for twenty-three years had arrived. Although, maybe not. Thousands went missing every year, you only had to watch television to know that.

Mark brought the mug of tea and placed both her hands around it. 'You'll have to phone the police in Edinburgh.'

She tried to lift the mug to her lips but when it almost spilled in her shaking hands she lowered it again. 'What if I don't?'

Mark brushed her hair away from her face. 'You know you must. You must find out.'

She nodded. 'What was she...wearing?'

He shook his head. 'I've no idea, Sarah. John didn't have any details. He simply knows that the body of a young woman has been found.'

She jumped up, the chair wobbled and she staggered. Tea spilled and she didn't notice. 'Well, thanks for coming Mark, I must get my clothes organised for school tomorrow. It was very kind of him to phone but it won't be her.'

He grabbed the mug from her and put it on the worktop, then caught her by the arms.

'Sarah...don't...listen to me. I know this has been a shock. But you'll have to deal with it. You can't go to school tomorrow as if nothing has happened....phone Moira now.'

'Don't be ridiculous! I can't phone Moira at this time of night!'

'Sarah, Sarah...come on.' He held her and stroked her hair. 'A couple of aspirin and bed for you. I wish now I hadn't told you until the morning, but I was worried about the television...'

She rubbed her face. 'I'll be all right.'

Mark said, 'I know, but I'm not taking any chances, I'm staying.'

In bed, with Mark's arms around her, she allowed herself to think about what might be coming. While it was possible that it wasn't Ruth, it was just as possible that it was. And then it would be over. A mixture of relief and guilt swept through her and she prayed that she would be able to face what was to come. She listened to Mark's quiet breathing. As long as he was there.

Unable to sleep, her mind wandered through the nooks and crannies of her childhood, from before Ruth went missing. She thought they'd been a reasonably happy family; she couldn't recall much conflict in the home, for example. She knew that she and Ruth had been well looked after, their childhood secure. She recalled various holidays, mostly in Scotland, and her dad with his camera on them at every turn. She smiled into the darkness when she remembered a time when the family album had been on display for some visitor and she'd thrown a tantrum about pictures which didn't include her, and the shock of realising that they'd all had a life before she existed. She wondered, not for the first time, where those photographs were now. They hadn't been found when she'd cleared the North Berwick house after her mother's death.

In the morning her eyes felt full of grit and she had a headache. She huddled on the sofa in her dressing gown while Mark made coffee and toast. On the tray he placed the phone next to the cup and plate. 'Moira.' he said.

A spot of marmalade found its way on to the handset and Sarah took it into the kitchen. She wiped the smooth plastic, carefully, and Mark leaned against the sink, arms folded. 'You'll have to do it sooner or later, Sarah.'

'I know.' She laid the phone on the worktop. 'Oh, Henry, I haven't fed him yet.'

Mark put the phone back into her hand and wrapped her fingers around it. 'I'll feed Henry.'

'But what if isn't Ruth?'

'Moira will understand.'

'But...maybe I should phone the police first...and if it's not her, I could go to school.'

His arm around her shoulder Mark led her back to the sofa and sat down next to her. 'Look at me, Sarah.' He turned her chin so that he was looking directly into her eyes.

'For, what, twenty-three years? - you have agonised over what became of your sister. Now you have at least one chance to find out. The police won't tell you in a phone call, you know that, so you will have to go and see them. Whether it is Ruth or not, you have to go - and hiding behind your work isn't going to change that.' He caught her chin between his thumb and forefinger and gave it a little shake. 'You know that, don't you.'

Sarah nodded, took a deep breath and dialled Moira's home number. The deputy head was in agreement with Mark, Sarah had to find out. It was still early enough to get cover for Sarah's classes. At the end of the call she added, 'By the way, did you know that the Head's mother has died?'

'I didn't know he even had a mother. Was it sudden?'

'Don't think so. She was in a home in Angus somewhere. The funeral isn't for a day or two so he's coming in. He says he'll be better for working.'

When she switched off the phone, Mark said, 'Now, the police.' He handed her a piece of scribbled paper. 'John Phillips gave me the number.'

Sarah stared at the scrap of paper for a long time before she started pressing the keys, aware that every click could be bringing her closer to the end of her sister's story.

Chapter 14

The police station on the corner of Queen Charlotte Street in
Leith was a substantial Victorian building. When Sarah gave
her name it seemed to her that the desk sergeant looked at
her with sympathy and she found herself bristling. She
wasn't a victim's sister just yet.

'It's about the …the...'

'Yes, we knew you were coming. If you'll take a seat
Detective Inspector Grant will be here in a minute.'

Although sharing a rank, Steven Grant wasn't Steve
Hamilton: Sarah could see that at a glance as the tall figure
appeared, dressed in an expensive-looking dark suit. He
smiled with genuine warmth as he shook hands with her,
then Mark. 'I'm the Senior Investigating Officer in this
case.' There was a touch of Irish in his accent, which she
might have found beguiling on another day. He turned and
put out an arm to guide Sarah away as a couple of uniformed
officers hustled a reluctant youth into the reception area.

'Well, well, if it isn't our old friend Binky
Graham…' the sergeant was saying as they left the front of
the station and followed the detective through a maze of
corridors to a small room. The furnishings were basic to the
point of stark. - a scarred formica table with two grey plastic
chairs on either side, and what was obviously recording
equipment at one end of the table.

The inspector raised his hands. 'I'm sorry to bring
you here but there's a surprising lack of privacy in a busy
police station and we won't be disturbed here. I've sent for

tea.'

As he spoke the door opened and a young policewoman entered carrying a tray with two paper cups. Sarah's stomach lurched as she took in the girl's olive skin and dark eyes, and an image of Rubina Khan stabbed her. Rubina, who had been released for burial once Hakim had been charged. Sarah had a vision of her young body in the icy hold of an aeroplane as she was flown back to Pakistan for her Islamic funeral.

He nodded to the girl. 'This is PC Samina Kaur; she'll be sitting in with us.'

She smiled at Mark and Sarah and placed the tray in the centre of the table, pointing out the packets of sugar and little tubs of milk. Pale liquid swirled in the paper cups and there was a plate of worn-looking digestive biscuits on the tray. 'Please help yourself.' She sat down next to the detective.

He pointed to the recording equipment. 'Needless to say we won't be using that - if you can just tell us what you can remember about your sister's disappearance the constable here will take notes.'

Sarah's fist clenched on the cold table. 'But what can you tell us about the girl who's been found?'

The policeman folded his arms and leaned back in his chair, away from Sarah, and nodded at the tea. 'Please, do help yourself. At this stage not much, actually. The body of a young woman has been found buried under a ground floor flat in Leith. The pathology indicates that she has been there more than twenty years. So, if you can give us something about - Ruth wasn't it? - that might be helpful. After all, there's every possibility it's not your sister, but we won't know that until we have some definite means of identity.'

'But,' Mark said, 'How could such a...a terrible

thing remain undetected?'

The detective nodded. 'I know. The person - or persons - would have to live in the property long enough to...' He made a delicate movement with his hand, 'And by the time new tenants came...?'

Mark held Sarah's free hand under the table as she told her story once again, ending with what they had found out in recent weeks.

'And you're no closer to finding out who this boyfriend might have been?'

Mark said, 'You could try speaking to Dr Sheila Macdonald, I daresay something could have come back to her after we left.'

PC Samina Kaur wrote it all down and for a moment there was silence as she copied the Macdonalds' address in Broughty Ferry from Mark's notebook. The interlude was a turning point. DI Grant swung his chair upright and said, more briskly than before. 'Anyway, that might not be necessary at the moment, as I'm sure you'll understand. The first thing is a possible identification.' He leaned across the table towards Sarah. 'Do you feel up to this, Miss Blane?'

'Up to...?' Sarah gasped, and Mark put his arm round her shoulder.

The young policewoman looked up from her note-taking.

'What would she have to do, Inspector?' Mark asked.

The detective rubbed both hands across his face. 'There were certain items found which might help us to identify this young woman. If Miss Blane were to recognise any of these...well...'

'Right.' Mark's grip on her shoulder tightened. 'Sarah?'

She took a deep breath. 'When?'

DI Grant smiled and rose from the table. 'For us, now would be as good a time as any. I'll arrange a car to take you to the mortuary. Samina will go with you,' He glanced at his watch, 'And I'll see you when you get back.'

The speed of events shook Sarah, even to wondering when they were supposed to drink the pallid liquid in the paper cups and try the biscuits. Anyway, she knew she would have choked.

As they stood in the corridor waiting to be taken to the car, the DI put his hand on Sarah's arm. 'I know this is an ordeal for you, but we're grateful to you for getting in touch so soon. You'll realise that your sister's case has never been closed. But, I should just warn you - if this girl does turn out to be your sister then it won't be a missing person case any longer - but something quite different.' He looked at her steadily to make sure his meaning was clear. 'This death was murder.'

Sarah flinched, the word striking her like a blow, but what other explanation could there be for a girl buried under floorboards for more than twenty years?

On the way to the car she turned back, but Inspector Grant had moved away. She hadn't asked him about the cause of death. She hoped there was a cause of death before this poor girl, Ruth or not, had been buried. The alternative was unthinkable.

As the police vehicle squeezed its way through the busy streets of Edinburgh Sarah tried to retrieve a mental picture of Ruth as she was last time she'd seen her - before she left that night. Sarah hadn't been too interested in her sister's appearance when she expected to see her a few hours later. She thought she could remember jeans, and a dark green coat. Suddenly she heard her mother's voice arguing with Ruth, who wanted to leave the coat and go out in a thick sweater...an Aran sweater...but not warm enough to satisfy her mother on a December night.   Sarah couldn't remember who had won.

The Edinburgh City Mortuary was in Cowgate - an almost subterranean thoroughfare, relic of the old town. The mortuary itself, however, she would have walked past; it was an anonymous modern building. Dark trees surrounded the brick-built frontage, whose function was revealed in a discreet brass plate. As they got out of the car she could detect, faintly, the sound of bagpipes from the Royal Mile.

Inside, with Mark holding firmly to her arm, they followed Samina Kaur to an office where they were met by a middle-aged man, whose rimless glasses made his eyes seem disconcertingly naked. He held out a very clean, pink hand, 'Richard Miller, Professor, forensic pathologist. I'm sorry to bring you here in such sad circumstances, but please, take a seat. I'd like to have a wee chat with you before we proceed.'

Mark and Sarah sat opposite his desk, while Samina faded into the background. She was still there, none the less.

The professor coughed, and flicked through a folder of notes before he spoke again. 'We have here the remains of a young female, discovered under the floorboards of a dwelling house during the process of demolition.' He raised his eyes from the paperwork and Sarah nodded.

'While in an advanced state of decay, the young woman appears to have died from the application of a ligature to her neck.' He looked up again. 'Strangulation.'

Sarah could feel her shirt sticking to her back. She wanted to yell at him to end the suspense. She knew that she was digging her nails into Mark's hand but he held on.

The professor closed the folder and gave them his full attention. 'Frankly, Miss Marchegay...'

'Blane.' Sarah said.

He blinked behind the glasses and opened the folder

again. 'Yes, yes, of course. I'm sorry, Miss Blane. Your sister was Miss Marchegay - Miss Ruth Marchegay.' He paused, 'You must have been very young when she went missing.'

'I was ten.'

'And your parents?'

'Both dead.'

'I see.'

'Well, what will happen now is that I will take you and Mr McKenzie to the mortuary suite. It will be distressing for you, I'm afraid, but in this case we can't use the relatives' viewing room - I'm sure you'll understand why. Obviously we won't ask you to make a formal identification of the remains, but we would like you to look at some of the items which were found, clothing and so on, and you may recognise something. When we've done that we will ask you to provide a sample for DNA testing,' he looked over his specs. 'You are familiar with this practice?'

Sarah's forehead was damp. 'I know what it is, yes.'

'And we will do comparison tests with DNA taken from the remains.' He stood up. 'Right - we'll get on with it. If you'll just come with me.'

With Samina behind them they followed him down a corridor to a door which led into a small chamber with a glass wall. This looked into what was obviously the mortuary suite. It was a large, cold-looking room with blindingly white walls and what looked like a hard, lino floor. On the wall opposite were some kind of massive steel doors. Sarah's eyes were drawn to the three metal tables - all empty - gleaming like an operating theatre as they lay in wait for their next patient? Victim? Body.

The professor signalled to someone in the room and a technician in a white coat appeared on the floor of the mortuary suite with a large, plastic box.

'We can't risk further contamination of these items so you will be obliged to try to make your identification through the glass, I'm afraid. Williams will bring them as close as possible and you can say if you recognise anything. We have photographs too, if that will be easier.'

The brilliant overhead lights in the room bounced off the gleaming hair of the technician as he bent over his task. He was wearing thin rubber gloves and Sarah had the ludicrous thought that he was like a conjurer, about to produce some wonder from his magic box.

First he spread out on a table placed close to the glass partition a pair of badly soiled denims, small enough to belong to her sister but so ingrained with dirt and God knows what else that they would not have been recognisable by anyone. Sarah shook her head. Then came what might have been an Aran sweater once upon a time. She felt sick as she nodded, and when she went to speak she could hardly get the words out. 'Yes...I think...the sweater...I don't know....maybe.'

If Ruth had won the argument all those years ago.

But the technician wasn't finished. One by one unidentifiable pieces of clothing appeared on the table, and to all of them Sarah shook her head. Until the final item. This had been isolated in a little transparent envelope and the technician shook it out and held it up to the glass. There, lying in his gloved palm, was a gold ring with a pale green stone. In a furnace blast of memory the whole scene came rushing back to Sarah, and she gasped. How jealous she had been of that ring! Ruth had been given it by their parents for some musical success, and Sarah had sulked for weeks. They promised that she would get something just as good when she was old enough to deserve it, and to look after it, but she never did.

She realised that tears were running down her cheeks. 'The ring. It's my ...it's Ruth's.'

She felt Samina Kaur's hand on her shoulder, 'Are you all right? Would you like a drink of water?'

Sarah said, 'Thanks, no,' as she felt for a handkerchief. 'What happens now?'

Suddenly she couldn't wait to get out of this cold environment with its depressing smells of death and disinfectant and its ghastly purposes. For her beautiful talented sister to end here - a pile of bones and a few rags in a plastic box. She couldn't breathe; she had to get out.

She rose to her feet and Mark did the same. Professor Miller was solicitous –'Come, Miss Blane - we'll continue in my office. And we'll have some tea.'

The tea was hot and strong this time and came in comforting earthenware mugs. Sarah warmed her hands against the mug while the Professor observed her over the top of his rimless glasses. At last he said, 'I know this has been a dreadful shock for you, but you do understand that it's not yet certain that this young woman was your sister?'

Sarah said, 'I know, but...'

The Professor tapped the end of his pen on the desk for a moment, then he nodded. 'We'll wait for the results of the tests, then we'll be able to tell you more.'

Sarah stared at the rain, skittering down the windscreen like tears, as they drove back to Glasgow. Her thoughts were a kaleidoscope of real images from the past and imagined pictures of the present. From time to time Mark would glance at her or gently touch her hair, but for the most part he drove in silence.

At last she said, 'I'm living in the nightmare now, Mark. It's come true.' She ran her tongue around the inside of her mouth, still tasting the swabs they had used to take samples of her saliva. She shook her head. 'What you said, before, about ...murder. I couldn't let myself even think it.' Her hands were fists on her lap. 'How could Ruth have known someone so...so evil?' Her voice rose. 'What was she doing in that house? Why didn't we know?'

'How could you know? You were a child, Sarah.' It was Mark's turn to shake his head, 'As for your parents...was there never any clue that Ruth was seeing someone they didn't approve of? Arguments about time-keeping, that sort of thing? I mean that's normal with teenagers in any household, isn't it?'

'Mark, I've been racking my brains for twenty-three years, even harder after we saw Sheila Macdonald. I can vaguely remember arguments about Ruth wearing too much make-up when she was going for her music tuition, but I thought it was lovely and couldn't see what all the fuss was about. But, just maybe, they had an inkling that she wasn't been totally honest with them about who she was meeting...'

'Anyway, perhaps we'll find that out now.'

She stared at him while the import of his words sank in. 'Of course, the building. Will they have records, do you think? For that long?'

Mark nodded, 'Council tax, poll tax, whatever it was then...1988? I'd reckon the council records go that far back.'

'Should we...?'

'Not now. The police will deal with everything now.' He grasped Sarah's hand.

'That part's over, for you...for us.'

*

Next day Sarah insisted on going back to school, in preference to sitting around the house waiting for more depressing news, and Mark agreed. The question of a funeral for Ruth would have to be dealt with at some time, but not soon. First, the positive findings from the DNA were required - it was just conceivable that it was not Ruth who was wearing the ring. Sarah had been able to help with the name of their Edinburgh dentist for tracing Ruth's records, but several other strands of the investigation had to be satisfied before her sister's remains would be released for burial.

D I Grant had shown great fortitude for an officer faced with an extremely cold case to pursue, when there was obviously no shortage of very live investigations demanding his attention. Nevertheless, he assured her, they would make every effort to bring Sarah's ordeal to a close as soon as possible. Sarah was sure that Steve Hamilton wouldn't have been so compassionate.

She was making her way along the corridor to Moira's room, reflecting that it seemed more than one day she'd been away from school, when she realised that the tall young man approaching from the other direction was not a pupil, but was Gordon Birkmyre, the Head's son. Then she remembered about the death in the family.

'Gordon. It is you. For a moment I thought you were a pupil.'

He stopped and shook hands with her. 'Miss Blane. How are you?'

The boy had matured in his few months in the USA. He looked taller and heavier and his hair was longer than it had been when he was a schoolboy. There was also a trace of an American accent.

'Yes, all right. I was sorry to hear about your …grandmother? I was out of school yesterday when I heard. How is your dad taking it?'

'Not very well, I'm afraid.' The boy folded his arms and leaned against the wall. There was an assurance about him which reminded her of his father. 'Malcolm and I hardly knew her, but Dad's gutted. It seems she brought him up by herself after his father did a runner.' He shrugged. 'My mother's telling us all this now, how Granny struggled to put him through a good school - the university - you know the kind of thing.' He rolled his eyes. 'How she sacrificed everything for her boy.' He pushed himself off the wall. 'Anyway, we've to go to Arbroath or somewhere tomorrow for the funeral. Mum wants Dad to come home , she doesn't think he's in a fit state to be here. She's at work and I've been sent to see how he is.'

'Have you come home for the funeral?'

'Not really, I've been here for a few days. It's the end of the semester.'

'And how is it going?'

'Absolutely fantastic - much better than school.'

'Your father tells us you're doing well.'

Gordon pulled a face. 'Well, he would say that, wouldn't he? Actually I am doing well. I love being at MIT.' He waved a hand around. 'It's so different from here.'

'Well, that's good. Give your father my condolences, will you? He'll be glad of the Easter break.'

'He will. He'll probably go off to the cottage for some peace, after - this.' He waved a hand along the corridor.

'I'm sure it's a lovely spot.'

He grinned. 'It is, if you like lots of sky and seals. Not for me - or my mum - give us the bright lights every time. I'm back off to America as soon as my gran's funeral is over.'

She moved away, but the boy's cheerful disregard for a sad situation remained with her; a sharp reminder of the resilience of youth. Sarah thought of Mark, and herself: they weren't so old either. There would be plenty of time for

266

them, when Ruth's story was over.

Moira hugged her. 'You know how I feel, Sarah. And if there's anything else you need - more time off, don't worry about it, I'll see that you get it. Anyway, what's to happen now?'

After Sarah filled her in on the situation, she asked, 'What about the department. Do they know what's happened?

Moira ran her hands through her mop of hair and screwed up her face. 'Yes, Sarah. I had to tell Roger because I thought, you know, there might be complications and you'd need more time and so forth...I couldn't lie about it.'

'No, no, of course not. What about Keith?'

'Well, I did try to tell him but he was so distracted by his own problems that he didn't seem to take in what I was saying, so I'm not sure. You know how dismissive he can be.'

'Pupils?'

'No. Definitely not.'

There was an air of relaxation in the school, and Sarah was reminded that it was just over a week until the Easter break. It seemed to be coming at her with speed, and not long after the February holiday, but Easter was particularly early this year. No matter what, the prospect of escape for a couple of weeks had an irresistible effect on even the most dedicated of teachers, and the English department was no exception. As she approached a loud burst of laughter came from behind the closed staff-room door.

When Sarah entered however, conversation stopped and the laughter drained away. Every head turned in her direction. She understood the difficulty for her colleagues. What do you say in a situation like this? What's the etiquette? As a diversion for herself she had taken a pile of exercise books to bury her head in.

Roger was first to move. He got out of his chair and took the jotters out of Sarah's hands. Laying them on the bench he said, 'Sarah, come and sit down.'

She stood for a minute more. 'I know you've all heard about what has happened.'

There were nods from around the room.

'Well...all I can tell you at this stage is we don't know if this girl is...my sister. There's still a lot to be done. But I'd really appreciate it if none of the pupils finds out.'

There was a chorus of, 'No, of course not.'

Sarah went on,' I'm sure you'll understand that I want to get on with my life as normally as I can meantime, and that just wouldn't be possible if all the pupils heard about... this.' She breathed deeply. 'It's pretty awful.'

William Armstrong said, 'We'll do our best, Sarah, you can be sure.' He tapped his empty pipe on the arm of his chair. 'Apart from the fact that our dear charges have a most unsettling tendency to find things out.' He sniffed and fumbled in his cardigan pocket for a handkerchief. 'You know, I remember when your sis...that girl went missing, all those years ago.'

Sarah sat down. 'That's quite a feat of memory, Willie.'

'No, no - it was a big story at the time - and she had such an unusual name. Marchegay, wasn't it?'

'Marchegay?' Judith said, 'So that's your name too, Sarah?'

'Yes, my father always told us it was a Huguenot name.'

Willie continued over the interruption. 'Yes, I was teaching in Dunfermline at the time.' He shook his head. 'It was such a sad story - lovely girl, talented musician, everything to...'

Judith looked at Sarah's expression and to her credit, cut Willie off. 'Well at least you'll have the break, Sarah, and by the time we come back it won't be spoken of here; the pupils won't connect you to the girl, and it may not be her anyway.'

Sarah nodded, and Judith turned the conversation again to where she was going on holiday.

But on Friday, Sarah was called to the school office to take a phone call. It was Detective Inspector Grant.

'Sorry to disturb you at school, Miss Blane, but I didn't want to use your mobile number in case you were in the middle of a class.'

'That's all right. I'm free at the moment.'

'Well, there are couple of things. First of all, I have to tell you that the test results are back and...'

'Yes?'

'The young woman is a DNA match for you.'

Sarah's mouth was dry and she struggled to speak.

'So...?

'The girl does appear to be your sister. The dental records also confirm that she was Ruth Marchegay. I'm very sorry.'

'Don't be, Inspector. In some ways it's a relief to know where she is at last. But it's just so...'

She became aware that the school secretary was staring intently at a blank computer screen. A detective inspector, who was not Steve Hamilton, asking to speak to member of staff was not something she heard every day. Particularly in the light of recent events in Fruin High.

'There are another couple of things we need to discuss. Would you be able to come through to see us again?'

'Would tomorrow do?'

'Tomorrow will be fine.'

The secretary's screen burst into life as Sarah left. She returned to her empty classroom to phone Mark with the news that they had both been expecting.

'Damn! I don't think I can go with you this Saturday. But I'll try...I'll change with...'

'No.' Sarah stopped him. 'I'll go alone. It's time I did some of this on my own. I've taken up too much of your time with my problems as it is.'

Mark was silent for a moment. 'You know that's not true. You know I want to be with you whatever you have to do.'

Sarah sighed. 'Oh, of course I do. It's just that ...well, if I hadn't met you I'd still have all this to face on my own, wouldn't I?'

She heard his soft laugh. 'But you did meet me. Anyway, call me when you get back to Glasgow and we'll have dinner. Are you driving?'

'No, I think I'll take the train and a taxi. It will be easier.'

Sarah was less sanguine about her decision to take public transport when the taxi emerged from Waverley Station into a downpour. She had an impression of the driver cursing quietly as pedestrians dodged in front of him through the maze of junctions that led from Princes Street to Leith Walk. It was still early, but shoppers and tourists appeared to be out in force.

As the taxi passed through Leith she looked out on the frenzy of redevelopment, and wondered which of these desolate tenements had become her sister's last resting place. What would Ruth have made of the glossy frontage of the new Scottish Government Office - or the great palace to consumerism that was Ocean Terminal? How had she fitted into a place which had been steadily decaying amidst the social problems of the residents even then? This had never

270

been Ruth's world.

DI Grant was waiting for her in the police station at Queen Charlotte Street, and he led her to the same dreary room as before. A different policewoman joined them this time, however, minus the tea and biscuits, and Sarah thought briefly that female officers were probably always present at interviews with women. The Inspector introduced her as PC Isobel Kerr. She was a plain girl, with dull brown hair scraped back from her forehead and an unusually square jaw. There was obvious sympathy in the smile she gave Sarah, who felt as if she must have 'sad person' stencilled on her forehead. The Inspector was still speaking and Sarah chided herself...

'I've asked you to come here today for two reasons, Miss Blane.' This time he was wearing slacks and what looked like a golfing sweater and Sarah reflected that she was probably eating into his off-duty weekend. If so, he gave no sign.

He clasped his hands on the table and seemed to be choosing his words with care.

'You were what age - 10? - when your sister went missing, is that so?'

'Yes, but...'

'I know, we already have that information. But what I'm actually trying to establish here is what kind of relationship you had with Ruth.'

'What kind? What kind of relationship do most youngsters have with their siblings?' Sarah hadn't known what to expect from this meeting but she certainly hadn't bargained on some sort of forensic examination of her relationship with her sister.

He smiled. 'I take your point. What I mean is, did she confide in you at all - or was the age difference too great?'

271

'I see.' Sarah didn't answer for a moment, then she said, 'Well, I do remember her complaining about things like having to practice her music, or being expected to help with the ironing or whatever, but,' she shook her head. 'if the point of your question is did I know she was seeing some boy...man... then the answer is a definite no.'

'I thought that might be the case, but it was necessary to ask.'

'Inspector Grant, if I'd had the faintest idea that Ruth was involved with someone I would have told my parents, even the police. Anything which might have helped to find her...'

'I understand.' He nodded. 'And you don't remember any other friends your sister may have had.'

'No, at Ruth's age a little sister was just a pest. And, recently, we've found Sheila Macdonald, and Julie Robertson, of course...' A shaft of pain cut through her at the thought of these two young women, Ruth and Julie, both of whose lives had ended here, in the rubble of Leith.

'We are in touch with Doctor Macdonald now.'

Sarah felt impatience welling up; when would it be her turn?

'What I want to know, Inspector, is what you've found out about that building - the one where she was found?'

He raised an eyebrow. 'The building?'

'Yes, surely there must be records of who was living there at the time - tax records or whatever.'

'Yes, we're working on that. Actually, it appears that the tenement changed hands more than once over the past quarter of a century or so - to the point where at one time that building and a few others were owned by some kind of conglomerate based in the Bahamas. Of course, its most recent owner has been the development company.'

'Doesn't the Council keep records?'

'Yes of course, as does the Land Register, but while we might establish title for the period in question it doesn't tell us who was living in the individual flats. Those records are harder to trace.'

'But there must have been some ...agency or other who collected rents, no?'

'Miss Blane, you can take my word for it that this aspect of the case is being followed up as we speak, and if there's the slightest chance of tracing who was living there at the time of your sister's disappearance, we will find it. We do know at this stage that many of the flats were rented out to students, on a multi-occupancy basis, but that just makes things more difficult. Students, as you are well aware, tend to be a transient population.'

'It was a student Ruth was involved with.'

'We believe that to be very likely, and that brings me to another of the reasons for asking you here today. And, in fact, my questions about your relationship with Ruth.'

Sarah's heart gave a little leap.

'Miss Blane, your sister was pregnant.'

Sarah's gasp had the policewoman out of her seat.

'Pregnant?'

DI Grant signalled to the girl, who left the room and was back in a few seconds with a glass of water which she laid before Sarah.

'We couldn't tell you before, until we had established her identity without doubt, but yes, she was pregnant. Between two and three months.'

Bile rose into Sarah's throat, this couldn't be her sister they were talking about? At times Sarah had almost driven herself mad struggling with what might have become of Ruth, but nothing could have prepared her for this.

'At the moment we're keeping an open mind,' the

Inspector went on, 'but we suspect with some justification that this might have been the motive for your sister's killing.' He spread his hands. 'A young man, a relationship with an even younger girl - a student - possibly struggling financially - makes a mistake and his girlfriend becomes pregnant. Who knows, probably panicked...'

The apparent detachment of the DI's speculation brought Sarah back.

'You make it sound very simple. Almost understandable.'

The DI shook his head. 'Don't get the wrong impression. It may well have been that simple, but that doesn't mean that we won't do everything in our power to track down the perpetrator of this dreadful crime. Murder is never understandable.'

Sarah got up. 'I'd like to go now.'

The policeman and the girl rose too. 'Of course. But, before you go, ' he held the door for her. 'how do you feel about taking part in a press conference?'

'A press conference, after all this time. What can you possibly hope to gain?'

'You would be surprised by what people can remember when their memories are put to the test.'

Willie Armstrong came to mind.

'And, you'd want me to take part in this?'

'Only if you are comfortable with the idea. We will set up the conference - but we know it would be greatly enhanced by your presence.'

She longed to be out of this building, with its grim décor and odours of stewed tea and stale crimes. But she had one last question. 'Will you give me the address?'

'The address?' He looked at her for a moment, then, with seeming reluctance, gave it to her. 'And you'll give some thought to the press conference?'

Typically, the weather had changed during the short time Sarah had been inside. The rain had been replaced by a strong wind from the firth and scudding grey clouds in patches of blue sky. The desk sergeant had called a taxi for her when she'd declined the offer of a police car back to Waverley, and it was ticking at the pavement as she exited.

In the taxi she checked her phone. There was a text message from Mark, hoping that everything was going well. She replied briefly that she'd be back in time for dinner: the rest would have to wait until they met, then she sat back until the taxi stopped at her request at a flower-shop.

The building was practically gone: in its remains there were cranes and earth-moving machinery, idle today, but brooding over the scene like some kind of monsters waiting to devour all the history which had once been here. There was blue and white police tape around the site, but no police presence. After all, anything to be gleaned from this crime scene must have vanished in the dust and debris of the demolition.

She laid her flowers on the ground below the tape then stood for a little while, the wind cutting through her raincoat and bringing tears to her eyes.

As he pulled away the driver said, 'Used to stay there, did you?'

'I didn't.' Sarah replied.

Their route took them past the building that Julie Robertson had lived in. It too, had become a skeleton of old fireplaces and shreds of wallpaper, and was well on the way to total oblivion. Just like the people who'd once lived here - to be replaced by shiny young executives in shiny new flats.

She left the taxi at the station and went into the bar of the Balmoral Hotel. While she waited for her sandwich and coffee she looked around her warm surroundings and at the well-fed diners. She reckoned some of them would be ideal candidates for a luxurious harbour-front lifestyle in Leith.

Chapter 15

Sarah awoke alone and found herself staring at an abstract painting on the wall opposite the bed. It was a swirl of deep, disturbing colours which troubled her until she remembered where she was. It was the first time she had stayed overnight in Mark's flat.

The familiar smell of coffee and toast reassured her and she was swinging her legs out of the bed when Mark appeared with a tray.

'No, no - stay where you are. This is for starters. Bacon and eggs coming up.'

'Oh Mark, I never have breakfast in bed.'

He set the tray down on a bureau, and sat beside her on the bed, smoothing the sleep out of her hair. 'Then it's about time you did.'

She smiled. 'I should be getting home. Henry will be furious!'

He tapped her nose. 'He'll forgive you. Anyway, it's just to change your clothes before we go out somewhere for a lovely, long Sunday lunch.'

Sarah lay back on the deep pillows and felt the tension ease out of her body. It had been her constant companion for so long. It was a pleasing sensation and she gave silent thanks for the day Mark McKenzie had come into her life. She tried to imagine facing the last few months without him.

Suddenly hungry, she sat up and straightening the big tee-shirt Mark had loaned her, reached for the toast.

*

Henry was furious. He stalked around Sarah with his tail in the air, complaining volubly while she forked food into a clean bowl and replaced the little biscuits which he only ate in emergencies. The biscuit dish was empty; last night had been an emergency.

Mark said. 'There are a couple of messages on your phone, Sarah.'

Her stomach lurched. Surely the press conference hadn't been set up already?

She was filling the cat's bowl with fresh water. 'Play them, Mark, will you?'

Angry sounds filled the room. The bowl overflowed and water poured on to Sarah's hands as they stared at each other. Mark pointed to the machine. 'Who on earth...?'

Sarah laid the dish down on the floor beside Henry. 'I don't know, play it again.'

The machine wasn't all that clear at the best of times, but the caller's volume was distorting the sound so much it was difficult to grasp the words. Sarah stood next to the phone and at the third playing realised that the voice belonged to Elizabeth Cameron.

'I think it's Lynn Cameron's mother. She's asking if I know where Lynn is? Why should I...God, Mark, I wonder when she left the message...?'

'Look, there's another message - maybe it's all right.'

The second caller was Moira. 'Hi, Sarah, I'm really sorry to be doing this but I thought you might be back from Edinburgh by now. It's ...just after nine o'clock...she hesitated, 'Saturday night.' She sounded very tired. 'I can't believe I'm saying this...but it seems Lynn Cameron hasn't been seen since yesterday. I know there's nothing you can do - I'm sure you'd have told me if you knew about any sort of ...plans... Lynn had to do something like...but her mother is boiling over. I know she's going to contact you. And...DI Hamilton...' Her voice trailed away as if the words were becoming too heavy.

Sarah sank on to the sofa and covered her face with her wet hands. The nightmare was back. She opened her eyes and looked at Mark. 'Not again.'

He sat next to her and held her shoulders in a tight grip. 'What can we do?'

Sarah shook her head. 'I haven't the faintest idea. Except to phone Moira.' She drew a long breath. 'Lynn might have turned up by now.'

But she hadn't. Moira was spending the weekend fielding outraged calls from Elizabeth Cameron, who seemed convinced that Lynn's disappearance had to be linked to the school. And from the press, who had quickly got hold of the idea that something distinctly untoward was happening around Fruin High. This time the police were taking the matter seriously, and the school was to be searched today while the pupils were absent. 'It's just a process of elimination,' Moira said, 'Why would she be in the school?'

'I know. But I suppose they have to start somewhere.' She had a sudden picture of David Smythe's grim expression when they had spoken of Lynn, and she remembered that for some inexplicable reason the girl had confided in him.

She hung up and turned back to Mark. 'I had intended to ask Lynn about why she had spoken to David Smythe, but then,' she shrugged, 'Leith intervened.'

'Did you see Lynn on Friday?'

'Ye-es, I'm sure, she was at registration.'

'How was she?'

Sarah thought for a moment. 'I can't remember anything different about her. But my head's been everywhere for the last few days. Her friends would be the ones to ask.'

'And they are?'

'Well, to be honest, I don't know. Since Rubina...if anyone she seems to spend most time with Leslie Watkins, doesn't she?'

'Of course, her crusading companion.'

Mark got up and stretched. 'Let's have some coffee while we make a plan.'

'A plan?'

'Well,' he nodded his head at the phone. 'I think to begin with you should brave the lioness in her den - if she's not out looking for her daughter.'

'But...but...'

'Yes, I know, but it's the quickest way to convince her that you know nothing about Lynn's disappearance. Besides, we might pick up on something to do with her home-life.'

Sarah made a face. 'It won't be pretty.'

Mark turned from filling the kettle, and smiled. 'I'll be there too.'

Apart from a couple of cars parked in the street outside, the Cameron's bungalow looked as untouched as ever. The garden seemed to have behaved itself throughout the winter, avoiding the confused look of greenery coming to terms with another spring. Even the daffodils stood at attention in regimented rows.

Lynn's mother too, had escaped the ravaged look of any parent whose child had been missing for three nights. Her face was immaculately made up and her hair in a smooth chignon. No fluffy dressing gown and tear-soaked hankies for Councillor Cameron. At the sight of Sarah and Mark her eyes narrowed, and for a second Sarah thought they were to be kept on the doorstep. Until her look went past them to the cars at the kerb.

She took them into the same, clinically decorated room at the front of the house. Elizabeth Cameron sat down on the spindly sofa and, when Mark had been explained, waved them to the other one. The fabric was cold, and Sarah shivered.

'So, what can you tell me?'

'Actually, nothing, I'm afraid.' Sarah said.

'Then why are you here?'

Sarah looked at the woman closely for signs of distress, but there was nothing to see beneath the smooth coating of make-up. Unless it was the anger in her eyes.

'You phoned my house, and I thought it best to come and tell you that I haven't seen Lynn either since Friday. Nor,' she hurried on as the woman opened her mouth to speak. 'have I had any personal contact with her for quite some time.'

Eyebrows raised, Elizabeth Cameron said, 'But you've made a habit of 'personal contact' with my daughter, haven't you?'

Sarah hesitated, then said quietly, 'You know how upset she was by what happened to Rubina. She spoke to me about that.'

The implication that Sarah had provided a listening ear was not lost on the girl's mother.

'But you know perfectly well, Miss Blane, that the sorry end of that girl had absolutely nothing to do with my daughter. I made that clear to Lynn more than once.'

Mark said, 'Wasn't Rubina Lynn's best friend?'

She looked at him as if he'd just crawled in from the garden. 'Mr...what?...McKenzie, is it?'

Sarah saw Mark draw himself up.

'Anyway, Mrs Cameron, this isn't helping to find Lynn. I just want you know how sorry I am, and to see if there's anything we can do to help. You must be desperately worried!'

For a second the mask slipped and a shadow crossed Elizabeth's face. She stood up and turned away from them. 'My husband is on his way home. His ship's in Buenos Aires but I've spoken to him. He's devastated.'

Sarah spoke softly. 'Have you any idea where Lynn might have gone?'

The other woman shook her head.

'I mean, what happened? When did you know...?'

Elizabeth Cameron walked to the window and spoke with her back turned. 'I...I didn't know until Friday night. I'd...been in London on council business from Tuesday. I knew Lynn would be all right, the cleaning woman comes in on Tuesday and Thursday. She turned to face them. 'And she is almost eighteen.'

Sarah nodded.

'She wasn't here when I got back and I thought she was out somewhere. But when she wasn't here yesterday morning I called...I had to phone Moira Campbell, apparently the Head's away. We...got the police then, because I couldn't think where she might be. I've been so angry at her ...thoughtlessness...' She turned to face Sarah. 'I even thought she might have stayed with you...' When Sarah shook her head she went on. 'I know. Then I thought at least she might have confided in you.' She returned to the window.

As Mark opened his mouth Sarah signalled to him.

She spoke to the woman's back, choosing her words with care. 'I don't suppose, anything happened here, at home? I mean, teenage girls can be pretty temperamental about house rules...' Ruth flashed into her mind.

Elizabeth Cameron turned, and actually smiled. 'If you mean has she run off after a row then the answer is a definite no. 'In fact, I've been so busy with my…council work…I've hardly seen Lynn for…'

'What about her mobile phone? She would answer that, surely?'

A faint flush appeared under the cosmetics. 'I've tried it a hundred times, but it's switched off.'

'Does Lynn have any access to money, Mrs Cameron?' Mark asked.

She looked puzzled. 'Why? Oh, I see - if she has run off…yes, she has a bank account, an allowance.' Her voice rose. 'But she has no reason to run away.'

Outside, Mark said. 'In other words a poor rich kid who is left to get on with it. Her father off at sea most of the time, her mother fully occupied with 'council' business. The cleaner in charge.' He nodded to the driver of one of the parked cars. 'Clarion' he muttered to Sarah. 'And her best friend murdered.'

'Still, the ice maiden was beginning to crack, I thought.'

'You're right. I thought so too. But it's hard to say exactly where her priorities lie. Is it as a mother, or a public face of this town? Not good if her daughter has run away.'

Sarah put her arm through his. 'I hope she has run away. Anything else is unthinkable.'

They made their way back to the flat. It was a leaden day, the sky so heavy and dark that noon seemed like evening.

'What about that lunch then, Sarah?'

'I don't think I could. I'm sorry, Mark. How about a sandwich?'

He was behind her on the steep staircase and he rubbed his hand over her back. 'I knew you'd say that. It's no problem. Sandwiches are fine.'

While Sarah stood at the counter buttering bread

Mark looked through the Sunday newspaper. 'There's nothing here that I can see. I suppose the guys don't want egg on their faces if she turns up, but at the same time they'll hang around for any sensational discoveries.'

Sarah was struggling with the recalcitrant packaging of some cold ham. 'Dammit! You'd think this blasted stuff is an art object! Not meant to be opened and eaten.'

Mark smiled and put the paper on his lap. 'Can I help?'

'No, no. I'll manage. It's just that I …what do you think can have happened to her, Mark?'

He got up and came round the counter to her side, taking the packet from her. 'Go and pour us a drink, Sarah. I think a wee sherry, don't you?'

'Don't you mean a big G&T?' Sarah was at the drinks trolley.

'Not if we're going out again, no.'

She stopped, the sherry bottle in her hand. 'And where are we going?'

'I thought perhaps we'd go and see Leslie.'

Sarah placed Mark's drink on the worktop beside him. 'Leslie?'

'Look Sarah, you know you won't be able to lie around this afternoon watching TV or reading the papers. You know you'd rather try and get some answers about Lynn, don't you?'

She sat on the leather chair. 'I can't believe this is happening again. Just this morning I was feeling so…relieved because the end was in sight. And now this.'

Another winter hadn't improved the caravan. A few spring flowers straggled along the roadside but the site itself was as depressing as ever. Still, Sarah thought, I'll bet Lynn Cameron would swap her sanitised surroundings for this cosy squalor any day. Franny Watkins cared about her son.

But said son wasn't at home.

Franny said, 'He's been away since Friday. He's at a motorway demo, isn't he?' As if this was a perfectly normal weekend activity.

Mark and Sarah looked at each other. Was it possible?

Franny pointed and they sat down on the bench seat.

She said, 'What is it? Has something happened?' She stayed on her feet. Her voice was hoarse, almost a croak.

'Oh, sorry. It's not about...was anyone with Leslie, Mrs Watkins?'

She nodded her head in the direction of the other caravans. 'Yeah, there's a group from here. What is it?' She began to twist the hem of her sweatshirt.

'It's Lynn Cameron. She hasn't been seen since Friday.' Sarah crossed her fingers under the table. 'Is there any chance that she might have gone with Leslie?'

Franny slumped down on the end of the bench. 'Oh Lord! No, I'm sure she's not with Leslie. I was supposed to be going too, but I got this flaming bug.' She put her hand to her chest.

Mark said, 'Would he have told you if Lynn was going with him?'

'Oh yes, definitely.'

'Could you phone him...does he have a mobile?'

Franny smiled and got up to fill the striped teapot from a boiling kettle. 'No mobile. He doesn't have any time for what he calls the trivia of consumerism.' She swirled the water around in the teapot. 'No more do I.'

Sarah resisted the temptation to point out how obvious that was. 'Where is he staying?'

'Was. He'll be on his way home now. They've built a tree house, haven't they?'

Mark looked at his watch. 'We'll come back later

then, if that's all right with you.'

Franny reached for a brightly coloured packet. 'Don't you want tea?'

Sarah smiled. 'Thanks, Mrs Watkins. No, we've disturbed you enough. When do you expect Leslie?'

Franny glanced up at a clock on the wall. A pair of clenched fists were visible beneath the hands and numerals. From where she sat Sarah wasn't able to read the slogan underneath.

'About an hour, I'd say.' She sniffed. 'If they don't get arrested.'

In the car Mark said, 'Phew! Thanks for saving us from the bramble tea, or whatever.'

Sarah poked his side. 'Don't scoff! At least she offered. Unlike Chez Cameron.'

'Yes.' he smiled. 'I think Franny's all right.'

They carried on to Arrochar and stopped at the hotel for coffee. The service was slow and they had easily filled an hour by the time they had finished.

On the way back the gloom had lifted a little and the gunmetal waves of the river flickered in the early evening light.

A battered dark blue mini-van stood beside one of the other caravans and Sarah assumed that had been Leslie's mode of transport.

He opened the door, unsmiling. 'Mum's just told me about Lynn. Come in.'

It was obvious from his appearance that the boy had had a rough weekend. He was grubby, and his hair looked as if he'd spent the time inside a bush. Bits of dried grass clung to his dreadlocks and his trainers were caked in mud.

Franny said. 'Get the shoes off, old son, before you settle down.'

To Sarah, the toes of Leslie's thick socks looked wet,

but he ignored them and sat opposite. This time Franny didn't ask, but set about making tea.

Leslie said, 'What's happened to her, Miss?'

Sarah sighed. 'We thought you might be able to help with that, Leslie. I know you spend quite a lot of time with Lynn.'

He glanced at his mother. 'She's not my girlfriend or anything.'

'We know that, son, but you are friends, aren't you?' Mark nodded. 'Similar interests, eh?'

Leslie flushed. 'Well, I suppose. It was really to do with Rubina.'

Sarah said, 'When did you last see Lynn?'

'Friday afternoon. After school.'

'After school?'

'Yeah, well, just outside the gate.'

'Did she tell you anything? Was she her usual self?'

He shook his head. 'She didn't tell me anything, but she definitely wasn't her usual self.'

Sarah felt a jolt. 'What do you mean?'

'She was really excited. I tried to get her to spill but she wouldn't. She just said things would be happening soon which would explain everything. She said she might go to see you - but I said that was a bad idea.'

'Why was it such bad idea?' Sarah asked, quietly.

He shuffled his stockinged feet on the floor. 'Well, Miss, we knew you were upset. We'd heard about...the...the'

'The body in Edinburgh?'

Franny gasped.

Leslie looked down at the table and nodded.

'In that case, do you know where she was going?'

Leslie shrugged. 'That's it. She said she was going home and she went in that direction.'

Franny placed a tray on the table with four mugs, the teapot and milk and sugar.

Sarah heard Mark's little sigh of relief when the liquid which poured into his mug looked and smelled like ordinary tea. A packet of biscuits rattled on to a plate and Franny shoved it in front of Leslie. 'Feel free.' She nodded at Mark and Sarah. 'And what's this about a body in Edinburgh?'

'Mum! Don't ask!'

Sarah said, 'I lost my sister many years ago, Mrs Watkins. Now the police think they've found her.'

'Oh, my God! No wonder you've been so concerned - about the Asian girl, and now this other poor girl.' Franny sat down, edging Leslie along the bench. 'Rack your brains, boy, are you sure you can't remember anything else?'

He looked down at his hands, which were filthy, dirt riming every nail. 'I'm sorry, Miss.'

Sarah laid down her mug. 'Tell me Leslie, if you were to go looking for Lynn, where would you start? Has she any other friends from school?'

'Not since Rubina. She's been sort of out of it, since...that happened. And she really misses her dad.' He snapped his fingers 'Sometimes she stays with her gran! That's her dad's mum.'

Sarah's breath caught. 'And where does she live?'

He shook his head and a couple of bits of straw drifted on to the table. 'I don't know. Somewhere in the country, I think.'

Mark said, 'Don't worry. We'll ask Mrs Cameron.'

Franny snorted, 'Is that the same as Councillor Cameron? The one that carries all the weight of that monstrosity,' she pointed towards the base, 'on her designer shoulders? If she paid more attention to her family instead of spouting support for a 'new generation of nuclear defence' maybe her daughter would still be at home!' She got up from the table and slammed the teapot on the stove.

'Mu-um, stop it!'

Sarah leaned over and patted the back of the boy's grubby hand. 'Don't worry, Leslie. You've been a great help.' She and Mark stood up. 'I'll see you tomorrow.' They squeezed their way to the door. 'And, just so that you know, the police are involved.'

They made their escape to the sound of Franny giving her opinion of that development.

Sarah said, 'I wonder how the kids found out about Ruth?'

'Yeah, you didn't ask Leslie.'

'The moment didn't seem right.'

It was wholly dark now. They drove along the front, the river twinkling in the lights from across the water. 'What do you make of the grandmother theory.' Mark asked.

'That's just it. I'm reluctant to ask. Surely Elizabeth Cameron would have started there.'

'We'll have to ask her, all the same.'

'Mmm...' Sarah was peering beyond Mark to the street on his side. 'Wait...I think that's ...it is ...it's Roger, and he's coming out of that house I saw him at before.'

Mark looked at the dark figure hurrying along the pavement. 'What? Roger from your department? But why shouldn't he be there?'

'Dorothy thinks he's out walking several nights a week, she never said anything about him making visits.'

When Sarah phoned, Elizabeth Cameron had regained her normal chilly manner. Of course Lynn hadn't gone there or they wouldn't still be searching for her.

Sarah moved away to sit on the leather chair. 'There's something we haven't talked about, isn't there, Mark?'

He sat on the sofa and leaned forward, scratching his chin. 'Frankly, I don't know what to think about it.'

Sarah said, 'And I can't bear to think about it. For if Hakim's innocent, what has happened to Lynn?'

Chapter 16

Deferring to Sarah's working hours the Edinburgh police scheduled the press conference for Monday evening. When he phoned, DI Grant said they understood the demands of school life. Even without cameras - it was not to be televised since it was not deemed urgent enough to justify the costs - Sarah felt sure it would be an ordeal all the same.

'Don't let any of these guys rile you,' Mark said, as they drove to Edinburgh for what seemed like the umpteenth time. 'In fact, I'm bound to know some of them.'

Sarah smiled. 'Well you can snarl at them if they do try to give me a hard time.'

'It's just that they are always on the look -out for good copy. The more sensational the better, so they don't mince their words.'

It was a bitterly cold night, and when they entered the hall where the meeting was to take place they took the icy air inside to swirl around in the dismal room. It was poorly lit, with a plain wood table at one end, a microphone on a stand and several bottles of mineral water.

DI Grant and Constable Kaur were already there, the young policewoman laying out note pads and pens at the three places behind the table. The inspector shook hands with Mark and Sarah, and thanked her for coming on such a night, and for agreeing to take part in the press questioning. He pointed to a few rows of chairs amongst which several individuals were scattered. 'If these chaps give us some

291

content in their morning papers it's amazing what might come out of it. Some people have long memories.'

Sarah thought the 'chaps' looked uninterested to a man. Mark had joined a couple in the front row and they at least were in animated conversation when DI Grant rapped the table for the conference to begin.

The inspector told of the body found under the demolished flat in Leith and that it had been established by forensic testing that these were the remains of Ruth Marchegay, aged 17 at the time, missing since the night of December 13th,1988,when she had gone, ostensibly, on a school visit to the theatre and had failed to return. A few of the reporters looked curiously at her when the policeman pointed out that it had been shown beyond doubt that Sarah Blane was the victim's sister, and that she had agreed to take part in this meeting because she was anxious to help in the inquiry. He made no mention of Ruth's pregnancy. 'As yet, the only people who will know about it are ourselves, and whoever killed your sister.'

The questions which followed were pretty desultory, Sarah thought. Twenty-three years is an aeon in press time, and juicier tales came out of the woodwork every day. In the end it wasn't the ordeal Sarah had expected, and the conference ended with a couple of the reporters promising a piece in the morning newspaper.

On the way back Mark pointed out again that even a small item in the press could have the effect of jolting a memory. 'Especially while the property trail isn't as fruitful yet as we'd hoped.'

Inspector Grant had told them with regret that they had traced the last owner of the building, who had bought it as a development opportunity. 'Over the years the flats had been sold off to individuals so we'll have to go through title deeds. We've also put the council on to tracing the ratepayer at that time, and that might bring some results.' He'd spread his hands. 'If only she'd been found while the building was still occupied...'

On Tuesday morning Sarah bought the Edinburgh papers on her way to school and, dropping her bag on the staff-room floor, began turning the pages for references to Ruth. Early, she had the place to herself, and she was wincing at the headline 'Grisly Find in Leith Tenement', when the door opened and Judith almost fell into the room. Sarah looked up.

'What a beauty! Who would have thought!' She slung her jacket towards the coat-stand and missed, laughing as she bent to try again. 'It's just incredible, isn't it?'

'What's incredible?'

'You mean you haven't heard?'

'Heard what, Judith?'

'Yes, heard what?' Roger came in behind Judith.

She stopped with her jacket in throwing position. 'You neither? It's the Heidie! He's been arrested!'

'Arrested!' Roger and Sarah gasped in concert. 'Keith?'

While Judith was speaking the rest of the department arrived and she went over the story again. Which was that Keith Birkmyre, with Annette and the boys in the car, had become involved in a road rage incident on the way back from his mother's funeral. Apparently incensed by the attitude of the other driver he had lost control and punched the man in the face.

The wife then phoned for the police, who arrested the Head and charged him with assault. Annette called Moira late last night to say that he was in custody until this morning, when he would be released on bail.' Judith's eyes sparkled. 'Incredible, isn't it?'

There was a disbelieving silence, then the questions

started. Where, when, what exactly happened?

But Judith had told them all she knew. Moira, whom she'd met in the car park, had been her source of information. She hoped for discretion, but knew that there was little chance of this latest disaster staying hidden.

'Poor Moira.' Sarah said, 'This on top of Lynn Cameron.'

'Oh Lord, I'm sorry,' Judith flopped into her chair, 'I'd forgotten about the girl for the moment.'

Willie Armstrong chewed hard on the stem of his empty pipe and Mary Stephens had turned several shades of puce while they listened to Judith. Now the reminder that there was another pupil missing was the last straw. Mary pulled a handkerchief out of her sleeve and was dabbing at her tears as the bell rang for the start of the day.

Sarah slipped the newspaper into her briefcase. 'Mary, will you be all right? Do you have a class first period? I can cover for you if…'

'No, no Sarah, that's kind of you, but I'll manage.' She stuffed the hanky back where it had come from as she left the staff-room. 'Must soldier on, mustn't we?'

Yes, Sarah thought, soldier on we must. Especially when we're confronted by DI Steve Hamilton. The policeman was heading towards her along the corridor. Sarah gritted her teeth.

'Ah, Miss Blane. Just the person I was looking for. You weren't at home last night when I called.'

'Whatever it is I'm afraid it will have to wait, Inspector, since I have a class and that won't wait.' Not strictly true, since her first class was second period, but she'd be damned if she was going to dance to his pompous tune.

He nodded coolly. 'I'll see you at the break then. If you'd just come to Mr Birkmyre's office.'

It wasn't a request. Sarah was tempted to remind him that a break was supposed to be just that, but reckoned it was best to have it over.

She hid a smile as she entered the office.

Steve Hamilton was behind the desk fiddling with the Head's swivel chair. Keith Birkmyre was a much taller man than the detective.

'Oh, right, Miss Blane. If you'd just sit over there.' The other chair was the one kept for interviewing difficult visitors, and was distinctly lower than the Head's. Sarah had never sat in it before but she knew that it was designed to put the interviewee at a disadvantage. Like a man on a horse.

The seating arrangements to his satisfaction, the Inspector sat down, clasped his hands on the desk and said, 'How did the press conference go last night?'

Sarah was taken aback. 'I thought you wanted to ask me about Lynn Cameron?'

'Oh, I do, of course, but you must have known that there would be contact between Lothian and ourselves about your other,' the bushy eyebrows jiggled, 'involvement with the police.'

'The press conference was satisfactory, as far as I can tell, having had no previous experience of such things.'

He smiled. 'Not even when your sister went missing?'

'Inspector Hamilton, I was ten years old at the time. Anyway, what are you suggesting about my - 'other involvement' - with the police? I know nothing about Lynn Cameron's disappearance.'

The policeman leaned back in the chair and stretched. 'Well, you may remember that when Rubina Khan went missing you were very anxious to help us with our inquiries. Even came to the station, didn't you? So it can't be a surprise to you that we're wondering what you may be able to tell us this time.' He swung himself upright. 'There's seems to be something about you and ...vanishing teenagers, is there not, Miss Blane ?'

Sarah's face was burning. She shook her head.

The DI raised a finger. 'Now, now, I know you've been to see Lynn's mother, so you can't get away with that.'

Sarah breathed deeply. 'Mrs Cameron had left a message on my answer-phone, so my visit to her was a matter of courtesy. She thought I might know something about Lynn.'

'But you don't.'

'No, Inspector, I don't.'

The bell rang for the end of the interval; the DI waved a hand as Sarah stood up, 'Just let me remind you that if you do find out anything it is your responsibility to bring it directly to us. Is that clear?'

'I am well aware of that.' She started to leave, then she put her head back round the door, 'But tell me, Inspector. What's to happen now to Hakim Ashrif?'

'He was absolutely furious! I think he might have done me some harm if he'd been able to get out of the chair fast enough!'

Sarah laughed as she heard Mark's sharp intake of breath on the phone. 'I'm not surprised! That's not the sort of question you're supposed to ask the cops. Anyway, I take it there's no news about Lynn?'

'Nothing yet. It's not looking good. This is the fifth day without a trace. It's awful.' She was silent for a moment, 'Listen Mark, I'm toying with the idea of going back to see David. What do you think?'

It was his turn to be silent. 'Not on your own, Sarah. From what you tell me he's a rather disturbed young man.'

'But he doesn't know you. I'm sure he'd find it totally unacceptable if I turned up with a complete stranger in tow.'

'Someone else then. What about Moira? Or Mary Stephens?'

Sarah said, 'No use. Moira has accepted that David had nothing to do with any of it, and Mary would have a fit at the very idea. David Smythe is above suspicion to the point of the angelic where Mary is concerned. Besides, they would wonder why I wanted an escort?'

'Judith?'

'You must be joking!'

'Well in that case, perhaps you should forget it for the moment. Anyway, you've enough to think about. What about the report in the paper?'

Sarah sighed. 'You mean the one 'grisly find' report? I was disappointed, to tell you the truth. I thought there would be more than that?'

'I know. But you'd see there was a new murder sensation to report.'

'Yes, the young lad found stabbed in one of the closes on the Royal Mile. I suppose that was bound to put Ruth off the scale. It won't be in any of the later papers either, will it?'

'No, Sarah, I'm afraid it won't. It's about hot irons, and all that. Still, someone may come forward. We can't give up hope.'

When the phone call ended Sarah found herself restless; she paced about the flat, then put up the board and heaved a pile of laundry on to the sofa, but didn't get as far as switching on the iron. She fed herself on a microwavable ready meal - in the freezer for emergencies and times like these when she couldn't summon the effort to cook.

Her meal eaten and Henry happily nestling into the pile of un-ironed clothes, Sarah left the flat and drove to David Smythe's house.

While it was less than two weeks since she had last seen him, great changes had taken place in that time. Sarah was surprised to find the flat bare, all pictures and ornaments removed and the living room almost impassable with packing cases. So taken up with this was she that she hardly heard David's greeting. When she looked closely at him she could see a difference in him too. His skin had lost its deathly pallor and although he was still very thin, his whole demeanour seemed altogether brighter.

Sarah found herself stating the obvious. 'You're moving!'

'You're clever!' He laughed when he said it, then waved Sarah to the armchair which was still in position. 'Sorry, the gin's packed, I'm afraid. What brings you back so soon, Sarah?'

'Have you heard about Lynn Cameron?'

He groaned, 'Not Lynn again! I told you last time...'

Sarah interrupted, 'She's been missing for four days.'

David Smythe sat down suddenly on one of the packing boxes. 'Lynn? Why Lynn?'

'That's a strange question, David? Might as well ask, 'Why Rubina?'

'I know, but...that was different. I mean, her...well Hakim and the culture thing. That just doesn't apply to Lynn Cameron.'

'So the police haven't been here?'

He shook his head. Some of his new-found vitality had deserted him. 'Why would they?'

Sarah shrugged. 'They seem to be covering the same ground as last time. Lynn had found out something, you know, but she didn't get the chance to pass it on before she disappeared.'

David rubbed his hands over his face. 'I can't believe this is happening again. Just when it seemed to be all over, this...' He took his hands away from his face and spread his arms. 'What's it about?'

'Anyway.' Sarah said, 'Where are you moving to?'

'Glasgow.'

She raised her eyebrows. 'That's not so far.'

'I'm...moving in with a...friend.'

Sarah nodded. 'I see.'

Suddenly he took a deep breath. 'Actually, you don't, Sarah. It will be more convenient for my...treatment there.'

She could only repeat, 'Treatment?'

He looked down at his shoes and Sarah did likewise. Gucci loafers, she was thinking, as David said,

'I'm HIV positive.'

She looked up from his feet and said the first thing that came into her mind.

'I'm very sorry, David.'

Suddenly a lot of things became clear. The clubs, the exotic trips, even the attempted suicide. And, being the son of Colin Smythe, the guilt. Judith was right all along. Rubina or any other girl had nothing to fear from this man. A conclusion obviously reached by the police too when they investigated his lifestyle.

Sarah got up. 'I'll go now. And, I wish you luck with...everything.'

As he held the door open for her, he said, 'Actually, you haven't told me why you came. Was it just to tell me about Lynn? Or was it to question me about her?'

'No, but I did want to ask...what you meant last time when you told me Lynn had confided in you about Rubina's friend?'

Even in the low lighting of the doorway Sarah could

see him flush. He mumbled something and she said, 'What did you say?'

'It wasn't true.'

Sarah leaned back against the balustrade of the landing. It was a chill March evening but shock held her against the cold railing. 'What wasn't true?'

'Lynn didn't tell me anything about Rubina. I...saw her myself, with... a boy.'

'A boy? Who?'

'Gordon ...the Head's son.'

Sarah thumped the railing, hurting her hand. 'David Smythe, how could you! When did you see them together? Why didn't you say? Did you tell anyone?' She didn't know which question she wanted answered most.

He leaned against the door jamb and hugged himself against the cold, 'It was down at the boatyard. They looked as if they'd been on Keith's boat - in the yard I mean.'

'So why didn't you say?'

'Well, it was long before Rubina went missing. And Gordon wasn't here then. He obviously had nothing to do with it. And it would have meant Keith finding out. I can't imagine he'd have been too pleased about Gordon and the girl. Besides, it might have been nothing.'

Sarah shook her head. 'I can't understand you. Everyone was bending over backwards to help and you knew something like this and didn't tell anyone!'

'To be honest, Sarah, it had sort of slipped my mind. If I'd thought it was important I would have told - after all, don't forget I was under suspicion myself. And,' he placed his hand on his chest. 'let's face it, I was a bit preoccupied. It was only when Hakim Ashrif was arrested that I remembered about Gordon, and I wondered if Hakim had found out and ...well...you know the rest.' He sniffed and turned away into the flat.

When she got home, there was a message from Mark on her phone.

He said, when he answered her call, 'Don't tell me, you went to David Smythe's, didn't you?'

She tried to laugh. 'Right first time.'

'I knew it, when I got no reply. So, was it worth it?'

'Actually, Mark, I don't know where to start, but apart from the fact that he's moving and he's got HIV he told me this weird story about seeing Rubina with Gordon Birkmyre, the Head's son, and admitted he'd lied about the earlier conversation with Lynn.'

'That's strange. Why tell now, when Lynn's gone missing? Do you think he's telling the truth now?'

'Oh! He said it had slipped his mind. It never occurred to me that he might be lying.'

'He lied about the previous conversation.'

'Ye-es. I know. But why now?'

'To divert attention from Lynn's disappearance perhaps?' Mark groaned. 'No, that doesn't make sense. He's not under suspicion for that, is he?'

'Not at all, apparently. Being gay has let him off the hook where the girls are concerned. But Mark, remember the expensive watch in the photograph. A Dreyfuss, wasn't it? I never thought to look when I was speaking to Gordon Birkmyre'

'Well, why would you? He's never been in the scene at all before now. Anyway, I've got something to tell you. That's why I was phoning.'

'Oh, sorry.'

'Someone has called the paper about Ruth.'

Sarah dropped on to the pile of ironing on the sofa.

Mark went on, 'Roddy Smith, that's one of the guys I spoke to at the press conference. He got the call. For some reason this person went straight to the paper, rather than the police, God knows why. Unless she's looking for money.'

'Money?' Sarah's tongue felt thick. 'You said 'she'.
A woman?'

'So it would seem. Roddy called me because he
thought that there might be a slim chance that the woman did
have a story to tell, and they might buy it. She wants to meet
with you.'

Her head had begun to thump. 'A marketing
opportunity all round. What a world!'

'I know Sarah, I'm sorry. We don't know what kind
of person this woman is, but if you insist on the police she
might just vanish into the ether. And you need to know what
happened to Ruth, don't you?'

The woman didn't want to meet in Edinburgh. If
they would refund her train fare she was happy to come to
Glasgow. Mark arranged that they should meet her in Queen
Street station at six the following evening. And when he said
café, she said, 'Bar.'

Sarah's day at school was fractured by the worry of
Lynn's continued absence, David Smythe's revelation about
Rubina - if that's what it was - and the forthcoming meeting.

After school she drove to Mark's flat and they took a
taxi to the station. 'Leaving nothing to chance,' Mark said,
'since parking can take an inordinate amount of time.'

In the taxi Sarah chewed the inside of her lip and
thought about how strange her life had become in recent
months. Even now, on the way to a clandestine rendezvous
with some unknown woman.

'How will we know her?'

Mark smiled, 'She won't be carrying a copy of The
Times, I promise. No, I said I'd be sitting near the door with
a gorgeous girl and she'd spot us right away.'

Sarah poked his arm.

'And, just in case, I'd be wearing a brown leather jacket.'

'That's more like it!'

Sarah's mouth was dry as she watched the Edinburgh train slide into the platform.

The nearly incomprehensible station announcements could have been the gabbling of a flock of geese, for all she cared. She tried to pick a likely woman from the passengers but it was almost impossible, this was commuter time. The only distinguishing factor was that she was looking for a woman, and there were hordes of them. She dismissed the very young ones - this was someone who'd been around twenty-three years ago, but there were still plenty of appropriate vintage.

Then Mark said, 'There she is!'

Sarah said, 'How did...' and stopped. This would be the one.

The woman was probably in her fifties, but could have been older. Her hair was the colour of cranberries and she was wearing a metallic silver anorak with an abstract design, a short green skirt and a pair of fake fur boots which could have done service in the Antartic. At its kindest, her face had seen a lot of life.

Her perfume preceded her into the bar, where she hesitated until she saw Mark, who'd got up to greet her.

'Hi, I'm Mark and this is Sarah, Ruth Marchegay's sister. Before I sit down, can I get you a drink?'

The woman smiled at Sarah as she answered Mark. 'A malt would be good. No' too much water.'

Sarah said, 'Thank you for coming.'

The woman sat next to her. 'Aye, you're her sister all right. I can see the likeness.'

Mark came back with the whisky and a separate glass of water. 'I thought this was best, eh...what's your name?'

'Just Angie.' She produced a pack of cigarettes from a shiny black bag, then threw them on the table. 'Ach, I keep forgetting.'

'Right then, Angie. You called the paper?'

'Aye. I was just glancing through it like, and I see this wee story about the body. It gave me a shock, ken, because I used to live in that same close.' She put a hand to her cheek. 'Then when I saw the lassie's name, I knew right away who it was.'

'How did you know Ruth?'

'Well, see, she used to come in wi' one of the students who lived across the close from me. He was a snooty bugger, ken, but the lassie was always nice.'

Sarah closed her eyes, 'What was he called?'

Angie touched her arm. 'There were two of them for a while. One was Michael, Michael Vaughn - I always mind that because there was a singer with that name, Frankie Vaughn. He was English. The other one was called Max. Mik and Max I called them. The Michael one left but Max was there longer. Wee Ruth came a lot then.'

Sarah said, 'Was Max English too?'

She sucked air through her teeth and shook her head. 'Nope, I don't think so. He had a posh way o' speaking, like I say, but no' English.'

'So, let me be sure. Ruth still came to the flat after this Michael left?' Mark asked.

'Oh, aye, for a good while.'

'You seem to have been on quite friendly terms with Ruth.' Mark had narrowed his eyes, and Sarah knew he was suspicious.

She said quickly, 'You saw my resemblance to Ruth right away, didn't you, Angie?'

'Aye. You don't get that many wi' the blonde hair

and they black eyebrows. I used to kid Ruth that she coloured them but I mind she said her wee sister's were the very same.'

The words made Sarah's heart leap.

Angie's chin went up. 'And I was friendly wi' her because maist of them had nae time for the likes of me, if you ken what I mean?'

Mark nodded.

'But Ruth would always stop for a blether if we met in the close. Once I asked her if she had a machine gun in the fiddle case. Like the gangster movies, right? And she laughed like anything.'

She cast her eyes down and tapped the cigarette packet on the table, 'She was a lovely wee lassie.'

Sarah felt herself on the verge of tears. 'So what happened to her?'

Angie looked up. 'Well, that I canny tell you. I only wish I could. All I know is I heard them shouting, and her slamming out of the house one day and when I looked out the window she was running down the road. She was greeting awful sore. I'd have ran after her but the wean was on the pottie, like, and I couldny leave him.'

'She must have come back, though.' Mark said.

Angie sighed. 'Aye, she must have. After I went to work. I used to leave the wean wi' my mother at night, ken, so that I could get out.'

Sarah said, 'Didn't you wonder why you never saw her again?'

'Aye, I did, hen, but I thought they'd just had a fall out, you know what I mean?'

'What did this Max look like?' Mark asked.

She screwed up her face. 'Oh, tall, and kinna posh. Dark hair, no bad-looking. He was going to be a doctor, Ruth told me.'

Sarah gasped, 'A medical student!'

'No, I don't think so. It was some other kind of doctor.

'Can you remember what subject?'

She shook her head and her ruby locks caught the neon light from over the bar.

'It didn't really mean anything to me?'

Mark stood and gathered the glasses. 'Another drink?'

When he went off, Sarah said, 'And you had no idea of this Max's second name?'

'I'm sorry, love, I didn't. They never had a nameplate or anything, the students, because they were just renting the house from somebody else.'

'Who was your landlord, Angie?'

For the first time the woman looked uncomfortable. 'Eh, I had a guy that, you know, looked after me, ken? I just paid the rent to him.'

'And he was?'

Angie smiled. 'No, no. Nae names, nae pack drill.'

'But it was so long ago! What can it matter now?

Angie gave Sarah a look that said everything about the differences between them.

'Certain folk have long memories, and they're still about. How d'ye think I didny go to the polis?'

Sarah slumped back in her seat. 'So that's it. Max left the flat never to be seen again and nobody knew my sister was ...' Her breath caught.

Mark came back with the drinks, his wallet in his hand. 'While we're at it, your train fare.' He laid out several twenty pound notes. 'But, Angie, I don't think you have enough information to sell to the paper.'

She looked at the money on the table, then at Mark. 'I didny do this for money! I've got my own reasons for, no going to the polis, but I'm selling nothing.' Her mouth was a thin line. 'I came because I thought it might help the wee lassie's sister, to meet somebody that liked her…and saw her just before she…she died?'

Sarah had a thought. 'Didn't you know that Ruth was missing? There were posters around…in police stations and…'

Angie laughed, 'You can bet I wasny looking at posters any time I was in the nick, hen, sorry.' She drained the whisky, put the money into her bag and stood up. 'I just hope they get that bastard. She was a lovely wee lassie.'

She stood to catch next Edinburgh train, and Sarah got up too and gave her a quick hug. Then she ran, beams of light bouncing off the silver jacket.

Mark emptied his glass, 'A hooker with a heart, as the Americans say.'

'Well, it was good of her to come. Even if it doesn't take us much further.'

He put his hand over Sarah's. 'You think? What about Michael Vaughn? If anyone is going to know this bloke's name it's him.'

'Yes, but if he's seen news about Ruth he hasn't come forward.' Sarah shook her head. 'Anyway, how do we find him?'

'What about good old Google, for starters. If this man has made any mark on the world since 1988 he'll be on the web. Meantime, the police might come up with names, but we can still get on.'

Sarah shrugged. 'Or we could try Sheila Macdonald again?'

Mark whistled, 'I think Google might be more responsive than that lady! Anyway, let's eat. Rico's? We're near enough.'

As they walked through George Square in the

direction of Merchant City and the restaurant, Sarah pulled her phone from her bag. 'I want to know if there's any news of Lynn.'

'Moira? Hi, it's me. Is there…no, somehow I didn't think there would be. Where? In Glasgow. I'm just going to eat with Mark. Listen Moira, there's something I'll need to discuss with you. Can you set aside some time tomorrow? We need to talk before we all disappear in different directions at the weekend. Yes, that would be good.'

Mark slipped his arm through Sarah's when she had returned the phone to her handbag. 'She's not back?'

She shook her head. 'No. I have a terrible feeling about this, Mark. It took two weeks to find Rubina's body in the loch…'

He squeezed her arm. 'Come on, love, this doesn't have to be the same.'

Chapter 17

'So, what do you think I should do?'

Moira laid her coffee cup in the saucer with care, then looked out of the hotel window at a clutch of seagulls squabbling over what appeared to be a discarded burger carton on the grass of the esplanade.

She took her eyes from the scene outside and looked at Sarah. 'Honestly, I just don't know.' Her face was pale, her normal ebullience nowhere in evidence.

Sarah felt bad that this quick lunch out of school was heaping more troubles on Moira's shoulders.

'I can't ignore it, can I?'

Moira shook her head and sighed. 'I suppose not, if you think David is telling the truth.'

Sarah's cup clattered on to its saucer. 'That's just it! I would have had a quiet word with the boy himself if I'd known before, but he flew back to America yesterday, I believe.'

'Oh yes, I'd forgotten that. But I just can't see Gordon Birkmyre with Rubina, somehow. It doesn't seem to fit.'

'Moira. They were young, and she was very attractive. What's to say Gordon didn't fancy a little flirtation before he went off to MIT?'

'Well, maybe...' Moira was drawing circles on the wooden table with the end of her spoon.

'But, do I speak to Keith about it? That's the big question.'

Moira dropped the spoon with a clatter. 'Of course not! Even if Gordon was seen with Rubina it has no bearing on what happened to her. They've got Hakim Ashrif for her murder, haven't they? So what's to be gained by taking gossip to Keith when he's so very upset. Even if it did come from David Smythe.'

Sarah didn't reply.

'Anyway, Keith won't be back at school until after the holiday. He's grieving terribly about his mother...' Moira ran both hands through her mop of hair, 'and about the arrest. I can't get over such a thing happening to him...' There were tears in her eyes.

Sarah got up, 'I'll settle the bill.' As she waited at the bar she thought about the effect all the events of this school year were having on Moira. She seemed close to cracking, and Sarah didn't intend to make it any worse. She would have to find a new strategy to deal with the affair of Gordon and Rubina, if that's what it was.

Back in class for the afternoon she tried to put it out of her mind, but if she was going to follow it up with any of her colleagues it would have to be before school closed for the Easter break at lunchtime next day. Judith didn't live locally so she was no use, and Mary Stephens' judgement wasn't the soundest. Willie Armstrong? Too objective for speculation, since that's what she would be asking for. It would have to be Roger Bullough. And who knows, if he thought there was someone else in the Rubina story he might come clean about what he was doing that October night when he claimed to have been meeting the bus. After all, it wasn't Hakim Ruth was going to meet, regardless of what followed. She decided not to tell Mark about her plan. He would probably think it a risky strategy.

However when she broached the need for a chat Roger surprised her by inviting her out to lunch on Friday after the school closed. Mark wouldn't be around until the evening so it would be done and dusted before he had to know.

'But, don't you have to hurry home, Roger?'

He gave a slow shake of his head. 'I'll explain tomorrow.'

On Friday morning there was another whole school meeting before the pupils dispersed for two weeks. Once again Steve Hamilton was centre stage, accompanied by Moira.

The purpose of this assembly, he pointed out, was to ensure that there was not the tiniest scrap of information any of them might have which would help in the search for Lynn, who had now been missing for a week. With his usual heavy manner he laid it on thick that girls liked to confide in each other and it that he found it very, very hard to believe that there wasn't a single friend of Lynn's who could help. As ever there were a couple of sobs from the more impressionable girls but no information. The DI's eyebrows were at their most active, and he waited in an uncomfortable silence until Moira added her pleas to the inspector's. Again nothing, then she dealt with a few administrative items before wishing everyone, staff and pupils, a good Easter break.

Roger had suggested that the lunch should be somewhere out of Helensburgh and they settled on the Glen Falloch. As she parked her car Sarah was reminded of her first lunch with Mark on that grim November day. Today, however, the weather was sunny, with a brisk wind scudding banks of cloud across a blue sky. Even the waters of the loch looked inviting.

Sarah was impressed by how relaxed Roger appeared to be, chatting casually about the department and about the Head's misfortune as they waited for their food. He even

311

indulged himself in a glass of white wine to celebrate the end of a very difficult term. Sarah declined and ordered mineral water instead. Wine in the early part of the day tended to make her sleepy, she said, and she wanted to be fit to drive home. 'However, had it been the evening…'

He nodded, then waited until the drinks came. 'Yes, well, let me explain. I don't normally get out for a meal and drink in the evening, as you know, Sarah. But Dorothy is in hospital at the moment.'

Sarah spilled a little of her mineral water. 'Oh, Roger, why didn't you say? What happened?'

He was clasping his glass in both hands. 'Nothing, really. She is definitely getting worse, but she's gone into hospital mainly to get a bit of a rest, and to give me a break.'

'Oh, I see. How long will she be in?'

'The two weeks of the holiday. The doctors thought perhaps I should try to get away for some sunshine myself.' He tapped his chest. 'For the benefit of the old ticker, if nothing else.'

Sarah studied him. It occurred to her now that no-one ever had time to closely study colleagues on the merry-go round that was the school day. He was looking better than she'd ever seen him, she realised. Much of the strain which normally marked his expression was gone and he had the festive aspect of a boy let out of school, which in a sense he was.

'And where are you..?'

He raised his eyebrows, and she smiled. 'Going to have that sunshine?' He flushed slightly. 'Oh, Tenerife.'

'Well, you should certainly get the sun there.'

'What about yourself, Sarah?'

She pleated the edge of her napkin. 'I'm just glad not have school for a couple of weeks. There's still a long way to go with …my sister.'

Roger gave her hand a light touch. 'I'm so sorry. How could I forget that you're in the middle of that ordeal.'

She nodded. 'And then there's Lynn Cameron.'

His brow creased and he looked into his wine-glass. 'I know. I feel so helpless about that.'

The waiter laid their plates in front of them and it broke the thread of the conversation. They ate in silence for a time then Sarah said, 'Roger, have you really no idea at all of what might have happened to her? I mean you've been in the school so much longer than I - you know everyone much better than I do.'

'Actually, that's not true, Sarah. In the time you've been in Fruin High I think you have established a remarkable rapport with your pupils...' He smiled. 'And your colleagues. Look how kind you've been to Dorothy, for example. And how you worried about David.'

'You know about David?'

He laid his knife on his plate. 'Yes. I've always known. Even when there was all that nonsense about Rubina Khan - taking her out of his class, I mean - I had to let it happen because I couldn't say anything.'

'Does Willie know too?'

'Yes, but not Mary, God help her. Judith, I think, suspects, but she's never said anything to me.'

'So, right from the start, when Rubina disappeared, you knew that David would not be involved.'

He did a maybe, maybe not, movement of his hand, 'Well, not unless she had found out something about his...preferences.'

'Tell me, Roger, what do you think did happen to her that night?'

'That night?'

'Yes, when you went to meet the bus and missed it.'

He choked on a piece of chicken and Sarah waited

until he washed it down with a mouthful of wine. His eyes were watering.

'Yes,' he said slowly, 'that night.'

He laid his cutlery on the plate and propped his elbows on the table. 'I think you know that wasn't true, Sarah, don't you? That I didn't go anywhere near the bus. I could tell, that time when you came to the house.'

She nodded, but didn't say anything.

'I was somewhere else.'

She nodded again, 'And?'

He took a breath, 'I was visiting a friend. A woman friend.' He looked intently into Sarah's face. 'You understand?'

Sarah sat back on her chair, 'Yes. And she lives on the front, doesn't she?'

His eyes opened wide. 'How do you know that?'

'I've seen you more than once, Roger. When you were supposed to be taking your 'constitutional', as your neighbour calls it.'

'Dorothy has been ill for a long time.' He rubbed his hand across his face. 'It's difficult, if you know what I mean.'

Sarah knew that it meant he was being unfaithful, but what was there to say? It was his burden. She shrugged, 'It's your business, Roger.'

'You won't say anything - to Dorothy - or in school?'

'No, I certainly won't.' She wiped her hands on her napkin. 'Anyway, there's another matter I want to discuss with you.'

His relief was palpable, and she understood why he'd suggested the lunch. He knew she'd seen through his 'alibi' for that October night and was testing her discretion. Unaware, of course, that he'd been on Sarah's list of

314

suspects for Rubina's death.

'Were you aware of any connection - relationship - or whatever, between Rubina Khan and Gordon Birkmyre?'

'Rubina Khan and Gordon, the Head's son?' He picked up his cutlery. 'Absolutely not. What makes you say that?'

'David Smythe told me he saw them together.'

He chewed thoughtfully for a moment. 'Now you mention it, Gordon was around the school rather a lot in that last term before he went to America, but I never saw him with Rubina. Anyway, what's your point? Gordon was long gone by the time Rubina was killed, and they've got their murderer, haven't they?'

Sarah drank some water. 'Quite frankly, Roger, I've been wondering about motive.'

'I don't see why, but never mind, Sarah, you must do what you will.'

'As must you, Roger. And while we're on that subject, are you going alone to Tenerife?'

This time he flushed deeply. 'Well...no.' Then in a rush, 'Actually, you might as well know. I'm going with Miss Carter.'

It was Sarah's turn to be caught unawares. 'What? Miss Carter from Home Economics?'

He nodded. 'It's why I didn't mention Dorothy and the hospital in school. I didn't want any awkward questions.'

'Well, you've been very discreet up until now, and I won't say anything.' Sarah smiled. 'I wish you a happy holiday.'

'You know, I've always felt a little envious at holiday times, since Dorothy became ill, that is. Everyone going their separate ways while I was stuck at home.' He took another swig of his wine. 'Of course, I'd never let Dorothy know how I felt, I wouldn't do that to her.'

No, Sarah thought, you just found yourself some solace in the Home Economics department.

'Have you never fancied a little holiday home, here in Scotland, Roger? Where perhaps Dorothy could go too. Like Keith has apparently, somewhere up north.'

He nodded. 'We still have a caravan - down at Portpatrick. I seldom get there these days - since Dorothy has become so ill.'

When Mark arrived in the evening and she told him of her conversation with Roger he simply smiled and shrugged.

'I thought you'd be gob-smacked!'

'I don't know the guy but I do know what it is, to be... on your own, in that way.'

'Oh Mark, I'm so sorry.' Sarah sat next to him and placed her hand on his cheek. 'I just didn't think.'

'No, it's all right. I was truly alone. Roger is physically alone, but his wife is still there. It can't be easy.' He tapped her forehead. 'So, what other dastardly secrets have you winkled out of your male colleagues? You've dealt with David, and now Roger. Next you'll be telling me that the lugubrious Willie is a transvestite, when he isn't growing carrots.'

She slapped his hand away and rolling Henry off her lap, went to pour drinks for them.

Mark said, 'In any case, I've got some news. I've found Michael Vaughn. He's an archaeologist in Australia - Melbourne University. I emailed him.'

Sarah stopped, the gin bottle poised to pour. 'And?'

'Well, he's not too keen to co-operate. Says he can barely remember this Max and wants to know who I am to be asking questions, why I'm asking questions and what I plan to do with the information.'

'What have you told him?'

'The best thing I could think of. I suggested he got on to the Scotsman archive for the last few weeks and read about the young girl found at his former address.' He pursed his lips. 'It might work, or it might drive him further away.'

Sarah went back to pouring. 'You know, it's just a possibility that the Max character is on the other side of the world too. I hadn't thought of that.'

'Right enough, nor had I. Still even if he is, we'll find him.' Mark said, 'Or the police will. Anyway, what are your plans for these next two idle weeks, Miss Blane?'

She handed him a drink. 'I daresay I could spend the time doing a bit of spring cleaning here, Mr McKenzie.' She craned her neck to look up at the corners of the ceiling. 'Good Lord, is that a cobweb?'

Mark copied her actions, twisting his neck to look at the spot. 'I see no cobweb.

No, actually, I have a better idea. Why don't you pack a bag and come and stay with me for the next fortnight?' He smiled. 'I mean, you can clean there if you like. I'm sure I have lots of cobwebs!'

Sarah threw a cushion at him.

'Seriously, Sarah, I think it would do you good to be away from here for a couple of weeks. I know you have to be around for the police and so on, but they can get you at my place. I can take some time off and we can do a few ordinary things - you know, cinema, concerts, theatre? What do you say?'

She sat down next to him again. 'It sounds lovely. But what about Henry?' Hearing his name the cat flicked his tail. 'It's too late to book him into the cattery. It's always jam-packed at school holidays.'

'He can come too. Can't you, old son?' Mark traced the line of Sarah's cheek. 'And before you say it, I will. You can keep in touch with the search for Lynn just as easily in

Glasgow as here. Moira isn't going away, is she?'

Sarah shook her head. 'Not this time. She looks as if she could with a 'bit of sunshine' more than Roger, but I honestly don't think she has the energy to go off on holiday, considering how hard this year has been for her.'

'She's not still worrying about drugs in the school, is she?'

The cat jumped back on to Sarah's knee and allowed himself to be petted.

'I don't think so. There haven't been any more incidents that we know of. But drugs are a worry in any school these days.'

Mark ran his fingers through his hair. 'I suppose. Anyway, back to the suitcase. Are you coming to stay at my place, or not? And you, Henry.' He stroked the cat's fur and Sarah's hand in the same movement. 'Off you go and pack up your bed and your dishes.'

Sarah laughed. 'All right, you win. I'll pack my bed and my dishes too. We'll go in the morning, ok?'

Mark was nodding as the phone rang. Sarah looked at her watch and made a face as she listened.

'Right, I see. Well, that's a bit of a disappointment, isn't it?'

Mark's eyebrows were raised questioningly as she hung up the phone.

'That was DI Grant. We've got further than he has, would you believe? They've found the person who owned the flat in Leith in 1988 but he has no records of the students he rented to. He had the flat for about ten years and a succession of students lived there but he couldn't remember who or when. He paid his rates, the council confirmed that, but it looks as if it was a bit of a tax dodge otherwise. He didn't keep records and rented out the flat on an informal basis.'

Mark smiled. 'And you didn't tell the inspector that we've found Michael Vaughn.'

Sarah bit her lip. 'I did think about it - but what if it's the wrong man? We don't want to involve an innocent party if he happens to have the same name as someone else.'

'No, fair enough.' Mark yawned and stretched. 'But I think it is the same one. He graduated from Edinburgh University in 1988. Will I phone the Chinese for dinner?'

Sarah was on her feet. 'Yes, great. I'll get started on my packing.' She walked to the door. 'Oh, by the way, DI Grant said he phoned my mobile and got no reply. I wonder what I've done with it?'

She scrabbled around in her briefcase and her handbag. 'Damn, I've just remembered. It rang during a class this morning and I switched it off. I must have stuck it in my desk drawer.' She shrugged. 'Oh well, I'll call in for it in the morning. Someone will be in the school, the cleaners or the janitor or someone, so the building won't be locked.'

In the morning Sarah left Mark in the car park while she went into school. The radio was on and Henry was howling his own accompaniment to the music. It was evident that he wasn't pleased to be in his basket, like luggage, going who knows where. Sarah was laughing at Mark's expression as she got out of the car. Over her shoulder she said, 'Well, it was your idea.'

Inside the building there was the sound of vacuum cleaners and distant whistling, which Sarah took to be the janitor. The odour of children was in the process of being wiped away by the fluid the cleaners used on the desks and hard surfaces. Her phone wasn't in her desk and she made her way to the staff-room, passing Moira's open door. She was pleased to see no sign of Moira. But further along the corridor the Head's door stood open too - and Keith Birkmyre sat behind his desk.

He caught sight of her. 'Ah, Sarah, isn't it? Do come in - I've been meaning to talk to you.' He gestured loosely with his free hand, 'Come in, why don't you? Come in!'

The whisky fumes struck Sarah the instant she stepped into the room. The desk was a mess of documents and newspapers. The head took a large gulp from the tall glass in his other hand, then waggled the bottle towards her. 'Care to join me?' The bottle was almost empty.

Sarah was astonished. His face had a bruised, sunken look, as if a heavy object had rolled over it, his eyes were bloodshot and he was unshaven. His tie was loose and he fished the end of it out of the glass where it was dangling in the whisky. 'Oops!' He waved at the seat opposite his desk. 'Sit down - take the weight off your feet, that's what they say, isn't it?'

Sarah moved towards the chair, but didn't sit. 'I…I was very sorry to hear about your mother.'

He laid his glass carefully on the desk and held out both hands. He shrugged. 'It happens. Sooner or later, it happens.' He wagged a finger at her. 'They tell me you had a sister. But, do you have a mother, Sarah?'

She hitched her bag on her shoulder. 'No, Keith. Not for a long time.'

He nodded, up and down, like a toy dog on a parcel shelf. 'Best friend, always best friend.' His eyes began to close and she feared he was about to fall off his seat.

She made a movement towards the door. 'Eh…I was just going to the staff-room to find my phone. I think I must have left it there yesterday.'

He was nodding again. 'Yes, yes…you do that.'

'Are you sure…will you be all right?'

His head snapped up so quickly that she jumped. 'Of course I'll be all right. I'm always all right. ' He prodded his chest so hard she could almost hear the thump on bone.

Sarah pointed to the clatter of cleaning, which was coming closer. 'It's just, Keith, the cleaners …it's the holiday…'

He smiled wetly. 'I know, I know.'

She had reached the corridor. 'I'll go then…' She turned back, 'Oh, I don't suppose there's any news of Lynn Cameron, is there?'

He frowned as if engaging in a serious feat of memory. 'Lynn Cameron? Now let me see - where might she have gone?' He winked at Sarah, then grinned. 'Not into Loch Lomond we hope, eh?' He gave a huge, expansive wave. 'Don't you worry about it - off you go and enjoy your well-earned holiday…Miss Marchegay.'

The name hit Sarah like a bullet. She walked to the staff-room in a daze of shock and repugnance. Her phone was lying on the coffee table. She had never cared for Keith Birkmyre but this was something else.

As she slumped into the car, Mark said, 'Did you get it?'

She held up the phone without answering.

'What is it, Sarah? What happened?' He took her free hand between his.

'The boss, he's up there.' She jerked her head towards the building. 'And he's blind drunk!'

'The Head?'

She nodded.

Mark said, 'He must be cracking up - his mother, the arrest - the things that have gone on here.' He shrugged. 'I've seen it before.'

Sarah bit her lip. 'Perhaps he is. I asked about Lynn, and he was horrible, and it wasn't just that - he…he called me - Miss Marchegay!'

Mark's eyebrows went up. 'My God!' Then he smiled. 'He knows about Ruth, of course, that she's your sister, and his wee chum Hamilton will have filled him in.'

She shivered. 'I suppose. But it was…such a shock.'
She turned. 'It's all right, Henry, we're going now.'

*

With Henry circling around his food and water in Mark's
kitchen as if he didn't trust his familiar dishes, Sarah went to
the bedroom to unpack. Mark was making lunch and there
was an interesting smell of garlic, not to the cat's liking.

Sarah's mind was still in Fruin High and the strange
behaviour of the Head. She was troubled by the idea that she
should have called his wife, or maybe Moira. Caught in that
state on the school premises would do nothing for his career,
on top of his charge of assault. She laid a skirt on the bed
and was leaving the room to share her thoughts with Mark
when the shout came.

'Sarah!'

Visions of Mark tipping boiling pasta over Henry as
he fell over him had her rushing along the long hall, only to
meet Mark coming towards her, clutching his Blackberry,
looking stunned.

'Michael Vaughn has replied. Look what it says!' He
pulled her arm. 'Come into the light in the living room.'

Sarah had to read the words on the screen twice.
Trembling, she grasped the small machine with both hands.

*'I have now checked the Scotsman, and can tell you
that the man who shared my flat in Leith in 1988 was one
Keith Maxwell Birkmyre, studying for a PhD in Physics. He
chose to be known as 'Max'. That's all I will
say at this stage. Let me know what transpires.'*

As if it were red hot, Sarah dropped the phone on the
sofa and collapsed beside it, panting, and almost incoherent.
'Keith?' She shook her head. 'Maxwell?'

She and Mark stared at each other. 'It can't be!'

Mark said, 'A coincidence?'

Nausea overwhelmed her and Sarah dashed to the bathroom. She didn't vomit but bathed her burning face with cold water. Back in the room Mark was sitting where she'd left him.

'Come and sit down, love.' He tried to smile at her. 'Sarah, it's got to be a coincidence. I mean, the name's not that unusual, is it?'

She nodded slightly. 'Should we tell the police?'

'Yes. But not Steve Hamilton. Let's think. What do you know about your Keith Birkmyre?'

She gave a dry laugh. 'If I hadn't seen him as he is today I would scoff at this...coincidence. But, Mark,' she tapped his arm with a clenched fist. 'He was so weird...he just wasn't his usual smooth self. And arrogant still, even although he was so drunk.' She caught her breath. 'And my God, he called me Marchegay!'

'Where did he go to university? Do you know?'

Sarah buried her face in her hands. 'I'm not sure...wait...somebody spoke to me about him...what was it?' She looked up, 'It was Dorothy! Roger's wife. She said...oh hell, what was it? Yes, she taught beside him many years ago.' She frowned, 'In Aberdeen.'

'That doesn't mean he wasn't at Edinburgh.' Mark jumped up from the sofa and walked about the room. 'You know, Sarah, that's the first thing we have to find out before we involve the police. I mean, the guy's in trouble enough as it is, and if we got the name wrong...' He spread his hands. 'Who can we ask without arousing suspicion? Moira?'

Sarah said, 'No...o...not Moira.   She's too protective of Keith...' She tugged at a lock of hair. 'I can't think of any...wait!' She sprang to her feet. 'His degrees and stuff are framed on the wall of his room! I always thought it was a bit tacky, but surely the University will be named on them? I never looked closely, always found it too embarrassing. His doctorate and everything. And that's another thing. Vaughn mentions the PhD.'

'Well, that's it.' Mark snapped his fingers. 'We've got to go back to the school and get into his office.'

Lunch abandoned, they set out again for Helensburgh. It was a black day in more senses than one, Sarah thought, as they drove alongside the boiling river. The sky was dark and waves slapped angrily against the shore. An inauspicious start to the Easter holidays. But as the school grew nearer the more unthinkable it seemed that Dr Keith Birkmyre, respected head teacher of Fruin High, could possibly have had anything to do with the long-ago murder of Ruth Marchegay. Sarah's scalp tightened. It was unreal.

It was after two o'clock in the afternoon. The school was locked.

Mark said. 'How do we get in?'

'I'll go the janitor's house and tell him that I left my phone in the staff-room. It was the truth, after all.' She opened the car door. 'Best you wait there. My excuse for being in the school would be pretty suspect if you were seen.'

Mark nodded. 'Just be careful.'

The bungalow was on the edge of the playing field. The janitor had gone to a football match, but Sarah apologised as sweetly as she could to his wife, who had her wet hair wrapped in a towel. She gave her a key to the only entrance which wasn't alarmed. 'Bobby needs to get in sometimes without disabling all the security. Just bring the key back when you're finished.'

Chapter 18

The deserted school was strangely unnerving and Sarah's footsteps echoed off the painted walls as she climbed the stairs. As she approached the Head's office she prayed that he hadn't locked his own door.

The smell of whisky was still strong in the room, which lay in shadow, the Venetian blinds closed. A faint gleam shone on the surface of several framed documents on the back wall, and she moved forward, kicking what she saw was the Head's whisky glass. It rolled on the floor until it clunked gently against the chair. Sarah held her breath and switched on the picture lights above the gold frames. A rugby success, two sailing triumphs, an MA from Aberdeen University, until there, in the most elegant frame and in beautiful cursive script, was the ghastly proof of her sister's death. 'Keith Maxwell Birkmyre, Doctor of Philosophy, Edinburgh University, 1989.'

Sarah's legs turned to jelly; she stumbled, and her foot came in contact with the whisky glass. She started to leave, then turned back to pick up the heavy tumbler. The deep patterns incised on the crystal swam before her eyes. Then, incredibly, a toilet flushed, and the Head appeared in the room.

Still intoxicated, his face still rubbery, he staggered slightly on sight of her, but his speech was clear, 'What are you...why are you still here?'

'I...I was worried after I left...I thought you might

be…'

He laughed, a harsh bark, and pointed. 'How kind? I see you have rescued my glass?'

Sarah looked down at the sticky tumbler in her hand. 'It rolled against my foot. I was just…going to put it on the desk.' She felt as if she might faint.

Shakily, he walked from the toilet door and sank into his chair. 'Now come on. Tell me why you are really here?' He gestured at the newspapers on his desk. 'After all, I'd have thought you'd be too busy solving the mystery of little Ruth?'

Rage welled up in Sarah and she wanted to smash the glass into his face. Her voice shaking, she said, 'I have solved it - Max.'

Confirmation of his identity threw a switch in Keith Birkmyre. His face became livid and he pushed the desk away. He rose to his feet. 'Give me that glass.'

Sarah backed towards the door. 'I don't think so.'

He lunged forward to take the glass from her and Sarah ran. In the wrong direction. Habit made her run in the direction she used every day of her school life, rather than to the door she had just entered by.

He caught her outside the staff-room and forced her inside and on to a chair. She'd never noticed before how much the room smelled of old paper and stale coffee. A shabby cardigan of Willie's hung on the coat-stand.

'I think…Bobby is coming.' She was breathless.

At this Keith Birkmyre laughed loudly. 'Everybody knows Bobby is a devout Rangers fan. Wouldn't miss a home game for anything.'

He settled down on another chair and crossed one leg over the other. 'What is it with you women? Nothing but trouble.'

Sarah thought of Mark outside in the car, and her

mobile phone, in her handbag - also in the car. How long until Mark would try to phone her and have to answer the ringing handbag?

'What do you mean - trouble?'

He leaned forward and stared into her face. 'I mean even an educated woman like yourself, Sarah, doesn't know where to stop. There's an excuse for a silly little bitch like the Cameron girl...'

Sarah gasped. 'Lynn? What have you done with Lynn?'

He put his head on one side. 'How do you know I haven't popped her into the loch, like the other one? Ruth, or whatever.'

Her skin crawled. 'Rubina?'

'Ha, yes. Rubina.' He pointed at her. 'Ruth was yours. You know, I've never liked you - that hair and those eyebrows. So like hers. It gave me the creeps.'

'But why?' She whispered.

He leapt up and started pacing about the room. 'Why? Why? I'll tell you why? That stupid ...Rubina girl came telling me that Gordon had been dealing drugs!' He thumped his chest. 'My son! She said they'd been seeing each other - and he'd told her just before he left that he'd been supplying a few drugs.' He laughed again. 'As if...'

He towered above Sarah.

'As if I would allow my son's future to be jeopardised by ...' a blob of spittle landed on her cheek. 'a creature like that! My God! He'd just gone to MIT. She wanted his address because she'd found out some of our pupils were taking the stuff. She said maybe I could speak to him about it.' He threw up his hands. 'It was only a bloody handful of ecstasy tablets!'

'A pupil died from taking those tablets.'

He grimaced. 'Don't I know it.'

'So you arranged to meet Rubina after the school trip - and killed her.'

He paused, and looked at Sarah as if she must understand.

'I had no choice.'

'Just as you had no choice with my sister.'

'Ah.' He put his head in his hands. 'I couldn't let that happen again...to my son.'

'You knew that Ruth was pregnant.'

'But that was the whole point.' He sat down next to her. 'I couldn't settle to being a father. Not after the sacrifices my poor mother had made.' He sighed. 'Your sister refused get rid of it, you know. I offered...but...' His face twisted. 'I wasn't meant just to be just a bloody schoolteacher, you know ...I was to...to reach for the ...'

Sarah's whole body was shaking. 'Why are you telling me this?'

'It's not rocket science. As soon as I heard about it I knew it had to be her. Then the minute I was arrested and they took my DNA?' He shrugged. 'Elementary my dear Watson.' He shook his head. 'After all the trouble I took to avoid DNA on the Asian girl. Then I let myself thump that idiot in the car. Sod's law, isn't it?' He leaned across to take the glass from her, 'So you won't be needing that after all, will you?'

Sarah put the glass behind her back. 'Tell me what you've done with Lynn?'

He thought for a moment. 'Lynn? The Cameron girl.' He scratched his head. 'She came prattling about Gordon's watch, and that Rubina... something to do with that damned photograph, and she wanted to talk to him about it. She asked me to arrange it...' He groaned. 'And I thought. Not again!'

'Where is she?'

He smiled.

Sarah tried to speak calmly. 'It's all over now, Keith, you know that. Tell me where she is.'

He was still reaching for the glass when he over-balanced on the erratic springs of the chair, the bane of every teacher who sat on them. Sarah helped with a push and scrambling up, ran from the room. This time she bolted in the direction of the right exit - but Keith Birkmyre was behind her. He caught up with her at the top of the stairs and they both watched, mesmerised, as the heavy glass fell from Sarah's grasp and smashed into pieces as it toppled down...from stone step to stone step.

Then Sarah heard Mark calling to her from below. Startled, Birkmyre turned wildly and, in imitation of his whisky glass, slowly fell the whole length of the staircase - over and over the shards of glittering crystal - to lie still at Mark's feet.

'Sarah, what the hell?'

She rushed down the stairs. 'Is he alive?'

Mark bent over the still figure. 'I think so.' Blood poured copiously from a patchwork of open wounds on his face – and his head lay at an unnatural angle.

Sarah shuddered. 'Quick Mark, call an ambulance! Oh God - he mustn't die!

Mark held her by one arm while he dialled, then he asked. 'Why?'

'Because he's got Lynn somewhere.   And if he dies...'

They followed the screaming ambulance over the twisting, undulating road between Helensburgh and the Vale of Leven, and sat in the hospital waiting room until DI Hamilton arrived, followed closely by Annette Birkmyre.

Hamilton glared. 'I'll deal with you later.' And strode away into the hidden regions of the emergency department.

Sarah got up and touched Annette's arm. 'I'm so sorry...'

Annette stared at her. 'I thought he was at the cottage. He said he was going there...what in the name of God ...?'

Sarah and Mark looked at each other, then Mark said, quietly, 'Where is that, Mrs Birkmyre?'

She looked at him as if he'd just dropped from the ceiling. 'Who are you?'

Sarah squeezed the woman's hands. 'It doesn't matter - please, tell us - where is the cottage?'

She pulled her hands away. 'Why are you asking this? Keith is in there and ...'

'Because he's got Lynn Cameron hidden somewhere.

'Lynn Cam...the girl who's missing?' She put her fist to her mouth. 'Oh no...why would Keith ...?'

Mark leaned towards her. 'Maybe we're wrong, but we need to find out...'

Annette Birkmyre was silent, holding Sarah's gaze, until a nurse hurried into the waiting area. 'Which of you is Mrs Birkmyre? You have to come now.'

She took a step to follow the nurse, then Keith Birkmyre's wife turned back and said, 'Toscaig - Wester Ross.'

*

The chilly sitting-room was as unwelcoming as ever, but Mark and Sarah were greeted so warmly by Lynn's mother that Sarah thought it was as if she was melting from the inside out. Her usually perfect hair was loose and untidy and she was wearing baggy jeans.

Lynn sat on the sofa in her teddy bear dressing-gown, the ubiquitous box of hankies clasped to her chest. Her eyes filled with tears when she saw her visitors.

Elizabeth Cameron said, 'I'll just go and make some coffee,' and left the room.

'Oh, Miss, I'm so sorry. I should have told you...after all you'd done.' Lynn pulled a tissue from the box. 'We'd just heard about your... sister... and that was so awful...'

'You were sparing my feelings, I know.' Sarah smiled. 'But what you did was very dangerous, Lynn.'

The girl's eyes widened behind her specs. 'I didn't know that, did I?'

Mark said. 'What had you found out, Lynn?'

She stared past them. 'I'd gone into the Golden Dragon for a takeaway Chinese, you know? My mother was away and I couldn't be bothered cooking. While I was waiting for my order to come I saw Gordon Birkmyre at a table with some friends. They were quite close, and I was just kind of watching them and listening to their joking and stuff, and someone asked about the time. Gordon pushed up his sleeve to look at his watch.' She breathed out. 'It hit me like a stone, Miss Blane, that fancy watch - even the sweater he was wearing. I was so rapt that I ran out of the restaurant without my food. It all made sense!'

She shook her head, as if amazed that it hadn't occurred to her sooner.

' I was going straight to your house when I remembered about your sister...then I thought I'd find Leslie, but he doesn't have a phone...' She stopped. 'So I thought, don't be too hasty Lynn, the best thing to do is wait and ask Gordon himself.'

'Ask him what?'

She waved the tissue. 'Like, if he'd been seeing

Rubina secretly before he went away. If it was him, you see, and Hakim had found out, it would explain it, wouldn't it? I thought it would maybe help Mohammed to understand why his brother had...' Her voice broke and she scrubbed her face with the tissue.'

Sarah said, quietly. 'Go on...'

She lifted her shoulders. 'I didn't know where Gordon Birkmyre hung out, and I knew he'd soon be going back to America, so there was no time to be lost. I went to see the Head and asked him if I could maybe speak to Gordon, I couldn't just go to the house!' She began to sound like a child. 'He told me to meet him at school about 8 o'clock on Friday night and Gordon would be there.' Her breathing quickened. 'When I got there he said he'd made a mistake and Gordon was at home, so we'd just pop into the car...' She began to cry. 'He hit me, Miss Blane - he hit me on the head and I was so scared...I fainted, and I woke up in this funny wee house. I was so scared.' She said again, her voice rising. 'He locked me in and told me if I tried to escape he'd...he'd kill me!'

Sarah got up and put her arm around the girl. 'Shh, it's all right, Lynn.'

Still sobbing, she said, 'And he'd taken my mobile off me. I cried and shouted, but there was no-one to hear me.' She put her face in her hands and her voice was muffled. 'It was horrible. I thought I was going to die!'

Elizabeth Cameron came into the room with a pot of coffee, and biscuits. She laid down the tray and stroked her daughter's hair until she quietened, then she smiled at Mark and Sarah. She poured the coffee. Commander Cameron was still with the police.

Over the rim of her cup, Lynn said. 'Can I ask you something, Miss?'

'Of course.'

'My mum has told me about Mr Birkmyre, and Rubina...and all that. But, how do the police know it was him, and not Hakim?'

'Remember the gloves that were found in the loch?'

Elizabeth Cameron shuddered.

'And how there was unknown DNA on one of them? Apart from Hakim's? When all this happened they found out that it was the Head's.'

Sarah had a vivid memory of that October night outside the police station; Hakim spitting with rage, his head almost inside the window, and Keith Birkmyre's gloved hand pushing him away from the car.

'But,' Lynn looked into her cup. 'Why did he do it?'

Sarah shook her head. 'I'm not sure. But, you know, he'd committed a terrible crime when he was a young man...'

Lynn interrupted, 'Your sister.'

'Yes. I can only suppose it preyed on his mind all these years, and then, when he thought that his son was involved with an - unsuitable girl - and she might tell about the drugs...I think he just lost control.'

Elizabeth Cameron said. 'I still can't get over the coincidence. That you would end up in the same school as...your sister's...'

Mark intervened. 'Yes, I suppose it's because Scotland's such a small country, and education seems to be an even surprisingly smaller world. Teachers' paths are always crossing, apparently.'

'That's true,' Sarah said. 'Why, Dorothy Bullough had taught in the same school as Keith in the past. And Mr Armstrong even remembered about Ruth – he'd been teaching nearby at the time.'

Lynn asked. 'Miss Blane, what is going to happen to the headmaster now?'

Elizabeth Cameron's cup clattered into her saucer. 'I haven't yet...'

Sarah held on to the girl's hand, 'Dr Birkmyre didn't recover from his injuries, Lynn. He died this morning.'

The End

About the author

Words – reading, writing (and talking) are Mary Edward's greatest loves. To this end she spent many years at Glasgow University, gaining two degrees and a diploma before she finally left, to enter a profession which was also all about words – teaching, developing teaching packages and talking to others involved in education. Now she writes mostly fiction, and before becoming president of the Scottish Association of Writers she won several of their trophies – The Pitlochry, The TC Farries and the Helensburgh Shield, in addition to many short fiction prizes there and elsewhere. She is the author of *Who Belongs to Glasgow?* a well-received history of immigration to her native city and she publishes short stories and articles, does a great deal of adjudication of other people's work and speaks about the craft to writing groups. She is an editor for New Voices Press, the publishing arm of the Federation of Writers, Scotland.

Also by Mary Edward

A Spider's Thread across the Tay. This is one of several long pieces Mary has written, and one which ticked all the boxes of her enthusiasms – the fascinating research into the events surrounding this unforgettable tragedy and the creation of the fictional context in which to tell the story.

About Author Way Limited

Author Way provides a broad range of good quality, previously unpublished works and makes them available to the public on multiple formats.

We have a fast growing number of authors who have completed or are in the process of completing their books and preparing them for publication and these will shortly be available.

Please keep checking our website to hear about the latest developments.

Author Way Limited

www.authorway.net

13239117R00188

Printed in Great Britain
by Amazon.co.uk, Ltd.,
Marston Gate.